2

Y0-BEO-415

SECRET SINS

SECRET SINS

JoAnn Ross

ST. MARTIN'S PRESS
New York

SECRET SINS. Copyright © 1990 by JoAnn Ross. All rights reserved. Printed in the United States of America. No part of this book may be used or reproduced in any manner whatsoever without written permission except in the case of brief quotations embodied in critical articles or reviews. For information, address St. Martin's Press, 175 Fifth Avenue, New York, N.Y. 10010.

Design by Judy Dannecker

Library of Congress Cataloging-in-Publication Data

Ross, JoAnn.
    Secret sins / JoAnn Ross.
      p. cm.
    ISBN 0-312-04145-4
    I. Title.
    PS3568.0843485S4   1990   89-77822
813'.54—dc20   CIP

First Edition
10 9 8 7 6 5 4 3 2 1

To Jay and Patrick—for all that you are, and all that you've given me. With all my love.

ACKNOWLEDGMENTS

No novel can be written without help, and I am fortunate to have been on the receiving end of an overwhelming amount of it. My heartfelt thanks to:

My agent, Maria Carvainis, who believed in this story from conception and guided me with sensitivity and insight through every draft.

Toni Lopopolo, whose astute editorial talents helped make *Secret Sins* the best it could be.

Cherry Wilkinson, Richard Willford, and Robin Lester, for their enthusiasm and support.

Karen and Thomas Grover, for being there when I needed them.

And finally, Bill Heywood, because I owe him one.

Hollywood
1981

Flashbulbs popped like gunfire the moment they entered the room. Along with all three major television networks, WBC had also sent a camera crew. The upstart network's investigative reporter, Peter Bradshaw, had broken the story, setting off the chain reaction that brought them all here today.

Jockeying for position with the network crews were jean-clad, T-shirted cameramen and -women from local television stations. Beside them stood the field reporters—the men bronze, blond, and handsome, the women tawny, blond, and beautiful. Behind these uniformly attractive golden individuals, notebooks in hand, were the print journalists, delegated, as always, to the back of the room.

Posted on either side of the doorway were two Brinks guards, their eyes alert, continually sweeping the crowded room. Only moments earlier the uniformed men had delivered a million dollars in newly minted thousand-dollar bills to

Leigh Baron. They had remained to ensure that none of those crisp green portraits of Grover Cleveland fell into the wrong hands.

Leigh was not surprised by the turnout. Viewed by many to be Hollywood's reigning royalty, she and Matthew had lived in glass houses for years. As heir to Baron Studios, she had grown up in the unrelenting glow of the spotlight, and while Matthew had a compelling background and had built himself a remarkably successful career, Leigh had the feeling he would have drawn attention to himself whatever he'd chosen to do. Put the two of them together and they were bound to make news.

She spoke first, enjoying the buzz of excitement her words caused. Excitement rippled through the crowd like a shot of adrenaline and it was obvious that the reporters were dying to dash out of the room and file the Story of the Year. But they wouldn't. Not until they'd heard from the man standing next to her.

Matthew St. James.

For much of the last decade the name had appeared on movie screens in darkened theaters all over the world: SCREENPLAY BY MATTHEW ST. JAMES. DIRECTED BY MATTHEW ST. JAMES. A MATTHEW ST. JAMES PRODUCTION. Once he had been the bane of Joshua Baron's existence. Today Matthew St. James was the ace of Baron Studios. In Hollywood vernacular, he had the world by the balls.

Her performance completed precisely as she'd rehearsed it, Leigh stepped aside to watch Matthew weave his seductive spell over his audience. In a town where blond was the norm, where men and women alike strove to achieve the image of sunny beaches and Mercedes convertibles with the tops down, Matthew St. James stood out like a blizzard in July. His thick, wavy hair was as dark as anthracite coal and thick brows jutted over eyes the color of smooth, aged whiskey. Those intriguing eyes could turn dangerously dark at a moment's notice or flame amber with unequaled passion. Leigh had experienced both in their years together.

He was a natural-born actor, she thought, not for the first time, as she watched him play his audience with an innate talent that could never be taught. Bogie had had it. Gable had had it. So did Newman and Redford. Matthew St. James had it in spades. One by one the reporters tumbled into his hands, professional detachment disintegrating like morning sea mist under a bright Malibu sun. Leigh had seen it too many times not to know exactly what was happening.

The women were all imagining what it would be like to be in bed with Matthew St. James.

The men were all imagining what it would be like to *be* Matthew St. James.

And Leigh? She was remembering.

Those early intoxicating, passionate days. The barren, in-between years of separation. The sun-filled glory days of their marriage. And then . . .

Betrayal.

Divorce.

Regret.

Her gaze drifted slowly over the rapt crowd, returning momentarily to a man standing at the front of the room, his eyes unblinkingly riveted on Matthew. The lack of a camera revealed that he wasn't a photographer. And he wasn't carrying one of those long, slender notebooks favored by reporters the world over. Nor did he have a portable recorder in the hand that was visible. His other hand, she noted with slow-building apprehension, was tucked away in the pocket of his faded denim jacket.

A moment later she saw it. The gun. Pointed directly at Matthew.

Events seemed to slow to the agonizing pace of ten frames per minute. She grabbed the bronze bust of her father, Joshua Baron, from its marble pedestal beside her and hurled it at the gunman. Then she screamed.

The sudden sound of the shot ricocheted around the room like the snap of a firecracker. The riveting explosion was immediately followed by another. Then a third.

After what seemed an eternity, the reporters began to react, shouting and shoving violently, trying to force their way to the front of the room. A blood red haze covered Leigh's eyes; someone a long distance away was calling for an ambulance.

A cold, dark mist enveloped her, and Leigh wondered if she was dying.

Instinctively she reached out for Matthew. Just as their fingers touched, Leigh surrendered to the darkness.

BOOK ONE

Los Angeles
1972

1

t was a Friday afternoon in late July—dog days—and the City of Angels was caught in the grips of the worst heat wave in fifty years. Hot shimmering waves rose from the asphalt freeways, radiated off the mirrored surfaces of downtown buildings, and made everyone miserable. The unrelenting record-breaking temperatures were a great equalizer, proving that everyone—from the privileged glitterati of Beverly Hills to the teenage hookers roaming Sunset Boulevard on their impossibly high platform sandals—sweat.

Those who could escape work early streamed down to the beaches like lemmings. On Zuma Beach, golden girls in minuscule crocheted bikinis played volleyball with boys whose classic physiques resembled statues of young Greek gods. At Venice's famed Muscle Beach, bodybuilders worked to surpass perfection, while nearby, thousands of tanned, stunningly fit, half-naked people were stretched out on gleaming yellow acres of sand like prime meat sizzling on a gigantic grill.

At Malibu's Surfriders State Beach, the surfer was undisputed king. Young men, along with those few women daring enough to invade what had always been a male-dominated realm, sported sun-bleached hair and swaggering attitudes. They welded their bodies to floatable Fiberglas and waited for the perfect wave.

While the surfers bobbed on the sun-silvered swells, beach bunnies rubbed Coppertone into one another's already bronzed backs, preened, and planned their weekend parties. Don McLean's "American Pie" and cuts from the Rolling Stones' *Hot Rocks* album blared defiantly from portable radios.

To these archetypes of California's sun-filled myths, the beach was not only home. It was Endless Summer personified.

Matthew St. James had been out on the water since noon. He'd come to the beach today to exorcise a deep, familiar feeling that had seethed inside him for as long as he could remember—a low, rumbling virulence, like a volcano on the brink of erupting. In his younger days, this anger had resulted in frequent fistfights; wiser now at twenty-eight, he chose to purge the demon with demanding and often dangerous physical activity. Challenging the vast power of the sea fit this criterion perfectly.

After five hours his arms and legs ached, his body was covered with sea salt, and he had a small cut over his left eye where he'd been hit by his board after being caught by a riptide that had engulfed him in tons of churning water and sand. Matthew hadn't been afraid; he had survived two tours of duty in Vietnam; he felt strangely invincible. Once he'd surfaced, he'd retrieved his board and rode the very next wave all the way to shore.

Now, when more and more surfers had paddled out to join him on the turquoise swells, Matthew decided to call it a day. He'd never identified with these purely recreational surfers. Besides, he had to work this evening, and it wouldn't do to show up in Beverly Hills with sand in his shorts.

He waded toward shore with a lazy, hip-swaying stride. Unlike the baggy Hawaiian jams favored by most surfers,

Matthew was wearing a pair of black Speedos that left little to the imagination, even as they made girls yearn for more.

Nubile young nymphets, looking like Southern California travel posters, thrust out their oiled breasts, extended long, gleaming legs, licked Vaseline-coated lips. Those who had managed to learn his name (which wasn't easy, the word was out that this guy was definitely a loner) called out to him, receiving only a vague wave in return. Matthew St. James was not into beach bunnies.

"Damn, dude, but you are fuckin' A," a muscular young man wearing blue swim trunks and a faded gray Sex Wax T-shirt exclaimed. Matthew dropped his board and sank down onto the hot sand. "Where'd you learn to ride a wave like that?"

" 'Nam." He took the beer Jeff Martin offered and, tilting his dark head back, poured it down his throat.

"Almost makes me wish I'd gone to war."

"No, you don't. It's a rotten war; you're lucky to have gotten out of it." A high draft number, along with three juvenile marijuana busts, had successfully kept Jeff from obligatory military service.

"I suppose so," Jeff said, thinking fondly of all those Thai sticks. "Still, any country whose major industry is drugs can't be all that bad."

Leaning back on his elbows, he watched a blonde a few feet away roll over onto her back. When her unfastened bikini top fell away, he got a glimpse of a pair of bouncy tits he rated as high 8s on his personal scale of 1 to 10.

"Contrary to popular belief, Vietnam isn't all surfing, drugs, and bar girls." Matthew crushed the empty Coors can in his hand, tossed it into a nearby green barrel with a high, looping toss, and immediately reached into the cooler for another one.

If it hadn't been for the Marines, promising to pay his college tuition when—and if—he returned from Vietnam, he sure as hell wouldn't have volunteered. Not that he could have kept from going. Matthew's own less than pristine juvenile record had included fights, truancy, and running away with almost monotonous regularity. Nothing to make the military turn him away. And he certainly hadn't been one of those fortunate rich kids with powerful fathers who knew whose palms to grease, what strings to pull.

Matthew St. James had never known his father. Or his mother. In true Hollywood melodrama, he'd been left in a cardboard box on the steps of St. James's Catholic Church when he was three months old. Pinned to his blue receiving blanket was a note that read:

> *I can no longer take care of my son. Please find him a home with people who will love him. Thank you and God bless you. P.S. His name is Matthew.*

Since no last name was given, social workers named the infant Matthew St. James and placed him in the Sacred Heart Boys' Home where, unadoptable without his mother's signature on a multitude of official forms, he lived for the next seven years.

Innately unable or unwilling to accept life without questioning the status quo, Matthew came to dread Saturdays, when he would enter the dark, velvet-draped confessional and recite his childish sins to a rigid, moralistic priest who would sentence him to a long afternoon of penance. While the other boys would be outside enjoying the California sunshine, Matthew would be on his knees in the chapel, reciting a litany of Hail Marys and Our Fathers.

The single bright spot in his life was Sister Jude, a young nun who had taken a special interest in Matthew from his first day at Sacred Heart. She rocked him to sleep, dried his tears, smuggled in Fig Newtons from the kitchen for secret, late-night snacks. It was Sister Jude who taught him to read, to pluck out a few simple chords on the guitar, and to play baseball, her heavy black skirts flying wildly around her ankles as she ran the bases.

Most important, it was Sister Jude who taught Matthew about the power of love. Every night, when she bent down, brushed his dark hair off his forehead, and kissed him tenderly, he inhaled the crisp, clean scent of Ivory soap and felt his heart expand in his chest. To Matthew, Sister Jude was Love itself.

Unfortunately he learned at a very early age that love was fleeting. When a fire gutted the interior of the red brick orphanage shortly after Matthew's seventh birthday, the State of California decreed that the boys of Sacred Heart would be better off residing in "normal family settings."

That decision led to Matthew's placement in the revolving door of the California foster care system, and he was shuffled from home to home, school to school. During the 1950s, when television defined the nuclear American family, Matthew was an obvious outsider. He quickly became a target of the other kids and it was Jimmy Collins, a porky fourth-grade bully with mean, squinty eyes, who first called him a bastard. The taunt, immediately picked up by Collins's loyal admirers, followed Matthew for years, fueling his smoldering inner anger.

In Beverly Hills, Joshua Baron's French Regency mansion was hidden behind high stone walls. In the center of the wall were a pair of heavy iron gates, ten feet tall, with spikes at the top. In the center of each gate was an elaborate filigreed crown positioned above curlicued letters that spelled out *Baron.* Black-and-white signs posted on either side of the electronically controlled gates warned that intruders would encounter killer guard dogs and an armed response. The signs, de rigueur in this neighborhood, were Beverly Hills' answer to the welcome mat.

Behind the gates Japanese gardeners clipped away at a lush emerald lawn that could have doubled as a putting green. Workers, clad in blue coveralls with orange lettering on the back, were erecting an enormous yellow-and-white-striped tent over the garden while the pool man skimmed rose petals from the shimmering blue surface of the water.

Inside the mansion Leigh Baron calmly faced down a hysterical florist. "David, you have to get a hold on yourself. This is simply not the catastrophe you're making it out to be."

David Thomas dragged his sensitive, manicured fingers through his thinning hair. His heart was pounding a million miles an hour—Christ, what he wouldn't give for a Valium right now—and he could envision his entire career going right down the toilet.

"What an optimist you are, Leigh darling," he said, gesturing toward a table where two dozen matching Baccarat vases sat empty. Empty! "Perhaps you didn't hear me, dreamheart. The refrigeration on the truck broke down; all my lovely Sterling Silver roses have died! They're gone. Kaput. Finished!"

He slumped into a spindly gilt chair. "Just like me. Finished. What am I going to do? My reputation will be absolutely destroyed. I'll have to move to Burbank. Or, God forbid, Encino!"

Leigh cast a glance at her watch; there wasn't time for David's theatrics. Joshua Baron insisted on perfection and Leigh had always done her best not to fail him.

She had been serving as her father's hostess for the elaborate parties the head of Baron Studios liked to throw since her sixteenth birthday, only days after her mother's death. Since her parents' marriage had been merely one of economic and social convenience, the untimely crash of the Mercedes sports car that took Signe Baron's life on the winding road to their Malibu Colony beach house hadn't been reason enough to call off a party months in the making, Joshua had argued.

However, the lack of a proper hostess had been annoying— until he gave Leigh another long look. Fortunately, his firstborn daughter possessed an air of poise not acquired by many individuals in a lifetime. Drafted into service, Leigh filled the role so well that nine years later she continued to add the perfect woman's touch Joshua considered vital to his social occasions.

"David." Leigh put her hand on the sleeve of the distraught florist's mauve linen jacket. "This isn't the end of the world."

He looked up at her with bleak, sorrowful eyes. "Leigh, dearheart, have you ever *seen* Encino? Restaurants there actually put plastic flowers on the tables." He shuddered dramatically at the horrible thought.

Leigh thought fondly of her favorite Italian restaurant with its cozy decor: a mural of the Coliseum, candles in Chianti bottles, and artificial grape leaves twined around white trellises. "You're not going to end up in Encino, David dear. You're entirely too important. Why, none of us would know what to do without you."

"Really?"

"Really. Now, about this little setback—"

"Setback? How can you call nearly three hundred dead roses a setback?"

"It might be a problem for someone else," she admitted. "Someone without your special talents. But I know you can do it. You'll simply have to replace the roses with something else."

"Replace twenty-four dozen roses? In the next two hours? With what?" He wasn't entirely convinced, but Leigh thought she could hear the wheels beginning to turn in his blond head.

"We still have the caspia," she coaxed prettily. "And the baby's breath. Surely that's a start. What else can we round up?"

David rubbed his bearded chin as he seemed to be considering her question. "I could probably locate some lily of the valley."

"I love lily of the valley."

"And wild daisies are plentiful this time of year."

"My very favorite."

"If I get on the phone right away, I suppose I could track down a few dozen tiger lilies."

"Perfect; the arrangements will look like spring."

"They should be carefree, even whimsical." His eyes brightened with a creative light. "Like a fresh April breeze, ideal for these stultifying days. Why, by tomorrow morning every florist in town will be dying to copy the look."

Leigh knew her problems were over when he kissed her warmly on both cheeks. "Dreamheart, you are an absolute genius!"

"Not me." Leigh's smile was echoed in her calm gray eyes. "You're the genius, David."

"I know," he bubbled, scurrying off to make his calls.

Another catastrophe averted. Leigh was just congratulating herself when a strident clash of pots suddenly shattered the momentary calm, followed by shouting and a string of heated curses strong enough to turn the refrigerated air blue. Stifling a sigh, she headed in the direction of the kitchen.

"Earth to Matt. Hey, man," Jeff complained, waving his hand in front of Matthew's face, "what planet are you on, anyway?"

Matthew refocused his thoughts on the present. "Sorry. I was thinking about something."

"From the look on your face, it must've been a bummer."

He shrugged. Matthew had never shared his past with anyone, and he wasn't about to begin with this beach bum—aspiring actor. And full-time hustler. If there was a buck to be made anywhere in town, Jeff would probably try to horn in on the deal. Matthew had known guys like him in Vietnam; most of them had returned to the States with a bundle made on the black market and a profitable East Asian drug connection.

"Hey, if you don't wanna talk about it, that's cool. I just wanted to let you know that I wouldn't be riding with you tonight. Nothin' against your wheels, dude, but I'm arriving at that party in style." He grinned. "Wait till you see how good yours truly looks in a stretch limo. Just like Redford. Hell, better."

They'd been hired to tend bar at a party in Beverly Hills. The money wasn't bad, but neither was it anything to get excited about. "What did you do, work out a commission deal for the liquor you pour?"

"I guess I forgot to tell you, I'm not working the bar to-night. I hooked on to another job. One that pays a helluva lot better than mixing martinis for a bunch of Hollywood pho-nies."

"Doing what? Pushing dope?"

"Nah, you know I'm not into that scene anymore," Jeff lied unconvincingly. "I'm working for an escort service."

Stud service was more like it. Matthew had admittedly been down and out in his day. Being male and human and not looking for any long-term involvements, he'd even suc-cumbed to temptation and gone to bed with some of the tanned, eager, and oh-so-lonely Beverly Hills wives who hired him to work their parties. But he'd never considered hustling lonely old ladies for a buck.

"For chrissakes, what're you doing that for?"

"Lighten up, willya? The way I figure it, I'm gonna be screwing anyway, so I might as well get paid. Jesus, Matt, get with it. Half the guys in my acting class work for Patsy."

Matthew took another long pull on his beer. He was getting tired of hearing how out of it he was. Perhaps if Jeff had spent some time in the jungle, he'd be out of it too. "So who's Patsy?"

"Patsy Judd. She works out of a place on Wilshire. Nice thing about Patsy is that she only deals in first-class clientele. You get to go to all the groovy parties and the tips are a helluva lot better than what you'd make in a month of pouring booze." Jeff gave Matthew's hard, bronze body a brief, professional appraisal. "Shit, the chicks all creamed their bikini bottoms when you came strolling out of the surf. You could really clean up working for Patsy. How about I introduce you and—"

"I think I'll pass. But thanks for the offer." Matthew stood up and brushed the sand off his legs. "I'd better get moving. I still have to get today's scene written before the party."

"Hey, man, summer's supposed to be time for the three Ss—Surfin', Sunnin', and Screwin'," Jeff said. "And you know as well as I do that the Writers Guild is practically a closed shop. Those hotshots running the show aren't about to share any real power with an outsider. So how come you keep working so hard?"

Matthew tossed the second empty can into the barrel and picked up his white Fiberglas board. "I'm in a hurry."

Tina Marshall was in a hurry.

She had spent the entire day cruising the Golden Triangle—Bel Air, Beverly Hills, Brentwood—with an absolute gorgon of a woman who wouldn't know a decent house if it bit her on her surgically corrected nose. The air conditioner in the Rolls was excellent, keeping the interior of the car at an optimum seventy-four degrees. But since you couldn't sell a house from inside a Rolls-Royce, Tina was forced to brave the blistering heat while she listened to a litany of complaints.

The silent movie star's estate in Bel Air—a steal at two million—was too old. And it lacked a tennis court. Privately, Tina didn't believe the obese woman physically capable of dragging herself around a court without inviting a massive heart attack, but she wisely kept her thoughts to herself as they trudged back to the car. The exquisite, two-story English manor, surrounded by nearly three acres of parklike grounds in Beverly Hills, was too small; the Spanish-style hacienda in Brentwood too far from the Polo Lounge.

For five hours, including the obligatory lunch at La Scala during which time the woman whined nonstop about the lack of movie stars in attendance, Tina had been forced to inhale clouds of Youth Dew, listen to disparaging remarks about California from the native Texan whose husband had recently purchased a number of California oil wells, and try to control the impulse to wring the woman's fat neck.

They'd finally given up for the day, agreeing to meet again in the morning. Now Tina had exactly thirty minutes to shower, do something with her wilted hair, put on her makeup, dress, and make it to Joshua Baron's party before all the good gossip had been exchanged.

Could she do it?

You bet.

Tina Marshall was an expert at overcoming seemingly unbeatable odds.

Matthew balanced the case of Tattinger Rose champagne on his shoulder and cursed under his breath as he looked around for the Mexican woman who'd opened the kitchen door only a moment earlier. After reluctantly allowing him entrance to the house, she'd disappeared, leaving him without any idea where Joshua Baron wanted the bar set up.

He was just about to start shouting—not that anyone could hear him over the cacophonous sound of the rock band warming up nearby—when a young woman entered the kitchen with long, purposeful strides. Her tailored silk business suit was unrelieved by any jewelry, her blond hair twisted into a practical knot at the back of her neck, and an oversize pair of tortoiseshell-frame glasses rested on the slender bridge of her nose. From the notebook she was holding in her hand, Matthew took her to be one of Joshua Baron's legion of secretaries.

"It's about time someone showed up," he said. "You wouldn't happen to know where Baron wants the bar set up, would you?"

Leigh's swift, judicious inventory was as much force of professional habit as personal interest. His face was dark and lean, with angular planes and shadows; jet black hair flowed to the top of his collar. He was astonishingly handsome, but she had grown up on the back lot of Baron Studios, where handsome men were the rule rather than the exception, and Leigh had long been immune to masculine good looks.

She glanced past him. "There were supposed to be two bartenders."

"There will be. The other guy ditched at the last minute. Jesse told me to tell Mr. Baron that he's looking for a replacement and will send someone over as soon as possible. Meanwhile, I'm it."

Leigh hoped that Jesse Martinez, owner of Martinez Temporary Personnel, located a second bartender before her father arrived home from Baron Studios. "I suppose we'd better put you out by the pool," she decided, turning to show him the way. "When the second bartender arrives, we'll put him in the music room."

Matthew followed her through a series of rooms that possessed all the ambiance of a baronial manor. Gilt-framed paintings hung on silk-draped walls; satin-upholstered French period furniture rested on Sarouk carpets. "I sure hope Baron's paying you a bundle, sweetheart. Because you're obviously worth every penny."

"I'll keep that in mind the next time I ask for a raise," she murmured.

"You do that." Matthew nodded his satisfaction. "It's important to realize your worth."

Curious at his quietly deliberate tone, Leigh glanced back over her shoulder. "Spoken like a man who knows his own."

His compelling amber eyes met hers. "I do."

Marissa Baron hummed along with the rock music blasting from her bedroom stereo. She was intent on scrutinizing her reflection in the dressing table mirror. The mirror was surrounded by round white bulbs that made Marissa feel like a movie star. Determined to look like one as well, she had been diligently working with the colorful pots, sable brushes, and gold tubes for the past hour.

"Lookin' good," she murmured with an admiring smile, smudging a wide swath of kohl eyeliner with her little finger.

Her fingernails, painted a vivid, daring scarlet, had been bitten to the quick. Taking a drag from the joint she'd left burning in a Waterford ring holder, Marissa drew the hot, acrid smoke deep into her lungs, holding it there while she stood back and examined her handiwork.

Above the ebony liner her lids glittered with metallic gold shadow; she'd applied two pairs of false eyelashes, one above, the other below. Her cheekbones, which she'd always considered too round—what she wouldn't give for Leigh's perfectly chiseled bones—were expertly highlighted with varicolored shading pencils and gleamed with a frosted amber blush. Her lips glistened with a rosy gloss. The face smiling back at her, surrounded by shaggy copper hair, was admittedly striking, but this was Los Angeles, movie capital of the world, where equally striking faces were a dime a dozen. What was unusual about this one was that it belonged to a girl not yet out of her teens.

Her makeup finally completed to her satisfaction, Marissa took the dress out of its hiding place in the back of the closet. She'd just tugged the sparkling gold lamé over her hips when there was a knock on her bedroom door.

"Marissa? Are you in there?"

"Just a sec." Marissa ground out the joint, tossed the ring holder into a dressing table drawer, and sprayed the air with perfume in an attempt to hide the sweetly scented smoke. A dense cloud of Opium wafted over the room when she opened the door.

"Lemon Cokes," Leigh said, holding up twin glasses filled with dark liquid over ice. "Just like the old days."

Leigh took in her younger sister's outré makeup and skin-tight dress and wondered why it was that Marissa seemed unable to believe that she was a naturally beautiful girl. The gold lamé hugged Marissa's ample breasts, girdled her hips, strained against her thighs. Leigh had to stop herself from suggesting that her sister dispense with at least one pair of false eyelashes.

Lemon Cokes. Marissa couldn't believe it. "Whatever happened to champagne?"

"You know Daddy would ban me from this house if I encouraged you to drink. Especially after the accident."

"So I dented the fender of his precious Porsche," she said with a defiant toss of her tawny head. "It was only a teensy-weensy dent. There wasn't any reason for him to behave as if I'd totaled it."

Crossing the room, she twisted the volume dial on the stereo, defiantly flooding the room with Neil Young's "Heart of Gold." Marissa identified with the rock superstar because he wrote about the frustrations of not being able to achieve what you want—a feeling she knew well.

All her life Marissa had lived in Leigh's luminous shadow, waiting for a single word, a touch, a smile from her father. After seventeen years she was still waiting, while her older sister had not only been elevated to Queen of the Manor, but was reputed to be Baron Studios' Wonder Woman as well. The jealousy eating away at Marissa's heart had become a habit. A type of bondage that got her through the lonely days.

"He wasn't upset about the car, Mar," Leigh said, not quite truthfully. At the time Joshua had certainly appeared more concerned about the indentation in the gleaming black paint than Marissa, who had required two stitches over her right eyebrow to close the wound made when her forehead hit the steering wheel. She'd been too stubborn to buckle her seat belt.

Leigh knew that Marissa's psychologist—the third one this year—had warned Joshua that his younger daughter's accident may have been an attempted suicide. Or at the very least a dramatic cry for help.

"Perhaps he's right," Leigh had answered carefully, when her father had informed her of the psychologist's opinion.

"Bull," Joshua had countered. "Marissa's only problem is that she's spoiled rotten. She just needs a firm hand." He scowled as he held out his glass for a refill. Leigh immediately obliged, filling the glass with Scotch—a Glenfiddich single malt—from a nearby Baccarat decanter. "The girl's incorrigible; I'm tempted to wash my hands of her."

"That would be a terrible mistake. You know Marissa's incapable of taking care of herself."

"If she wants to remain in this house, she can damn well straighten up and obey the rules." Joshua frowned into his glass. "Otherwise, she's out of here. The choice is hers."

That conversation had been two weeks ago and, as far as Leigh could tell, her younger sister had been behaving herself. For the time being. The trouble with Marissa was that she was like a lit fuse on a keg of dynamite. The question was not *if* she was going to explode, but *when.* Although Leigh yearned for a home of her own, she dutifully remained under her father's roof in an ongoing attempt to keep Marissa and Joshua from one another's throats.

"He really was concerned about you," she said now.

"Sure. Tell me another fairy tale, why don't you?" Marissa turned back toward the dressing table mirror, busying herself unnecessarily with sable brush and powder.

The flippant words were spoken with bravado, but Leigh could hear the pain behind them. The two sisters' images, reflected in the pane of silver-backed glass, were a study in contrast. Leigh was tall and willowy, her Nordic coloring— light gray eyes, porcelain complexion, and sleek, pale hair inherited from her mother—bringing to mind jagged mountain peaks cloaked in ripples of sequined snow, iridescent glaciers, and ice blue winter light.

If Leigh was ice, Marissa was fire. Her thick copper hair blazed like wildfire, her skin gleamed a deep, tawny gold, and her bright green eyes glittered with emotions that continuously teetered on the brink of control. Her body was lush, voluptuous, inviting erotic fantasies from the most soberminded of men.

"Honey, driving after you'd been drinking was a foolish, dangerous thing to do," Leigh said.

"So I shared a couple of six-packs with the pool guy. Big fucking deal."

"You could have been hurt. Even killed."

"And give the old man the pleasure of having me out of his life for good?" Marissa's petulant expression turned speculative as she gnawed on a ragged fingernail and observed her sister with renewed interest. "Speaking of our beloved pater, have you had a chance to ask him again about my screen test?"

Marissa's desire to become an actress was no secret. After having been steadfastly refused work at the family studios, she'd tried to finagle a screen test with the competition. Unfortunately, the word was out that the head of Baron Studios did not want his daughter working in films and, everywhere she went, Marissa found doors closed. Ever since graduating from Beverly Hills High School two months ago, she had adopted a more circuitous route, asking her sister to intercede for her. Leigh, as always, had agreed to help.

"Not this week," Leigh said. Marissa's answering oath was short and rude. "But he's been in Las Vegas," Leigh added quickly. "I thought we'd have a better chance if I waited and asked him again in person."

"The bastard will just say no, like he always does."

"You don't know that for certain." Leigh wished that her words held more conviction; in truth, she was afraid that Joshua would reject her renewed pleas on behalf of her sister. Something she could not—would not—allow to happen. Because she had her own reasons for wanting her father to test Marissa.

"That's my big sister, always the optimist. But I suppose it's not so surprising, since you've had our dear daddy wrapped around your little finger all your life." Marissa took a long swallow of the iced cola drink, then grimaced. "This stuff sucks; I'm going downstairs for some champagne."

"You used to like lemon Cokes."

"I used to be a kid."

Despite the way the conversation had turned yet again to the discomforting subject of her favored status in the family, Leigh couldn't resist a slight smile. "Seventeen is so old?"

Marissa's gleaming lips curved in a caustic smile. "Old enough."

Her sister's words, carelessly tossed back over her shoulder, stirred a long forgotten memory inside Leigh's head.

"She's damn well old enough to be here."

Joshua Baron's eyes had flashed with silent warning as they circled the room, daring any other foolhardy studio department head to complain about his nine-year-old daughter's presence. Although Leigh had practically been weaned on the movie business, accompanying her father to the studio since her third birthday, this was the first time Joshua had allowed her to sit in on an executive meeting. She'd been so excited when they left Beverly Hills this morning; never had she expected to be met by such a group of unsmiling, stern faces.

Now, as she sank down into the too large leather chair her father held out for her—significantly at his right hand—Leigh's legs were shaking.

Across the vast expanse of the polished ebony conference table, the dour man who had initially objected to Leigh's presence, Richard Steiner, head of distribution and marketing operations, leaned back in his chair, lit a cigar, and scowled.

Unreasonably nervous, Leigh crossed her legs, squeezing off a sudden, insistent need to go to the bathroom. Her fingers brushed at nonexistent wrinkles on the daisy-sprigged cotton skirt of her favorite Kate Greenaway dress. Her hair, tied back with a navy ribbon, cascaded down her back, Alice-in-Wonderland–style. Her feet, clad in white anklets with lace trim and gleaming black patent-leather Mary Janes, did not reach the floor, and it took a major effort to keep them from swinging back and forth.

Surprised by the vivid detail of this sixteen-year-old memory, Leigh wandered over to the French windows and stared out over the formal gardens. But she was not seeing the elaborate party preparations taking place on the grounds of the vast estate; instead her view turned inward, her attention riveted on the scene playing in her head.

The business meeting had been acrimonious, even by Baron Studios' trenchant standards, the department heads vocally divided upon discovering that their upcoming musical, *The Playboy Prince*, had been penned under a pseudonym to hide the fact that the author of the screenplay was actually a writer who'd been blacklisted after refusing to name his "pinko" friends before HUAC—the House Un-American Activities Committee.

"Why the hell didn't anyone catch this?" Joshua growled. "How come nobody noticed that this Robert Ransom guy was actually Richard Reinhart?"

"Ransom was always kind of a phantom," Ira Katzenbaum, in charge of production, explained. "The script came through Corbett Marshall over at William Morris. Marshall's always been your pal. Who'd suspect him of sneaking a Red past the studio gate?"

"You know, now that you mention it, that guy never has

been much of a flag waver," Steiner pointed out. "If he's not careful, he's going to end up in the Bible." He held up a dog-eared copy of *Red Channels*, that infamous, mimeographed pulp manual of blacklisted artists. Leigh knew that the list, published by former FBI agents and conservative businessmen who'd organized into a group calling itself AWARE, was updated weekly, sometimes even daily. Only last week she'd gone downtown to buy a birthday present for her mother and had had to push her way past the crowd at the newsstand at Hollywood and Vine, lined up for the latest edition. "I say we put the damn thing on the shelf and try to slip it into a few backwater theaters sometime in February or March."

"You got some kind of death wish?" Katzenbaum argued. "Sneaking it out like that'd kill it for sure."

"This movie's got Oscar potential," Norman Levy countered. "If it wins and Hedda Hopper gets wind of who wrote it, we might as well shut down the studio." Levy's complaint showed him to be firmly in Steiner's camp. "Hell, Reinhart wouldn't be the first commie to have his career torpedoed by that broad. Why let him take the studio down with him?"

"Fuck Hopper, McCarthy, and the horse they rode in on," Katzenbaum spat out with unaccustomed anger. He glanced over at Leigh. "Whoops! Sorry for the bad language, darling."

Leigh nodded, understanding that one of the reasons the men hadn't wanted her at their meeting was the feeling that they wouldn't be able to curse with her in the room. As if she hadn't heard far worse during her father's frequent tirades.

The argument continued. As the hours wore on, Leigh never once wiggled in her chair or fidgeted. Instead, she sat upright, her hands folded in her lap, watching the proceedings with fascination.

She knew about the blacklist, of course. She'd watched in shock when the newsreels had shown the Hollywood Ten being taken off to prison for refusing to say whether or not they were communists and refusing to name others. She knew those people; they'd been guests at her parents' home, they'd brought her birthday presents, and every time Richard Reinhart visited, he brought along a new magic trick to show her.

Only last month, he'd made a silver dollar disappear behind her ear. Then he made it come back and gave it to her for a kiss. If they could go to jail, who was safe?

Somehow, when no one was looking, terror had become a Hollywood watchword. Even now, fear welled up in Leigh's young heart at the idea that Senator McCarthy might send her father to jail. A bleak, dangerous jail, the composite of every prison movie she'd ever seen.

When it looked as if they'd reached an impasse, Steiner, frustrated by his inability to sway the opposition, suddenly turned to Leigh. "So what do you think?" he growled around the stump of his black cigar.

Surprised to have her presence suddenly acknowledged, Leigh blinked owlishly. "Me?"

"If you're old enough to be here, you're old enough to have an opinion." He glanced at the others, the first humor he'd revealed thus far flashing in his eyes.

"Leigh is merely here as an observer," Joshua broke in.

"Hell, Josh," Steiner argued, "if the kid's actually gonna run this place someday, you may as well let her get her feet wet."

Joshua gave her a long look. "Okay, princess," he decided. "Why don't you share with these gentlemen what you told me on the drive into the studio this morning?"

It was one thing to talk business with her father, alone in the car, another thing entirely to voice her opinion to this group of grownups who were eyeing her with a mixture of good-natured condescension and out-and-out scorn. She rubbed her palms on her crisp skirt, wondering how ice-cold skin could be so sweaty.

"*The Playboy Prince* is a wonderful film," she began falteringly, glancing toward her father for confirmation. Joshua nodded his encouragement. "It's got everything audiences love—a marvelous score, a romantic setting, adventure, romance . . ."

"You tell 'em, darling," Katzenbaum said in a big, booming voice that revealed his Brooklyn roots. He grinned at Leigh and winked broadly.

At the outward show of support, Leigh blushed. "I think it would be a mistake to bury it."

"You got something against your old man, little girl?"
Steiner asked. "You want to see him end up in the slammer?"

The horrid man was talking like a character from a James
Cagney movie. Leigh hated him. "Of course not," she said
with a coolness that the others would later learn to recognize
as controlled anger.

"Well, you sure as hell could've fooled me." Steiner shook
his bald head with ill-concealed disdain. "Why don't we just
agree to dump the thing in a few small-town theaters in February and see how much we can recoup?"

"Wait just a minute." Josh Miller, in charge of foreign acquisitions, had remained silent during the heated meeting.
"Why don't we let the little girl explain her reasoning?" His
blue eyes were kind as they met hers.

Leigh took a deep breath. Giant butterflies were flapping
their wings inside her stomach and her legs were shaking so
badly that she knew she'd never be able to stand. She pressed
her hands tightly together beneath the tabletop and reminded
herself that her father had honestly seemed to like her ideas
this morning.

"Baron Studios has made a lot of money making films about
the good guys against the bad guys." She echoed the words
she'd heard her father say time and again with a high, clear
voice that only trembled slightly. "In all our movies the good
guy always wins and when he does, all the people cheer,"
Leigh said. She was beginning to pick up steam. "I've seen it
happen lots of time. Just last week, even, at Grauman's. And
since Senator McCarthy is meaner than any villain in any of
our movies, maybe if we stand up to him, people will decide
that Baron Studios is one of the good guys." She glanced
tentatively around the table. The sight of heads nodding gave
her a much needed burst of confidence.

There was a long moment of thoughtful silence. "You
know," Norman Levy murmured, "that's not an entirely off-
the-wall idea."

"Whose side are you on, anyway?" Steiner spat out, irritated by one of his supporters suddenly shifting allegiance.

"The studio's side," Levy answered. "And what the little
lady says makes sense. So what if the word does get out about
Ransom's true identity? Maybe the folks in Topeka and Peoria

are as sick to death of McCarthy as we are. Maybe they'll see Baron Studios as a bastion of truth and light in a dark sea of innuendo and intimidation."

"We could take a real bath," Steiner insisted. "Hell, a stunt like this could get all of us called before the Committee."

"My grandfather and father always said that Baron Studios doesn't run with the pack." Her opinion succinctly stated, Leigh sat back and watched, flushed with an infectious feeling of stimulation as the arguments hit new levels of acrimony. She was nine years old, and she'd just experienced her first taste of power. She loved it.

An hour later, when the smoke had cleared, Baron Studios' five department heads had voted 4 to 1 to adopt the "little lady's" suggestions.

The Playboy Prince went on to win an Oscar, as predicted. Hedda Hopper, ever vigilant in her search for communists lurking behind the silver screens of Tinseltown, eventually managed to uncover the true identity of the author and the charade became front-page news until it was replaced by a story about a black woman in Montgomery, Alabama, who had refused to give up her seat on a bus to a white man.

If Americans were confused and divided about what was happening in the South, they seemed to be of one mind when it came to Baron Studios' refusal to buckle under to the infamous blacklist. They showed their approval at the box office, giving Baron an unprecedented fourth-quarter profit.

And in a town where geniuses were as common as starlets, Leigh Baron's reputation as a Hollywood prodigy became legend.

But Leigh hadn't known what the future would bring that long-ago afternoon. She'd only known that her father was proud of her. As a reward for her sterling performance, he'd taken her to the Santa Monica Pier, where they rode the carousel. Astride a gleaming white horse, embellished with fanciful medieval armor, Leigh leaned back against Joshua's chest, reveling in the raucous music of the calliope, the salty ocean breeze, and the strong, reassuring feel of her father's arms around her.

"How about some ice cream for my princess?" Joshua asked after they'd ridden three times.

"Nanny doesn't let me have ice cream after five o'clock. She says it spoils my dinner."

"Screw Nanny." Joshua lifted a giggling Leigh atop his shoulders and marched over to the vendor who'd set up shop under a bright red-and-white umbrella.

Funny, the things you remember, Leigh considered now as she watched David Thomas overseeing the arrangement of his flowers beneath the garden tent. More and more lately, these images of her childhood had come unbidden into her mind, like scenes from some forgotten movie. Some were clear, others misty. But all had remained hidden in her mind until this summer.

"Daddy had vanilla," she murmured. "And I had strawberry. And we shared licks. And then we laughed, and Daddy hugged me and told me how proud he was of me and then we went . . . where?" The vivid image faded, veiled by the shadows of time.

Try as she might, Leigh could not recapture the memory.

But for some reason she could not discern, on the hottest day of the year, Leigh began to shiver.

3

oshua Baron was not in a party mood.

His flight from Las Vegas had been delayed due to a malfunctioning fuel gauge on the studio jet. He'd arrived back in L.A. in time to get stuck in afternoon traffic on the drive to the studio, and no sooner had he finally reached his office when Corbett Marshall had phoned with a new list of demands from one of Hollywood's hot new stars. And on top of that, the rep from the damned WGA had the nerve to threaten him with a strike.

"The bastards are trying to bring me to my knees," Joshua muttered as he marched out to the Porsche parked in its reserved space. Leigh's adjacent parking space was empty, revealing that she'd gone home early to prepare for the party. Joshua hoped she had everything under control; he didn't know how many more problems his stomach could handle for one day.

"They know damn well that a strike could shut the studio

down," he continued talking to himself. "And then where would all those fucking prima donna writers be?" Joshua Baron considered screenwriters to be in the same devil's league as actors and agents. He hated the whole greedy lot.

When the security guard called out a cheery good night as he drove through the gates, Joshua managed only an absent wave in return. He was piloting the Porsche west on Sunset Boulevard when he remembered Leigh's instructions to offer birthday greetings to the elderly man. It had been only this morning that she'd phoned him at his hotel to remind him of Harry Potter's sixty-fifth birthday.

Sixty-five years old. Only five years his senior. Christ, was he going to look that ancient and grizzled?

Stopping for a red light at the intersection of Sunset Boulevard and La Cienega, where one can, on a clear day, see one of the most panoramic views L.A. has to offer, Joshua took a judicious survey of his reflection in the rearview mirror. His thick white hair was expertly styled by his personal barber, who came to his office every Thursday afternoon. His complexion was the requisite Hollywood bronze, acquired from afternoons spent on the tennis courts or golf course at the Hillcrest Country Club. Although a faint network of lines surrounded eyes shaded by Ferrari sunglasses, women always assured him that the lines added character rather than age to his features. An admittedly vain man, Joshua chose to believe them. Still, he'd had the puffy bags under his eyes removed last year by the most expensive plastics man in Beverly Hills. The exorbitant cost of the surgery had been worth every penny; it took ten years off his looks.

In this gold rush industry of moviemaking, in a place boasting of at least one plastic surgeon every four-and-a-half blocks, it was imperative that people on both sides of the camera look young. Vital. Joshua was all too aware that Hollywood was built on fantasy and illusion. Image was everything; a healthy appearance equaled a successful business.

Business. An unseen hand twisted his gut. Reaching into the pocket of his white-on-white silk shirt, Joshua pulled out a pack of Rolaids and popped two antacids into his mouth. As he crunched down on the chalky tablets, he contemplated that if things didn't turn around pretty soon, he'd have to begin buying the damn things by the case.

He wondered if Harry Potter had ulcers and decided he probably didn't. How much stress could there be in sitting in an air-conditioned booth, checking names off a list, and watching Dodger games on a portable TV? Potter, hired by Walter Baron, Joshua's father, had come to work at Baron Studios forty-five years ago, a decade after Walter had founded the studio.

Using tactics usually attributed to Eastern Seaboard robber barons, Walter had single-handedly wrested power from a loosely connected group of silent filmmakers and turned the new enterprise into the largest, most profitable movie studio in America. In the world.

It had not always been easy, Joshua mused. As he headed up into the green hills overlooking Los Angeles, Joshua thought back to those dark days of the 1940s. The studio had lost most of its leading men to the armed forces, and although they'd continued to make War Bond films, union troublemakers had begun eating into their profits. Then, as if they hadn't had enough problems, in 1946 a British film—Olivier's *Henry V*—was nominated for the Oscar, making British acting, costumes, cinematography, and accents all the vogue. The floodgates had been opened. Soon the Academy began nominating French and Italian films, along with the British. When foreign films won four Oscars in 1947, American studios nearly had a collective coronary.

The subsequent influx of foreign films proved such a menace that in 1948, the heads of all six major Hollywood studios—Warner Bros., Paramount, MGM, 20th Century–Fox, RKO, and Baron Studios—banded together for the first time since the labor crises of the 1930s and voted to withdraw their sponsorship of the Academy Awards.

It was during those unsettled times that Walter had come up with his latest scheme to keep the studio afloat. He instructed his son to court the daughter of Jens Eldring, a Norwegian-born, San Francisco–bred shipping magnate and financier. Joshua, who had been enjoying a lusty existence as playboy heir to the Baron Studios throne, was not eager to settle down. And even if he were, Signe Eldring would not have been his first choice for a wife.

Still unmarried at the age of thirty, Signe was tall and painfully thin, with a waspish tongue that had discouraged more than one potential suitor over the years. But Joshua was not your usual, easily rebuffed young Romeo; he was a man on a mission. Save Baron Studios, whatever the cost.

Two weeks after their first date, Joshua proposed, flashing a ten-carat emerald-cut diamond set in platinum from Cartier. The money for the extravagant piece of carbonized stone came from Baron Studios' advertising budget.

As it turned out, Walter and Joshua needn't have bothered risking their valuable capital. Signe, always the pragmatist, realized that the man sitting across the candlelit table was her last chance to escape a lifetime of playing maiden aunt to her numerous nieces and nephews. After making him wait until the following morning, she accepted Joshua's proposal.

When Joshua Baron exchanged vows with his stoic, Dior-clad bride twelve weeks later, the majority of guests invited to the elaborate ceremony understood that what they were witnessing was more merger than marriage. At the extravagant reception dinner held in the gold-leaf splendor of the Biltmore Hotel's ballroom, Jens Eldring, relieved to have his daughter finally married off, handed his new son-in-law a check in excess of ten million dollars, effectively yanking Baron Studios from the ravenous jaws of bankruptcy.

As he pulled the sports car into the curving driveway of his Canyon Drive estate nearly thirty years later, Joshua found himself wishing that the answer to his current financial dilemma could be solved with similar expediency.

4

Baccarat glittered, Limoges gleamed. Perfumes—floral, spicy, oriental, as exotic and individual as the women who wore them—mingled with blue clouds of tobacco smoke and the sweet scent of lily of the valley. The yard, illuminated with softly glowing lanterns, was abloom: magenta bougainvillaea blossoms competed with orange Cape honeysuckle for claim to the most colorful, while creamy hibiscus added a quiet sophistication to the displays of riotous color. Beneath the gaily striped garden tent, flamboyant bouquets of spring flowers in crystal vases garnered appropriate *oohs* and *aahs* as everyone agreed that this time David Thomas had outdone himself.

Damask—yards and yards of it—was adorned with ornately patterned trays fashioned of gleaming silver. Thin, long-stemmed crystal glasses captured the light and split it into a thousand shimmering rainbows. The draped table held the weight of a vast assortment of dishes beautifully presented with the formal arrangement of a still life.

Rosy slices of lamb sprigged with watercress rested on gold-rimmed Royal Copenhagen porcelain. The ubiquitous chèvre lay on a bed of crisp, dark green spinach leaves. There were tiny circlets of smoked eel on brioche, squares of dark pink salmon dabbed with glossy black Iranian caviar, and peppery paté lavishly spread on circles of toasted Italian bread.

At the far end of the table were sweet temptations—puff pastry wrapped around cognac-flavored pastry cream and a hazelnut torte, the meringue layers sandwiched together with butter cream and topped with Swiss chocolate curls. The champagne flowed freely, the guests' tulip glasses continually replenished by tanned young men clad in dark formal wear.

In the lush, silk-draped sanctuary of the music room, the complex strains of baroque music, performed by a string quartet hired from the Hollywood Symphony, accompanied the steady drone of conversation, while outside a driving rock beat pounded unrelentingly on the fragrant night air.

The guests, like the atmosphere and the food, possessed a distinctive California flair. The men were casually, albeit expensively dressed, the women dressed equally as pricey, but more flamboyantly, in gowns by Norell, Halston, Yves Saint Laurent, and Givenchy. Conversation, as always, centered solely on the industry.

Those Americans unfortunate enough to reside outside the movie colony were currently caught up in rumors that the CIA had orchestrated last month's break-in at Democratic headquarters in Washington's Watergate Hotel; Martha Mitchell's sanity (or lack of it) provided juicy cocktail party speculation and everyone from Seattle to Sarasota waited to see how long it would take George McGovern to drop Thomas Eagleton from the ticket, now that news had been leaked to the press revealing his hospitalization for psychiatric care (complete with electroshock treatment!). The long hot summer of 1972 had more than its share of gossipy intrigues, but in this close-knit, secular society, movie deals were all that mattered. With the right vehicle you could burst forth like a blazing comet to become the brightest star in the Hollywood firmament. One wrong move and casting agents would forget your name, the maître d' at Chasen's would suddenly find new bodies to seat at your table, and producers who only weeks ago had been crawling all over themselves to package a deal with you were too busy to come to the phone.

It was nothing if not an intensely competitive atmosphere. Power was the game. And parties like this were the playing field.

"Believe me, sweetheart, one look and you're gonna be begging to cast him in your new project. He's a blond Al Pacino . . ."

". . . a brunette Carol Lynley."

". . . a young Peter O'Toole."

". . . a taller Shirley MacLaine."

". . . a shorter Rock Hudson."

Over the years the names had changed, but the game always remained the same.

Matthew had been working the poolside bar for about thirty minutes when he saw her. Actually, he heard her first. The band, Suicide Express, had taken a break, and her laughter rang out in the sudden silence. Searching out the owner of the musical sound, he saw her standing between two actors, obviously enjoying something one of the men had just said.

For a moment Matthew didn't recognize the vision in the white silk Grecian-style gown with the rippling, spun-silver hair. But then her soft gray eyes met his and he realized that this siren with the face of a Botticelli angel was a long way from the secretary he'd initially taken her to be. His eyebrows rose only a fraction as he acknowledged his error. Leigh's response was a faint, enigmatic smile.

A tuxedoed waiter arrived with an empty tray and an order for drinks; Matthew turned his attention to mixing a pitcher of frozen margaritas. The next time he looked up, she was gone.

Tina was seated beside her husband in his gold Rolls-Royce Corniche with the vanity plates spelling out DEALS. They were in a long line of limousines snaking their way up the curving drive.

"Have I told you that you look gorgeous tonight?" Corbett Marshall asked.

"You have, but that certainly shouldn't stop you from saying it again," Tina answered with an appreciative grin. Knowing that bright colors complemented her light olive
complexion, she'd dressed for the party in a swirling silk hot
pink and violet Pucci sheath. Plum stockings displayed her
legs to advantage, as did the strappy purple sandals with their
skyscraper heels.

For a woman who barely topped five-foot-one, Tina possessed surprisingly long legs. Her husband had often been
heard to profess that Tina's body consisted mainly of legs and
tits. Which seemed to please Corbett immensely. The tall,
handsome, graying-at-the-temples agent was an anomaly in
Hollywood—one of the few husbands who didn't play around.

"Oh, God, I don't believe it," Tina groaned.

Corbett put his right hand on Tina's firm thigh. God, how
he loved this woman's legs! He loved looking at them, touching them, tasting them, and he especially loved the way they
felt wrapped around his hips.

"What?" he asked somewhat distractedly as he felt his body
stiffen in response to his sensual thoughts. Fifteen years and
she could still make him hard. The woman must be a miracle
worker. Or a witch.

"See the woman who just got out of that limo four cars in
front of us?"

Corbett took in the enormous individual clad in a voluminous beaded red-and-gold caftan. Diamonds dripped from
her ears, throat, wrists, and fingers. Climbing out of the
stretch white limousine behind her was a man young enough
to be her grandson, wearing a nubby, cream silk leisure suit.
His tight pants were widely flared, his lavender paisley shirt
was unbuttoned to the waist.

"The one who looks like Moby Dick in drag?"

"That's her," Tina agreed grimly. "Mrs. Edith Halladay, of
the zillionaire Dallas Halladays."

Corbett lifted a dark eyebrow. "She's the shrew who ran
you all over town today?"

"In the flesh." And so much flesh too. Acres and acres of
it.

"Small town," he murmured thoughtfully. "I take it that's
not Mr. Halladay."

"Hardly. Old man Halladay's in his seventies, bald as a billiard ball under his two-hundred-dollar Stetson, and reeks of cigar smoke." Tina's wide brown eyes, framed by sleek dark hair styled in a trendy Vidal Sassoon geometric cut, turned thoughtful. "They've only been in California a few days; I wonder how she managed to wangle an invitation to this party."

"Maybe her tycoon husband is tired of oil wells and wants to buy a movie studio."

"Well, if that's the case, and I doubt it, he's wasting his time on Baron Studios. Joshua would never sell."

"Money tends to be a mighty powerful motivator."

"Spoken like a true agent. Josh has more money than God. Besides, everyone knows he's grooming Leigh to take over."

"Let's hope all his efforts aren't in vain."

"I know she's young, but she's incredibly bright. And she has a natural flair for the business. By the time Josh is willing to relinquish control, Leigh will be more than capable of carrying on the family tradition."

Corbett was not surprised by the unflagging support of Joshua's older daughter evident in Tina's tone. Leigh had been a child the first time he'd taken his new bride to the Baron mansion. Ten years old, with wide, sober gray eyes and a grave manner that Tina later told him had made her want to hug the little girl right on the spot. Instead, Tina had simply shaken the small outstretched hand and stated her desire to be friends. Something she had the feeling that Leigh Baron had needed. A lot.

During Leigh's adolescence, Tina served as a kind of surrogate mother, offering the love and support that the glacial Signe Baron seemed incapable—or unwilling—to give. After Signe's death, the bond between the quiet young heiress and the outspoken real estate broker became even stronger.

"I've no doubt she'll be able to fill her father's—and her grandfather's—illustrious shoes when the time comes," he acknowledged. "I just hope there's a studio left for her to run."

"Then the rumors are true? About Baron Studios' financial difficulties?"

"According to Joshua, they've experienced a rough year,

but all he needs is one really strong vehicle to get them back on the fast track." He paused. "One like *Dangerous*."

Dangerous was a compelling novel written by one of Corbett's lesser-known clients. The story of a charismatic terrorist cult leader who kidnapped an heiress, only to fall in love with her, and she with him, was so compelling that Tina had devoured it in one reading. Although a far cry from the epics that had long been the signature of Baron Studios, Joshua had taken an option on the work, immediately turning the project over to Leigh, who had lobbied unceasingly for the acquisition in the first place. That had been three years ago. Thus far, she had been unable to bring the project to the screen.

"If any one movie could turn a studio around, *Dangerous* is the one to do it," Tina agreed. "It's a marvelous novel."

"I know. The problem is that the money men in this town don't read anything except *Variety* and audit sheets. They're only interested in the bottom line. They also tend to get nervous when you try to pitch a project without stars."

"I take it Leigh's still insisting that the two key roles be played by new faces."

"Of course. You know as well as I do that Leigh rivals her grandfather when it comes to that damnable Baron intransigence," he answered with a frustrated grimace. "She's tested everyone in town for the parts of Marilyn Cornell and Ryder Long—I should know because I sent most of them to her— and she still hasn't come up with either character."

Tina had lived with her husband long enough to know when he had something on his mind. Something he wasn't saying. "And?"

"I'm thinking of suggesting Josh test Marissa."

"You are kidding."

"Not at all. You saw how she stole the show last month with her performance in *Bus Stop*."

"Darling, that's a great role; it would make any fairly competent actress look good. Also, may I point out that we're talking about a high school production."

"A lot of stars have come out of Beverly Hills High School. And for the record, Leigh just happens to like the idea of Marissa in the role."

"Really?"

"Well, it took a while for the idea to sink in," he admitted reluctantly. "But she called me this morning to tell me that after having reread the novel—twice, as a matter of fact—she believes I may have hit on something."

Realizing that her husband was serious, Tina considered his surprising statement. The role of the pampered heiress-turned-terrorist for love would be a good one. It could even win an Oscar for the young woman fortunate enough to be given the part. But even more important, it could mean instant stardom. Tina knew all about Marissa's acting ambitions. Just last week Corbett had come home with a remarkable story about the girl showing up at his office, wearing nothing but a pair of high heels, a bold, dangerous smile, and a white mink coat. He had no sooner risen to greet the teenage daughter of his oldest friend when Marissa had shrugged out of the coat, flung it dramatically down onto the Aubusson carpet, and said, "What's the matter, Uncle Corbett? Haven't you ever fucked on a mink before?"

Still shaken from the encounter hours later, Corbett had assured Tina that he'd somehow convinced Marissa to put the coat back on and hurried her out of his office. Although Tina was furious at the sexually charged teenager for having attempted to seduce her husband, she was not particularly surprised by Corbett's story. After all, Marissa was determined to succeed in a town where tales of beautiful young starlets rising to the top on their backs were legion; unfortunately, there continued to be enough success stories, even these days, to make the idea attractive to a woman willing to sell her body for a part.

"Josh would never permit it," Tina predicted. "Everyone knows he's dead set against Marissa becoming an actress."

"I know," Corbett said on a reluctant sigh as they reached the parking valet. "But I'd love to have that girl as a client. With ten percent of her potential earnings, we could buy that island in the Caribbean you're always talking about retiring to."

Tina didn't answer. There was no need. One of the few things she and Corbett had in common was the fact that they were both incurable workaholics.

The parking valet, wearing a royal blue T-shirt bearing the

crown logo of Baron Studios, was obviously an out-of-work actor. His wavy blond hair had been professionally sun-streaked, his toothpaste-commercial teeth were capped, and Tina had no doubt that he had the obligatory all-over Holly-wood tan. He was undeniably gorgeous. He also looked like every other guy his age in town; throw a stick on a Malibu beach and you'd hit a dozen of them.

Not for the first time, Tina Marshall—nee Theresa Salerno—was grateful that her youthful dream of becoming an actress had failed to come true.

Jeff Martin was in his element. Expensive booze, bitchin' food, and the best-looking chicks in town. Everything would have been perfect had it not been for the nonstop whining of the great white whale hanging on his arm. From the moment he'd picked Edith Halladay up at the flamingo pink Beverly Hills Hotel, the evening had been one long gripe session.

The champagne stocked by the limousine company was domestic, the limo itself wasn't long enough, they had to wait in line to gain admittance to the party, how come he wasn't introducing her to all the movie stars, why didn't he get her a drink, some food, dance with her? On and on until he was tempted to push the fat bitch into the pool and watch her sink to the bottom and stay there.

Relief came when they entered the music room. Recogniz-ing the bartender immediately, Jeff left the diamond-draped monster expertly boring a producer from Warner Brothers with tales of her futile search for a suitable house while he made his way to the portable bar.

Jeff waited impatiently for an over-the-hill matinee idol and his obviously hired-for-the-evening blond bombshell to make up their mind between vodka martinis or Manhattans. Finally they left, martinis in hand.

"Hey, man," he said, "I am in desperate need of some downers. You got any Nembutal or 'ludes?"

The bartender glanced around. "Sorry, man, but you know as well as I do that parties like this usually go for coke or grass."

"Shit." Jeff scowled as he glanced back at the whale.

"Come to think of it," the bartender said, "I do have a

Noctec that I was savin' for a special occasion." Noctec was a brand-name form of the sedative chloral hydrate; the combination of chloral hydrate and alcohol was notorious as the Mickey Finn. "I could let you have it for a ten spot."

The price was highway robbery, but Jeff was in too much of a hurry to waste precious time bartering. "Sold."

He handed over some of the expense money Patsy had given him this afternoon in exchange for the orange capsule. No one noticed as he surreptitiously dissolved the capsule into the frothy pink strawberry margarita.

As he crossed the room, doctored drink in hand, Jeff Martin was smiling.

ina Marshall was the undisputed queen of the Hollywood game of musical houses. In a town infamous for conspicuous consumption, the forty-five-year-old real estate maven traded pieces of property like a wily Las Vegas dealer shuffling through a deck of cards in search of an ace.

Gossip invariably played a key role in her success; whenever Tina heard that an actress had signed for a blockbuster movie, she sent a bottle of Dom Perignon along with a little note stating that she had "just the perfect house" for the actress's important new image.

A series cancellation earned an invitation to a home-cooked dinner. Since the movie community was a very superstitious place, failure was perceived as contagious, which caused the hapless former star to be treated like a pariah. By everyone but Tina Marshall.

Over a casual, friendly meal of linguini, avocado salad, and a crisp Napa Valley Chardonnay, she would mention that she'd just listed the most darling bungalow in Beverly Hills, whose anxious owner was desperate to sell. Before dessert was served, the out-of-work actor had convinced himself that he was actually trading up by moving to a smaller, more manageable place.

While the capriciousness of the film industry provided constant up-and-down movement, divorce was the mother lode of her real-estate business. Every night, as she climbed between her silk Pratesi sheets, Tina thanked God for California's community property laws. Always careful not to take sides, she would commiserate with the angry wife over lunch at The Bistro Garden, patiently listen to the husband's complaints during Sunday brunch at the Polo Lounge, and inevitably end up with another listing and two new sales.

By the time she'd been at the party an hour, she'd chatted with a recent Academy Award–winning director, a rock star whose latest album had just gone platinum, and the castoff third wife of a hot talk-show host, all of whom expressed interest in changing residences. Tina, naturally, knew just the house for each of them. She was also approached by Brendan Farraday, one of the few actors left in town who could qualify as an old-fashioned movie star.

Back from one of his star-studded Vietnam excursions, Farraday was in the market for a small house in the Valley. For a friend. Since the San Fernando Valley was conveniently separated from his vast Bel Air estate—and his wife—by the Santa Monica Mountains, Tina had a good idea exactly what type of friend the actor was talking about. Murmuring something about being too busy to take on any new clients, she plucked his wandering hand off her hip and walked out to the pool in search of a stiff drink. She'd gotten enough work done for one evening.

It was then that she first saw Matthew. Standing behind the bar, mixing a pitcher of frozen daiquiris. Tina couldn't believe her luck.

"You are just the man I've been looking for."

"Looks as if you've found me," Matthew said agreeably. "What can I get for you?"

"The question, you impossibly sexy young man, is what can *I* do for *you?*"

Matthew took a long look at the woman standing before him. Her smile was open, her dark eyes vivacious and unabashedly friendly. She didn't look the type to pick up strange men at parties, but experience had taught him that looks were deceiving.

"Have we met?"

"I'm Tina Marshall," she said with a bold, infectious grin. "The fairy godmother who is about to change your life."

"You've outdone yourself, princess," a deep voice offered in Leigh's ear.

Leigh turned and greeted her father with a faint smile. "I'm glad you approve."

"You know I approve of everything you do. Speaking of parental approval, have you seen your sister's dress?"

"It's not that bad," she hedged with careful loyalty.

"She looks like a slut."

"I suppose you told her that?"

"Of course."

Of course, Leigh echoed silently. And by doing so, her father had merely validated Marissa's rebellious behavior.

"Have you given any more thought to letting her test?" she had to ask carefully. After Corbett's unexpected suggestion, Leigh had reread the novel with Marissa in mind and discovered a striking similarity between the temperamental, love-starved young heiress and her sister.

Joshua scowled. "I've already told you, it's out of the question."

"But she's incredibly talented. If you'd only come to her senior play last month—"

"You know I had to go out of town that night."

Leigh didn't believe Joshua's alleged need to rush off to New York, and she knew Marissa hadn't bought the flimsy excuse either. She'd always tried to calm the choppy waters between her father and younger sister, but the chances of the two strong-minded individuals ever getting along seemed to grow more impossible with each passing day. Leigh wished that she could do something, anything, to bridge the widening gulf between them.

"Have you talked with Corbett?" she asked, seeming to change the subject. Leigh was counting on Corbett's practiced, persuasive ways to succeed where she'd failed.

"Not since this afternoon when he called to inform me that Johnny Banning wanted six points of *High Country Riders*.

Johnny Banning had proven one of last year's few success stories when he'd appeared in a low-budget Western. The enormously handsome former bull rider had made the genre popular again, thanks to all the women who sat in the theaters and fantasized about playing saloon hall queen to Johnny Banning's sexy gunfighter. What none of them suspected was that during the filming of the movie, the macho actor had spent his nights being handcuffed by the movie's equally handsome sheriff.

"What did you tell him?"

"That there was no way I was going to agree to Banning's demands. Then I reminded him about the morals clause in that faggot's contract."

Her father would never enact that clause while Banning was still on top; it would be killing the goose that gave the golden egg. "Meaning that you're willing to give three points?"

His eyes gleamed with parental pride. "Three and a half. Am I that obvious, or do you know your old man so well?" As he put his arm around her shoulder, Leigh experienced a vague stirring of misgiving that was as familiar as it was undefinable.

"We know each other," she murmured.

The princess was locked in a tall stone tower. When she heard her name called, the princess obediently lowered her long blond hair out the window. As she felt the familiar weight on her golden tresses, the princess grew afraid.

Strangely shaken by the childhood fairy-tale image that flashed through her mind, Leigh was relieved to hear someone calling her name. Glancing around, she saw a tall, dark-haired man standing on the other side of the pool, enthusiastically beckoning to her.

"I'd better see what Jimmy wants," she said with a great deal more aplomb than she was feeling. "Did you know he's up for Marlon Brando's role in Olympus Studio's remake of *On the Waterfront*?"

"I believe Corbett mentioned something about it."

"Oh, that reminds me, Corbett's looking for you." She tossed the words back over her shoulder, as if they were a mere afterthought. "Something about *Dangerous*."

Leigh's words caught Joshua's instant attention, expunging the jealousy he'd felt when his daughter had flashed her bewitching smile at that muscle-bound actor.

Although initially he hadn't been enthusiastic about the story, after a great deal of nonstop lobbying (in her own calm way, his daughter could wear away a stone) Leigh had managed to convince him that the intense, electrifying drama possessed Academy Award potential.

Those were the magic words. In recent years, an Oscar had begun to demonstrate an astonishing—or frightening, depending on your point of view—power at the box office, and it didn't take a Wall Street banker to realize that the little statuette had turned from gold to platinum. An Academy Award–winning film guaranteed massive money harvests—as much as five million dollars to the picture's gross income. If a movie won several important Oscars, the payoff was easily doubled.

Joshua rubbed his hands together with anticipation. All he needed to do was get *Dangerous* into production to surpass his father's exalted place in Hollywood history.

When he'd first taken over the studio after his father's death, the consensus was that Walter Baron's philandering, free-spending son would run Baron Studios into the ground within two years. But he'd proven them all wrong. Out from under his father's shadow, he broke new ground by expanding into foreign markets, creating films for the lucrative television market, and traveling to remote, exotic locations earlier producers had eschewed as too expensive. Studio coffers had swelled; his detractors had been silenced.

The Rolodex in Joshua's head was filled with names—Wall Street's top bankers, power brokers, politicians, agents, newspaper publishers in Los Angeles, New York, London, Paris, and Rome. His face was immediately recognizable at all the Beverly Hills bistros; there wasn't a maître d' or parking attendant who didn't know that Joshua Baron expected his table and his car to be waiting. The guest lists of his Sunday brunches read like a *Who's Who* of the industry and tales of Hollywood's most respected citizens battling with the ferocity of pit bulls to win an invitation to his acclaimed Academy Award extravaganzas were legion.

For the past twenty years, Joshua Baron had reigned over Tinseltown from the loftiest peak of Hollywood's Valhalla.

Then things began to unravel. Like every other Hollywood studio, Baron Studios had undergone a period of change, no longer making a hundred movies a year. Instead, they were producing less than a dozen, and since all but one of last year's releases had proven financial failures, the wolves had begun to gather hungrily at the door.

Lord, how he hated the new, murky financial conglomerates that were threatening to take over the movie business. What he wouldn't give for the good old days, when the studios produced, the directors directed, the actors played their parts, and long lines extended outside huge, elaborate theaters. When dollars seemed to come from a gigantic money-making machine, stimulated by the steady stream of successful, profit-producing movies. These days all his time seemed to be spent deciding who was going to get what percentage of the profits before the damn screenplay even rolled from the typewriter.

Somehow, when he wasn't looking, Baron Studios' profit-and-loss statement had begun to hang like a sword of Damocles over his head, and his life had declined into a shitawful mess.

Except for Leigh. Beautiful, steadfastly loyal Leigh.

Plucking an icy martini from a passing waiter's tray, Joshua forged his way through the ebullient crowd, searching out Corbett Marshall.

Marissa was seething. She stood in the shadows, chewing on a bloody cuticle as she watched the hunk behind the bar watch Leigh. As if he thought the high and mighty Miss Studio Executive would even look at a common bartender. And even if Leigh did deign to diddle the hired help, Joshua would have the guy in question run out of town on the nearest rail.

The thought of her father reminded her of his furious ex-

pression when he'd seen her new dress. The memory caused
a small, mean flame of satisfaction to glow inside her. The
dress had proven every bit as effective as she'd planned; it had
garnered a reaction. If the mean-spirited bastard thought that
was something, Marissa considered, smiling, wait until he got
the bill. She could hardly wait for the upcoming explosion.

She had achieved her goal of aggravating her father. Now
Marissa spent twenty minutes walking back and forth in front
of Matthew, during which time he remained frustratingly oblivious to her presence. When Tina began flirting with him,
Marissa decided the time had come to take the bull by the
horns. Running her hands over her gold lamé–clad hips, she
tugged the clinging bodice even lower and made a beeline for
the bar.

Brendan Farraday downed a martini—his fifth of the evening—and watched Tina come on to that oversexed bartender. Who the hell did she think she was, walking away from
him? He was Brendan Farraday. A star. While she was nothing
but a failed actress turned real-estate agent. And an aging one
to boot. Despite her long legs and sensational knockers, she
had to be at least forty. Probably older than that. She ought
to be damned grateful he'd given her a second glance.

As a rule, Farraday preferred his woman young. The
younger the better. But there was something intriguing about
Tina Marshall. Something almost primitive; her polished skin
exuded a mysterious melange of oriental perfume, musk, and
sex.

That's why, when he saw her looking and smelling like the
star of every man's favorite wet dream, he had come up with
the idea of having her locate a suitable love nest for his latest
mistress. Of course he and Tina would have to try the place
out first, just to make sure the vibes were right. So what did
the bitch do when he brought up the idea? Told him she was
too busy to take on any new clients, then walked away.

A red-hot anger boiling in Farraday's blood, he marched
toward the poolside bar. No over-the-hill cunt was going to
turn him down and get away with it. Tina Marshall had a
lesson to learn. And he was just the guy to teach it to her.

*   *   *

"I'll have a champagne cocktail," Marissa ordered imperiously. So what if the hunk and Tina were engrossed in their private conversation? He was hired to mix drinks, not hustle the guests.

Irritation flashed in Tina's eyes, but she banked it as she turned to Joshua Baron's younger daughter. Good heavens, she thought. That dress is remarkable. If the girl so much as sneezes, she'll provide some unexpected entertainment.

"Hello, dear. What a stunning gown." Eyeing the scrap of glittering fabric, she decided that Marissa appeared to have been dipped in a vat of metallic paint.

Marissa laughed, tossing her hair back over one shoulder with a practiced gesture that Rita Hayworth had perfected in *Gilda.* "That's not exactly the word Daddy used."

"I can imagine," Tina murmured.

"Poor Daddy can't get used to the idea that I'm a grown woman. Capable of making my own choices." Marissa picked up the glass Matthew had silently placed in front of her, took an appreciative sip, and eyed Tina over the crystal rim. "Did Corbett tell you that I'm going to be an actress?"

"I believe my husband mentioned that you were interviewing agents." Tina felt guilty for playing games with a child. But this particular child had the voluptuous body of a woman. A body she'd attempted to use to seduce a married man. Tina's man. "Tell me, dear, have you found someone to represent you yet? Or are you still going door to door with your—uh—portfolio?"

The attack was like a stiletto sheathed in silk. Marissa's bright green eyes narrowed as she tried to decide what Tina had been told about the incident. Her mane of flaming hair fanned out combatively as she tossed her head back, polishing off her drink.

"Why should I be talking to other agents when Corbett was absolutely wonderful?" Marissa's wide, kohl-rimmed eyes turned blissfully reminiscent. "And so very encouraging." Her voice was lush with sexual undertones. "Why, after how close we've become, I can't imagine anyone else ever representing me."

Tina assured herself that this underdressed, overendowed teenager was lying. If anything had happened between them,

Corbett never would have told her about Marissa's seduction attempt in the first place. Unless he was trying to establish an alibi, a niggling little voice in a back pocket of her mind pointed out. For chrissakes, look at this girl, the voice insisted. How many men do you think could resist taking her to bed? Or, in Marissa's case, to mink.

The tableau—a silent, watchful Matthew, an uncertain Tina, a vindictive Marissa—appeared to have been captured on freeze frame. Nearby the rock band's female vocalist—yet another Cher clone—broke into what Matthew decided was an appropriate chorus of "Gypsys, Tramps and Thieves."

The charged moment was broken by Farraday's arrival. "Damnit, Tina," he said, slurring his words, "since when do you turn down a chance for a fuckin' commission?" His fingers curved around her arm with a force Tina knew would leave bruises; his booming voice garnered instant attention from nearby guests, including a columnist from the *Hollywood Reporter.*

As the columnist fluffed her cotton-candy hair and looked inclined to join them, Tina's worried gaze went from Marissa to Farraday, then back to Marissa, as she attempted to decide which troublemaker to deal with first. Finally she glanced over at Matthew, deciding that he probably wasn't going anywhere.

"Don't you dare leave without talking with me," she instructed.

"I wouldn't think of it."

Tina turned to Farraday. "Come on, Brendan, let's get you out of here before you blow your chances of making SAG president." She didn't give a damn about the upcoming Screen Actors Guild election, but she did care a great deal about their hostess, and wasn't about to let this bastard ruin Leigh's party. Taking hold of his arm, she practically dragged him away.

"Leigh, dear, it's an absolutely marvelous party." Richard Steiner flashed Leigh a patently false smile. "You never cease to amaze me."

Leigh forced a polite smile of her own. "Thank you, Richard. I'm so pleased that you're enjoying yourself."

As she exchanged brief party pleasantries with the recently retired head of distribution and marketing operations, Leigh thought back to that summer after her graduation from college, when Joshua had assigned her to Steiner's department.

Steiner, intent on sabotaging Leigh's fledgling career, put her in charge of a merchandising campaign for a time-travel movie that was over budget and behind schedule. Undaunted, Leigh traveled to toy conventions and merchandise trade fairs, where she pitched the movie unceasingly. Living out of a suitcase, she rinsed out her underwear and stockings in hotel room sinks each night as she shook the trees, finding money in locations that Steiner, on his most imaginative days, had never thought of.

While her unflagging enthusiasm created undeniable interest, she still had one immense hurdle to overcome. With the movie behind schedule, Leigh had no film to show potential licensees. And without the film, it was difficult, if not impossible, to entice any astute businessmen into signing on the dotted line.

Although Leigh knew that Richard Steiner was secretly waiting for her to fall flat on her face, she refused to give her adversary the pleasure of reporting failure to her father. Just when it looked as if she was going to run out of time, in a stroke of genius, she leased Disneyland for one memorable night. The magnificent presentations she staged in each of the fanciful venues succeeded in setting the standard for future industry promotions.

To the delight of onlookers in Fantasyland, a stuntman double for the adventurous time traveler suddenly appeared in the midst of a dazzling fireworks display, drifting to the ground in front of Sleeping Beauty's castle beneath a silver parachute.

Another stuntman wrestled with live alligators on Adventureland's famed jungle ride, while in Frontierland, a buckskin-clad actor exchanged gunfire with a trio of desperadoes who'd just robbed the Disneyland train.

But the pièce de résistance was what Leigh had arranged for Tomorrowland. There, on an elaborately designed sound stage built specifically for this party, guests sat on the bridge of a starship and battled alien spaceships on a three-dimensional screen that made the special effects appear dazzlingly realistic.

The party was an unqualified success. Months before the

film's release, *Time After Time* T-shirts, ashtrays, key rings, bumper stickers, and plastic action figures appeared in all the stores—along with a colorful board game that took the nation by storm. McDonald's featured *Time After Time* characters on their cups and hamburger containers; Pepsi ran TV commercials featuring the picture's intrepid hero carrying the familiar red, white, and blue can on his journeys through time.

Utilizing a surfeit of superlatives, *Variety* proclaimed that Baron Studios' marketing department had never known an energy vortex like Leigh Baron. She was talented, creative, ingenious. She was indefatigable. Brilliant. And best of all, she was beautiful.

Media gushing aside, Leigh proved very good at her job. Enough so that when she left the marketing department six months later, Richard Steiner—who'd resented her presence at Baron Studios since that long-ago afternoon when he'd made the mistake of crossing swords with a nine-year-old girl—was almost sorry to see her go.

"Pushy old cow." A blistering scowl marred Marissa's carefully made-up face as she watched Tina and Farraday leave. The scowl was instantly replaced by a dazzling smile. She handed Matthew her empty glass for a refill. "You're very good," she purred, watching him mix the drink.

"And you're a brat." He placed the champagne cocktail in front of her.

His derogatory words were not what she'd been expecting. She lifted her chin. "Do you know who I am?"

Matthew shrugged. "Nope." His tone indicated that he also didn't care.

"I'm Marissa Baron."

"Congratulations."

"My father owns this house."

"Nice place," Matthew said pleasantly.

"This is his party." When he didn't answer, she leaned forward, offering him an unrestricted view of her perfumed breasts spilling over the top of the gold dress. "Which makes you his employee."

"So?"

"So he can fire you."

"Since it'd leave him a bartender short, I doubt if he'd do that. Besides, from what I can tell, it's your sister who's in charge around here."

Leigh again. It was always Leigh. "You mix a lousy drink." She slammed her glass down on the top of the bar with such force that the delicate stem shattered.

Matthew watched the exaggerated swing of Marissa's hips as she flounced away. The idea that such disparate individuals could be sisters proved that Mother Nature was more than a little fond of practical jokes.

Cleaning up the broken glass, Matthew wondered what Tina Marshall could possibly want with him. Other than the obvious, of course. Despite a lambent sexuality that clung to Tina like a particularly stimulating scent, Matthew didn't have the impression that she was looking for a quick roll in the hay. No, instinct told him that she had something else in mind.

Something more serious.

Something she insisted would change his life.

So what the hell was it?

He poured a Chivas on the rocks for an aging character actor and mixed a Harvey Wallbanger for the actor's young wife. Matthew decided that it was going to be a very long night.

6

"What the hell is this? A goddamn conspiracy?"

Joshua's stomach clenched; he popped an antacid into his mouth and chased it with a long swallow of Scotch and milk. "First Leigh tries to talk me into giving Marissa a screen test. Then you come up with the insane idea of having her test for *Dangerous.* Christ, that'd be like casting Mae West to play the leading role in *The Nun's Story*."

Corbett had suggested they go into the library, where they could talk in private. He had hoped he could convince the studio head that the answer to his casting dilemma was living right under his nose.

"Look, I know Marissa's unconventional—"

"That's a new word for tramp."

An image of a dangerously seductive seventeen-year-old, nude save for a pair of high heels, flashed into Corbett's mind. He'd known Marissa Baron from the day she was born; his feelings for her had always been paternal. Except for that one fleeting moment of temptation when his traitorous body had responded to her allure like a lecherous old man.

"You're too hard on the girl, Josh. Underneath that sexpot glamour, Marissa possesses a deep-seated insecurity that would make an audience believe that she'd do anything— even kill—to win Ryder Long's love."

Joshua slammed his glass down onto the antique mahogany bar. Liquid splashed over the top and went unnoticed. "Now you're sounding just like her shrink."

"Perhaps all those psychologists are right. When was the last time you actually sat down and talked with her?"

Joshua Baron's glare could have cut diamonds. "None of your damn business. Besides, I don't have to talk to her to know that she's entirely wrong for the part."

Corbett had negotiated enough contracts with Joshua to know when he'd hit the brick wall of the movie executive's intransigence. "Hey, she's your kid," he said with a shrug.

Busy refilling his glass from the heavy crystal decanter, Joshua failed to answer.

Tina dragged Farraday through the throng of guests to the front driveway, where she instructed the parking valet to call a cab for the inebriated actor. Not that she'd mind the bastard killing himself in that new Lamborghini he'd been bragging about all evening; she just didn't want him taking any innocent drivers who might happen to be on the road tonight along with him.

"Your place or mine?" Farraday slurred, reaching behind her to grab a handful of Pucci-covered ass.

"In your dreams." Tina yanked his groping hand off her body.

"Anyone ever tell you that you're too friggin' old to play coy?"

"Go to hell," she said, turning away.

He pulled her roughly around by the arm, holding her against him. "You know you like it."

Tina's dark eyes blazed with hatred. Even as drunk as he was, Farraday read their blistering message and quickly released her before taking an unsteady step backward.

"You listen to me, Brendan Farraday," she said, thrusting a plum-tinted nail into his chest. "And listen good. If you ever so much as look at me crosswise again, let alone try to touch, I'll get a gun and blow your fucking balls off. Is that clear?"

Sweat beads formed on his brow as Farraday tried to remember that he was a major star. And stars didn't take shit from nobodies. "I can break you, bitch. A few words from me and you won't be able to get a job pushing tract homes in Compton."

"Give it your best shot. But lay one finger on me and you're a dead man." With that she spun around and marched away, her four-inch-high heels tapping brisk staccatos on the flagstone.

"Uh . . . excuse me, but your cab's here, Mr. Farraday," the valet offered with an encouraging smile.

The first thing the rookie actor had learned upon arriving in Hollywood eighteen months ago from Denver was to humor all the old farts. Although the balance of power was beginning to shift to a new generation, some of these guys still wielded a helluva lot of power. Brendan Farraday more than most. "By the way, Mr. Farraday, your performance in *The Star Seekers* was brilliant."

His unpleasant altercation with Tina Marshall was instantly forgotten as Farraday turned his attention to the young man with the wavy blond hair and hard, muscular body. Christ, he thought, the competition was getting younger every day. At least this one knew a bona fide star when he saw one. Although it took a major effort, he pulled himself up to his full height of six-foot-four-inches tall.

"You an actor?"

His sudden interest earned a flash of white teeth. "Yes, sir, Mr. Farraday."

"What's your name?"

"Royal Harmon."

"Belong to SAG, do you?"

"Yessir. And you've definitely got my vote for president."

Brendan nodded as he pressed a crisp green bill into the young man's hand. "Well, hang in there, Royal Harmon," he advised expansively. "Thanks for your support. And tell all your friends to vote." Having gotten his pitch in, he allowed the valet to help him into the backseat of the cab.

As soon as the taxi's amber taillights returned back down the curving drive, Royal checked out the tip. As a rule, drunks tended to be generous. Especially ones running in the upcoming Screen Actors Guild elections.

The valet's oath was harsh and succinct as he viewed the one-dollar bill. Brendan Farraday's opponent had just won Royal Harmon's vote by default.

Marissa's arms were wrapped around Jeff Martin's tanned neck and her body clung to his as they swayed to the music. "Did you come here with someone?" she asked, moving her pelvis sinuously against his erection.

Jeff hadn't seen the whale lately. He hoped she'd passed out in some quiet corner where he could retrieve her later. Much later.

"No one important." He slid his knee between her legs. Marissa sighed happily.

"I'm glad. I'm don't like to share."

The way the chick was rubbing her crotch against his leg, Jeff half expected her to have an orgasm any moment. "Don't knock it till you've tried it," he suggested, cupping her buttocks and lifting her more firmly against him. "You know what they say."

"What?"

"Double your pleasure." His teeth nipped at her neck; Marissa went weak from the knees down. "Double your fun."

Marissa was not inexperienced; she'd willingly surrendered her virginity shortly after her thirteenth birthday to one of the estate's gardeners. She'd found the experience painful, messy, and not nearly as thrilling as described in the banned books she kept hidden beneath her mattress.

But she couldn't deny that the look in the old man's eyes— raw lust—had excited her. It was the same way her father looked at Leigh when he thought no one was nearby.

"Hey, sweetcakes." Jeff's tongue played wetly in her ear. "How about you and me ditch this dull old crowd and go somewhere we can make our own party."

His penis was pushing demandingly against her dress; dewy moisture gathered between her legs. "The pool house is

being remodeled.'' She gasped when his dark hand slid between them to press against her heat. "It's empty."

Jeff grinned. "Darlin', I thought you'd never ask."

Matthew was frowning. He mixed a pitcher of martinis.
Tina Marshall had returned, as promised, with a proposition
that was as surprising as it was impossible.

"Let me get this straight," he said slowly, a hint of suspicion
underscoring his words. "You're offering me—a guy you've
never seen before—a role in Baron Studios' new picture."

"I'm offering you a chance to test," Tina corrected. She
plucked an olive from the bowl in front of her and popped it
into her mouth. "But believe me, you're a shoe-in for the
role."

"But you're a real-estate agent."

"You've found me out."

"It'd be difficult to miss your signs; they're on all the best
lawns in the city."

"More prevalent than crab grass," she agreed cheerfully.
"But my husband is Corbett Marshall—"

"The agent."

She bobbed her sleek dark head. "That's him. And he's the
one who'll arrange the test. You see, Corbett and I are a team.
When I'm not pushing overpriced real estate, I freelance as
his scout, just like all those retired jocks who travel around the
country discovering new talent for the Dodgers."

Matthew remained unconvinced. "Corbett Marshall only
handles stars."

"That's true, but—"

"I'm not a star."

Tina's grin was immensely confident. "Trust me, kiddo,
you will be."

A faint line etched its way between his dark brows. From the
looks of Tina Marshall, Matthew would have expected the
woman to be more imaginative. "Nice line. Not terribly original, but I've been told it's effective. On some people."

Tina decided not to be offended by his accusation. She was
certain a man as good looking as this one must have a constant stream of women throwing themselves at his feet. Or
some other more vital part of his anatomy. "But not you."

"No." The long, level look he gave her was calm. Assured. "Not me."

The waiter returned for the martinis, interrupting their conversation. Once they were alone again, Tina smiled to ease the suspicion she viewed in his eyes. "I'm afraid I haven't made myself clear. As sexy as you admittedly are, my interest in you is strictly professional. Besides, I love my husband. I'd never screw around on him."

Watching the way her wide brown eyes had turned earnest when she mentioned her husband, Matthew wondered if Corbett Marshall realized that he was a very lucky man.

"Look," he said, his tone gentler now that he'd determined she was telling the truth, "I appreciate your interest, but I'm not an actor. I'm also one of the few people in this town with no dreams of stardom."

"Am I supposed to believe that bartending is your life?"

Matthew smiled, realizing he fit into her stereotype more closely than he'd thought. Was there anyone in Hollywood not playing a role? he wondered. "Okay, you've got me. But I'm not an actor."

"So what are you? A singer?"

"A writer."

He saw no need to mention the nightmares that began occurring with increasing frequency during his second tour of duty in Vietnam. Instead of turning to drugs as so many others had, on the advice of a sympathetic nurse he'd begun to write down the nightmares in a small notebook he always carried with him. For some reason, putting the horrifying images down on paper seemed to sap their strength, enabling him to get on with the day-to-day business of living. And killing. He had returned home with notebooks filled with stories. Stories he intended to tell to the world.

"Novels or screenplays?"

"Screenplays."

She leaned her elbow on the bar, rested her chin in her palm, and observed him thoughtfully. "Are you any good?"

"Yes. I am."

Tina liked the way he answered simply, without embellishing. If he was going to make it in this business, a steely self-confidence was vital. On the other hand, nothing could do a person in quicker than an overinflated ego. She'd watched more than one career founder on the shoals of swollen vanity. "You'd make it a lot faster if you could devote all your time to your writing."

She wasn't telling him anything Matthew hadn't told himself hundreds of times. After getting out of the Marines, he'd taken advantage of his GI benefits and enrolled at USC. For the next three years, he'd attended classes in the morning, parked cars at the Beverly Hills Hotel in the afternoons, and tended bar at night. He eventually gave up the hotel job when it became too much of a hassle to explain to a seemingly continuous parade of sexually liberated females why he had no desire to while away his few free hours with them in the hotel's bungalows.

"Believe me," Tina insisted, "you are perfect for the starring role in *Dangerous* because you're every parent's worst nightmare. You ooze sex appeal and, best of all, you're totally unknown, which is exactly what Josh Baron's looking for."

"I'm not sure I appreciate that part about being every parent's nightmare."

"It sure as hell didn't hurt James Dean's career," Tina shot back. "Look, with the money you'd make from *Dangerous*, you could quit these part-time jobs and concentrate on your real work."

Matthew couldn't deny the idea of ample funds had merit. But an actor? "I'll give it some thought," he agreed finally as he realized Tina was waiting for an answer.

She nodded, satisfied for now. Twenty years of selling real estate had taught her when not to push. She'd seen his reluctant look of interest when she'd mentioned giving up his part-time jobs. It was enough. For now.

"You do that," she said agreeably. Reaching into her plum satin evening bag, she pulled out one of the business cards she was never without. "Here's my husband's card. Give him a call when you're ready to talk, okay?"

Matthew shrugged. "I'm not promising anything," he warned. "Except to think about it."

"That's all I'm asking." She flashed him a parting smile, more brilliant than any he'd witnessed from her thus far, and turned away. She'd only gone a few steps when something occurred to her. "What's your name?"

Matthew wasn't surprised that she hadn't bothered to ask before. He was an unknown. And in this town, that translated to a nobody. "Matthew. Matthew St. James."

"Matthew St. James." She repeated his name slowly, as if savoring the taste and feel of it on her tongue. "I like it." She nodded in satisfaction. "I can't wait to see it up on that big silver screen in Westwood."

With that she was gone, leaving Matthew holding the gray business card and wondering why in the hell he was even considering Tina Marshall's outlandish proposal.

7

Jeff Martin was ruled by his cock.

He went through life pistol hot, his sexual radar honing in on a target with the speed and accuracy of a Minuteman missile. And it didn't take a rocket scientist to figure out that Marissa Baron was one hot piece of ass.

"Take off your clothes," he said, the moment they entered the deserted pool house.

Marissa, eager to oblige, lowered the zipper at the back of the dress. She wasn't wearing underwear and as she wiggled out of the clinging gold lamé, his predatory gaze settled on each newly exposed piece of flesh—on her high round breasts, her rosy nipples surrounded by dark brown areolas, the curve of her waist, the fiery nest of hair nestled between firm gold thighs. The sharp scent of chlorine assailing the night air was rapidly being replaced by a warm, musky aroma emanating from Marissa's skin.

"Turn around."

Hot desire rose higher and higher as she turned her back, exposing her round buttocks to his silent appraisal. Marissa knew that if he didn't take her soon, she'd come from the force of those intense blue eyes.

"Okay, you can turn around again." His voice was steady. Impersonal. As if they were two strangers sharing idle conversation while waiting for a bus. But as she watched him take off his own clothes and viewed his swollen sex, Marissa knew that he was not as unaffected by her naked body as he was pretending to be. Such knowledge made her inner fires burn even hotter.

When she started toward him, he held up his hand. "Not yet."

"But I want you."

"Don't worry, you'll have me," he said. "All in good time." He reached out and traced her lips with a fingertip; Marissa, eager for some physical contact, drew the finger inside her mouth and sucked it. "God, you are a greedy little thing, aren't you," he said on a low laugh, retrieving his finger and trailing it wetly across the top of her breasts. "Just like a bitch in heat."

Marissa did not like being laughed at. "I thought you wanted me," she pouted.

"I do. But I can wait." He surveyed the room, his gaze settling on a white wicker lounge chair. "Sit down over there." Marissa sank gladly onto the wicker seat, ignoring the piece of broken cane that dug into her naked buttocks. His eyes held a cruel note of amusement. "Touch yourself, baby. Let me see you play with your tits."

There was something about his dangerously authoritative tone that Marissa found impossible to resist. She cupped her hands over her breasts, pinched the hardened buds, and felt a respondent tug between her legs.

"Good girl. Lift your legs up over the arms of the chair." When she obliged, he nodded. "Now fuck yourself."

She'd never masturbated in front of a man, but now, as her fingers caressed the tender pink folds exposed to his unrelenting gaze, Marissa found the experience a definite turnon. Cream flowed heavily over her hand as she twisted her fingers together and pushed them deep into her moist warmth. Her hips tilted up involuntarily, her head rolled back as a jolt of electricity burst forth from her vagina, catapulting her into the throes of climax. When it was over, she lay wantonly sprawled, dampness glistening in the russet curls between her outstretched legs.

"Feeling better?" Jeff asked in that same casual tone.

Her eyelids fluttered open. He was standing over her, looking at her with a smug satisfaction she found hateful. "You're a bastard."

"And you loved every minute of it."

She couldn't deny it. But that didn't mean she had to like him acting like such a cocksure son of a bitch. "I could make you crawl."

His mouth quirked. "Next time."

The lounge chair groaned in protest as he forced her thighs even farther apart and moved inside her with one hard thrust that made her scream. He was so big. Before her body had a chance to adjust to the enormous phallus throbbing inside her, he began to move, pulling away and reentering her with a force that created pain pulsating through her entire body.

His fingers dug deeply into her soft, yielding flesh, his teeth left purple marks on her perfumed breasts. He pounded into her like a jackhammer for what seemed like hours and, when he finally came, he seized fistfuls of her tangled hair and yanked them hard enough to bring tears to her eyes. But before she could cry out, he crushed an ampule of amyl nitrite under her nose and as the incredible, intense rush exploded between Marissa's parted legs, she forgot all about the pain.

Tina heard it the moment she entered the gilt and mirrored powder room. A low, whimpering moan. Looking around, she saw the woman in the corner of the plush gold carpet, slumped against the wall.

"Mrs. Halladay?"

Edith Halladay's beady, pink-veined eyes pleaded with Tina from folds of pale green flesh. "I'm sick. You have to take me back to my hotel."

Kneeling down beside the woman, Tina took hold of her fleshy wrist and felt for a pulse. Edith Halladay's skin felt clammy, but her heartbeat, when Tina found it, was steady. "Can you stand up?"

The woman made a feeble attempt that failed. As she folded back to the floor, the voluminous red-and-gold beaded caftan settled around her body like a collapsed hot-air balloon.

"I'll never be able to get you out to the car by myself," Tina complained. "You'll have to wait here while I find my husband."

She hurried back down the winding staircase, thinking that tonight had definitely been one of contrasts. Marissa, Farraday, and Edith Halladay all represented the down side. Matthew St. James, on the other hand, was proof that even the gloomiest cloud possessed a silver lining.

The house was quiet. The guests had departed, the caterer had taken his pots and pans away, Joshua had retired to his den, and Marissa had disappeared to God only knew where.

Leigh was in the kitchen, watching Matthew count the partially filled bottles of liquor. "You did a terrific job tonight," she said.

Matthew's only response was a muffled "Yeah." He was making notations in a small wirebound notebook.

"I received several compliments on the margaritas."

"The trick is to use fresh limes."

"Oh. I'll remember that."

Silence.

She decided to try again. "Are you an actor?"

"No."

"But I saw Tina give you one of Corbett's cards."

Matthew cursed under his breath. He had lost count of the Wild Turkey bottles. "Look, Jesse's charging you by the hour. So do you want me to talk or work?"

"Can't you do both?"

Not when her damn perfume was infiltrating his senses like an inhaled drug, Matthew could have answered. "Apparently not."

She appeared to consider that for a moment. "Then I believe I'd like to talk," she decided. "If you don't mind."

Matthew shrugged. "It's your money." Leaning against the counter, he crossed his arms over his chest and gave her a long, appraising look.

Leigh wondered why she was even bothering to attempt conversation with such an impolite, brusque man. Then she remembered that time, midway through the party, when their eyes had met and held. In that suspended moment Leigh had imagined that she heard the clash of cymbals.

"If you're not an actor, why did you take Corbett's card?" she asked, genuinely curious.

"I hadn't realized my behavior was being so carefully monitored."

"A good hostess keeps a close eye on everything."

"And you're a good hostess."

"One of the best."

"And modest, too," he said dryly.

"Someone once told me that it's important to know your worth."

Matthew suppressed a smile. "That's good advice."

"I know. So, if you're not an actor, what are you?"

"A writer."

For some reason Leigh did not want to take time to discern, she was pleased that he wasn't just another handsome face hoping to make a fortune by cashing in on his good looks. And he was incredibly good looking, she admitted. In a disturbing sort of way.

"Baron Studios is always looking for writers. Are you any good?" she asked, echoing Tina Marshall's earlier question.

"I suppose that would depend on personal taste."

His eyes locked onto hers, and Leigh felt a strange tightening in her stomach. She willed herself to look away, but couldn't and felt herself drowning in those smooth amber depths, like a swimmer caught in an undertow.

Christ. What the hell did he think he was doing, standing here in Leigh Baron's Beverly Hills kitchen, wondering what, if anything, she was wearing under that virginal white dress. Would her skin feel as soft as it looked? Matthew wondered. Would it taste as good as it smelled?

Matthew was no stranger to the purely physical need that suddenly flared between them. He had willingly given up his virginity during his sophomore year of high school to a horny, big-breasted foster mother who seduced him on the steps of the family swimming pool while her husband was fishing with the guys at Lake Arrowhead. At first Matthew found sex for two a decided improvement over jerking off in the shower, but then the woman grew increasingly possessive—entering his room without knocking, sneaking into his bed at night while her husband snored unconcernedly in the next room, squeezing his groin under the table during Sunday dinner.

And although Matthew had never been fond of his hatchet-faced social worker, when she showed up with the news that it was time for him to move on to a new family, he could have kissed the woman on her grim, orange-painted lips. Having learned at an early age to avoid commitment, over the years Matthew had settled for one-night stands with an occasional brief affair. He'd given his body in those short-lived relationships, but never his heart.

But now, as he became lost in Leigh Baron's wide gray eyes—eyes that brimmed over with reluctant desire and something else that looked strangely like fear—all his instincts told him that this woman was a siren who could lure him into dangerous, uncharted waters.

"I'd better go," he said abruptly. "It's late."

"It's not that late," Leigh protested, wishing that she hadn't sounded so damned eager. "I haven't had a moment to relax all night; I'd love some company while I unwind. Besides, I've already agreed to pay Mr. Martinez for your time."

Matthew wondered if Leigh Baron always got everything she wanted and decided that she probably did. The woman had been born with a silver spoon in one hand and a fistful of credit cards in the other. It was only sheer luck that she was born into Hollywood royalty, mere good fortune that she was being groomed to succeed her father as head of Baron Studios instead of having to struggle like everyone else. Ancient resentments came swirling up from deep inside him.

He gave her a slow, assessing glance. "I never would have taken you to be the type of woman who'd have to pay for company, Ms. Baron."

His contempt hung heavily on the refrigerated air. The only sign of her distress were the bright splotches of scarlet that appeared high on her cheekbones. Leigh tilted her chin and looked into his uncivilized eyes.

"You're right." Her tone was glacial. "It *is* time for you to go." She handed him an embossed envelope. Inside was the generous tip she had decided on before his insulting remark.

"I'll tell Mr. Martinez that your performance was exemplary."

After six years in the military, Matthew could recognize a command when he heard it. "It's always gratifying to hear a woman has found my performance exemplary."

Lifting the box with the remaining bottles onto his shoulder, he gave her a brief salute, which she took like a slap in the face, and turned sharply on his heel. He was out the door, swallowed up by the darkness, before Leigh noticed that he'd left the envelope behind on the counter.

The princess was trapped in a dark, damp dungeon. The dank odor in the dungeon emanated from a monster with flaming eyes and dragon's breath. Ignoring her desperate pleas for mercy, the monster chained her wrists and ankles to the algae-covered stone wall, then began ripping at her flesh with his razor-sharp talons, again and again.

Leigh's terrified screams woke her, rescuing her from the monster's brutal savagery.

8

Venice, California, was a theater of the absurd. Although Mack Sennett's bathing beauties no longer cavorted on the beach and the days of Sarah Bernhardt, Charlie Chaplin, and Mary Pickford performing in the city of canals had faded into memory, the exotic beachfront town still maintained its share of entertainers.

Magicians, musicians, and white-faced mimes made the streets their stage while bicyclists and roller skaters raced along Ocean Front Walk. Although the energetic scene provided a continual delight to the senses, on this particular July evening Matthew remained oblivious to the action swirling past him.

He was sitting on the porch of his rented Venice home, nursing a beer and gazing out over the vast expanse of Pacific Ocean. The tide was coming in, the water tinted brilliant shades of crimson, lemon, and amethyst by the setting sun. On the horizon a catamaran rode at anchor and Matthew imagined he could hear the water faintly slapping at the boat's sides.

Under normal conditions, the ever-changing panorama of the Pacific soothed him, cleared his mind and calmed his senses. But not tonight. Matthew was unreasonably edgy. He'd been like this since Joshua Baron's party two days earlier. It was more than Tina Marshall's surprising proposition that had him feeling so uptight, and if he were to be perfectly honest with himself, he'd have to admit that the money she had promised sounded better with each passing day.

Matthew would enjoy the freedom that such money would bring, but he found it almost impossible to imagine himself as an actor. He was a writer, he reminded himself. Still, if playing one role in one film allowed him to work full time at his craft, wouldn't he be a fool to pass up what so many struggling would-be actors would consider a golden opportunity?

Temptation warred with a deep-seated pragmatism. Matthew's mind tossed the problem around, like a fallen leaf in a whirlpool, circling and circling, attempting to work free. Frustrated by his atypical vacillation, he turned his thoughts to another problem. Leigh Baron.

He'd rerun their brief conversation in his mind and was forced to admit that perhaps he'd come across too surly. Thinking back on it, nothing she'd said indicated that she was looking down on him. It was only his own frustration—and that dark, castrating fear of failure, which had attacked without warning—that had caused him to treat her so brusquely.

It was common knowledge that Leigh was being groomed to replace her father. Joshua Baron was a dying breed: the last of the Titans, those legendary studio heads who wielded unchallenged power. They were brutal men and Joshua, like his father before him, was no exception. Matthew wondered idly if Leigh—who reputedly possessed her father's intelligence—had also inherited Baron's ruthless streak.

"Hey, Matty," a bright feminine voice called out, shattering his introspection.

He turned his attention toward the woman waving energetically at him from the porch next door, her waist-length chestnut hair backlit by the setting sun. She was wearing her usual outdated flower-child costume—an ankle-length peasant skirt, a scoop-neck blouse that allowed an enticing, shadowy hint of nipple through the thin gauze material, and bare feet. Dressed as she was, no one would ever guess the attractive young hippy's income came from a hefty portfolio of blue chip stocks inherited from her maternal grandmother.

"Hi, Lana," Matthew greeted her without enthusiasm.

Lana Parker, daughter of San Francisco stockbroker Leland Parker, had one credo: to enjoy life to the fullest. She hated seeing anyone unhappy. Especially Matthew St. James. Although nothing had ever come of the brief fling they'd had when she first moved to Venice, she still thought he was one of the sexiest—and here was the surprise, *nicest*—men she'd ever slept with.

"You look a little down."

Matthew shrugged.

Lana had grown used to her neighbor's enigmatic silences and, while she knew they might intimidate a lesser woman, she believed that keeping your feelings bottled up led to bad karma. "So, how's the screenplay coming along?"

"Okay, I guess."

"I'd love to read it."

He tilted the beer bottle to his lips and took another drink before answering. "Maybe. When I'm done."

"I can't wait. I know it's going to be wonderful."

Matthew's only response was a shrug.

"Are you working tonight?"

"No."

"Then why don't you come over? I just got back from Acapulco with some primo grass that'll blow your mind, and if I've ever seen a man in desperate need of some serious partying, Matthew, it's you."

Matthew wondered what it would be like to have all the money you'd ever need at your fingertips and all the time in the world in which to spend it. When he'd first expressed surprise that someone as wealthy as Lana was living in such a modest place, she had answered simply that people in Venice knew how to party. It was only later that he learned her family owned the entire block of rental houses, his included.

Rich women. He was certainly meeting his share of them

lately. Yet, other than their wealth, Matthew decided that Leigh Baron and Lana Parker had very little in common. As far as he knew, Lana had never worked. After dropping out of Berkeley three years ago, she'd drifted aimlessly from town to town, man to man, enjoying life to the hilt. While Leigh was reputed to be a workaholic.

"Sorry," he said, "but since I've got a rare free evening, I'd better take advantage of it and pound the typewriter keys."

"A girl could get jealous of that horrible old mechanical rival," Lana pouted prettily. Then she shrugged her tawny shoulders. "Well, if you change your mind, the door's always open."

"I'll keep that in mind."

"You do that." She flashed him an appealing grin, then turned around and went back into the house. A moment later, the scratchy sound of Bob Dylan's "Blowin' in the Wind" drifted out onto the sea air, as it did every night about this time, making Matthew wonder why, with all her dough, Lana couldn't at least spring for a new record.

Leaning back in the chair, he twisted the dial on the portable radio beside him. As Vin Scully announced the second game of a Dodgers-Giants twinight doubleheader, Matthew sipped his beer and allowed his thoughts to drift.

To Tina Marshall.

And Leigh Baron.

And what getting involved with either one of those attractive, powerful women could mean to his life.

It was nearly eleven o'clock at night. The studio was quiet, everyone having gone home hours ago. Everyone but Leigh.

She was seated at her desk, reading glasses perched on the end of her nose, her stocking-clad feet curled up under her on the leather chair, reading a novel. It had been a week since the party and for the last four of those seven days Joshua had been in Las Vegas, seeking funding for *Dangerous*. During that time she'd struggled to do not only her own work, but his as well, along with reading the myriad novels Baron Studios had optioned. Over the past few days, she'd begun to feel as if she were searching for a single brilliant diamond in an ever-expanding sea of zircons.

Tonight's novel was a dark and depressing story of a back-woods Kentucky child repeatedly and horrifyingly raped by her stepfather. For seven years the girl bore her abuse in stoic silence, until she became pregnant. It was then that something inside the girl finally snapped. Picking up her father's squirrel gun after a particularly brutal attack, she shot him. Again and again. Until the rough-hewn walls of the rustic cabin were covered in blood and ragged bits of human flesh.

The story, especially the horrifying ending, was riveting. "But too depressing," Leigh murmured, taking off her glasses. The headache teasing behind her right eye for the final three chapters had arrived full blown, threatening to escalate into a migraine. "It'd die at the box office within a week."

Reaching into her center drawer, she took out a bottle of aspirin, poured two into her palm, and swallowed them with a glass of mineral water. Then she leaned back in her chair and closed her eyes.

The princess stared at the gilt doorknob. She watched it rattle, her wide gray eyes pale with terror. The hands were coming again; nothing would stop them, not even a locked door. The princess hated the hands. She hated the way they smelled: of hair tonic and aftershave, tobacco and brandy. She hated the way they made her feel: frightened and dirty, guilty and ashamed. Trembling, she reached beneath her satin pillow, feeling for the dagger she'd hidden there. Her fingers curled tightly around the jeweled hilt. Someday she would kill the hands. She would stab them with the dagger. Again and again, until they were dead. Then she would finally be safe.

Clouds of sweetly scented smoke hung over the bedroom. The slow, sultry fire of Roberta Flack's voice throbbed from the stereo.

"That's it, baby," Jeff crooned. "Give me some of that sizzling sex you're so good at."

Marissa, nude save for the milky string of pearls Joshua had given Leigh for her twenty-first birthday, leaned back against the black polyester, satinlike pillows and smiled enticingly at the camera lens.

Jeff eyed her appraisingly. "Almost, but not quite." He

arranged her hair over one naked shoulder. "Think heat."

Marissa thought about her father. And how he'd react if he ever got a glimpse of these photos.

"That's it," Jeff murmured encouragingly, misunderstanding the restless pleasure that flooded into her eyes. "Now think about how it feels when I kiss you." He covered her softly parted lips with his, forcing his tongue deep into the inner recesses of her mouth. "When I touch you here." When his hand cupped her breasts, causing her nipples to tighten, Marissa wondered if Jeff's film would correctly depict their warm, rosy hue.

Since that first night in the pool house, Marissa had continued to enjoy the outrageous sex Jeff offered while deftly manipulating the affair so that he believed himself to be in control. He even thought this photo session was his idea. She spread her legs, imagining her father's reaction when he received the photographs. She'd overheard Leigh fussing over his diet, fretting about his high blood pressure. Wouldn't it be wild if he had a stroke? Or a heart attack? If the stone-hearted old bastard actually croaked, she wouldn't have to worry about him giving her a part in one of his lousy pictures; she'd inherit half of Baron Studios. She'd have real power, the kind spelled with a capital P.

Power. God, how she loved that word!

Unaware of her thoughts, but pleased with the way Marissa was practically setting the sheets on fire, Jeff lifted the camera once again. She was caught there, like a quarry in the cross hairs of a scope. "Imagine me fucking you, baby. Think about my cock inside you, how good it feels."

Rather than contemplate Jeff's mental image, Marissa instead imagined the unblinking lens to be the steely gaze of her father and licked her lips lasciviously. When her hand fluttered to her engorged clitoris, the camera shutter opened and closed.

The thought of how much dough he was going to get for this batch of photos stimulated the most magnificent erection in Jeff's recent memory. "That's enough for today," he said, tossing the camera aside. When he stripped off his jeans and approached the bed, Marissa arched her hips off the slick ebony sheets.

Ignoring her silent invitation, he flipped her over onto her stomach and spread the cheeks of her plump round ass. She gave a short surprised gasp when his teeth sunk into her flesh, but then he was inside her and there was only his pounding, relentless energy and heat. When she came, it was a violent series of convulsive spasms.

Later, lying beside Jeff on the musky, sex-rumpled sheets, sharing the joint he passed her, Marissa couldn't remember being happier.

9

After a restless night's sleep, Leigh was back at work, feeling as if she'd gone fifteen rounds with Muhammad Ali. She had just completed a meeting with a group of SAG representatives when she found herself picking up the novel she'd finished late last night. Rereading selective sections, she found it every bit as mesmerizing as she remembered. It was also entirely unsuitable for the big screen. Audiences wanted happy endings in return for the price of their tickets; if they wanted grim reality, they could stay home and turn on the evening news.

A deep voice broke into her introspection. "So how's my right-hand girl?"

Leigh glanced up to see her father standing in the doorway. So he'd finally returned from Las Vegas. It was about time. "Myopic. This is the fifth novel I've read this week. I'm beginning to wonder why we bothered to option any of them." She took off the dark-rimmed glasses, revealing the fatigue in her eyes.

"To keep anyone else from bringing them to the screen, of course." He consulted the diamond-studded Rolex on his wrist. "How about going out to lunch with your old man?"

She smiled apologetically. Her hand swept over a stack of hardcover novels taking up a good portion of her desk. "I'd planned to send down to the commissary for a salad. But thanks just the same."

Joshua frowned. "I thought we should catch up on what happened while I was away."

"Fine." Leigh reached for the phone. "Want me to order two salads?"

"I made reservations at Musso and Frank's."

It was an order. Couched in silk, but an order just the same. Rising immediately from her dove-gray leather chair, Leigh tucked a few errant blond hairs back into the twist at the nape of her neck. "Give me two minutes to freshen up and I'll be right with you."

"Take five minutes," he allowed expansively. "And have Meredith clear your calendar for the rest of the afternoon."

"But I have a meeting with Pamela Winter at three. She's designing the costumes for *Kaleidoscope* and has some sketches she wants me to approve."

"*Kaleidoscope* isn't even going to begin shooting until October. Instruct Meredith to reschedule Pamela. You and I are celebrating."

"Celebrating?" She belatedly realized that her father's eyes were actually twinkling. How long had it been since she'd seen him looking so pleased with himself? Too long.

"I'll tell you all about it over lunch," he promised, shooing her from the room. "Now hurry and get ready; you know I hate to be late."

Leigh didn't budge. "And you know how I hate secrets."

Joshua's exaggerated sigh resembled a deflating blowfish. "Stubborn," he muttered, "just like her grandfather. All right, I'll give you one hint: it's about *Dangerous*."

Her heart leaped into her throat. "Tell me it's good news."

"The best."

It was all she needed to hear. As she hurried from the room, Leigh felt as if she'd just been given a shot of adrenaline.

Corbett Marshall had never considered himself to be a superstitious man. Still, he had noticed that his most profitable deals had been made over the sauerbraten at the Musso & Frank Grill. Not one to tamper with success, when Matthew telephoned one week after Joshua Baron's party, Corbett suggested that they meet for lunch.

The Musso & Frank Grill was a bastion of L.A. nostalgia. It opened its door in 1919, making it the oldest restaurant in Hollywood. Its clientele consisted mostly of writers, directors, and actors who came to bask in the lingering ambiance of Faulkner and Fitzgerald. Corbett hoped that as an aspiring writer, Matthew St. James would find the atmosphere intoxicating. If he was as perfect for the part of Ryder Long as Tina professed—and he'd never known his wife to be wrong—the man could solve a great many problems. And make them all richer in the bargain.

As soon as Matthew arrived, the maître d' led him to the high-backed, red-leather booth. Even seated, Corbett Marshall gave off an impression of tremendous strength and power. Not just physical power, but the steely self-determination of a man used to getting his own way. The agent's silent, judicial study made Matthew feel like a side of beef on display.

"Perhaps this was a mistake," Matthew said.

Corbett blinked, then shook his head. "I'm sorry," he said. "I'm afraid that once every decade I'm guilty of professional bad manners."

Although he'd learned long ago to trust Tina's judgment, Corbett hadn't honestly expected to meet Ryder Long in the flesh. Christ, he thought, wait until Leigh saw this one. He felt like shouting out *eureka*. Now if Matthew St. James only talked half as good as he looked . . .

He held out his hand, his easy smile belying his earlier impersonal behavior. "I'm pleased to meet you, Matthew. My wife has talked of little else since Josh's party last week."

Matthew shook the older man's hand before taking a seat in the red booth. "It's good to meet you too, Mr. Marshall, but—"

"The name's Corbett," he corrected amiably. "Whenever anyone calls me Mr. Marshall, I'm tempted to look over my shoulder for my father."

"Was your father an agent?"

"An attorney. Actually, he represented the greats: Selznick, Theda Bara, Doug Fairbanks. My grandfather was one of D. W. Griffith's personal bankers."

"That's very interesting." Matthew wondered what the hell he was doing sitting here in a landmark Hollywood restaurant with one of the most powerful people in town.

"Yes, my family's been involved with the movie business in one way or another for as long as there's *been* a Hollywood," Corbett said. "In fact, when my grandfather got involved in the industry, it was still based in New Jersey. The talent was all working in New York theaters at the time and the actors would sneak across the river to earn the money the movie producers were paying."

"Sneak?"

"They didn't want their names attached to anything they considered a bastard industry," Corbett explained. He paused briefly when the waiter arrived to take their drink orders. That out of the way, he picked up his story where he'd left off. "They made a helluva lot of movies in those early years. Griffith, during one five-year stretch, directed over five hundred movies. Some theaters changed entire shows every day." His eyes took on a faraway, reminiscent glow, as if he were imagining working during such a boom time. "All those pictures resulted in the birth of Hollywood."

Matthew leaned forward, intrigued. Although he liked to believe that he'd remained unaffected by the glitter of Hollywood, in his more honest, introspective moments he wondered if anyone could live in Los Angeles without fantasizing about those early glory days.

"Most people think the weather was the underlying reason behind the move west," Corbett continued, enjoying the opportunity to impart his vast knowledge of the business. "And granted, our bright California sunshine was a major factor. But the initial reason was that the studios had to pay Thomas Edison a fee for each and every film. The motion picture was his invention, you know."

Matthew nodded as he took a drink from the frosted mug of dark German beer. "Moving three thousand miles from New York made it easier for pirate studios to steal," he guessed.

"Exactly." Corbett plucked an olive from the glass the waiter had delivered with his martini. The glass of extra olives was routinely bestowed upon the regulars by the management, a perk Corbett had never questioned. As a lifelong Hollywood insider, he was accustomed to being treated with the type of reverence reserved elsewhere for visiting royalty. "Some things never change," he pointed out reflectively. "Which is why agents exist. To protect actors' interests from greedy studios."

Matthew had decided that he owed it to Corbett Marshall to be up front about his lack of acting ambition. "I have to be honest with you," he began carefully.

Corbett waved an impatient hand. "One important lesson my father taught me was never to discuss business on an empty stomach." He motioned for the waiter, who appeared instantly with their menus.

"You can't go wrong with the homemade chicken pot pie," Corbett suggested, not bothering to open his own menu. "Although personally, I'd recommend the sauerbraten."

Although Matthew had vowed never to play Hollywood games, neither was he a complete fool. "The sauerbraten sounds great."

Even as he reminded himself that he was not a superstitious man, Corbett couldn't hide his satisfaction.

"Well?" Leigh asked, picking at her zucchini Florentine. It was delicious, but anticipation had dulled her appetite.

Joshua eyed her mildly. "Well, what?"

He was so damn smug. It could only mean good news, Leigh considered. So why didn't he just come out with it? She waved a breadstick threateningly at him. "You realize, of course, that you could be accused of mental cruelty."

Joshua chuckled. "First things first," he said, taking a small, gift-wrapped package from his jacket pocket.

Leigh recognized the robin's-egg blue wrapping instantly. Tiffany was one of Joshua's favorite haunts; her father had always believed in going first class. She shook her head as she slipped off the white satin ribbon. "You spoil me."

"Nonsense." He touched a fond finger to her cheek. "It's impossible to spoil a princess."

Leigh drew her head back slightly, breaking the delicate physical contact. She had come to the conclusion a long time ago that the world was divided into two groups of people— the touchers and the nontouchers. Tina Marshall, for instance, seemed unable to keep her hands to herself. Like graceful birds, they continually fluttered, caressingly, reassuringly. It was not any attempt to invade personal space; it was simply Tina's way. Marissa was also a toucher. As was Joshua.

Leigh was not.

"Oh." She stared in awe at the peacock-hued black pearl earrings. The perfectly matched pearls were so large it was almost impossible to believe they were real. But of course they were.

Joshua frowned. "You don't like them."

Unable to resist their iridescent luster, Leigh ran her finger over the gleaming surface of the gemstones. "How could I not?" she murmured. "They're lovely. But surely they were also horribly expensive?"

Joshua shrugged. "Don't worry about it; I had a run of luck at the baccarat tables. Besides," he said, covering her hand with his, "you've grown into a beautiful woman, Leigh. And beautiful women deserve pearls. Of all the gems in the world, pearls are the most feminine. And romantic."

As she avoided his eyes, Leigh felt the color rise in her cheeks and wished that her father wouldn't talk to her this way. Oh, she knew that underneath his brusque, impatient exterior dwelt the heart of a true romantic—why else would he be so drawn to the film industry? Still, his continually flattering statements always embarrassed her.

"Really, Daddy," she protested on a quiet, not-so-steady laugh, "how you do carry on. I hate to think what would happen if people discovered what a soft touch you are."

Leaning back in the booth, Joshua chuckled as he sipped his Scotch. "Probably ruin me," he said agreeably.

Casting one last fond glance at the pearls, Leigh slid the box into her Gucci alligator bag and folded her hands on the table. "Don't you think it's time you told me what, exactly, it is we're celebrating?"

"We've got the funding for *Dangerous*."

She'd been hoping that was the case. But there had been too many times during the past three years when she'd allowed herself to get her hopes up before, only to have them subsequently dashed. "Who?"

"It's not exactly a who, but a what. I've been promised all the money we need from a land development company that wants to branch out into new areas. Fortunately for us, they liked the idea of investing in your movie."

"Who are the principals in this land company? And why, out of all the scripts floating around today, did they choose *Dangerous*?"

"Really, Leigh, the answer to your second question should be obvious. After all, you're the one who's been insisting that *Dangerous* has Academy Award–winning potential. Besides," he pointed out gruffly, his annoyance evident, "your old man just happens to be one helluva salesman."

"I'm well aware of your vast talents," she said. "But you still haven't told me who, exactly, these generous, farsighted people are."

Joshua was not accustomed to finding himself on the defensive. He bristled. "No one you'd know. Does it really matter? We've got the money, Leigh. That's the important thing."

Leigh could not understand why her father was being so evasive. Knowing better than to push him into a corner, she opted for a more circumspect tack. "I'll want to meet with them," she warned.

"Of course," he answered curtly. His features were rigidly set. "Now, if you don't mind, I believe I'll order dessert. Unless my daughter would rather drag me down to the Beverly Hills police station and submit me to a polygraph test?"

Leigh stifled a weary sigh. For a man who wielded such extensive power, her father could certainly take things personally. "Don't be so dramatic," she said mildly, "I was only trying to get a grasp on the details of the deal."

"Details are for lawyers. The important thing is that you've got your funding."

"But—"

He cut her off with an almost imperceptible narrowing of his eyes. It was a warning gesture she'd come to respect. "I believe I'll have the cheesecake," he said to the waiter, who had appeared beside the table instantaneously, as if pulled out of one of Joshua Baron's bag of tricks. "Leigh?"

Leigh bit back a curse, knowing that to create a scene with her father in public would not only set tongues wagging all over town, but start rumors about even more problems at Baron Studios. "I believe I'll pass on dessert," she said with a great deal more equanimity than she felt. "I'd better be getting back to the studio; I still have a lot of work to do."

Although he'd been the one to insist that she clear her calendar for the remainder of the afternoon, Joshua seemed disinclined to continue their conversation. "Fine. I'll see you at home."

As she rose from the table, Leigh viewed the flash of disappointment in her father's eyes. She knew it hurt him when they argued, and although their working so closely together was bound to generate conflict, Leigh was always left feeling guilty. Giving in, she bent down and gave him a quick peck on his tanned cheek.

"Thank you for the earrings," she said, feeling genuine warmth. "They're absolutely beautiful."

Their earlier dispute forgotten, Joshua beamed. "Not as beautiful as my girl."

While Corbett pitched the same line Tina had at the party, Matthew's gaze wandered across the room to Leigh Baron. She was, he admitted, beautiful: a slim, chisel-featured blonde in the finest Scandinavian tradition. She was also not his type.

"What makes you think I can act?" he asked, returning his attention to the conversation.

Corbett shrugged. "To paraphrase Spencer Tracy, all there is to acting is learning your lines, showing up on time, and trying not to bump into the furniture."

Matthew remained unconvinced. "I'll admit that the money you're offering is attractive," he said slowly. "But I still can't believe what you're suggesting is even possible. I wasn't one of those kids who took drama courses in school; hell, I never even played a tree in any grade-school plays." He didn't mention that attending eight different grammar schools had precluded such youthful opportunity.

"Let's just take things one step at a time," Corbett said with careful casualness. He was trying to hide his building enthusiasm.

During the leisurely lunch, Matthew St. James had proven himself to be an intelligent, level-headed, albeit intensely restrained, individual. Under normal circumstances, such a reserved attitude might work against an actor, making him seem shallow, or even worse, dull—a cardinal sin in this town.

Yet there was something different about Matthew; he possessed an unnerving aura of explosive energy lurking just beneath his steely, controlled surface. And, as Tina had been pointing out for days, the guy was gorgeous. In a dark, unsettling kind of way. Matthew St. James, Corbett mused, like Ryder Long, was definitely not the type of man a girl would want to take home to Daddy.

He did not trust easily, nor was he a man who took anything at face value. The deep-seated personality trait would serve him well, Corbett considered, if he intended to work in this town where ethics were often skin deep. He also was an expert at keeping his emotions to himself. Matthew St. James would not be here today if he wasn't at least moderately intrigued with the idea of acting in a major motion picture. But his face had given nothing away.

Almost nothing. There had been that one time, when his eyes had drifted over to Leigh and Joshua Baron, and a fleeting interest had flickered in those tawny depths. It had come and gone so quickly that if Corbett hadn't been watching Matthew closely, he would have missed it.

"You'll need photos."

"Photos?" Matthew asked unenthusiastically.

"A portfolio to send over to Baron Studios. To pique their interest."

"I can't afford a professional photographic session."

Corbett brushed the problem aside, as if it were a pesky fly. "No problem, I'll advance you the funds—"

"I don't borrow money."

Corbett could respect Matthew's stubbornness, since he possessed a fair share of that trait himself. But enough was enough. "Don't be so damnably hard-headed; you'll pay me back after Baron signs you to star in *Dangerous*." He took out a gold Waterman fountain pen and scribbled a telephone number down on the back of one of his gray business cards. "Jill Cocheran's the best in the business," he said, handing Matthew the card. "When Jill's finished, Leigh Baron will be on her knees, begging for you."

Matthew couldn't resist a smile at that particular mental image. "Where do I sign?"

Corbett didn't hesitate. "Right here," he said, penning the brief agreement on a paper cocktail napkin.

Matthew perused it quickly, took the pen Corbett offered, and signed his name in a bold, spiky script.

"Now that our business is concluded," Corbett said, "we should order champagne."

Matthew shook his head. "Thanks, but since I'm working tonight, I have to go by the warehouse and pick up the liquor."

The agent looked inclined to argue, but quickly changed his mind. "I've always admired a man who knows how to put work before pleasure. It's a rare trait in this town." He rose, extending his hand once again. "We'll have the champagne after the pictures are finished."

"After I get the part," Matthew corrected firmly, a statement with which the older man immediately concurred.

Matthew had just reached the door when he came face to face with Leigh. Experiencing an immediate—and disturbing—sexual tug, he frowned and nodded brusquely as he stepped aside to let her pass.

Leigh recognized him immediately. This was not the type of man a woman would meet and easily forget. Recalling their last encounter and the unpleasant way it had ended, she was no more eager than he to engage in a feigned polite conversation.

Lifting her chin, she preceded him out the door without a backward glance. Once outside the stone-and-glass block restaurant, Matthew headed in one direction, Leigh in the other. Neither had said a word.

Yet as she drove her racing green Jaguar sedan back down Hollywood Boulevard toward the arched Spanish gates of

Baron Studios, Leigh recalled the instantaneous flash of anger in the look he'd given her and wondered at the cause.

Later that afternoon, in a warehouse across town, Matthew shoved a dime into the slot of a pay phone. He was not surprised when the woman on the other end of the line assured him that she'd love to have him drop by after he got off work tonight.

As he replaced the receiver in its wall cradle, Matthew tried to convince himself that Lana Parker had been his first choice all along.

10

"Are you sure you want to do this?"

Leigh sat on the edge of Marissa's bed, watching her sister haphazardly throwing things into the Louis Vuitton cases.

Marissa held up two bikinis for consideration—one consisting of little more than two pieces of yellow yarn, the other crocheted from black string. After a moment's hesitation, she tossed both into the suitcase.

"I've never been so sure of anything in my life."

"But it's only been what, ten days? How can you be ready to live together?"

"I've been going with Jeff for two weeks. Which is thirteen more days than I needed to make up my mind." She chewed on a ragged coral thumbnail and observed the clothing strewn over the pink-satin spread. "God, I need some new threads. Jeff's taking me to a party and this junk is so ancient."

Leigh didn't point out that, less than two months ago,

Marissa had spent a king's ransom practically buying out Neiman-Marcus's entire junior department in search of a suitable wardrobe for the Beverly Hills High School's senior trip to Maui.

"Where's the party?"

"I don't know." Marissa was purposefully vague. "Somewhere in West Hollywood or Malibu. I forget . . . I know!" Her expression brightened as she turned to Leigh. "How about letting me borrow your black dress?"

It was a Bill Blass, simply fashioned of black crepe, beautifully draped and ridiculously expensive. Leigh had fallen in love with it at first glance while shopping for a new suit at Bonwit Teller last week and had managed to justify the exorbitant price tag by assuring herself that its classic lines would allow her to wear it forever. "But it's brand-new. I haven't even had a chance to wear it yet."

"So? I'm not going to go surfing in it or anything. God, sometimes you sound just like Daddy. No wonder you're his favorite; you're turning into a damn Joshua Baron clone."

Years of acrimony hung heavily on the air as the two sisters faced each other across the bed, cool gray eyes dueling with gleaming green. Marissa blinked first, managing to look almost contrite.

"I'm sorry." Her soft voice begged absolution, her lips trembled. "You know what a bitch I am right before my period."

Even as Leigh admired Marissa's performance, she wanted to believe her sincerity. "Don't worry about it; we've all been under a lot of stress lately."

"Tell me about it! Can you keep a secret?"

"Of course."

"Cross your heart and hope to die?"

Leigh smiled. "Cross my heart."

"It doesn't count unless you actually do the motions."

Marissa looked just like a little girl again, reminding Leigh of the years she'd mothered her, made allowances for her, defended her rebellious behavior to their father.

Leigh crisscrossed her index finger over her left breast. "Cross my heart."

"And hope to die."

"And hope to die."

Marissa nodded, satisfied. "This party is really important, Leigh. I haven't said anything because I was afraid nothing would come of it, but Jeff took some pictures of me last week and showed them to a producer, who wants to meet me."

"Really? Who?"

"Jeff didn't tell me his name; he said he wanted it to be a surprise. But he's the one throwing the party, and Jeff thinks I've got a great chance for a part in the picture he's casting."

Although Leigh hadn't seen a great deal of Marissa these past two weeks, she had noticed that every other sentence her sister uttered began with "Jeff says" or "Jeff thinks." She'd seen the man in question only twice, and then only briefly. A little over six feet tall, he was tan, athletic-looking, and handsome, in a California beachboy sort of way. His sun-bleached hair had hung well over his collar and a trio of gold chains had filled in the open neck of his shirt. Actually, Leigh had considered at the time, Jeff appeared to be a male version of Marissa.

"Do you know what picture?" As much as Leigh wanted to believe that her sister was being offered a legitimate part in an actual motion picture, she couldn't help wondering if there was a producer left in town their father hadn't gotten to in his effort to keep Marissa from becoming an actress.

"Jeff didn't say. But he promised it was a good part. And the producer liked my still shots a lot."

"You know, honey," Leigh cautioned, "there are a great many unscrupulous people in this town. And you are awfully young."

Marissa's face hardened. "I'm old enough to know the ropes. You're not the only one who grew up around a movie studio, you know." As if immediately regretting her harsh tone, she flashed Leigh her sweetest smile. "But the thing is, all my clothes look like kids' stuff. I need something really sophisticated."

"Like my black dress." Leigh could feel herself weakening.

"Exactly." Marissa's smile turned positively angelic. "Please, Leigh? I promise not to eat or drink anything all night, so I won't spill on it. And I swear I'll take it to the dry cleaners before I return it."

Leigh relented, as she'd known all along she would. "Wait

here," she said on a sigh. "I'll go get it."

Marissa clapped her hands together in childish delight. "You are an absolute lifesaver!" She came around the end of the bed and impulsively kissed Leigh's cheek. "When I'm a big star, I'm going to tell everyone that I owed my first break to my wonderful, beautiful big sister."

Leigh sighed. "Just try to bring the dress back in one piece."

For Matthew, who had expected a cold, intimidating photography studio, Jill Cocheran's loft proved a revelation. The cavernous interior was cluttered with furniture, books, ancient props, and photographic equipment. Bright sunshine poured through a skylight, flooding the room with soft yellow light. An enormous orange cat lounged on an overstuffed sofa, basking in the warmth of the sunbeam. When Matthew entered the studio, the cat opened one eye and studied him with an attitude of feline superiority.

Photographic prints covered the walls: expected photos of movie stars and rock performers shared space with candid shots of heads of states, farmers, factory workers, captains of industry, miners, and migrant workers.

At five-feet-ten-inches tall in her bare feet, Jill possessed just enough curves to prevent her from appearing angular. Her expressive face, framed by a tangled mane of sun-streaked honey hair, possessed a firm chin and cheekbones any cover girl would kill for, and her eyes were a remarkable china blue. Tanned legs, clad in a pair of brief white shorts, went on forever. Her only flaw, if it could be considered a flaw, was her overly full, unpainted lips. Deciding that they added a ripely sexual appeal to her idealized, American girl-next-door looks, Matthew was surprised that with all she had going for herself in the looks department, Jill Cocheran had opted for the business end of the camera.

"My daddy gave me a camera for my eighth birthday," she explained when he offered his opinion midway through their photo shoot. Matthew had been uncomfortable when he had first arrived at the loft, but Jill's open personality and comfy, down-home West Texas drawl gradually eased his discomfort.

Over coffee served in earthenware mugs, she explained that she never approached a shoot as just another job. They were here to do something together. To establish a rapport. Eventually he almost managed to forgot the unblinking lens. Almost. But not quite.

"It was just a little ole Kodak," she said as she moved a light stanchion. Studying her hand-held light meter, she frowned because the reading disallowed his face to be in sharp focus. "But Ah was hooked before Ah finished my first roll of film. All ducks."

"Ducks?"

She adjusted the silver Mylar fill. "You know, sugah, those fluffy white things that float on ponds and eat standing on their heads with their flat orange feet in the air. Ducks."

"Sounds as if you started out to be a wildlife photographer."

"Not at all." She began to click the remote camera switch. A bare bulb flashed from behind a sheet of blue background paper. "We lived next door to a golf course water hazard. Since Ah wanted to use up all the film and get it developed before my daddy left town again, the ducks proved the handiest subjects."

Pleased with how the arrangement of the lights added additional sparkle to his intriguing amber eyes, Jill decided that the time had come to add a little beefcake to the portfolio.

"You can take off your shirt now."

"Why?"

She wasn't surprised when he balked. Just as she'd instructed when setting the appointment, Matthew was wearing a faded blue chambray shirt and a pair of jeans worn white at the stress points. Aware that this was a man unaccustomed to displaying his body for an audience, she softened her tone. "Because you're going to need a torso shot in your portfolio."

Matthew folded his arms across his chest. "If getting the role depends on how I look without my shirt, I think I'll pass. This is a ridiculous idea, anyway."

When he looked inclined to leave, Jill suffered a momentary sense of panic. Although she wouldn't know for certain until she developed the film, all afternoon she'd been getting a sense of something special evolving. She couldn't let Matthew get away.

"Look here, sugah," she coaxed, coming from behind the bank of lights to place her hand lightly on his arm. Beneath her fingers his muscles were tensed hard as boulders. "Ah promise not to take any shots that might come back to haunt you. Or embarrass you. But hell, honey, beefcake—uh, torso shots—are part of this business." Her Texas twang had thickened to the consistency of maple syrup and her guileless smile offered reassurance. "Casting directors jus' want to be sure that y'all don't have some tattoo of a naked lady etched across your pecs."

Matthew smiled as she'd hoped he would. "I really hate this."

Jill nodded. "Ah know." Her bright blue eyes held sympathy. And resolve. "And Ah truly do promise to make it as painless as possible."

Matthew weighed his options and decided that since he'd already come this far, he may as well see this farce out. "How about making it as fast as possible?"

"It's a deal." She managed to avoid looking too triumphant. "Ah thought we'd put you by the window," she suggested, moving across the room. Matthew noticed that once she'd gotten her way, her drawl grew less pronounced. "The natural light's fantastic and the block wall and unpainted windowsill will add a rustic charm."

She turned around and was momentarily stunned into silence. Lordy, Jill considered, with a body like that, she wouldn't be at all surprised if the guy was hung like one of her Grandpappy Cocheran's Texas Longhorns.

"No tattoos," she said finally.

"Nary a one," Matthew agreed.

There was a moment of shared silence. "Well," she said, "let's get this here show on the road."

The remainder of the afternoon flew. She had read the novel Corbett messengered over to her, and knew from the beginning what she wanted to achieve from the session. And now, when everything clicked into place, it was like a shot of electricity shooting through her. A high-energy person, she was able to draw the best from a subject. And Matthew St.

James, she mused, as she took a few final parting shots, had more than most.

"How about dinner?" she asked as she went around the loft, turning off the bright lights. "Ah make a mean chiliburger. If you're not afraid to try genuine West Texas chili, that is."

Matthew realized that they'd worked straight through lunch. "A chiliburger sounds great."

The brilliance of her smile rivaled the sunset streaming through the windows. "Y'all are a risk taker, Matthew St. James," she decided. "Ah've always liked that in a man."

Later that evening, they were sitting on her overstuffed couch, listening to James Taylor and sipping brandy. Matthew was pleasantly surprised to discover that this afternoon's energy-driven dynamo could also be quietly companionable. A pleasant silence settled down around them and, as Matthew's gaze swept the room, he noticed a group of riveting photographs he'd missed the first time.

"Did you take those Vietnam shots?"

"Uh-uh. Those are my daddy's."

Matthew left the comfort of the sofa to study them in greater detail. All the photographs were of soldiers, the young, dirt-streaked faces achingly familiar. "They're damn good. But I suppose that's to be expected."

"Daddy was the best. He was an AP photographer who was—"

"Wounded during a firefight at Chu Lai in '69. His death ten days later was officially attributed to peritonitis and pneumonia resulting from his wounds."

Jill stared at him. "How on earth did you know that?"

Matthew shrugged. "I knew Bill Cocheran. He was a great guy. And the only man I ever met who could say 'Don't shoot, I'm a journalist' in eight different languages. There was this one time . . ." His voice trailed off as he belatedly realized he should be more circumspect. After all, Wild Bill Cocheran had been this woman's father.

Jill was curled up in the corner of the couch, her long legs tucked under her. "Y'all don't have to watch your words on my account, Matthew. I'd like to hear something about those days."

Matthew sat down beside her, cradling his glass in his palms. Jill waited as he stared into the brandy, collecting his thoughts.

"It was shortly before all hell broke loose during the Tet Offensive. This guy in my unit had just gotten word he was a father—a girl, seven pounds, three ounces. Funny the things you remember," he mused out loud. "Anyway, your dad decided that we should take him to Cholon to celebrate."

"Cholon?"

"The Chinese section of Saigon. Somehow—don't ask me how—Bill had gotten hold of this case of Seagram's. After all the homemade hootch and Saigon Tea, that damned colored water the bar girls were always pushing," he explained at her questioning glance, "that premium booze was cause in itself for a celebration. We ordered grilled chicken, boiled shrimp, and plates piled high with what sure as hell tasted like real beef, all paid for by your father with the beneficence of his Associated Press expense account."

"Daddy always was a generous man," Jill agreed matter-of-factly. "Particularly when he was spending some Yankee's money."

"So I discovered. Wild Bill Cocheran's expense account sheets will probably go down in literary history as some of the Vietnam era's most creative writing. Anyway, after dinner we all sat around drinking and smoking cigars and talking about kids and families—all that homey stuff."

Then Matthew's expression changed. He recalled the envy he'd felt, listening to the others reminisce about loved ones waiting for them back home. Jill took note of the fleeting frown and decided not to comment on it. She'd already determined that Matthew was an intensely private man.

"This pretty little whore, dressed in one of those shiny, paper-thin silk dresses so many of the bar girls wore, had obviously figured out which of us had the dough. She climbed up on your dad's lap and began biting his ear and running her fingers through his hair. We were all going crazy, watching this, but Bill didn't seem to notice. Instead, he kept on talking about his daughter who—and this is a quote—had more talent in her pinky than he had in his entire body."

A warm feeling flooded through her. Warmth and a nostalgic longing that she'd learned to live with. "Daddy said that?"

"He sure as hell did. I remember because about that point the girl got tired of being ignored and assured your father that she had more talent in *her* pinky than any American baby-san."

"Baby-san?"

"Virgin."

"Oh." Jill had to ask. "What happened next?"

Matthew shrugged. "I can't remember. It was probably about that time we all passed out."

Jill had the distinct impression that he was being deliberately circumspect on her account and appreciated his concern for her feelings. "Thank you for sharing that with me," she said quietly. "Ah never knew my father very well. My parents were divorced when Ah was still a baby and Daddy was always off chasing his photo stories—Selma, Birmingham, Vietnam." She shivered, remembering the scenes of the dogs, the fire hoses, those terrifying crosses blazing in the night, the death and destruction of war.

Matthew didn't say a word. He simply reached over and put his arm around her. Jill put her head on his shoulder.

"Whenever he'd come visit, he'd scoop me up and hold me against his chest. He was so big and strong that Ah let myself believe no one could ever hurt him."

She turned her head upward, gazing directly at his lips. Lowering his head, Matthew tasted the softness of her mouth. He kissed her once, lightly. Then again. Slowly, artfully, hungrily.

After a long, pleasurable time, Jill tilted her head back. "Do you want to make love to me, Matthew?"

Matthew had always believed in being straightforward. "Yes."

She stood up, extending her hand. "Well, then, what are we waiting for?"

They undressed each other, hands lingering over warming skin, lips caressing newly freed flesh. When they lay facing each other on the bed, Jill's hands skimmed the planes and hollows of Matthew's body, her fingers tracing long, corded muscles that contracted under her exploring touch. In turn, Matthew moved his hands over her slender curves, drawing out a slow, smoldering need that had her aching for release.

He stopped only long enough to put on the condom he was never without—no bastard kids for Matthew St. James—and then his tongue slid into her, creating explosions of mind-blinding pleasure. Unable to remain passive while he was driving her mad, Jill's touch grew greedy. She dragged him up to lie full length on her, drawled dirty words in his ear as she wrapped her long, tanned legs around his hips and guided his penis home. The fluffy comforter slid unnoticed onto the floor; the sheets became hot and tangled.

Control disintegrated as the power swept them away, their bodies fused, moving in unison until they climaxed together in a hot flood of release. When it was finally over, they lay beside each other on the rumpled bed.

"That was," Matthew said, still breathing heavily, "one of the most intense sexual encounters of my life."

"Sugah," she said, on a low, throaty chuckle, "you ain't seen nothin' yet." She was smiling as she bent her head and took him deeply into her mouth.

When his half-limp penis rose to her intimate demands, Matthew decided that truer words had never been spoken.

Much later, while Matthew slept, Jill crept from the bed and disappeared into the darkroom. After developing the day's work, she sat in the eerie glow of the red light and studied the contact sheets for a long, silent time. Then she began dialing the telephone she'd taken into the room with her.

"Ah'm glad Ah caught you home," she said when the male voice on the other end of the line answered. "What? No, Ah most certainly have not been drinking. As a matter of fact, Ah've been working. How the hell should Ah know what time it is?"

Again that gruff voice.

"Really? Four A.M.?" She paused, allowing the man to give her a few choice suggestions as to what she could do with both her camera and the telephone. Finally, she broke into his heated monologue. "Don't you dare hang up on me, Corbett Marshall," she insisted. "Not until you hear my news about your new client, Matthew sexy-as-all-get-out St. James."

That got his attention. Jill had known it would. "Tell you

what, sugah. Y'all get Baron Studios to give me an exclusive on all his still work and Ah'll comp you a set of publicity shots that'll knock your socks off.''

Satisfied with Corbett's response, she belatedly apologized for waking him up, hung up the phone, and went back to work.

Watching the eight-by-ten image of Matthew slowly appear beneath the developing fluid, Jill experienced a satisfied burst of pleasure at the idea of having made love to Hollywood's new sex symbol. And hot damn, she'd found him first.

aron Studios brought to mind a California mission. Entrance to the hallowed grounds was through a pair of tall white arches; the buildings were gleaming white stucco topped with rust-red Spanish tile. Looking at the architecture from the visitors' parking lot, Matthew expected to see a flock of swallows swooping down on the towering belfry.

If the exterior of the studio was reminiscent of long-ago settlers, the interior blended old-time Hollywood opulence with modern California chic. The walls were covered in soft suede the color of sand, bark brown leather chairs with curved brass arms rested beside ebony end tables inlaid with ivory. The ornate gold-and-crystal chandeliers could have come from the prop room of an early Cecil B. De Mille epic; the paintings with their heavy gilt frames could been taken directly from the walls of Selznick's Tara; and the enormous glass display case filled with Oscars—the little gold statuettes standing in rows by movie and by year—was evidence of the longevity of Baron Studios' success.

A receptionist attractive enough to be one of the studio's starlets examined Matthew with interest as he approached her desk. "I'm Matthew St. James. I have an appointment with Mr. Baron at four o'clock." It was one minute to four.

Lines furrowed the young woman's brow. "I'm sorry, Mr. Baron's out of town. Perhaps you mean Ms. Baron," she suggested helpfully.

She ran a carmine-tinted nail down the page of the appointment book. Matthew's heart thudded in his chest. If he had been uncomfortable talking with Leigh Baron in the kitchen of the Baron mansion, the idea of reading for her was abhorrent.

"Here it is," she said happily. "I was right; your appointment is with Ms. Baron at four o'clock." She picked up the phone and announced Matthew. "Ms. Baron's secretary will be with you in a moment."

Only pride kept Matthew from leaving. That and his unflagging ambition. He'd come this far, there wasn't any point in turning back. When a striking young redhead stepped into the reception area, Matthew wondered if good looks were a requirement for working at Baron Studios.

"Good afternoon, Mr. St. James," she greeted him with a welcoming smile. "I'm Meredith Ward, Ms. Baron's secretary. I'm so sorry for the misunderstanding; someone should have informed you that Ms. Baron is conducting all the reading auditions for *Dangerous*."

"So I just discovered."

She seemed surprised by his grim tone. "Do you have a problem with reading for Ms. Baron?"

A problem? That had to be the understatement of the century. "Not at all."

She nodded. "I'm glad. Ms. Baron will see you now." Matthew followed her down the hall. The suede-covered walls of the hallway were lined with framed black-and-white glossies of the galaxy of Baron Studios stars. The faces, covering four decades, were so immediately recognizable that Matthew wondered what the hell he was doing here.

"By the way, Mr. St. James," Meredith Ward offered sotto

voce, when they reached the ornately carved set of double doors at the end of the hallway, "I thought you might like to know that you're the sexiest man to read for the part of Ryder Long yet." Her smile was brimming with feminine invitation.

Matthew wiped his sweaty hands on his slacks and managed a weak smile of his own. "Thanks."

Leigh Baron was seated behind a lovingly tended burr walnut desk that gleamed with the patina of age. He walked across the plush beige carpeting, and she rose to greet him.

"Hello, Mr. St. James. It's a pleasure to meet you." Her smile remained distant and displayed no warmth.

Matthew wondered on whose account she'd decided to forget their first two meetings. His? Or hers? She was wearing a slate-gray suit, severely cut, and a trim white blouse. Her hair was back in its tight twist at the nape of her neck and as her cool gray eyes observed him through her glasses, Matthew had no doubt that her entire look had been carefully chosen to make her appear remote and forbidding. Unlike the highly agreeable Meredith Ward, who settled into a chair across the room, crossed her legs, and continued to show her warm, Cheshire-cat smile.

"It's a pleasure to meet you, Ms. Baron," he said evenly and shook her outstretched hand. Some perverse masculine instinct made him rub his thumb lightly against the soft skin of her palm; Matthew was rewarded when her eyes, shielded behind the oversize lenses, revealed a mild shock of female awareness.

She recovered quickly. "Please have a seat." Retrieving her hand, she gestured toward an Eames chair on the other side of the desk.

Leigh sat back down, somewhat relieved to put the expanse of polished walnut between herself and Matthew. He'd come to the audition in a black shirt and lean black slacks that made her think of pirates, radiating a dangerous unpredictability she found as intriguing as it was unnerving.

"Have you had any acting experience, Mr. St. James?" she asked with a glacial politeness. It was important—vital—that she establish control. Having learned at her father's knee that Hollywood was filled with people looking for signs of weakness, Leigh was adept at hiding her feelings.

Bitch. Matthew knew that Corbett had sent his résumé over with his photos. She knew he didn't have any previous acting experience. She only wanted to make certain both of them knew exactly who had the upper hand. "No."

She folded her hands atop the desk. Her fingernails were buffed to a glossy sheen. No rings, Matthew noticed. No bracelets. Her only jewelry consisted of a slim, gold-banded watch with Roman numerals and a pair of perfectly matched black pearl earrings. He'd spent enough time in the East to know that the pearls were genuine and wondered if the earrings had been a gift from a lover.

"*Dangerous* has the potential to be an important film, Mr. St. James. I can't risk casting it with unqualified individuals." Her gray eyes flicked over him, submitting him to a long, impersonal examination. Then she opened a manila file, taking out what Matthew recognized to be the studio shots Jill Cocheran had taken. Leigh remained silent for a long, nerve-racking time. She appeared to be comparing the original with the photos. "No matter how attractive any of those individuals might be," she finished up finally.

For an executive at a studio that had made a fortune on the appearance of its stars, she made good looks sound like a dirty word. Matthew rubbed his jaw thoughtfully. A day's growth of beard cast a dark shadow on his chiseled features. "I'm certainly glad to hear that, Ms. Baron. Since I've never considered myself to be particularly good-looking."

Perfectly shaped blond brows rose above the dark frames. "Oh? Yet Ryder Long is a very handsome man."

Matthew leaned back in his chair and locked his hands behind his head. The muscles in his upper arms swelled against his black shirtsleeves. "Far be it for me to argue with you, Ms. Baron, but you're wrong. Actually, Ryder Long isn't at all handsome. At least not in the conventional sense."

Leigh could feel the beginning twinges of a headache in her right temple. "Don't tell me that you've gotten hold of a screenplay. All of the copies are supposed to have been kept under lock and key."

"I read the book."

"Really." Her acid tone was laced with blatant disbelief.

"Really. I've always enjoyed reading. And you're right

about *Dangerous* being an extremely compelling story."

Leigh was momentarily nonplussed. Although she had spent her life surrounded by professional storytellers, she knew very few individuals who actually read for pleasure.

"Yes, it is," she said at length. "Well . . ." She glanced significantly at her watch. "I'd hoped to have someone else here, but since she seems to be late, I suppose we may as well get started." She handed him a sheaf of papers. "Will you need time to prepare?"

Before he could answer, the door to the office burst open and a whirlwind wearing tight black jeans and a bright red silk T-shirt studded with emerald rhinestones dashed into the room. "Christ, the traffic in this town just gets worse and worse," she complained, throwing her petite body into the chocolate brown chair next to Matthew. "I swear, one of these days the entire place is going to come to a screeching halt." Combing her fingers through her long, sleek black hair, she turned to Matthew. Although her quick study was just as professional as Leigh's had been, her brown eyes immediately brightened with feminine admiration. "Where in the hell did Leigh find you?"

"In her kitchen."

"That does it," the woman muttered. "I'm going to learn to cook if it kills me."

"First you'd have to locate your kitchen," Leigh countered with the first flash of humor Matthew had witnessed. "Mr. St. James, Kim Yamamoto. Mr. St. James is reading for Ryder," she added unnecessarily. To Matthew she said, "Kim has agreed to edit *Dangerous*."

Matthew gave her a rare, genuine smile. "I can't think of a better person for the job," he said. "Your work on *Street Smarts* was brilliant."

Kim's almond eyes narrowed as she studied him with renewed interest, obviously surprised that he'd mentioned one of her lesser-known projects. "Thanks, but in case you've forgotten, that little gem bombed at the box office."

"Only because marketing blew their job by promoting what was obviously a coming-of-age story as just another action film."

Kim preened visibly. "That's how I always viewed it."

"It was the only way possible." He looked at her curiously. "Isn't it unusual for an editor to come onto a project this early?"

"Most editors."

"But you're not most editors."

"No. I like to come onto a film in the beginning, so I can be involved through the evolution of a story—through all the various scripts—so that by the time the director begins shooting I have a firm grip on the story. Contrary to popular belief, editing isn't about taking out. It's about putting all these random scenes filmed from a hundred different angles into a workable, believable story. And I can't do that until I know what I'm doing and why I'm doing it."

"Sounds a lot like writing."

Kim bobbed her ebony head eagerly. "Exactly! Good looks and brains too," she enthused on a tone of exaggerated disbelief. "How would you like to get married?"

They could have been the only two people in the room. Deciding that the meeting of the Matthew St. James–Kim Yamamoto mutual admiration society had gone on long enough, Leigh cleared her throat.

"Excuse me for interrupting, but Mr. St. James was just about to begin reading," she said with clipped deliberation.

The spirited editor grinned. "Sorry, Leigh. But it was all this marvelous man's fault for getting me started." She nodded toward Matthew. "Please carry on; I promise not to open my mouth."

The friendly exchange with Kim Yamamoto had managed to banish his early tension. Matthew skimmed the pages, noting that Leigh had chosen the scene where Ryder Long explains his behavior to his terrified yet unwillingly fascinated hostage.

Once he began, the words came remarkably easily. Having reread the novel several times in preparation for this audition, Matthew discovered that not only did he empathize with the kidnapper, but he also shared many of the antihero's feelings of anger, isolation, and frustration.

"I believe that it all comes down to power," he said as the lengthy monologue came to a close. His quiet voice was more deadly than the harshest shout. "Power's the key thing. I was just a kid when I discovered I have it in my personality. I used to be afraid of it."

"But you're not any longer?" Leigh asked, prompting him from her own copy of the script.

"No." As his eyes met hers and held, she felt vaguely like a mongoose hypnotized by the unblinking, painted eye of the cobra. "I'm not." Beneath the steely outward arrogance, Leigh could see the tangled undergrowth of Ryder Long's— or was it Matthew St. James's?—dark soul. She shivered imperceptibly.

The room was hushed; everyone in attendance appeared stunned by Matthew's performance. Out of the corner of his eye, he viewed Meredith Ward applauding silently. Next to him, Kim flashed a thumbs-up sign. Only Leigh appeared unmoved.

"Thank you, Mr. St. James," she said, her tone as cool and polite as it had been when he first walked through the door. "Your interpretation was very interesting. And I'd like to discuss it further, but unfortunately, I have some pressing business to attend to first. If you'll just allow Meredith to direct you to the commissary, I'll join you there as soon as possible."

Matthew felt drained. As if he'd taken a knife and poured his guts out all over the impeccable surface of Leigh Baron's antique desk. The fact that the haughty bitch had encased herself in enough ice to cover Jupiter did nothing to improve his mood.

"I'll be happy to wait," he said, rising abruptly from the leather chair. "For ten minutes."

"Ten minutes?"

This time, as he met her disbelieving gaze, Matthew's eyes held a direct challenge. "That's right. Ten minutes. If you haven't completed your business by then, I'll have to leave. You see, Ms. Baron, I have a few pressing matters to attend to myself this evening."

"Another bartending engagement, I presume?" The words were no sooner out of her mouth than she regretted the catty put-down.

"No," Matthew corrected. "I'm having dinner with friends. I believe you know them."

"Oh?" Leigh's tone suggested that the possibility of their having mutual acquaintances was slim to none.

"Corbett and Tina Marshall."

His look reduced her to six inches tall. Before she could respond he was gone, leaving Meredith Ward to hurry after him.

Leigh realized that this was the second time Matthew St. James had walked out on her with the last word. One thing was certain: if he came to work for Baron Studios, that was going to change.

"Well?" Kim asked as soon as she and Leigh were alone.

"Well, what?"

"What are you going to do about that gorgeous guy?"

"I don't know. How are you coming along with the trailer for *Scattershot*?"

Kim shrugged. "Shit, Leigh, that movie is overflowing with sex and violence. If I can't edit a trailer out of it, I can't edit a trailer. And you're begging the question."

"I know."

Seeking something, anything to do, Leigh began straightening the few items on her desk. Both women knew the sudden display of tidiness was unnecessary. The crystal paperweight, the only sign of femininity Leigh permitted herself in her office, was precisely where it always was, three inches to the left of the leather-bound appointment book. The gold pen-and-pencil set was in its assigned place six inches from the front of the desk; memo pad, Rolodex, and brass paper-clip container right beside it.

"He *is* gorgeous," Kim offered.

"I know."

"And he's without question the best so far."

"I know."

"In fact, in a lot of ways, the guy actually seems to *be* Ryder Long."

Leigh sighed. "I know. And that's precisely what has me so worried."

"And intrigued?"

She and Kim Yamamoto had met when Joshua assigned the editor to Leigh's first feature-length movie four years ago. The film, a controversial World War II story about a young

Nisei newspaper reporter and the married navy captain who fell in love with her, had garnered rave reviews. From their very first meeting, it had been as if the two women had known each other all their lives. Leigh knew better than to try and keep a secret from her best friend.

"This town is filled with so many shallow people that a complex person is bound to be a bit intriguing," she argued.

Kim crossed her arms across the front of her rhinestone-studded shirt. "Don't pull that Ice Maiden routine with me, Leigh Baron," she warned. "We go back too far." Kim appraised her frankly. "Contrary to what those nuns at parochial school taught you, lust isn't really a mortal sin. If it were, ninety-nine percent of this town's population would have been turned into blocks of salt years ago."

"How did we get started in on lust?" Leigh began twisting a paper clip into figure 8s.

She did not want to think about how she'd been held spell-bound during Matthew's reading; she did not want to remember how she'd looked at his hands holding that script and wondered what they would feel like on her body. Such thoughts—such sensual feelings—were dangerous, threatening to undermine what she'd worked so hard to become.

"If Matthew St. James didn't start your juices flowing, you are in desperate need of sexual rehabilitation," Kim said. "Why, when he started in on that power bit, it was all I could do to keep myself from jumping his manly bones."

"You've got a dirty mind."

"Guilty. And thank God. The way you've kept me working my tail off the past six months, fantasizing about screwing is as close as I've gotten to the real thing." She smiled. "So how many projects are you working on now?"

"Ten," Leigh answered promptly, relieved that the conversation had returned to work. "Most are in the early development stage; *Scattershot*, as you know only too well, is in final editing; *Frenzy* hits the theaters Friday. We begin shooting *Kaleidoscope* in October and *Dangerous* . . ." She shook her head again, this time in frustration. "And *Dangerous* is, as usual, up in the air."

"Which brings us back to that guy you've kept waiting in the commissary for six"—Kim glanced down at her wide-banded diver's watch—"make that seven minutes. And counting."

"I know."

"So are you going to have him test?"

Leigh hesitated. "I haven't decided," she admitted as she tossed away the mangled paper clip. "I'll make up my mind on the way to the commissary."

12

Leigh changed her mind at least a dozen times on her way to the commissary. Entering the elaborately appointed dining room, she weaved her way past two uniformed motorcycle cops, a trio of doctors clad in green scrubs, and an exuberant group of extraterrestrials who were playing liar's poker with dollar bills.

From his vantage point at the back of the room beside a towering potted palm, Matthew watched as Leigh approached, stopping to exchange a few words, a smile, a casual hug. He noticed that despite her outwardly friendly behavior, she stiffened almost imperceptibly at each occasion of physical contact.

"Thank you for waiting," Leigh said as she sat down across the table from him.

"No problem." Twelve minutes had elapsed since he'd walked out of her office. Since she had entered the commissary precisely on time, he decided to be generous and give her the extra two minutes.

Leigh waved away the waiter who approached with a sterling silver coffeepot. Her nervous system was already horribly agitated; she didn't need any caffeine to make things worse. "I thought you were a writer," she said abruptly, dispensing with small talk and getting right down to business.

"I am."

"Yet here you are, reading for a part in a movie. Why?"

"Perhaps I didn't have anything better to do this afternoon."

Damn the man for baiting her. "Have you had any theatrical training?"

"None at all."

"Your performance was very interesting."

"So you said."

"Kim Yamamoto was quite impressed."

"Thank you. Given the quality of her work, I'll take that as a compliment."

Leigh folded her hands together atop the table. The deep-toned claret and forest green tablecloths echoed the colors of the trompe l'oeil woodland scenes on the far wall. The scenes had been copied from a 1930s Baron Studios' Robin Hood movie. "That was Kim's opinion, you understand."

She sure as hell wasn't going to make it easy on him. Wondering if she was the type of little girl who had pulled the wings off butterflies, Matthew refrained from answering immediately. Instead, he took a long sip of his coffee. "Oh, I believe I understand, Ms. Baron." He looked directly at her over the rim of the Spode cup. "Perhaps more than you think."

Leigh didn't appreciate his insinuation that she was taking their earlier encounter personally. "I like to believe that my reputation for being a fair businesswoman is deserved, Mr. St. James. If you're implying that I'd hold your previous behavior against you, you're mistaken."

"Ah," he said. "I was wondering how long you planned to continue that little charade."

"Charade?"

"Pretending that we'd never met."

"I thought you'd appreciate the others not knowing the circumstances of that meeting," she said, not quite truthfully.

"I'm not afraid of honest work, Ms. Baron," Matthew countered. Although his voice was calm, his eyes were not. "And unless memory fails me, I seem to recall some mention of bartending during our brief conversation."

Color darkened her cheeks as Leigh looked down at the table. When she lifted her gaze to Matthew's, her eyes expressed genuine regret. "I'm sorry about that."

He waved away her apology with a lazy flick of his wrist. "Don't worry about it."

There was a slight pause. "Obviously you weren't exaggerating about having read *Dangerous*." Matthew was accustomed to having women gaze at him with blatant feminine admiration. Leigh's grave gaze seemed to be measuring him. "You seem to have very strong feelings about Ryder Long."

"You could say that."

She knew Matthew was waiting for her decision and wondered what he'd say if he knew she still hadn't made up her mind. She fell silent once again as she studied him for a long, drawn-out moment. His face, while impossibly handsome, was chiseled and full of character. Lines fanned out from deep-set eyes the color of dark amber; at close glance, his nose appeared to have been broken, and a thin white scar cut across a square jaw. It was the face of a man used to living life on his own terms, even if those terms at times included violence and danger. But was it, she wondered, the face of a man she could trust?

"Do you identify with the character?"

Her wary implication hung heavily on the refrigerated air. Matthew decided that there was no way he was going to admit that in order to prepare for today's reading, he'd had to open some very personal doors and venture down some dark cellar steps.

"What's the matter, Ms. Baron, are you afraid of being kidnapped?" There was something new in his voice. A cold, precise anger that could have come from Ryder Long himself.

Leigh repressed a shiver. "Certainly not." She tugged her slim gray skirt over her knees as she crossed her legs. "I was merely wondering how you managed to hit upon precisely the right note. Especially since you've had no formal training."

"Perhaps I'm a natural."

"Perhaps."

As she looked into his uncivilized eyes, Leigh was suddenly reminded of her recent rash of nightmares. She'd experienced the bad dreams off and on since childhood, but lately, ever since Matthew St. James had entered her life, stirring emotions that were better left untapped, they'd begun tormenting her with increasing regularity.

Viewing the distant panic that flashed into her eyes, Matthew was struck with the realization that he'd seen that look from too many of the villagers in Vietnam not to recognize it. The unappealing truth of the matter was that on some basic level Leigh Baron was afraid of him.

"Whatever else you may think of me, Ms. Baron," he said quietly, "I'm not a sociopath like Ryder Long."

Leigh was beginning to realize that she was dealing with a very complex man. She had no doubt that Matthew had experienced his share of violence. Those rigid lines bracketing his mouth and fanning out from his eyes were proof of that. At the same time, however, instinct assured her that he'd never harm a woman.

"I'm pleased to hear that, Mr. St. James." She managed a faint smile that only wavered slightly. "We already have all the sociopaths we need in Baron Studios' legal department."

Matthew nodded his satisfaction with having gotten that little matter clarified. "So," he said, "where do we stand now?"

"I'd like to arrange a screen test." A voice in the far reaches of her mind screamed out *What are you doing?* Leigh ignored it. "Are you free tomorrow afternoon?"

"I'll make it a point to be."

"Fine. I'll make an appointment for you in makeup at one-thirty; your test will be at two. If that intensity you portrayed in your reading today translates to the screen, you may just turn out to be an actor after all." She glanced down at her watch. The pointed gesture was not lost on Matthew. Brushing a palm frond out of the way, he stood up.

"I'll try not to disappoint you," he said agreeably, extending a hand that, as much as she wanted to, Leigh knew she could not ignore.

It was only a hand, she told herself. Like any other. But when his fingers closed around hers, she was dismayed by the thrill that rocketed through her. Desire and something else. Fear? Shame? Whatever it was, Leigh knew that this was neither the time nor the place to dwell on it.

"Just don't get your hopes up," she warned. "Frankly, Mr. St. James, the odds aren't in your favor."

The smile he gave her was tinged with irony. "Don't worry, Ms. Baron. I'm used to that."

Leigh watched him walked away with a lazy, arrogant gait that fit the outlaw Ryder Long to a T. Her palm still tingled. It was not, she decided, the most propitious of omens.

Leigh had spent a lifetime suppressing her feelings; some instinct had warned her since childhood that emotions had a way of making you vulnerable, causing life to veer out of control just when you least expected it. She'd never met a man capable of triggering such a volatile sense of sexual awareness. With a single look, a mere touch, Matthew St. James had proven himself capable of arousing passions she'd been unaware of possessing.

She found herself saying a silent prayer that tomorrow's screen test would be a dismal failure. Once Matthew St. James proved unsuitable for the role, he'd be out of her life. Out of her thoughts.

It was a scene from the lowest circle of Dante's hell. VC, dressed in black pajamas, bandoleers strung across their chests, hand grenades on their belts, AK-47 assault rifles in their hands, streamed into Khe Sanh village. There were hordes of them—hundreds, thousands, tens of thousands. Incoming artillery screamed out of the sky, the hill was ablaze with napalm, the mortaring and rocketing went on and on, growing louder and louder until the earth shook.

Matthew fired, but his rifle jammed after only forty rounds. All around him living, breathing men and women were reduced to nothing more than lumps of red clay. The fighting continued while Matthew stood in the center of the chaos, alone and impotent. When it was finally over and silence settled over the village, the heavy, sweet smell of death flooded his nostrils. Mangled bodies littered the landscape, sprawled in pools of dark blood. The only sign of life was the rats that had come out of hiding.

It was then that he heard the baby. Lying beside its dead

mother, the child was screaming his lungs out. Matthew approached. Then stopped in his tracks when he saw the Russian pineapple grenade tied around the infant's neck. Another person staggered into the center of the village. Matthew instantly recognized the stunned soldier as one of the cherries who had joined up with K Company the previous day. The kid was headed toward the baby, obviously intent on salvaging some semblance of humanity from a ridiculously inhumane war.

Matthew tried to shout out a warning, but the words were stuck in his throat. He tried to move, but his feet were mired in the concretelike mud. He could only watch in horror as the teenage soldier gently picked up the crying baby. The world exploded.

Jerked out of his tortured sleep, Matthew pushed himself up to a sitting position and wearily leaned his head back against the wall. He was alone and shaken and drenched with sweat. The nightmare was not unfamiliar; having begun during the seventy-seven-day Siege of Khe Sanh—the longest battle of the war, where eighteen hundred Marines were killed and wounded—it continued to invade his sleep whenever he found himself in a situation out of his control.

It had been nearly six months since he last had the nightmare. Which was, Matthew reminded himself, a distinct improvement. When he first arrived stateside, the visions had tortured him on a nightly basis.

Getting out of bed, he went into the kitchen and made a cup of instant coffee. While he sat in the predawn darkness, drinking coffee and waiting for morning, Matthew was forced to admit just how badly he wanted the part he was testing for that afternoon. It wasn't good to want anything so badly. It smacked of weakness. And Matthew had never considered himself a weak man.

He didn't want to win the part in order to become a star; if he thought such a thing was even remotely possible, Matthew never would have walked into Leigh Baron's office in the first place. No, what he wanted was freedom. The freedom that could be bought with the money the role offered. Freedom that would enable him to direct all his energies toward his goal of becoming a screenwriter.

Although Matthew would be the last person to describe

himself as a mystic, over the years he'd come to believe that movies marked lives. He could remember exactly where he was—and who he was—the first time he saw *High Noon*. *Citizen Kane*. *Rebel Without a Cause*. From the time the neighborhood theater had first given season passes to the residents of the Sacred Heart Boys' Home, he'd been hooked on movies.

The summer of 1950 had been hot. Hot enough to break records all over the country. By July most Californians had taken to the mountain lakes or the beaches. Others, seven-year-old Matthew St. James included, escaped to the air-conditioned sanctuary of movie theaters.

In the third row of the balcony of a theater in Glendale, Matthew sat alone. Coming from behind him, a bright white beam cut through the darkness and lit up the giant silver screen. First the newsreel—fighting on the 38th Parallel in North Korea; Joseph McCarthy brandishing an FBI report he claimed exposed communists in the State Department; the New York Yankees leading the American League pennant race; previews of fall fashions in Paris revealing women's skirts rising to mid-calf. A narrated short showed off the new Fords, which boasted a new, revolutionary power-steering system. An advertisement pushed buttered popcorn and ice cold Coca-Cola available at the snack bar. The cartoon: Bugs Bunny foiling a befuddled Elmer Fudd. And then (finally!) the feature film—Walt Disney's *Treasure Island*.

The movie was like a magic carpet, whisking him away to a land of fantasy and adventure. No longer Matthew St. James, an unwanted bastard shuffled from foster home to foster home, he'd become Jim Hawkins, boy-hero, outwitting the villains on a hair-raising search for buried treasure. When the door behind him opened, emitting a brief flare of light, Matthew prayed that the beam of the usher's flashlight would continue down the aisle.

Up on the screen, Jim hid in a barrel of apples and listened as Long John Silver told the story of blind Pew. In the theater, Matthew slumped lower in the red velvet seat and held his breath as the usher drew nearer.

"There you are," a harsh, feminine voice crowed triumphantly. His social worker, the grim, relentless Miss Tomlin, had found him. Again. As she jerked him to his feet, a light-ning sharp pain shot through his arm. His latest guardian, Helen McCrea, had caught him drinking out of the milk bottle this morning. Screaming incoherently about germs, she'd twisted his arm behind his back and tossed him out the kitchen door, where he'd fallen headlong down the rickety wooden stairs and sprawled on the parched yellow grass.

"Do you have any idea how much trouble you've caused, young man?" Miss Tomlin huffed as she dragged him out of the theater into the bright California afternoon. Although he couldn't help blinking at the sudden harsh sunlight, Matthew refused to flinch, despite the pain that felt like fire shooting up his arm. He remained silent, his hands curled into fists in the pockets of his faded jeans.

"Do you think that I have nothing better to do than spend all my time in movie theaters, tracking down some runaway kid who doesn't appreciate the effort people have gone to to give him a home? I've a good mind to take you right down to the Hall of Detention, since that's undoubtedly where you're going to end up, anyway," Miss Tomlin predicted. "With all the other juvenile delinquents."

Her tirade continued nonstop all the way back to the house. Matthew didn't bother to listen; he'd heard it all before. He wondered idly if Helen would be passed out when he got back to the house. Her husband, a traveling salesman, was out on the road this week, which meant a constant string of men coming and going. He knew from bitter experience that some of those men would get drunk and try to knock him around. Still, he reasoned, with a pragmatism that had become second nature, if Helen stayed smashed, she might not discover the fifty cents he'd stolen from her purse for movie tickets.

They were passing Beverly Hills. As he looked out the car window at the palatial estates and imagined the perfect, pam-pered lives of those lucky enough to have been born to wealth and privilege, a sense of injustice and angry rebellion rose up inside him. The social worker's words were like wasps, buzz-ing noisily in his ears. Matthew returned his mutinous gaze to his ragged sneakers and imagined Long John Silver cutting Miss Tomlin's head off with his cutlass.

* * *

August 1965 had been hot and steamy. The monsoons had arrived and the afternoon rain came down in torrents. The constant mist in the air made the red, white, and green flares over Pleiku look soft and hazy, like falling stars. At the 71st Evacuation Hospital, the still air was pregnant with moisture, rendering the rusty paddle-blade fan next to useless as it creaked slowly overhead.

But the wounded men in the hospital ward were oblivious to the stifling humidity, their attention riveted on the World War II movie being screened on a sheet nailed to the wall.

"Go get 'em, Duke," a grunt sitting in a wheelchair beside Matthew shouted out as John Wayne's battleship chased down the Tokyo Express. "Splash those fuckin' Zeros," an SP/4 hollered. The soldier's head was bandaged, tubes coming out of his mouth and nose, and he could only see out of the corner of his left eye through a ragged hole cut in the bloody tape. Yet his enthusiasm was no less than if he'd been on that battleship himself. Other battle-weary and wounded soldiers, caught up in the story, yelled similar encouragement.

It was amazing, Matthew considered. Only an hour ago, the ward had been filled with moaning, screaming wounded. Kids, mostly, missing arms and legs, their heads smashed in and pieced together, their eyes lost and their hearts broken. Yet somehow, this uncomplicated, ninety-minute film had managed to transport its audience to a better place, a less complicated time.

Although the suspension of reality lasted no longer than the movie, Matthew wondered what it would feel like to have such an impact on people's lives.

By the time his second tour of duty was over, the idea of becoming a screenwriter had become fixed in Matthew's mind. These days his goal remained the driving force in his life, and although he knew it was a long shot, Matthew also knew that he wouldn't fail. He wouldn't allow himself to fail.

Now if only he could make it through Leigh Baron's damn screen test.

13

Matthew needn't have worried. His test was riveting, the electricity from his perform-ance arcing through the air. As she viewed the film with her father in Baron Studios' screening room, Leigh knew that they'd found their Ryder Long.

"Do you have any idea what you've done?" Joshua asked slowly as the lights came back on.

Leigh's palms were damp. Matthew—or Ryder, she couldn't quite tell where one left off and the other began—had seemed so blatantly masculine, with his mesmerizing eyes and strong hands. No. She didn't want to think about him that way. There was too much living etched onto his angular face; a woman would be insane—or a masochist—to let a man like Matthew St. James into her life.

Shaking off her thoughts, she brushed her palms against her slim navy skirt. "What have I done?"

"You've discovered the life raft that's going to save this

studio from drowning in red ink. Women will show up at theaters in droves to see Matthew St. James, while their husbands and lovers will sit beside them and fantasize having so much power over a woman she'd be willing to kill for you." He looked at Leigh with unbridled admiration. "That bartender is going to prove to be the find of the century. And the way you found him, working one of our parties, is going to be a gold mine of publicity."

"I didn't really discover him at the party," Leigh felt obliged to point out. "Tina was the one who recognized his potential."

Joshua shrugged as he pulled a cigar out of his pocket. "Lana Turner wasn't really discovered sitting at the counter of Schwab's Drugstore either," he reminded her over the flame of the gold lighter. "But who the hell remembers? Or cares?"

He frowned in concentration as he lit the cigar. "So, you've got the funding. And your protagonist. Now all you have to do is come up with your heiress and your project will definitely be a go. Have you thought about my suggestion?"

"About using an established actress to play Marilyn?"

"I still think it's a good idea."

"Both Ryder and Marilyn need to be played by unknowns," Leigh said mildly. It was not the first time she'd stated her position on the matter; Leigh doubted that it would be the last. "If we use someone whose image is familiar, it will only distract the audience from what I want this film to convey."

"If you want to send a message, use Western Union," Joshua quoted the memorable Goldwynism. "Besides, unknowns are a box office risk; casting a star would guarantee a hedge against disaster. Get yourself the right name and even if the movie turns out to be a turkey, it'll still open."

Although Leigh hated the practice, she was all too aware that a key way of judging a picture was by the opening weekend box office receipts. It was an industry conclusion that star appeal would cause people to flock to the theater. If the public stayed away, word immediately got out that the movie "didn't open." Which, in movie parlance, was a death knell.

"It's not going to be a turkey."

Joshua eyed her through a veil of blue smoke. Even as he

found her steely intransigence frustrating, he couldn't help admiring her strength. Holding the cigar out in front of him, he studied the glowing end for a long, thoughtful time. "How about we cut a deal?"

"What type of deal?" she asked cautiously. When her father suddenly turned agreeable was when he was the most dangerous.

"I convince our backers that you're right about using unknowns in the major roles and you agree to sign a name for the part of Dirk Young."

The role of Dirk Young, the obsessed FBI agent determined to track the pair down, was a pivotal part of the movie. But it had been written in a way that kept it from diminishing the main conflict between the protagonists.

"All right. You've got yourself a deal."

Joshua knew that Leigh never began a day without a detailed list of things she wished to accomplish, never entered into any venture without a distinct goal. She was also not a woman to make snap decisions.

"You knew all along what I was going to propose and were already prepared to concede on that point, weren't you?"

She couldn't resist a slight smile. "I don't know what you're talking about."

Joshua leaned over and squeezed her fingers with parental affection. "You're damned good at bluffing, sweetheart. But don't ever try an out-and-out lie," he advised good-naturedly. Matthew St. James's electrifying screen test had left him feeling more optimistic than he had in months. "Your face gives you away. Every time."

Leigh slipped her hand from his. "I'll keep that in mind."

"You do that," he agreed easily, leaning back in the plush seat. "So, what are you going to do about your sexy new star?"

"I'll call Corbett in the morning and get negotiations started."

"Fine, fine." He puffed thoughtfully on the cigar, clouds of smoke rising to the ceiling. "I also think you should telephone this St. James fellow. Invite him to lunch. Or better yet, dinner. An intimate dinner with wine and candlelight would probably be in order."

In all the years she'd been coming to the studio, her father had never—not once—suggested that she spend personal time with an actor. In fact, there had even been an unpleasant incident when she was fourteen and had a crush on the twenty-two-year-old star of Baron Studios' popular teenage surfer movies, Chance Murdock. Joshua had caught the two exchanging a kiss behind the sound stage one summer afternoon. The resulting fireworks had practically set the studio ablaze.

Two days later, Chance was discovered in a Santa Monica motel room with a fifteen-year-old girl. The girl's mother had no qualms about telling her story to the press; the hapless actor was charged with statutory rape and, although his attorney managed to get him off with probation, Chance Murdock's career as a teen idol came to a screeching halt. Rumors had persisted around Hollywood that Joshua Baron had set his young star up. A rumor Joshua denied.

"Why on earth would I want to have dinner with Matthew St. James?"

"Matthew St. James is the answer to our current financial difficulties. It's important to keep him happy." His eyes turned hard. Calculating. "Never underestimate the insecurity of an actor, Leigh, especially one destined to be a star. Being revered is a dual-edged sword—although fans' adoration brings stars fame and fortune, it also gives them that much farther to fall. Which most of them do. But while they are on top, my dear, they can make a studio one helluva lot of money."

Joshua placed the cigar in the ashtray located in the chair's arm and turned toward Leigh, shaping her tense shoulders with his palms. "It's not like I'm asking you to marry this St. James fellow," he assured her, thinking back on that fateful day when his father had instructed him to court Jens Eldring's frigid daughter. "Just take the man under your wing. Have dinner with him. Use your feminine wiles to keep him contented."

"Are you asking me to go to bed with him?"

"Of course not. You're a big girl, Leigh. Surely you can flirt a little with a man without having it get out of hand. All I'm asking you to do is see that St. James doesn't get away before we've got him safely signed, sealed, and delivered." His hands moved up and down her arms, coaxing acquiescence. "You'll do it, won't you, princess? For the studio?"

Bull's-eye, Leigh considered bleakly. To her, Baron Studios was more than a three-generational business. It was her roots as well as her future. Joshua often claimed that if his daughter were Scarlett O'Hara, the studio would be her Tara. Which was, Leigh considered now, an incisively accurate assessment.

She loved Baron Studios. And she'd do anything to save it. Including being nice to a man she didn't like. A man who made her too aware of being a woman.

"All right. I'll do it."

Pleased, Joshua rubbed his hands together as if he'd never expected any other outcome. Which indeed, he hadn't. Marissa might continually question his authority, but not Leigh. Never Leigh. "That's my girl."

Leigh was proud of her work at Baron Studios. Despite the fact that it had taken three long and frustrating years to get *Dangerous* to this point, she had no qualms about her ability to bring the film to the screen. She was confident enough to believe she could handle any situation that might arise.

But Matthew St. James was turning out to be another story altogether. Because Leigh had the uneasy feeling that the man was going to prove inordinately more challenging, radically more dangerous, than his fictional counterpart.

It was a classic morning at the beach. A clean swell was angling in out of the west at six to eight feet, the wind was calm, and long, hollow waves peeled off left and right. Although conditions were near perfect, the lineup was almost empty of surfers, due to the great white shark scare.

The rumor mill was well greased this time. Only one day after the initial sighting, the shark was reported to be twenty-five feet long and sixty feet off Manhattan Beach, fifteen feet long and two hundred yards off Redondo Beach, caught and killed off Topanga, responsible for the disappearance of a UCLA student off Zuma Beach. In the last alleged incident, all that the lifeguards were reportedly able to recover of the hapless surfer was an egg-shaped Bonzer board with an enormous bite taken out of it.

Stalking the border between supreme confidence and absolute disregard for life and limb, Matthew was not about to retreat and leave the surf to whatever shark may or may not have been lurking in the murky early-morning waters. Besides, he considered after cracking a wave all the way to shore, as angry as he was, any shark that even tried to attack him would be shit out of luck.

Whenever he thought about Leigh Baron, that icy rich bitch who had grasped control of his life, it was all he could do not to drive to Baron Studios, march into her sterile office, and wring her neck. Forced to admit that he was the one who had handed the reins over to her by testing for her goddamn movie, Matthew was thoroughly disgusted with himself and the situation he'd gotten himself into.

"Hey, man," Jeff Martin called out from his perch on the wet morning sand, "you look super-bummed."

"That's an understatement." Matthew picked up the Fiberglas board, intending to wade back out into the surf when he spotted the broken fin. "Shit."

"Just as well," Jeff said pragmatically. "Go back out there again and you could end up shark bait."

"The way my life is going lately, that could only be an improvement."

"Well, dude, your luck is about to change."

"Oh, yeah?"

"Yeah. I've been looking all over for you." Jeff's attention wandered as a tall platinum blonde strolled by walking a magnificent matched pair of Harlequin Great Danes. "Jesus Christ, would you look at that ass."

Matthew cast an appraising glance at the impressive rear end clad in a pair of skintight hot pants. "Not bad."

"Not bad?" Jeff leered, looking inclined to go after her. "What I wouldn't give for just one bite."

"If I were you, I'd try to control my appetite." Matthew nodded toward the two men trailing a short distance behind the woman. Dressed incongruously in dark business suits, they scowled at the wet sand clinging to their alligator shoes.

"Sal Licata and Dominic Alioto, two of Rocco Minetti's soldati," Jeff observed with respect.

Matthew was not particularly surprised that Jeff recognized

the Las Vegas gangster's henchmen; everyone in town knew that the Mafia controlled the porno racket in California, bringing in more than a hundred million dollars a year.

"So why were you looking for me?"

Jeff cast one last covetous look at the curvaceous blonde in the ass-clinging shorts as she continued down the beach. Some guys had all the luck. Not only did Minetti own the Lucky Nugget Hotel and Casino in Las Vegas, his trucking, real estate, and restaurant-supply businesses raked in enough bread to fill Fort Knox. And that was just the legal stuff.

"Because, dude, this is your lucky day." Jeff held out the joint he was smoking, offering a hit. When Matthew declined with a brief shake of his head, he simply shrugged. "It's god-damn true, you know."

"What's true?"

"That it's not what you know, but *who* you know. And you just happen to know a guy who can open all the right doors."

"I'm still not interested in working as a gigolo."

"I've graduated from that gig, man. Yessir, old Jeffy has moved on to bigger and better things. I'm into art films these days."

"Stag films, you mean."

"Hey, man, how long has it been since you've seen a really good adult film? The genre has grown up. We're using Tech-nicolor and soundtracks, fog lens, flashbacks, all sorts of artsy stuff. We're even putting plots in the stories."

"Look, the world might not be beating a path to my door in order to buy my screenplays. But that doesn't mean that I'd ever succumb to writing trash like *Bambi Blows Baltimore*."

"The money's bitchin', the work's a fuckin' breeze, and the side benefits are not to be believed." Jeff grinned, remember-ing last night's marathon. For a chick brought up in the rare-fied atmosphere of Beverly Hills, Marissa Baron sucked cock like a natural-born whore. "In fact, there's this tender young fox that I have big plans for. All I need is the right script."

"Which is where I come in, right?"

"I told Minetti all about you, really gave you a big buildup. So big, in fact, he's willin' to look at anything you've written."

Matthew scowled. "Forget it."

"Look, you want to write for movies, right? So everyone's

gotta start somewhere. Don't forget, Monroe posed for that girlie calendar and Joan Crawford, back when she was still Lucille LeSuer, is rumored to have starred in that unforgettable stag classic, *Velvet Lips*. Hell, even Clara Bow—"

"I get the point," Matthew said.

"All you have to do is come up with seven to ten scenes, six of them hard-core, throw in some lesbian pussy eating, and a couple of threesomes. How fucking hard can that be?"

Matthew was only half listening. He was thinking back to the time when he and Jeff were both sixteen and hanging out at the beach together, drinking beer, trying to score with girls, smoking (tobacco in those days), and acting tough.

A helluva lot can change in twelve years, Matthew decided, grateful that his life hadn't taken Jeff Martin's dubious path. He'd felt the energy in that room when he'd read Ryder Long's lines and, although Leigh Baron refused to admit it, he knew she wasn't going to find anyone else better for that part.

Despite the damn waiting game Miss Studio Executive was making him play, Matthew knew that what Tina and Corbett had predicted was going to come true. He was definitely on his way up—while his old high school buddy was on a fast slide down a very slippery slope.

"Thanks for thinking of me," he said, turning to leave. "But I'm still not interested."

"Damnit, Matt," Jeff complained. "I promised Minetti I could get him the hottest damn script ever written. But artistic, you know, which is what he's really stoked about, since it's a big step up from the shit he's been getting from his regular writers. If you cop out on me, what am I gonna do?"

"You'll think of something," Matthew shot back over his shoulder as he walked toward the parking lot. "You always do."

14

Marissa had prepared carefully for the party at the Malibu beach house. She had applied her makeup with an unusually light hand; her hair was tamed and flowed over her shoulders like a flame cascade. She looked, she thought with satisfaction, almost like Leigh.

Her camouflage did not fool anyone. Her voluptuous body did things to the simply draped dress that Bill Blass had never dreamed of. The black silk caressed her lush breasts and hugged her ass in a way that shouted out sex. With a capital S.

Basking in the pointed looks from the other party guests—blatant lust from the men, glittering envy from the women—Marissa made her way across the room to where her host was holding court. A six-foot-tall, impossibly stacked blonde clad in a clinging emerald green minidress and a pair of thigh-hugging, high-heeled black boots hung on his arm. A show girl, Marissa decided. Some bimbo he'd brought with him from Vegas. Nearby, guests were helping themselves to the cocaine offered on a large Baccarat tray tastefully surrounded by white cattleya orchids flown in from Hawaii.

"Mr. Minetti," she purred, interrupting Brendan Farraday, who'd been telling everyone who'd listen about his latest role in Baron Studios' new picture. "I wanted to tell you that I'm having a delightful time. Thank you for inviting me."

Rocco Minetti was a tall, lean man with the type of muscular body that came from a lifetime of working out. He was wearing a red silk shirt, tight white linen pants, loafers and no socks. His hair was dark, streaked at the temples with silver, his eyes as unreadable as a pair of hard black marbles.

"Those photos Jeffy took piqued my interest," he said. "When I saw them, I said to myself, Rocco, here is a girl we can make into a star."

"Do you really mean that?"

He shrugged. "Rocco Minetti never says anything he doesn't mean. Hell, if I could make a truckdriver into a household name, doing the same thing for a pretty young thing with knockers like yours should be a cinch, right, Bren?"

"Sure, Rocco," Farraday said unenthusiastically. Talking about the old days was not his favorite way to pass the time.

"Tell me, sweetheart," Rocco said, "don't you like to party?"

"Of course I do."

His eyes took a cold, judicious tour of Marissa, from the top of her fiery head down to her tasteful black silk Maud Frizon high heels. "So how come you're dressed for a funeral?"

She ran her hands nervously over her hips. "I wanted you to see that I have a lot of different looks. It's important for an actress to have range," she said, repeating the words of her Beverly Hills High drama teacher.

"Range, smange." Minetti exchanged an amused look with his minions, who immediately laughed on cue. "Look, sweetheart," he said, "you gotta understand, the kind of flicks I make, all that's required is that you be legal age, have the kind of body that makes men walk into walls, and like to fuck like a rabbit."

Marissa felt a flash of red-hot anger when everyone laughed again. They might see her as a source of amusement now, but one of these days, she vowed, she was going to get the last laugh.

She flicked her hair back over one shoulder and met his sardonic gaze with a patently seductive one of her own. "I'm eighteen." It wasn't really a lie; her birthday was in two short months. "I think my body speaks for itself." She ran her palms seductively down her sides from her full breasts to her thighs, successfully capturing the attention of every male present. "As for the last, I can supply references."

The show girl obviously decided that a poacher had wandered into her hunting ground. "Rocco, I want to dance."

Rocco's dark eyes didn't move from Marissa's. "Sure, babe. Bren, be a good boy and take my lady out for a spin."

It was an order. Softly couched, but carved in stone. Although neither Farraday nor the blonde looked all that eager, both wisely took to the crowded dance floor.

"So," Rocco said, "I guess the next order of business is to schedule a screen test." He pulled a card out of the pocket of his slacks. "Call my casting director Monday; he'll take care of everything."

Take risks, be bold, her father was always saying. Hesitate and you're lost. "Why wait until Monday when I can audition for you tonight?" She managed a manufactured smile and thrust her breasts toward him.

"Why not?" he said, shrugging. "Come into my office and we'll see what you've got."

They'd no sooner entered the book-lined room when Minetti told her to turn around, put her hands on the desk, and lift her skirt. "You got a nice ass," he commented conversationally as he yanked down her black bikini panties. "Not too skinny, like so many broads these days. Spread your legs."

Marissa liked sex; she enjoyed the high, the feeling of control. But this was different. As Minetti positioned himself between her rounded cheeks, she felt like a piece of meat.

Take risks.

Be bold.

Marissa closed her eyes and repeated her father's words over and over in her mind while Rocco Minetti pounded into her. It could have been a minute, an hour, an eternity, but finally he erupted and it was over.

"You're okay, kid," he said as he wiped off his limp penis with a white linen handkerchief. Marissa could now see he hadn't even bothered to take off his pants.

"Gee, thanks," she muttered and pulled her underpants back up, noting that he didn't offer the handkerchief so she could wipe the sticky semen off her buttocks. She felt dirty and used and was regretting her decision to come here in the first place. His next words instantly changed her mind.

"By the way, you got the part."

Warmth coursed through her. It was the chance she'd been waiting for. This time her answering smile was genuine. "Thank you, Mr. Minetti. I promise you won't regret it."

Marissa experienced an almost sexual tremor of anticipation when she considered that soon—very soon—her father would realize that she was more like him than his precious Leigh would ever be.

Joshua Baron sat alone in the library, nursing a tall glass of Scotch. The view from the arched ceiling-to-floor windows was spectacular; as the purple shadows of dusk gave way to night, the lights of Los Angeles looked like fallen stars. And the city certainly had its share of those, he mused, thinking of all the performers who had passed through Baron Studios' gates in the fifty-five years of the studio's existence.

They came and, if they were lucky enough to be in the right place at the right time, they could make themselves, and more important, the studio a lot of money. As soon as their name on a marquee ceased to bring in profits they were gone, back to the unemployment line, cattle calls, and these days, that most remote of all outbacks, television.

Fifty-five years. During that time ten men had served as Chief Executive of the United States; only two men had claimed the executive office of Baron Studios. And Leigh would be the first woman. Everyone else came and went, only the family lasted forever.

As his mind drifted to his elder daughter, Joshua thought about her remarkable new discovery and considered how ironic it was that once again the fate of Baron Studios had fallen on the shoulders of a single individual. And an outsider, at that.

This time the key to the studio's survival was Matthew St. James. Last time it was Signe.

Joshua remembered his wedding day and the disastrous wedding night that followed. He was not particularly surprised to discover that his bride was sexually inexperienced; after all, men hadn't exactly been beating a path to her door. What he hadn't counted on, however, was that she would behave like some goddamn sacrificial vestal virgin.

"My God, you're beautiful," he'd said in amazement when he viewed Signe, clad in a long white satin nightgown.

Her white blond hair, freed from its usual tight bun at the back of her neck, cascaded down her back. The plunging neckline of the clinging gown displayed high, firm breasts, and although she was thinner than the women he usually preferred, her wasplike waist allowed for an inviting curve of hip. Her face, free of makeup, appeared years younger and a great deal more appealing. It crossed Joshua's mind that perhaps this marriage wouldn't be such a sacrifice, after all.

When he would have drawn her into his arms, Signe held up her hands. "I know why you married me," she said stiffly.

The twin shadows of her nipples were visible though the gleaming satin. Joshua's body hardened. "I married you because I love you," he lied.

"No." When she shook her head, her silken hair settled over her breasts. Joshua wondered what that hair would feel like draped across his chest. "You married me so that my father would save your father's precious studio."

"That's ridiculous." He cupped her shoulders with his palms. Her perfumed skin was as smooth as porcelain. And every bit as cold. "You're a wonderful woman," he said, caressing her in an attempt to soothe, to warm. "Intelligent, beautiful." He nuzzled her neck. "Sexy. Christ, baby, any man would want you." Damn if it wasn't turning out to be the truth. As his lips moved slowly downward toward the swell of her breasts, Joshua couldn't remember ever feeling so horny.

Signe remained rigid in his arms. "Our marriage is one of economic convenience," she insisted, her slightly accented voice revealing her Scandinavian roots. "But I understand that men have certain biological needs." At that idea, her face twisted in distaste. "I will attempt to live up to my part of the bargain by being a proper wife in all respects."

Joshua's hard-on began to sag. "I appreciate your willing-ness to do your part to make our marriage work," he said, his own tone matching her formality. "And I promise to make our lovemaking as enjoyable for you as I know it's going to be for me."

Drawing her into his arms, he kissed her cold lips, stroked her hair, her shoulders, her arms. Although she didn't in-stantly respond, Joshua took heart in the fact that neither did she protest as he lowered her to the turned down double bed.

Joshua had never had to coax a woman into having sex. The women of his acquaintance were not afraid to admit that a female's body was every bit as capable of enjoying pleasure as a male's. His new bride, however, was proving to be the exception. When he touched her, she flinched. When he stroked, she trembled, but not in passion. And when his lips moved over her body in a futile attempt to warm her flesh, she turned as cold as a block of ice.

Tenderness gave way to frustration, frustration to irrita-tion, irritation to anger. Although Signe remained unrelent-ingly unresponsive, his own body, stirred by his continued attempts to rouse her to passion, ached for relief. Finally, unable to hold back any longer, he surged into her unwelcom-ing dryness, slowed momentarily by the taut, forbidding bar-rier of her virginity.

He came almost instantly. His penis had no sooner col-lapsed than Signe slid out from under him and rushed from the bed. A moment later Joshua heard the shower running in the adjoining bathroom.

When twenty minutes had passed and she still hadn't come out, he cursed, put his clothes back on, and went downstairs to the Biltmore Hotel's bar, where he proceeded to get royally drunk.

That first night set the tone for their marriage. For years Signe remained a coldly fastidious block of ice, submitting to sex only when he insisted. Although sexual satisfaction was easily found elsewhere, his father kept pointing out that it was necessary that Joshua's wife give birth to an heir in order to ensure the future of Baron Studios. The day Signe finally, petulantly, announced that she was pregnant, Joshua ceased going to her bedroom.

"It's just too damn bad the kid isn't a boy," Walter Baron had grumbled eight months later as he and Joshua stood beside the white wicker bassinet and looked down at the infant who bore a remarkable resemblance to her mother.

As if on cue, Leigh reached up and grabbed her father's finger with a strong grip that surprised him. When her somber gray eyes met his, Joshua sensed that those tiny pink hands would someday be capable of controlling an empire.

"Just wait," he promised his father. "This little girl will top us all."

Determined to give her a proper start in the business, Joshua began taking Leigh to the studio shortly after her third birthday, initiating her into the society of moviemaking. She proved to be a prodigy, surprising everyone but her father. He'd seen her potential from the beginning.

And now, as he sipped his Scotch and thought about Leigh's strength and dedication to the family business, Joshua only wished that her grandfather had lived long enough to see how well she'd lived up to the name of Baron.

When the phone rang the following morning, Matthew forced himself to let it ring once, twice, three times. It wouldn't do to look too eager.

"So when are we going to get together for that champagne?" Corbett asked without preamble.

"I got the part." Matthew was unaware of holding his breath until he heard the quick, relieved exhalation of air.

"Didn't I tell you that you would? We still have the details to hash out, but I'll take care of all that."

Although his tone was couched to reassure, Matthew could hear the repressed excitement in Corbett's voice. He knew that although Corbett, the man, appeared to be genuinely interested in his welfare, the agent's primary interest was in the deal.

Matthew recalled a joke he'd heard while tending bar at a party in Laurel Canyon. The way the story went, Corbett was on a cruise ship bound for La Paz when he fell overboard.

When an enormous shark came swimming circles around the agent, the passengers standing at the ship's railing began to shout and scream. Just when it looked as if Corbett was going to end up as brunch, the shark turned and swam away.

"My God," one of the passengers gasped, "it's a miracle."

"Not a miracle," another passenger corrected cynically. "Just professional courtesy."

Thinking of the story now, Matthew grinned. "I don't know how to thank you."

"Hey, it's my job. Just be free when Tina calls you for a celebratory dinner, okay?"

"Any time," Matthew confirmed. They talked for a few more minutes, during which Corbett outlined his plan of attack. When Matthew mentioned that a few of the items on the agent's agenda sounded overly optimistic, Corbett assured him that Leigh Baron was desperate enough to agree to just about anything.

As the conversation progressed, Matthew found it difficult to concentrate on details. All he could think of was that now, finally, he was free to write. Corbett assured him that it would be weeks before the movie went into production; plenty of time to finish the first draft of his screenplay.

After thanking the agent again, Matthew hung up. A minute later, he was making two more telephone calls. One to Jesse Martinez, quitting his job, the other to Beverly Hills Floral Creations, instructing the florist to send a dozen long-stemmed American Beauty roses to Tina Marshall. Those items of business out of the way, he went to the refrigerator, pulled out a can of Coors, and went out onto his porch.

Looking out over the vast expanse of cerulean water, Matthew realized that Corbett Marshall's phone call had inexorably changed his life.

Returning from lunch at The Bistro Garden with Kim Yamamoto, Leigh stopped in front of Meredith's desk. "Would you get Matthew St. James on the phone for me?" she asked her secretary.

"Are you going to sign him to play Ryder?"

"If we can reach an agreement with his agent."

"You will," Meredith said, flipping through her Rolodex.

"The guy was magnificent. God, I'd love to have him kidnap me."

"Let's hope that millions of other women feel the same way," Leigh said dryly.

She wasn't about to admit that she'd dreamed a disturbingly similar scenario just last night. She'd been sipping a piña colada on some scenic tropical beach, surrounded by a trio of attentive, sophisticated men who lived only to satisfy her every whim, when a pirate, clad all in black, suddenly appeared in the their midst and carried her off to his ship, where they sailed the high seas in search of dazzling treasures . . . Flash forward . . . Giddy with the richness of their bounty, Leigh allowed the pirate to drape her in heavy ropes of diamonds, rubies, emeralds, and pearls. His eyes gleamed with a primitive purpose as they took a slow, sensuous tour of her body, nude save for the dazzling plunder. She whispered not a word of protest when his firm lips captured her softly parted ones. He slowly, deliberately lowered his body over hers, then Leigh's clock radio switched on and the overly cheery voice of the morning DJ shattered the erotic image, leaving her feeling both ashamed and aroused at the same time.

"You're making the right decision," Kim said, once they were alone in Leigh's office.

"I know."

"Then why are you looking so down in the mouth?"

Leigh shrugged. "He's not an actor."

"So? The hunk's a natural."

"We don't even know if he can memorize lines."

"If that's all you're worried about, I'll volunteer to hang around the set and cue him."

"You just want to sleep with him."

"Of course I do." Kim's grin was one of friendly female lust. "Although sleeping wasn't exactly what I had in mind. After all, Leigh, how could any woman with blood stirring in her veins not want to go to bed with a man who's a dead ringer for Heathcliffe?"

Leigh wasn't about to touch that one. She was saved from answering by a short buzz on her intercom, signaling that Meredith had Matthew holding on the line. Was it her imagination, or was the blinking of the orange light actually beating with the same runaway rhythm of her heart?

Taking a deep breath that was meant to calm, but didn't, she picked up the receiver. "Hello, Mr. St. James. I assume Corbett has informed you of our offer."

"He's given me the bare bones." Matthew wondered if she actually thought him stupid enough to enter into negotiations himself.

His tone was every bit as remote and unfriendly as Leigh remembered. She had a good mind to hang up, when her father's instructions flashed through her mind. Matthew St. James was an unknown quantity, she reminded herself. He was also seemingly independent-minded enough to walk away before she could close the deal. And where would that leave Baron Studios?

"Are you calling for any special reason, Ms. Baron?"

"Well, yes, now that you mention it, I was. Actually, I called to invite you to have a drink with me."

"A drink?"

"That's right. Perhaps early this evening, around six? At the Polo Lounge?"

Would wonders never cease. "I don't know if that's such a good idea, Ms. Baron. If you want to discuss my contract, I'd suggest you call my agent."

Leigh wondered if the insufferable man was going to make her beg. "I promise not to discuss a word of business. This would be a purely social drink."

A social drink with Leigh Baron. Things were getting curiouser and curiouser. Matthew was reminded of the White Queen, who believed six impossible things could happen before breakfast.

"Are we talking about a date?"

"Oh, no, not a date," she said quickly. Too quickly, Leigh realized. "Our last two meetings haven't exactly been overly cordial," she reminded him unnecessarily. "Since we'll be working quite closely on this project, I thought it might be easier on everyone involved if you and I got to know one another a bit better."

"I suppose that couldn't hurt," Matthew decided after a slight pause. "Six o'clock, did you say?"

"That's right. If the time is convenient with you."

He'd promised to take Jill Cocheran out for Chinese to celebrate his contract. "I guess I could do some shuffling."

"I appreciate your fitting me into your busy schedule," she ground out between clenched teeth.

"No problem. I'll see you later."

"Later," Leigh agreed, returning the receiver to its cradle with more force than necessary.

"I knew it." Kim grinned devilishly. "You do have the hots for the guy."

"Don't be ridiculous."

"I can see it all now: drinks at the Polo Lounge, a long leisurely drive up the Coast Highway, dinner in some romantic, candlelit, out-of-the-way spot, a moonlight stroll along the beach. And before you know it, Ms. Leigh Baron, Baron Studios' renowned workaholic and professional celibate is smack-dab in the middle of a mad, passionate romance with her studio's newest star."

"That's ridiculous. Despite what I said, my meeting with the man is strictly business."

"Sure," Kim returned. "That's what Scarlett said when she rode off wearing the family drapes to talk Rhett into giving her the money to save Tara."

Deciding that such a ridiculous comparison didn't deserve a response, Leigh turned the conversation back to what they'd been discussing at lunch, Kim's work on *Dangerous*.

Across town, Jill looked up at Matthew's grim expression and wondered at the cause. The man had just been offered the hottest role in town. What on earth could have happened to cause him to scowl so? "Leigh Baron actually called you herself?"

"Her secretary placed the call. But, yeah, that was her. She wants me to have a drink with her."

"When?"

"This evening at six. At the Polo Lounge."

Jill whistled under her breath. "You really are on the fast track, aren't you?"

The unexpected telephone call had left him feeling both let-down and uneasy. What the hell was she up to? "Seems like it," he said on a shrug. "I guess we're going to have to go out to dinner later than we'd planned."

"Sure. Ah certainly wouldn't want to interfere with your chance to become rich and famous."

Matthew, looking for some sign of sarcasm, found none. "You really don't mind?"

"Matthew, Ah have told you Ah don't believe in messin' up a good thing with unnecessary obligations. Ah don't have any strings on you, sugah."

If only the rest of his life was as uncomplicated as his relationship with Jill. "You know," he said, drawing her to him, "you are one helluva woman, Jill Cocheran."

When she lifted her arms to link her hands around his neck, the rumpled sheet, which still carried the redolent scent of their recent lovemaking, fell away. "And you, Matthew St. James," she said, "are one helluva man."

15

Marissa lay on her back in the center of the round bed, trying to remember to groan on cue as two women—one white, the other black—made love to her. The glaring klieg lights hit the bed at hard angles, emphasizing every glistening pore.

"For chrissakes, put a little feeling into it, willya," the director complained, not for the first time. "We don't have all day."

"I'm trying"

Closing her eyes, Marissa willed her body to respond to the women's sensual ministrations. But it was impossible. The barren warehouse where the film was being shot was unbearably hot, she was sweating like a pig, and although she'd always fantasized about doing it in front of an audience, the disinterested attitude of the crew was not at all encouraging.

"Cut," the director shouted in disgust. "Okay, Martin," he said to Jeff, "you've got exactly five minutes to turn this broad around or we get ourselves another girl."

Jeff wiped the sweat off his brow. "Don't worry, Mr. B, I'll take care of everything."

"You'd better," Joe Bompensiero warned, chomping the stump of a fat black cigar. "Because every minute we sit around on our asses waiting for the chick to get it in gear is another bundle down the toilet. And Mr. Minetti don't like to see his money wasted. Capisce?"

"Yessir." Jeff grabbed a red satin kimono and threw it around Marissa's shoulders. He pulled her off the bed and behind a tower of boxes containing hijacked color TVs.

"What's the matter, kid?" His friendly tone didn't reveal that he was on the verge of knocking her ass across the damn warehouse.

"You try fucking in front of that bunch of Neanderthals," she complained. "And that blonde reeks of garlic. Every time she kisses me I feel like I'm going to throw up."

"It's just stage fright." He stroked her shoulders under the kimono. "All performers get it, even the big ones. But you don't have to worry, sweetheart, old Dr. Jeff has just the medicine to make everything all right." He reached into his shirt pocket and took out a small glassine envelope. Marissa watched as he shook some of the fine white powder out onto his palm.

"I don't do coke." Cocaine had scared her ever since a boyfriend—a drummer in a rock band—had died of a heart attack after snorting one too many lines at a party.

"Then you're missing the ultimate high, sweetheart." He dipped his little finger into the powder, then sucked it up one nostril, then the other. "Now it's your turn."

Marissa hesitated. She knew that this was her last chance. If she couldn't pull off this scene, Bompensiero would dump her and she'd never break into the business.

At first she had to press her finger against her nose to stifle a sneeze, but then suddenly, without warning, the cocaine swept to her brain like a trail of glittering diamond dust. Her body became unbearably sensitive and when she returned to the bed, her erect nipples tingled and her thighs quaked with excitement. Dark hands stroked her belly, glossy wet lips suckled at her breasts, sharp white teeth nipped at her buttocks. Fingers probed, explored, tormented the hidden niches of Marissa's body until she was writhing on the sheets. Out of the corner of her eye, she caught a glimpse of the crew watching with uncensored lust and, when release came, the applause magnified her climax.

It was six-twenty. After having spent the last agonizing twenty minutes trying to carry on a conversation with Matthew St. James, Leigh had come to the conclusion that she would have had better luck attempting to communicate with the Sphinx.

"Your résumé stated that you served in Vietnam. That must have been rough."

Matthew shrugged. He didn't believe that anyone who hadn't been there could begin to understand. "It wasn't a picnic."

"Corbett tells me that you're working on a screenplay about those days. I assume he's also warned you that the war is not a very popular subject."

"Not at the moment. But it's bound to end soon. And after a period of national denial, people will want to know the truth."

"And you intend to be the one who provides it?"

"Someone's going to write about it. It might as well be someone who was there, instead of a draft dodger who studied English literature at some nice, safe Canadian college."

"Point taken," she said. "But the way feelings are running right now, I think you're going to have a very long wait until the country's ready to look at this war without prejudice."

"Probably." He shrugged. "I'm used to waiting for what I want."

"But you don't necessarily like it."

"No." His eyes met hers and held. "Neither do you."

Touché. At this moment, it was a simple matter to imagine Matthew as a pirate, enjoying his stolen plunder and his women with the same lusty pleasure. Deciding it was time to change the subject, Leigh leaned back in the booth and observed him thoughtfully.

"Your résumé also said you're one of a rare breed—a California native."

"I was born in L.A." Matthew had always assumed he was born in the city, although his mother could have given birth to him anywhere before dumping him on the steps of St. James's.

His tone was less than encouraging, but Leigh had come here determined to get to know the man a little better and she wasn't going to let his sullen, uncooperative behavior stop her. "Do you have family here?"

"No." His abrupt tone did not encourage elaboration.

"None at all?"

"I never knew my family. I spent the first seven years at the Sacred Heart Boys' Home, the next nine in foster homes."

"I'm sorry," she murmured, wishing she hadn't brought the subject up.

"Don't be. From what I've seen, families aren't all they're cracked up to be."

"Sometimes they can certainly complicate your life," she agreed. "I realize that if my grandfather hadn't created Baron Studios, I could still be knocking my head against the wall, trying to prove that a woman can succeed on the business end of a camera. But on the other hand, there are times that I find myself giving in to my father; if he were any another boss, I'd probably be a little tougher."

She smiled, inviting a response. Matthew remained mute.

Frustrated by his continued silence, Leigh began talking about her work. Describing how she had been involved with the studio since childhood, her current duties, her lofty plans for the future, her every word underlined the difference between her privileged upbringing and Matthew's humble beginnings. And although Leigh realized that she was making him uncomfortable, she didn't care. He'd been unpleasant from the beginning.

Matthew wasn't really listening to her lengthy monologue. Instead he was wondering why the hell he had agreed to have a drink with this pampered bitch when he could be back home having a good time with the uncomplicated, agreeable Jill.

Joshua settled into in his customary power booth, facing the door. A quick glance around the Polo Lounge revealed that Leigh had followed his instructions concerning Matthew St.

James. He watched with interest, noting that although Leigh was chatting amiably and smiling right on cue, St. James was definitely not cooperating. Knowing firsthand his daughter's considerable charms, Joshua wondered if the guy was gay and made a mental note never to cast him in a film with Johnny Banning, just in case. He'd had enough trouble keeping the actor's sexual proclivities under wraps during the shooting of that damn Western last year, and although stories about love affairs between co-stars provided a big boost at the box office, as a general rule fans preferred their sex symbols to be heterosexual.

Of course if he was queer, Joshua decided, opting to look at the bright side, he sure as hell wouldn't have to worry about the guy trying to get into Leigh's silk panties. Not that he'd have a rat's chance of succeeding. Leigh was too smart a girl to get involved with a man who was so obviously from the wrong side of the tracks. When she did marry—and he assumed eventually she'd have to, if only to provide a fourth generation to run Baron Studios—she'd choose a mate who'd prove useful to the business. As he had done. Not that there was any hurry, Joshua assured himself. She was only twenty-five. There were still years to go before he'd be forced to share her with another man.

At that unwelcome idea, Joshua scowled.

The arrival of Brendan Farraday shattered his unpleasant introspection. "Sorry I'm late," Brendan said, sliding into the booth. "But I was at the club and the game ran a little longer than I'd planned."

"Golf or tennis?"

Farraday grinned. "Neither. These days I'm more into indoor sports."

Joshua was not surprised. Farraday's sexual appetites were well known. The only surprise was that he hadn't been shot in the ass by some jealous husband years ago. Joshua had often wondered if Sylvia Farraday kept a few discreet men on the side, or if she simply put up with her husband's affairs because being the wife of a star paid damn well. "Anyone I know?"

Farraday ordered a Scotch, rocks, before answering. "Would you believe Margie Wentworth?"

Margie Wentworth was the granddaughter of Giles Wentworth, one of Hollywood's biggest stars back in the golden
days of the 1930s. She'd been acting since appearing in an
Ivory Snow commercial when she was six months old. Recent
rumors had her hitting the bottle with increasing frequency.

"Christ, Brendan, talk about your jail bait. That kid can't be
more than sixteen."

"She turned fifteen last month," Farraday revealed, not
bothering to acknowledge the waiter who'd placed his drink
on the table, along with a second for Joshua. "But you'd never
know it. The kid's got moves even I couldn't believe."

"You're the one who was so hot for a part in *Dangerous*. If
you get your ass thrown in jail for statutory rape, Leigh'll
replace you before your lawyer shows up with the bail
money."

"Never happen." Farraday leaned back in the booth, appearing unconcerned, sipping the Scotch. "You're the boss of
the studio. She's just your kid."

"It's her project."

Farraday's eyes hardened. "Do I have to remind you where
the funding for this project is coming from?" His gaze moved
across the room to where Leigh was still struggling to carry
on a congenial conversation with Matthew. "Perhaps, if it's
really Leigh's baby, we ought to fill her in on a few of the more
critical details of the deal."

A hot flush rose from beneath Joshua's white silk collar. "I
told you before. We're keeping her out of this."

Farraday's answering smile didn't quite reach his eyes.
"Sure, Josh. Whatever you say."

So long as you play the game our way. The words were left
unstated, but they hovered threateningly in the air between
them. Joshua tossed back his Scotch, then stood up. "It's
getting late. And I've got that damn charity thing to get ready
for tonight."

"Sure. Sylvia and I will see you there. Oh, Josh, aren't you
forgetting something?"

"What?"

Farraday reached in the pocket of his pale cream linen
blazer and pulled out a plain white envelope. "Mr. Minetti
sends his best wishes for a successful film."

Christ, how he hated that smug look on Farraday's once handsome face. Looking as if the envelope was something that had crawled out from under a particularly slimy rock, Joshua took it, slipped it into his own pocket, and walked out of the restaurant.

Alone in the Polo Lounge, Farraday contemplated exactly how far he'd come. Who would have thought that he'd ever have a powerful man like Joshua Baron in his pocket? Like so many others who'd trekked to Hollywood in search of fame and fortune, Farraday, the former Arnie Stoller of Elko, Nevada, came from humble beginnings. Arnie's mother had been a seamstress who also took in ironing in order to make ends meet while his drunken father routinely drank up what little money Mary Stoller managed to earn. When Arnie was twelve years old, Mary packed her bags and disappeared on a Greyhound bus for parts unknown, leaving her son alone with an increasingly brutal father.

Arnie put up with the drinking and the beatings until his sixteenth birthday, when he greeted his father's arrival home from a drinking binge with an Ithica 12-gauge shotgun. Afterward, he walked out the door, never bothering to look back.

The sixteen-year-old changed his name to the ordinary-sounding John Brown, got a job driving a truck between Reno and Las Vegas, made some contacts at the casinos, and within eighteen months had turned to the more lucrative business of hauling contraband liquor and cigarettes. It was Rocco Minetti, owner of the Lucky Nugget Hotel and Casino, who first recognized the potential in the young truckdriver's all-American good looks.

Rocco changed Arnie's name again—this time to Brendan Farraday—and introduced him to Joshua Baron, a regular high roller at the casino. When Joshua, never known for his luck at cards, was offered an opportunity to cash out his markers in exchange for signing Farraday at Baron Studios, he didn't think twice before accepting the deal. He also, at Minetti's request, introduced Farraday to Corbett Marshall, an ambitious young agent at William Morris. Corbett took Farraday on as a client, Joshua signed him to play a hero in a World War II epic, and as they say in Hollywood, a star was born.

Farraday definitely liked being a star. He liked the perks: the fame, the money, the women, the power. And he definitely liked making Joshua Baron grovel.

"How the mighty have fallen," he murmured to himself with a slow, satisfied smile. He sipped his Scotch and took in the silicone-enhanced breasts of the actress in the next booth. Did Joshua realize that this was only the beginning?

Rocco Minetti's booth was in the corner of the Polo Lounge, allowing him to watch the action without drawing undue attention to himself. Sitting beside Marissa, he had seen Joshua Baron's discomfort during the brief conversation with Brendan Farraday. Farraday might be a world-class prick, but the guy was definitely useful. He'd have to tell him to ease up on Baron for a while, though, Rocco thought. Whatever he'd said, the old man had looked like he was going to have a heart attack or a stroke right then and there. Timing, Rocco mused, was everything.

Interesting how Baron had walked out without saying anything to his kid, Rocco considered, his gaze moving from Farraday to Leigh. It wasn't that her father hadn't noticed her; his eyes had kept drifting her way and, from the tight set to his jaw, Rocco determined that whatever Josh had been thinking, it sure as hell wasn't good. Wondering if there was a rift building between father and daughter, he made a mental note to make a few phone calls. If there were any more problems brewing at Baron Studios—problems he hadn't initiated—he damn well wanted to know about them.

The kid sure was a looker. She reminded him a lot of her mother—cool, distant, like a marble statue. But looks were deceiving, Rocco knew, wondering idly if the ever-so-proper Leigh Baron was as hot in the sack as Signe had been.

Marissa was getting sick of the way her sister drew everyone's attention without even trying. It was bad enough that she was having a drink with that hunk bartender from the party (in public, yet!), but their old man hadn't been able to keep his eyes from her the entire time he'd been talking with Brendan Farraday, and now even Rocco was looking at Leigh like he was considering casting her in his next skin flick.

"Hey, baby." She ran her ragged fingernails slowly up his thigh. When she'd reached her goal, she began seductively stroking his groin under the pink tablecloth. "I'm getting bored. Why don't we blow this joint and go back to your place and get it on in the Jacuzzi?"

"Later," Rocco said, pushing her hand away. What the hell was it that had turned this current crop of young chicks into crotch grabbers? Although he liked fucking as much as the next guy—hell, more than most—he was getting damn tired of being assaulted under tablecloths. Must be that damn women's lib, he decided grimly.

"But Rocco—" Marissa pouted prettily.

"I said later." He stood up. "Right now I got a business meeting with a friend of mine."

His eyes were hard. Unyielding, reminding her of the risks of arguing. She watched him walk over to Brendan Farraday's table and Marissa promised herself that once she became a star, she'd have any man she wanted. And one thing was for sure—that scumbag Minetti wasn't going to be one of them.

"Well, as much as I've enjoyed our little chat," Leigh said abruptly, "I do have a dinner engagement."

Matthew rose from the table, not bothering to conceal his relief.

They were standing at the entrance to the hotel, waiting for their cars when Matthew turned to her. "Thanks for the drink."

"You're welcome." Looking up into his dark eyes, Leigh had the feeling that the man was actually going to break down and say something personal, perhaps even profound.

When he continued to look at her for a long time without saying another word, Leigh found herself holding her breath. She was about to ask him if something was wrong when the valet arrived with her Jaguar; once again he disappointed her, leaving her to drive away from the restaurant, wishing she'd never have to see Matthew St. James again.

The club was packed. A blue cloud of smoke hovered over the room, along with the scents of perfume, sweat, and marijuana. The floor was awash with discarded cigarettes and spilled drinks. A driving rock beat accompanied by incomprehensible lyrics blared from monstrous speakers hung on every wall. Strobe lights flashed, adding a surreal feeling to the scene.

Matthew elbowed his way through the teeming sea of humanity, wishing he was anywhere else. Anywhere but wherever Leigh Baron was tonight, he amended as an afterthought. It had been Jill's idea to come here and, since he felt he owed her a good time after the way he'd left her this afternoon to go running off to the Polo Lounge, he was struggling not to let his distaste for the raucous scene show.

"Isn't this fun?" Jill shouted over the music, pulling him by the hand as she tugged him toward the crowded dance floor.

"Loads," he muttered.

"What?"

Her strapless sequined stretch top revealed a generous amount of golden flesh, the taste of which he still carried on his lips. Her hair was a wild tangle of gleaming blond, her eyes eager, her smile bright enough to light up the entire city. Matthew reminded himself that it wasn't her fault that his encounter with Leigh Baron had left him in a rotten mood.

"It's loads of fun," he assured her, grateful when the DJ in the tall booth switched to Neil Diamond's "Song Sung Blue." Although Matthew knew he could be considered a throwback to the dark ages, he had never understood the point in dancing if you couldn't hold the woman in your arms.

"Y'all are a rotten liar, Matthew," Jill accused as she lifted her arms around his neck. "But Ah like you anyway."

The flashing lights turned the dancers vivid shades of crimson, saffron, and purple. Matthew tried to relax, but his unsatisfactory conversation with Leigh kept running through his head, over and over again, like a record with the needle stuck in a groove. An hour later, he had still not managed to put it out of his mind when he heard a familiar voice behind him at the bar.

"Hey, man," Jeff said, "I thought you spent all your time sweating over a typewriter."

"Or mooning over women he won't ever get," a feminine voice added meanly.

Matthew slowly turned around. "I manage to get out from

time to time." His eyes narrowed and focused on Marissa Baron. "As for women, I like the one I'm with just fine."

"That's good, because any man who thinks he can get into my sister's pants is wasting his time." Her eyes were glazed, the shiny black pupils dilated. "Leigh has always had ice between her legs, isn't that right, sweetie?" She looked up at Jeff.

"Whatever you say, babe. So, Matt, what's a Mr. Clean guy like you doin' in a swingin' joint like this?"

"We're celebrating Matthew's contract," Jill said brightly.

"Contract?"

"He just got the starring role in Baron Studios' new film."

Both Jeff and Marissa stared at Matthew in disbelief.

"You're kidding," Jeff said finally.

"I don't believe it," Marissa echoed. "My father would never hire some bartender to star in one of his movies."

"The details still need to be ironed out, but it looks pretty good," Matthew confirmed.

Emotions washed over Jeff's face. Surprise, envy, anger. "Well, hey, dude, this calls for a celebration. Yo, bartender," he called out, "another round of drinks on the movie star here."

"We were just leaving," Matthew said, taking hold of Jill's elbow and turning her unprotestingly toward the door. He tossed a five-dollar bill onto the bar. "But have a beer on me."

Once in the car, Jill turned toward him. "Are you all right?"

"Sure." He gave her what he hoped was a reassuring smile. "It's just been a long day."

Returning his smile with a dazzling one of her own, she reached out and patted his hand. Matthew was grateful when she remained silent during the drive home.

Jeff was pissed. Here he was, busting his balls on those goddamn dead-end porno films and his old high school buddy just glides into Baron Studios, slicker than snot on a doorknob. It just wasn't fair. He sat in the dark, drinking himself into oblivion. He was alone because Marissa had locked herself in the bedroom after he'd gotten a little mean and knocked her around. Usually the chick liked it rough, but when he split her lip, she'd screamed at him like a banshee and raked her fingernails down his cheek, drawing blood.

Damn bitch. He tipped the bottle of Jack Daniel's back and swallowed deeply. If it wasn't for those pictures he'd taken of her, she'd still be waiting for her big break.

Deciding that she'd pouted long enough, he rose unsteadily from the chair and headed toward the bedroom.

Even as drunk as he was, the flimsy hollow-core door proved no obstacle. When he kicked it in, Marissa scrambled off the bed, clutching the sheet to her breasts. She was wearing the see-through black nightgown with heart-shaped cut-outs in provocative places that she'd surreptitiously stuffed into her voluminous shoulder bag after today's filming. "You'd better get out of here."

He was swaying dangerously. "This is my pad, remember?"

She reached into the drawer of the bedside table and took out the gun she'd seen the first night she moved in. "You come one step closer, you son of a bitch, and, so help me God, I'll use this."

He continued toward her, oblivious to the pistol pointed at him. "Come on, baby, quit playing hard to get. It's casting against type."

Marissa backed up until she was pressed against the wall. "I'm not kidding, Jeff."

"It's not loaded."

In one swift gesture he ripped her black nightgown to the waist. When he ground his mouth against hers, Marissa felt a surge of dangerous intensity, but before she could respond, Jeff suddenly went limp and slumped to the floor in an alcohol-sodden lump.

Her own head spinning from too many tequila sunrises, Marissa stared down at him for a long, incoherent time.

16

The waiting was driving him crazy as the pre-production days dragged on. Although Corbett had passed on to him what was promised to be the final draft screenplay of *Dangerous* (the third in the past week), and the director had been signed, the studio was a long way from beginning to shoot. Frustrated by the continual delays, Matthew spent the time learning his lines and writing. So far, moviemaking was about as exciting as watching two guys fish.

"You're what?" Joshua stared at Leigh in disbelief.

"I'm moving out," Leigh said, looking her father straight in the eye.

"The hell you are!" His face flushed, a vein pounding darkly at his temple. "We've been over this before. You have a home. With me. And your sister."

No. She wasn't going to let him do it to her again. She wasn't giving into emotional blackmail of any kind. It was strange how he only treated Marissa like a member of the family when it suited his own purposes. And although she was afraid that this time he'd actually have that stroke his doctors had warned her about, Leigh held her ground.

She was standing across his office from him, her hands resting on the back of one of the leather visitor's chairs. "I need a home of my own," she said calmly. "A place where I can be alone."

"To do what? Screw some ambitious stud who's only using you as an entry to me? To the studio?"

Leigh refused to be insulted. "Because I love you, I'm going to pretend I didn't hear that. And although I am honestly sorry that you're so upset, there's nothing you can say that will change my mind. Now, if you'll excuse me, I'm late for an appointment."

To her surprise and relief, Joshua didn't try to stop her. Thirty minutes later Leigh was standing on the balcony of the two-story house on Santa Monica's Gold Coast, looking past a pair of tall fan palms to the stretch of beach and the ocean beyond.

"Well? What do you think?" Tina asked.

"It's perfect."

"I have to be honest with you," Tina said. "The reason you're getting such a good deal is that after last winter's mud slides, a piece of the Palisades ended up in the owner's back-yard. Right after that, he chickened out and bought a place in Brentwood."

"His loss."

"Then there's the traffic. It's gotten terrible. Not to mention the tourists who will park illegally and block your drive-way, and drunks who spin out on the highway and land in your living room."

Leigh had heard the story. A few years ago a car had nearly done exactly that, crashing through the fence and landing in the compound of a scion of one of the old-time studios. The crash had been filmed by the owner's security cameras.

"I still love it," she insisted. "It's loaded with history."

Back in ancient times, when films were called moving pic-tures, it was this particular stretch of beach that was known as the Colony. Indeed, in those days, Malibu, a long haul away on a dusty, unpaved road, was for second stringers and those whose cars had sturdy shocks and rugged axles.

The house had once belonged to a silent film star infamous for his wild parties. She could look down at the beach, and almost imagine F. Scott Fitzgerald and William Randolph Hearst, dressed in white flannels, playing Ping-Pong while Marion Davies and Norma Shearer sipped dry martinis and cheered them on.

"It's also got dry rot," Tina felt obliged to point out.

"The wood can be replaced. I'm not looking for just a house, but something . . . more."

"A way of life." Tina wished she had a dollar for every time she'd heard that one.

Leigh nodded. "Exactly. Imagine waking up every morning to the Pacific Ocean."

"Along with flooding, damp air, salt corrosion, drunks sleeping it off in your front yard—"

"I'll take it."

Leigh needed a retreat. A place where she could escape Joshua and Marissa's constant battling, Baron Studios' ongoing financial difficulties, and her most distracting problem of all, the studio's new star. Although Leigh hated to admit it, lately she'd found herself thinking about Matthew St. James in ways that had nothing to do with business.

Not that there was anything wrong with fantasizing, she'd assured herself only this morning, after a particularly lengthy shower, during which time she'd closed her eyes and imagined the stinging hot water sluicing over her body to be Matthew's hands. After all, to believe *Cosmopolitan* magazine, entertaining sexual fantasies was perfectly normal behavior for modern women in these liberated 1970s.

But now, even as she reassured herself that she had nothing to be ashamed of, Leigh knew she'd feel better if the male starring in her erotic fantasies were any other man.

"Sold." Tina's satisfied voice broke into Leigh's thoughts. "You know," she said, slipping from the role of real estate broker to friend, "your father is not going to be pleased."

"I'm twenty-five. It's past time I had a home of my own."

"Still, it's obvious that Josh would prefer you to stay in

Beverly Hills. And your father has never been one to suffer defeat gracefully."

Leigh's calm gray eyes had a determined look. "Perhaps it's time he learned that he can't always have things his way."

Matthew was fuming as he strode through the hallowed halls of Baron Studios. By the time he reached Meredith's polished desk, smoke was practically coming out of his ears.

"Is she in?"

"Yes, but she's on the phone. Long distance. If you'll just take a seat—"

"I'll wait in her office."

One look at the fire in his dark eyes stopped any objection Leigh's secretary may have been about to raise.

Leigh glanced up as he marched into her office. Only a blond brow rising above the dark frame of her glasses revealed her surprise by his unexpected appearance.

"Peter," she said into the receiver, "something's come up. I'll have to get back to you on that, all right? Terrific. I appreciate all you've done."

"That was Peter Worth," she said as she hung up the phone. "There's talk in Washington of us losing the tax shelter from advertising expenses. If the investors get back their original expense, plus a guaranteed percent, the IRS may consider it a loan and disallow the tax deduction. If that happens, we'll have a more difficult time finding investors, which in turn would limit the number of films we could make each year. Baron Studios pays Mr. Worth a great deal of money to take our case to the appropriate members of Congress. I assume," she continued briskly, "that whatever has you charging in here today is equally important?"

He was already angry enough; Matthew knew if he allowed Leigh's cool, superior attitude to get under his skin, he'd explode. "We need to talk," he said, flinging his body into a chair.

Leigh took off her glasses, leaned back in her leather chair, put her elbows on the padded arms, and studied him over linked fingers. "About what?"

"About that twinkie you've got running the promotion department."

"Janet Bridges? That twinkie happens to have a master's degree in journalism."

"Undoubtedly yellow journalism."

Leigh ignored his sarcasm. "She's also the best in the business. I couldn't count the number of times she's pulled our chestnuts out of the fire."

"So let her handle *your* nuts. Just leave mine out of it."

"Did you come here today to impress me with your prowess of the English language? Or was there another reason?"

"She told *Variety* about the Silver Star I got in 'Nam."

"You got one, didn't you?"

"That's beside the point."

"It's hardly beside the point when Baron Studios' newest star is awarded a medal for gallantry in action."

"Aren't you afraid people will think Baron Studios' newest star is a baby burner?"

"Not after the follow-up story in tomorrow's *Variety* about your Purple Heart. Compassion for your wound should cancel out any antiwar feelings."

"You've got everything all figured out, don't you?"

"It was Janet who came up with the medal strategy. The war is a tricky subject. She decided it would be better to be upfront about your participation than to let some supermarket tabloid break the news."

"I can remember when serving your country could be construed as patriotism," he muttered.

"True. And as much as people would undoubtedly prefer to continue believing that war is like it was portrayed in all those heroic John Wayne movies, the evening news has brought reality home to the dinner table. What other complaints do you have?"

"How about her releasing that picture of me to the L.A. *Times*?"

"The one Jill Cocheran took? I selected that particular shot myself. It was quite good." Better than good. One glance and the image of the tight cords of his neck, the firm sinews of his arms, his powerful chest and washboard stomach, had been fixed on her mind for all time.

"Did you have to choose the only one where I wasn't wearing a shirt?"

"There's an old saying in this business, Matthew: If you've got it, flaunt it. Next?"

Somehow, without raising her smoothly modulated voice, she'd managed to subdue his rage. Matthew found himself admiring her technique. "The premiere tonight."

"Ah yes." She swiveled back and forth in her chair. "Don't tell me; you refuse to wear a tuxedo." She wondered vaguely what would happen if he showed up at the premiere dressed in those faded tight jeans and bare pecs. The women would go crazy; it'd be like throwing him into a bucket of man-eating piranhas.

Matthew saw a faint smile tease at the corners of her lips and wondered at its cause. "I'm not wild about the idea of dressing up like a headwaiter," he admitted. "But I categorically refuse to escort Cindy Raines."

"Cindy is one of our hottest young actresses. The press loves her; the publicity could do you a lot of good."

"She also has the IQ of a toaster."

"You don't have to talk to her, Matthew. You'll be watching a movie."

"Yeah, but I'm starting to get a handle on how you guys operate. All I have to do is show up at the theater with Miss Silicone in tow and the next thing I know your overeducated Janet Bridges will be leaking a blind item to the *Hollywood Reporter* that Cindy and I are having some hot affair."

"So?"

Matthew stared at her. Was he suddenly talking in Swahili? Why the hell couldn't he make her understand? "So I don't want people thinking I'm sleeping with Cindy Raines."

"Any people in particular?" she asked with studied casualness. If she had been worried about her unwilling attraction to Matthew, Leigh was aghast at her reaction to his being seriously involved with some nameless, faceless woman.

"How about everyone in particular? I'm not going, Leigh. Understand?"

Despite their initial lack of rapport, Leigh had met with Matthew several times to arrange carefully selected public appearances and interviews. If everything went as planned, by the time *Dangerous* made it to the screen, the public, enamored with the preproduction hype of Matthew St. James, would be eagerly waiting for the film.

Although their relationship had remained strictly professional, she watched how he worked, and was aware of how focused he was on his goal of becoming a screenwriter. Leigh couldn't help admiring Matthew's drive. She had also discovered that she could only push him so far.

"All right," she said, "I suppose we can arrange for Parker Masterson to escort Cindy. His new comedy is opening next week and, from the looks of the final cut, it's going to need all the help it can get."

"Thanks." Matthew stood up. "Sorry about interrupting your phone call." Now that he'd achieved victory on the most important of his demands, he could afford to be gracious.

"That's all right. Just don't make it a habit." Leigh stood up as well, coming around the desk to walk him to the door. "There is just one little thing."

"What's that?" Matthew asked, instantly suspicious at her casual, offhand tone. He'd already determined that Leigh Baron was never casual about her work.

"You're still going to have to attend that premiere."

"With whom?"

"I don't know. Why don't you call me back later this afternoon after Janet and I have time to work on it?"

"May I make a suggestion?"

Leigh glanced up at him curiously. Thus far, Matthew had displayed no interest in the promotional side of the business. On the contrary, she often felt as if she were using up a lifetime store of patience cajoling him into the few appearances he had agreed to make.

"Of course. Who do you have in mind?"

"You."

The single word ricocheted around them in the sudden stillness of the office. "Me?"

"That's right." He tested the waters a little further. "Got a problem with that, boss lady?"

Leigh studied him warily. Was this some kind of test?

"Not at all. It's just that the idea of you and I . . . of us . . . together . . . it never crossed my mind."

She was obviously uncomfortable with the sudden turn the

conversation had taken. Matthew had already come to the conclusion there were very few things that could fluster the ever-so-proper Ms. Baron. He decided he liked being one of them.

He regarded her with amusement. "What's the matter, Leigh? Does Baron Studios have a rule against the brass fraternizing with the talent?"

"Of course not."

"Good." His teeth flashed in a satisfied, wolfish smile. "I'll pick you up at seven-thirty." He turned to leave, then stopped in the doorway. "Wear something sexy. And get rid of that damn bun. I like your hair down."

With that he was gone, leaving Leigh to stare after him. Who the hell did he think he was? For a man who six weeks ago was tending bar and had yet to film his first scene, he had a lot of nerve, telling her how to dress and how to wear her hair.

She'd give him time to get home, then telephone with the news that something urgent had come up and she was going to have to cancel. No. That wasn't the way to handle it. She was Leigh Baron, heir to Baron Studios; she didn't owe the man any explanation. She'd simply tell him that he'd be attending the premiere with someone else—the most obnoxious actress she could find on such short notice.

That's exactly what she'd do, she decided, marching back to her desk. It was high time that Mr. Matthew St. James learned who, exactly, was boss. As Leigh picked up the receiver, a pair of thoughts occurred to her.

The first was that she really was the boss.

The second was that as boss, she could do any damn thing she wanted to.

"Meredith," she said, when her secretary came on the line. "Please clear my calendar for the rest of the afternoon, then call Julio and see if he can squeeze me in for a shampoo and blow-dry."

When Leigh hung up the phone, she realized she was smiling.

17

Carole King was singing "It's Too Late" on the car radio when Matthew drove through the studio gates. "You can sure say that again, Carole baby," he muttered, wondering what in the hell had possessed him to ask Leigh to go to the premiere with him.

Wasn't it enough that he spent too much time thinking about her as it was? Hadn't he wasted too many hours that he should have spent writing, staring at the blank piece of white paper and seeing her face materialize on the page?

Matthew knew that if he didn't sort out these feelings he'd been having about Leigh before tonight, he could end up with a helluva lot more trouble than he needed.

She was admittedly lovely, with her wide eyes and blond hair gleaming like silk in the bright California sun. But he knew other women just as lovely. She was intelligent, but no more so than some other women of his acquaintance. She was maddeningly stubborn and ambitious when it came to her work, but despite what he considered an unhealthy obsession with Baron Studios, the more time he spent in her company, the more she intrigued him.

One of the problems, he considered, taking the exit that led off the Hollywood Freeway to the Santa Monica, was that in all their dealings, all Leigh had ever permitted him to see was the tip of the iceberg.

Carole King gave way to James Taylor, and Matthew reminded himself that it was beneath what was the iceberg that had sunk the *Titanic*.

Smiling an apology to the driver she'd just inadvertently cut off, Leigh pulled her Jaguar sedan to a stop between a sporty little red Mercedes 280-SL and a gunmetal gray Rolls-Royce with the windows tinted black.

Leigh had never understood the appeal of Rodeo Drive, where impossibly thin, too rich women with too little to do shopped with a fervor that gave new meaning to conspicuous consumption. Personally, despite her high-image profession, she preferred buying classic styles made from good fabric that she could wear year after year. The idea of buying a spectacular, one-of-a-kind evening dress for a single occasion had always seemed incomprehensible.

"I've just the thing." The ultrachic saleswoman, clad in a black sheath, whisked a scarlet satin strapless dress with a short bell skirt from a nearby rack. "This would look absolutely divine on you, dear."

"Even if I could keep it up, which I doubt, I'd freeze to death before we made it through the first reel," Leigh said.

"Then how about this one? It's such a lovely color, don't you think?"

The emerald silk cocktail dress with a matching beaded jacket was closer to what Leigh had in mind, but the color was all wrong. "Green makes me look sallow."

The clerk switched gears with the deftness of a natural-born saleswoman. "Black is always appropriate."

The black floor-length evening dress was simply cut, with a slender skirt and tight sleeves ending in narrow points at the wrists. But the neckline was also slit to the waist in front, and there was no way she'd have the nerve to greet Matthew at the door wearing anything so blatantly revealing.

"I don't think so." Leigh was beginning to remember why she hated shopping.

"You're certainly slim enough to look marvelous in this," the woman suggested, displaying an abbreviated froth of pastel pink organza ruffles.

"It reminds me of cotton candy." Definitely not the image she wanted to portray to Matthew St. James.

"These are dazzling, don't you think?"

Leigh rejected the gossamer gold-and-flame harem pants and blouse with a firm shake of her head. "I'd feel like a reject from Central Casting. All that's missing are the seven veils."

The saleswoman remained undaunted. "Gracious, I nearly forgot. We received the most gorgeous dress this morning; it's still in the back room. Let me get it for you." She was gone before Leigh could tell her that she'd changed her mind.

"It's you," the woman proclaimed, returning with a triumphant gleam in her eyes.

Even as Leigh opened her mouth to thank the salesclerk for her trouble and explain that she wasn't in the market for a new dress after all, she drew in a quick, sudden breath.

"It's stunning." The dress, an ice blue silk Valentino, with thin silver threads, was the most ravishing thing Leigh had ever seen. "I've never seen a color like it."

"The threads were individually hand-dyed before the fabric was woven in Paris. Edith Head had a similar fabric made for Grace Kelly's 1955 Oscar appearance, but personally, I think this gown is even more divine than the princess's."

"It's beautiful. And undoubtedly ridiculously expensive."

The clerk deftly plucked the coded tag from the hanger. "Why don't you try it on?" she coaxed.

Leigh found the shimmering blue lure impossible to resist. The dress flowed over her like rippling water cascading down a mountain stream. The ice blue silk skimmed her body, hugging her slender curves in all the right places. The off-the-shoulder neckline framed a tantalizing display of creamy flesh, while the slit in the skirt displayed her legs to advantage. But it was when she turned around that the dress revealed its full potential: the neckline, which skimmed the crest of her breasts in front, plunged below her waist in back.

"How is it?" the woman called in to her.

"It's a little snug," Leigh lied, vowing to get out of the dress—and the boutique—before she gave in to temptation.

"Let me see." The saleswoman entered the dressing room without an invitation. "Didn't I tell you it was absolutely perfect? I almost feel sorry for that poor guy."

"Excuse me?" Leigh turned this way and that, studying her reflection, feeling like a little girl playing dress-up for the first time. She was enthralled against her will, amazed at the magic the dress had performed. She looked . . . sexy.

"Whatever man you're buying this dress for. One look at you and he's going to be a goner."

Leigh was stunned by the image in the mirror. Whereas moments before she'd entered the dressing room an attractive, sophisticated woman, now she was seductive.

Leigh surrendered to impulse. "I'll take it."

On some distant level, Leigh knew that she was probably making one of the biggest mistakes of her life. But she couldn't stop staring at the sexy stranger in the mirror.

Westwood was the movie capital of Los Angeles, boasting the most intense concentration of first-run theaters in the world. Surrounded by the posh communities of Beverly Hills, Bel Air, Brentwood, and Holmbly Hills, Westwood possessed a fascinating energy, derived in part from the cosmopolitan mix of students and young people drawn to nearby UCLA.

As they approached the theater, Leigh smiled with satisfaction at the serpentine lines of people curving around the block waiting to buy tickets. There was nothing quite like the enthusiasm of Westwood audiences; they had a way of reminding her what this business was all about.

Magic.

Excitement.

Make-believe.

Although searchlights no longer blazed across the night sky, the frenzied neon energy of the theater marquees created an excitement all their own. On a movie's opening night, the Paparazzi crowded near the entrance, cameras at the ready, and fans lined the sidewalk, hoping to catch a glimpse of a famous star.

Janet Bridges had done her job well. Although the first scene of *Dangerous* had not yet been shot, Matthew's face was becoming familiar. When he and Leigh emerged from the limousine, a clutch of teenage girls clad in stretchy Lurex tube tops and tight jeans excitedly screamed out his name.

"How does it feel to be famous?" Leigh asked. Necks craned to get a glimpse of the couple walking down the red-carpeted aisle.

"I feel like a trained bear in a cage."

"Does that bother you?" she asked as they took their seats.

"Of course. Wouldn't it you?"

"Having grown up in this business, I've learned to live with publicity. Of course, I've never had any interest in acting."

"Don't feel like the Lone Ranger."

"Yet you did end up auditioning for *Dangerous*."

"The dough you're paying me to make this movie will allow me to write full time. That's the only reason I agreed to test for the damn thing in the first place."

"You sound as if you're having second thoughts."

The contract negotiations had not yet been concluded. If Matthew got it into his frustratingly hard head to walk now, Leigh didn't know what she would do. His next words caused a frisson of fear to skim up her spine.

"I suppose I am."

The brief, unsettling conversation was cut short when the lights dimmed, the velvet curtain parted, and the screen filled with the familiar Baron Studios crown. Sitting in the dark, Leigh thought of all those thousands who had gravitated to the city from all over the world to try their luck at the incredible odds of becoming a star. She knew many aspiring actors and actresses would sell their souls for a single shot at the opportunity the man seated beside her had been given.

Two hours later, Leigh had no doubt that the featured film, *Scattershot*, would prove popular; as Kim Yamamoto had succinctly pointed out, the thriller was packed with sex and violence. It also had a complex plot, strong characterization, and fast-moving dialogue. All in all, a studio couldn't ask for anything more.

They got up to leave. "Looks as if you've got yourself a hit," Matthew said.

"I think we do," she agreed, smiling her thanks to the driver who'd opened the door of the limo. "Which just goes to show how much of this business is based on luck," she continued when Matthew joined her in the backseat and the car pulled away from the curb. "That script was turned down by six other studios before it finally ended up with us."

"Why?"

"Because so many different locations made it expensive to shoot, because the love interest is a multiracial couple, because the plot's too complicated; it moves so fast that if you leave your seat to buy popcorn, you'll miss something important. You name it, each studio had a different reason for turning the project down."

"But you bought it."

"I knew it was a movie people would enjoy."

"As simple as that?"

"Unfortunately, nothing is simple any longer," she said on a soft sigh. "These days most studio executives are selected for their business expertise rather than their feel for films. With them, everything is numbers, the bottom line. They just don't love movies."

"And you do."

"I'm passionate about them."

Belatedly realizing that it was the wrong thing to do, Leigh made the mistake of meeting Matthew's suddenly intense gaze.

"That's an intriguing idea."

"What?"

"You. Passion. The two together." He tugged lightly on the ends of her hair that tumbled freely over her bare shoulders.

Julio Mendoza, self-proclaimed hairdresser to the stars, had labored for the better part of two hours with shampoo, conditioner, gel, and spray, defying nature to force Leigh's straight blond hair into a mass of curls atop her head. Realizing that it was useless to argue with a hairdresser in the throes of creating, she had downed Julio's frothy confection under the shower immediately after returning home.

"I like your hair down."

"So you said. Not that I wore it this way for you."

"It makes you look softer. Warmer. More approachable . . .

Did I mention that I like that dress too?"

"I don't believe the subject came up." Her voice was calm; Leigh was not.

He shook his head and ran his fingertip along the neckline. "Damn. I must be losing my touch."

"Matthew—" When his fingers trailed up her neck, Leigh wondered if he could feel the increased beat of her heart.

He could. "Your heart's racing."

"Of course it is. You're making me nervous."

"Personally, I'd call it something more elemental. But I'm willing to settle for nervous. Until one of us comes up with a better word."

She watched, unable to move as his head descended, his intent obvious. Part of her mind told her to back away—both physically and emotionally—before things got out of hand. Another, more sensual part, the part that had succumbed to the seductive vision in the boutique mirror earlier this afternoon, welcomed Matthew's kiss.

His lips, now on hers, were clever, experienced, but that was no surprise. Leigh knew that a man as ruggedly handsome as Matthew would have had plenty of opportunity to perfect his technique. What was a surprise was that such a light touch could create such scintillating heat.

He deepened the kiss, degree by glorious degree. Matthew's broad hand cupped the back of her head. His mouth was firm, persuasive, his lips nibbling at hers, coaxing a response. Desires too long untapped rose to the surface, drawing her into a world of steamy, potent passion. She could get lost in this dark and smoky world, Leigh realized. Too easily.

Matthew knew that the kiss, which had begun as a casual sort of experimentation, was fast turning out to be something more intense. More dangerous. The attraction for Leigh had been there from the beginning, along with a basically sexual male desire he refused to apologize for. But no attraction had ever made him ache this way, and desire had never made him feel as if he were slowly, inexorably sinking into quicksand.

"I knew it," he murmured, lifting his head. Her eyes were filled with a confused desire that tugged at something elemental but unnamed inside of him.

"Knew what?"

"That there was fire under all that ice."

"That shouldn't have happened."

"You're right."

It was not what she'd expected him to say. "I am?"

"You sound surprised that I agree with you."

"I am."

Matthew shrugged. "Look, Leigh, you're a nice woman, when you're not playing that damn Joan Crawford, female-executive role. You're also remarkably intelligent, and as beautiful as any actress in this town. If you were a baseball player, you'd be a triple threat."

"Thanks," she murmured. "I think."

"It was meant as a compliment. And the truth is, if you were any other woman, you'd be spending tonight in my bed."

"You are incredibly arrogant."

"Perhaps. I'm also right. There were sparks there, and they weren't all mine. But I have a rule against sleeping with any woman who already has too much power over my life."

"And I have a rule against sleeping with anyone connected with Baron Studios."

"Fine." Matthew gave her a long, hard look. "Then we shouldn't have any problems, should we?"

"None at all." Her brisk, self-assured tone belonged to the icy studio executive Matthew found so unlikable.

But later, alone in the bedroom of her new home, Leigh pressed her fingertips against her lips, imagining that she could still feel the heat, and wondered.

18

Matthew was irritated when the memory of the kiss he and Leigh had shared lingered in his mind, teasing him with sensual suggestions that proved more frustrating with each passing day. She had infiltrated every corner of his mind, disturbing first his sleep, and then his work. And when he found himself facing an uncharacteristic writer's block for the third day in a row, he became furious at the idea of any woman having such power over him.

Swiftly calculating how long it had been since he'd made love to a beautiful woman, he realized the last time had been with Jill, the day he'd found out he'd won the part. That had been four weeks ago. Too long. That was all that was wrong, Matthew assured himself. He was simply reacting to Leigh because he was in need of a woman; it had nothing to do with her personally. Matthew began to feel better.

"So, what are you doing this weekend?" Kim asked over salads at The Bistro Garden the Friday before Labor Day.

"View some dailies, read some screenplays, walk the floor worrying about when and where I'm going to find someone to play opposite Matthew St. James in *Dangerous*," Leigh answered.

"Joshua is still dead set against Marissa?"

"He insists his feet are set in concrete." She speared an artichoke heart. "I'm still hoping to change his mind."

"Have you brought the subject up with her?"

"I haven't dared get her hopes up."

"How is she, anyway?"

Leigh put down her fork. "I don't really know. I told you she moved in with Jeff Martin."

"The beachboy."

"That's him. She mentioned something a few weeks ago about being up for a part, but I haven't heard anything about it since, and every time I call their apartment, there isn't any answer."

Kim took a sip of Chablis. "I wouldn't waste any time worrying about her. Marissa can take care of herself."

"She's more vulnerable than she looks. Or acts."

"That's probably what they said about Bloody Mary. So, how's the hunk?"

"I assume you're referring to Matthew St. James."

Kim's dark almond-shaped eyes observed her with renewed interest. "Some other good-looking stud you've been dating lately?"

"No. And I haven't been dating Matthew. I'm only seeing him for business reasons."

"That was quite some business suit you were wearing the night of *Scattershot*'s premiere. Don't forget, I was sitting behind the two of you and, believe me, the way that guy was looking at you, if you'd been a Hershey bar, you would've been a goner."

"Your imagination is not to be believed."

"It's the truth."

"It never pays to get involved with an actor," Leigh said, folding her napkin and putting it on the table. "They're all children."

"True. But Matthew isn't really an actor. He's a writer. And he's good, Leigh. Really, really good."

Leigh, who had been reaching into her wallet for her American Express card, looked across the table at her friend with undisguised interest. "You sound as if you've read his work."

Kim, avant-garde as usual, was wearing a kelly green silk-fringed cowboy shirt with mother-of-pearl buttons and a pair of navy blue hot pants with a cartridge belt worn low on her slender hips. Dressed as she was, with her gleaming black hair framing her smiling face, a casual observer would have taken her for a starlet, rather than the newly elected president of the Editors Guild. Leigh had watched the male heads turn when Kim had entered the restaurant. Now she couldn't help wondering if Matthew had also found the glamorous young editor irresistible.

"I was in Venice a couple days ago," Kim answered offhandedly. "And who should I run into but your sexy new star."

"Not unreasonable, since he lives in Venice." She quickly scanned the bill, then handed her card to the waiter.

"So I discovered. Anyway, we got to talking, then it got late, and pretty soon we were in his kitchen and I was reading his screenplay while he made lasagna."

"Sounds cozy." Something that felt too much like jealousy curled through her. Something she couldn't quite keep from her voice.

Kim grinned. "It would have been, if Matthew had cooperated. Unfortunately, he was a perfect gentleman."

"Now that is a surprise," Leigh said dryly. Try as she might, she hadn't been able to get that kiss they'd shared from her mind. She had spent too many sleepless hours since, trying to recall the last time she'd been kissed like that and had come to the reluctant conclusion that she had *never* been kissed like that. "I'm also surprised he let you read his screenplay."

"Well, to tell the truth, he didn't really let me," Kim admitted with an unrepentant grin. "It was on the counter and I couldn't resist glancing through it while he was down at the corner market getting the tomatoes for the sauce." Her smiling eyes turned serious. "It really was damned good, Leigh. Good enough that the guy's crazy if he gives up writing for acting."

"I hope you didn't tell him that."

"Are you kidding? Before I get a chance to edit him in *Dangerous*? The guy could be the next F. Scott Fitzgerald and

I wouldn't open my mouth until the wrap party."

Leigh nodded her satisfaction, added the tip, then signed her name to the charge slip. "Good."

"Oh," Kim said as they rose to leave, "I almost forgot. I'm invited to a cookout tomorrow at Doherty State Beach. How would you like to come along?"

"Don't you have a date?"

"The beach should be swarming with great-looking guys. Why take a bologna sandwich to a banquet? So, what do you say? It should be a lot of fun."

"I really should work."

"You know, you are in grave danger of becoming a drudge. Worse. A spinster drudge."

"Spinster? What Victorian dictionary did you get that out-dated word from? This is 1972, remember? I prefer to think of myself as a dedicated career woman."

"Fine. So what does a dedicated career woman do for sexual relief when she gets tired of going to bed with her stacks of scripts and optioned novels?"

Leigh considered herself to be a thoroughly modern woman, but conversations about sex—particularly when they involved her sex life, or lack of it—made her uncomfortable. "I do all right."

"For a Carmelite nun . . . At least give it some thought," Kim advised. "I'll call you later this afternoon."

"I have a meeting this afternoon."

Kim's frustrated sigh ruffled her sleek black bangs. "You are impossible. But I'm not giving up on you, Leigh Baron. Not until you learn to have some fun."

Back at her office, Leigh thought about Kim's words. The talented film editor managed to play every bit as hard as she worked, a talent that had somehow escaped Leigh. She had enough difficulty juggling the demands of the studio and her father and sister, without the added demands of a romantic relationship.

Leigh accepted the stack of phone messages from Meredith, and sitting down at her desk, experienced a fleeting wish that she could learn Kim's trick of keeping all the balls in the air.

* * *

Matthew had almost been able to convince himself that he was not interested in Leigh Baron. Until he walked into her office the Friday afternoon before Labor Day weekend.

"Good afternoon, Matthew," she greeted him with polite interest. "What can I do for you?"

Wanting her outrageously and cursing her heatedly for creating such heretofore unknown emotional turmoil, he turned inward. "Corbett told me you'd signed Brendan Farraday to play the FBI agent in *Dangerous*."

"That's right. We were lucky to get him; he had almost decided to do a thriller for Warner Brothers, but after he read the screenplay, I was able to persuade him to come over to us."

"Why wasn't I informed?"

"I suppose because I've been busy and the deal was just consummated. Besides, when you come right down to it, signing Brendan really doesn't have anything to do with you."

"The hell it doesn't!"

She tried to discern the reason for his gritty tone and failed. "We signed Brendan for star appeal. You may find this difficult to believe, Matthew, but your name doesn't bring in the big investment dollars."

"Not yet."

"That's right. Not yet."

There was a challenge in his tone that made Leigh worry that Matthew was beginning to believe his own press. Thinking that he was the last man she would have expected to have fallen prey to an inflated vanity, she frowned in annoyance. "There is nothing in your contract about casting approval."

"Common courtesy demanded that you tell me you were planning to cast Farraday."

"Would it have actually made a difference?"

"I never would have signed if I'd known I'd be working with that guy."

Leigh was surprised at Matthew's unprecedented animosity. Granted, Brendan could be pompous. And although he did tend to drink too much between pictures, he was a pro once the cameras began rolling. His recent election as president of the Screen Actors Guild proved that he was popular among his peers. In fact, Leigh considered now, the only person she'd ever met who openly disliked Brendan Farraday was Tina.

"I assume you have a valid reason for your aversion to working with Brendan?"

"Let's just say that after seeing a few of his Vietnam tours, I don't much care for the guy."

It was more than that. Something Matthew wasn't saying, but he'd encased himself in an impenetrable armor Leigh had come to know all too well. She folded her hands on the desk and observed him gravely. "You know, Matthew, military behavior was undoubtedly in order in Vietnam," she said quietly. "But it doesn't serve you very well in Los Angeles."

"What the hell does that mean?"

"It means that you go through life as if it's a journey behind enemy lines. You look at everyone, even those people who want to help you, with suspicion, and you face every day as a continuing series of battles to be won."

She'd hit a little too close for comfort. "I hadn't realized you had a degree in psychology."

"It doesn't take a degree to recognize hostility. I don't know what your problem is, Matthew, but it won't be long before *Dangerous* begins production and it's vital that harmony be established among the cast and crew. This attitude of yours could endanger my project." She gave him a long, warning look. "Which is something I will not, under any circumstance, allow to happen. I'm sorry that you're not happy about working with Brendan Farraday, but the bottom line is that we need his name recognition, so I suggest you just grow up and adjust to the fact that you can't always have things your way."

Her frosty, remote behavior only served to increase his own aggravation. "Doesn't it ever get old?"

"Doesn't what ever get old?"

"The Iron Maiden act. Centering your entire life around Baron Studios."

"Not that it's any of your business, but my entire life is certainly not centered around the studio."

"So what are you going to do this weekend?"

"I haven't decided."

"Let me guess."

Frustrated, Leigh pulled off her dark-frame glasses and sat back in her chair. "Be my guest."

"You're going to work. Like the good, nose-to-the-grind-stone little girl your daddy raised you to be."

"Excuse me?"

He wondered what had gone wrong with his mind that he'd wasted so much time thinking about such an icy, un-feeling woman. As difficult as he found talking about his feelings, he'd come here today to admit to his discomfort about working closely for months with a man he detested, yet all she could talk about was business. And the goddamn bottom line.

"When was the last time you actually took time to enjoy yourself?"

"I went to that premiere with you," she reminded him. "Or have you been with so many women since last week that you've already forgotten?"

"I haven't forgotten a thing. Including how you responded when I kissed you. You can say what you want about not sleeping with people you work with, but I could have had you that night, lady. In my bed, crying out, begging me to take you."

The provocative image was too close to Leigh's increasingly frequent fantasies for comfort. "I wish I'd never let you read for that damn part in the first place," she flared unchar-acteristically. "You're arrogant, egotistical, insufferable . . ."

"And right," he said when she paused to take a breath. "Don't forget that one, lady studio executive, because it's the most important of the lot. No matter what successful, Ice Queen face you show to the world, inside you're nothing but a confused mess of sexual inhibitions."

The truth stung more than Leigh ever could have imagined. She flung her head back. "You're a bastard."

Her careless words, spoken in anger, hit their mark. He flinched as if she'd hit him, his eyes turning to dark slits. Her cruel words reverberated about her head. Leigh sucked in several deep, calming breaths. What on earth was wrong with her? She never lost her temper. Never shouted. She was Leigh Baron. Cool, composed, dignified. Leigh Baron would never, ever, scream like a fishwife.

"I'm sorry."

"Actually, that one just happens to be the truth. Are you quite finished?"

"Quite," she said. "And you?"

"For now."

"What does that mean?"

"It means that we'll continue this conversation some time when you're more reasonable."

Temper flashed in her eyes until she realized she'd been expertly baited. "We really are going to have to settle this," she warned. "Or we might as well retitle *Dangerous* as *Disastrous*. Because that's how the movie's going to turn out."

"If you find me that difficult to work with, perhaps you ought to find yourself another Ryder Long."

"No." She shook her head. "You really are perfect for the part, Matthew. I also know how hard you've been working and how frustrating all these changes and delays must be."

"It's not having control over my life that's frustrating."

She managed a wry smile at that. "Tell me about it." She held out her hand. "Truce?"

Knowing exactly how Adam must have felt when Eve showed up in the Garden of Eden with that apple, Matthew found her coaxing smile impossible to resist. "Truce," he agreed gruffly.

Marissa was unusually calm sitting at the kitchen table in Jeff's apartment. Be bold. Take risks.

"That's exactly what I'm doing, Daddy dear," she murmured, leafing through the stack of photographs one last time, remembering how psyched she'd been when Jeff had taken them. She'd felt sexy. And sex, she considered, even more than money, was the animating factor in this world.

She slipped the photographs into a padded, oversize brown envelope, then addressed it to her father, care of Baron Studios. Across the bottom of the envelope, she printed PERSONAL in large bold letters, and underlined it three times.

Marissa smiled. She had made her plans. Now it was time to carry them out.

Her concentration shattered by her altercation with Matthew, Leigh finally threw in the towel late that afternoon.

Since she'd sent Meredith home early, in order to allow her secretary to get a start on the holiday weekend, she picked up the telephone and dialed the familiar number herself.

"Hello?"

"Hi, Kim," Leigh said, forcing a breezy tone she was a long way from feeling into her voice. "Did I interrupt anything?"

"Not at all. I was just watching the Olympics. Speaking of which, have you seen the Omar Sharif lookalike who's winning all those swimming medals?"

"Mark Spitz?"

"That's him. God, talk about star potential. If I were you, I'd be on a plane to Munich to sign him up before any other greedy studio gets its hands on him."

"I've already talked with his agent about a possible screen test," Leigh acknowledged. "But, believe it or not, I'm not calling about work."

"No?"

"Actually, I've decided to take you up on your offer."

"Terrific. I'll pick you around ten-thirty tomorrow morning."

"What should I bring?"

"Beer and chips are always good. Oh, and don't forget suntan lotion and your birth control pills."

"My what?"

"Hey, you never know when you're going to get lucky at one of these beach parties. And this former Girl Scout's motto is *Be Prepared.*"

"With an attitude like that, I'm amazed Matthew was able to resist."

"You're amazed?" Kim countered. "I was absolutely flabbergasted. Oh, my God."

"What?"

"You don't think he could be into guys, do you?"

Leigh thought about the heated kiss they'd shared in the backseat of the limo. And the way his eyes had turned dark and intense when his fingers had curled around hers this afternoon. "No. I don't think Matthew's gay."

"I hope you're right. Christ, what a waste that would be."

Hanging up, Leigh decided that, for once, she and Kim were in total agreement.

19

The mood was decidedly festive when Leigh and Kim arrived at Doherty State Beach shortly before noon. Rows of faded green tents lined the pine tree–shaded beach, making it look as if the Marines from nearby Camp Pendleton had chosen this weekend to go on bivouac. Hot dogs roasted over campfires, beer flowed from shiny aluminum kegs, dogs leaped into the air to catch bright plastic Frisbees in their jaws. Impromptu football and volleyball took up much of the sand.

Out on the water, surfers rode the breaking waves. One particular surfer captured Leigh's attention. Tall and muscular, with a physique that backed up any challenge the ocean might dare to make, his style was tautly controlled and precise, unlike so many of the others who were wiping out. She watched, entranced by the unknown surfer's combination of strength and grace riding the white surf all the way to shore. It was then that she recognized him.

"My goodness." She gave Kim an accusing look. "Of all the beaches in the state, what a coincidence that we just happened to show up at the same one as Matthew St. James."

Kim waved merrily at Matthew, who began walking toward them. "Isn't it?"

"Well, have fun."

When Leigh turned away, Kim grabbed her arm. "Where do you think you're going?"

"This is supposed to be my day off, remember? So I'm leaving before Matthew and I get into another argument."

"But you can't leave. Not now."

"Why not? Don't you want to be alone with him?"

"The guy's already turned me down; now it's your turn at bat."

"What are you talking about?"

Kim was forestalled from answering by Matthew's approach. "That was absolutely wonderful," she gushed.

He shrugged. "It's getting glassy; they'll be higher this evening." He glanced over at Leigh. "This is a surprise."

"Isn't it?"

"Well," Kim said quickly, "I see my friends; I'd better get over there before they run out of Fritos. You two have fun; Leigh, maybe I'll see you later." She ran off, leaving them alone.

"Why do I feel like high school?" Leigh asked.

Matthew managed a half smile. "Join the club."

She glanced down at his surfboard. "Don't let me keep you."

"I was ready for a break."

"Oh." Leigh reminded herself that she was an adult, an individual who wielded a great deal of power. So why was she suddenly behaving like a tongue-tied schoolgirl?

A charged silence settled over them while Matthew tried to think of something, anything, to say. "Want a beer?" The sea breeze blew a few strands of blond hair across her cheek; his fingers itched with the urge to brush them away.

Leigh tucked her hair behind her ears. "That would be nice. It was a long drive down here and Kim's Corvette doesn't have air conditioning."

"I've got a cooler back at my tent. It's just around the corner."

"Which means it's out of sight of this beach."

"Does that bother you?"

Her glance moved to Kim, who had joined a group of people Leigh recognized to be fellow editors and cinematographers. All of them were eyeing Leigh and Matthew with undisguised interest. "What do you think?"

Matthew chuckled. "I think that if we disappear, they're going to go crazy wondering what we're doing."

"Serves them right." Cast in the role of a fellow conspirator, she smiled up at him. "Lead the way."

"What took you so long?"

Marissa greeted Jeff at the apartment door wearing a filmy black negligee from Frederick's, matching crotchless panties and a plunge bra.

"Just delivering a few pharmaceuticals, babe." When she handed him a glass of champagne, Jeff dropped the athletic bag to the floor.

"I hope you saved some goodies for me."

"Don't I always? So how come you're not dressed?"

"Don't you like my new outfit?" she asked on a pout.

"It's bitchin'. I just thought we were goin' to the beach."

"I changed my mind. I decided that it would be more fun to stay home and celebrate." She shrugged out of the negligee, letting it drop to the floor.

Jeff's body stiffened at the sight of her nipples, darkly rouged, jutting impertinently through the lacy cutouts of the bra. "Baby," he said, yanking off his gray cotton gym shorts, "you're on."

Later, as they lay panting on the avocado green shag carpeting, Jeff thought to ask, "What the hell are we celebrating?"

"Didn't I tell you?" Marissa refilled their glasses with the Cristal champagne she'd filched from Joshua's wine cellar. "My daddy's going to make me a star."

Matthew's campsite faced the beach. The beer was cold, the sun hot, and the company surprisingly enjoyable. Leigh could see that the sea relaxed him. She sat cross-legged on the sand

and watched the waves roll in to shore. It smoothed off his rough edges, calmed his inner anger, wore away at the parapets that normally kept everyone at arm's length.

While they indulged in obligatory small talk, Matthew found Leigh much more accessible. She'd discarded the severely tailored suits she usually wore like a suit of armor in favor of a sunshine yellow T-shirt and white shorts. With her long blond hair free and blowing in the breeze, she was more natural.

"Mmm," she sighed happily, leaning back on her elbows and stretching her legs out in front of her, "I needed this." She took a deep breath, filling her lungs with the invigorating salt air. "I have this theory that if everyone took thirty minutes a day to walk along the beach, all the psychologists and psychiatrists in L.A. would go out of business in a week."

"The beach is one reason I live in Venice." He took a drink from the long-necked brown bottle. "That and the atmosphere."

More than anything, funky Venice, birthplace of fads, was what had given Los Angeles its reputation as La-La Land. A mixture of quaint and seedy, rich and poor, it had always been a home for dreamers, beginning with Abbot Kinney, whose vision had transformed the sleepy little ocean community into a miniature of its Adriatic namesake, replete with miles of canals, gondolas, and seaside hotels. Today all that remained of the Grand Lagoon was a traffic circle, but the town continued to attract more than its share of individualists.

"You're a dreamer," Leigh suggested softly.

Matthew shrugged. "I suppose, in a way, I am. After all, who else but a dreamer would be crazy enough to think he could actually earn a living telling stories?"

"Kim says you're very talented."

"Kim's a nice lady. And an excellent judge of talent."

Leigh laughed at that, as she was supposed to. Her gaze drifted out toward the lineup of surfers. "You were very good out there."

"Thanks."

"You don't move around as much as the others."

Matthew shrugged. "I believe in a less-is-more approach."

"It was beautiful. Almost elegant, but at the same time,

powerful." She turned back toward him. "I don't know much about the logistics of surfing, but I like your style, Mr. St. James."

"That makes us even. Because I definitely like your style, Ms. Baron."

"That's not the impression I got yesterday."

"It's a holiday." He took her hand and linked their fingers comfortably together. Matthew wondered if everything between them would be such a close and perfect fit. "Let's forget about work. Just for today."

"Just for today," she agreed softly.

"Great. Don't go away." He stood up and walked a few yards down the beach to where a couple was locked in a passionate clinch. After exchanging a few words, he returned, carrying a long white surfboard with a likeness of Ann-Margret wearing a shiny black-vinyl bikini laminated onto the back. "Come on, boss lady, we're wasting those waves." He reached out and pulled her to her feet.

"Wasting what waves? Are you talking about surfing?"

"Of course."

"I don't surf."

"You're kidding! You grew up in L.A. and you've never surfed?"

"You don't have to make it sound as if I've suffered a misspent childhood," she complained. "For your information, I have body surfed. Lots of times."

"Great. Board surfing is simply the next step."

When a trio of surfers disappeared under a wall of crashing white water, Leigh dug her heels into the sand. "Matthew, I don't think this is a very good idea."

"You'll be terrific, trust me."

"How do I know this isn't some sadistic scheme to pay me back for yesterday?"

"I told you, forget yesterday. That was then. This is now. And the question on the table is whether or not you're willing to trust me not to let anything bad happen to you."

Leigh looked up into the unrevealing dark lenses of his sunglasses and realized that what had begun as an offhand suggestion had metamorphosed into some sort of a test. A test that could determine the future of Baron Studios. Leigh remembered her promise to humor Matthew.

"All right. But if I break my neck, I'm going to kill you."

"You've got yourself a deal." For a fleeting moment, Matthew's self-satisfied grin reminded Leigh uncomfortably of her father.

"I know I'm going to regret this," she said, reaching for the hem of her T-shirt. She stripped out of her shirt and shorts, revealing a sleek body clad in a white bikini.

"You're going to love it," Matthew insisted, resisting the urge to drag her, caveman-style, into the nearby tent.

The house was quiet; wanting to be alone, Joshua had given the servants the weekend off. He was in the library, drinking Scotch and milk and staring down at the photographs that had arrived this afternoon at the studio, Special Delivery. After he had flicked through the glossy eight-by-tens of Marissa in a series of increasingly sexual scenes, Joshua's mind raced back to the day Signe had announced that she was pregnant again.

There was no way the baby could have been his; he and his wife hadn't slept together since she'd become pregnant with Leigh years earlier. If he'd given the matter any thought, Joshua would have guessed that Signe had remained celibate; to discover that she had had an affair was an unpalatable revelation.

When he suggested that she take her bastard and go live with whoever was responsible, Signe calmly replied that not only was the man in question already married, she had no intention of telling him he was about to be a father.

"You should at least make him pay for the doctor," Joshua advised. "Because I'll be damned if I'm going to spring for the cost of getting rid of some other guy's kid."

"Don't be ridiculous," Signe replied. "In case you've forgotten, Joshua, the one and only thing we have in common is that we were both raised as Catholics. Abortion is out of the question."

"But adultery isn't?" he shot back. "I want you the hell out of here by the time I get back from the studio tonight."

Signe surprised him by laughing. A cold, unpleasant sound that made him want to kill her. "Very good, darling," she said. "Just the right amount of husbandly outrage with a touch of wounded male pride. Perhaps you should have been an actor instead of a studio head."

His hands clenched into fists at his side. "You're a slut."

"And you're a pompous prick." Her smile was brittle ice. "I'd say we belong together." She crossed the room and placed her hand on his arm. Her scarlet fingernails looked like blood against the navy sleeve of his suit jacket. "Don't forget, darling, it was my money that saved your precious studio from bankruptcy. You owe me."

Joshua stared at her. "You actually expect me to stay married to a woman who made a laughingstock out of me?"

"You have no need to worry; I was quite discreet." Her fingers stroked the rigid muscles of his forearm. It was the first time she'd touched him in years. "There isn't anyone— including my child's father—who won't automatically assume this baby is yours. Besides, think of the advantages continuing our marriage would have for you."

"Name one."

"If you get enmeshed in a long, expensive divorce proceeding, Baron Studios could go right down the drain. But what even you should realize, Joshua, is that by remaining a married man, you'll have a ready excuse for not marrying all those young actresses you're always sleeping with."

Joshua reluctantly decided that Signe had a point. "All right," he said. "You can stay."

"And you'll claim my child as yours?" Signe had no intention of having her baby born under the stigma of illegitimacy.

He scowled. "It'll have my name. That's all I'm promising."

She smiled. "That's all I'm asking."

Over the next few months they entered into an uneasy truce. Unfortunately, the idea of some faceless man inflaming the frigid Signe to passion left Joshua feeling strangely inadequate. To his further dismay, he discovered himself to be sexually impotent.

It was then that he sought comfort in the one aspect of his life he could still control: Leigh.

After he crossed society's inviolate moral boundary, Joshua lived in constant fear of detection. Until he began to realize that Leigh had no memory of that night. Of the betrayal that had taken place.

Instead of destroying his life, as he'd feared, a secret bond had been created between father and daughter—a bond that possessed the tensile strength of silk. And although Leigh had no memory of how that silken cord had been woven, Joshua knew that she accepted the reality of its existence. She'd never leave him. He was the only man she could ever love.

He burned the pornographic photos of Marissa and thought of his beautiful, talented daughter.

20

It was not nearly as easy as it looked.

By the time she'd been out on the water for an hour, Leigh's arms and legs ached, her sinus cavities were filled with brine, and a bruise the size of Alaska was forming on her hip where she'd been struck by another surfer's board.

Matthew watched her struggle out of the sucking white foam to climb aboard the surfboard again and again, displaying all the tenacity of a bull terrier. He admired her grit. Most women—hell, most people—would have given up a long time ago.

"Feel like one more try?" he asked. They bobbed together in the gentle swells.

Leigh looked toward the horizon where the monster waves were being born. She had already discovered that what appeared to be small, ridable waves turned into gigantic, roiling mountains as soon as she tried to stand up.

"I'm going to do it this time," she swore, paddling toward

where Matthew said the wave would break. "This one's going to be it."

It had to be. Because she didn't know if she had the strength to climb onto that damned board one more time. Somehow, what had begun as Matthew's test had turned into her own personal challenge. She was no longer trying to prove anything to him; now she was struggling to prove something to herself. Something as powerful as it was unnamed.

She rose unsteadily to her feet, clinging to the rails, the board bucking angrily against the rolling water. Just when she thought she was going to land headfirst in the surf again, a sudden calm came over her, flooding her mind, soothing her senses.

After an hour of fighting it, she'd become one with the dark green sea, riding the curling wave, feeling as if she were flying. Free. Untethered. Her body and mind in pure harmony with the water. It was the most peaceful, yet thrilling, feeling she'd ever experienced.

"That was wonderful!" She grasped Matthew's hand, the surf creaming around their ankles. "Let's go out again."

"Don't you think you've had enough? You're going to be sore as hell tomorrow morning."

"It's a holiday." She pushed her wet hair out of her eyes. "And I fully intend to make the most of it. If I wake up stiff tomorrow, I'll spend the day soaking in the Jacuzzi." She gave him a challenging look. "Well, are you coming or not?"

Matthew shook his head. "Now I know how Dr. Frankenstein felt when his monster ran amuck."

The mellow, late-summer afternoon slowly ripened, then faded all too soon. The sky turned indigo, then ebony, illuminated by the glow of campfires up and down the beach. Rock music from portable radios and laughter filled the night air.

Leigh sat on a blanket on the cooling sand, gazing up at the soft, far-flung stars that seemed just out of reach and wondered if she'd ever experienced a more perfect day.

"Do you realize that we've managed to go all day without an argument?" she asked.

"The thought had crossed my mind." Matthew tossed another piece of driftwood onto the fire, causing a brief flare of orange sparks. "But I didn't want to bring it up for fear of breaking the spell."

Leigh took a sip of the red wine Matthew had produced from the cooler. He was right, she decided. It was as if a magic spell had been cast over them all day. A spell that lingered, even now.

They could have been the only two people on the beach. The moonlight streamed down, making the sand sparkle like diamonds. Music drifted on the salt-tinged air, accompanied by the distant sound of crashing surf. Just beyond the blanket, little wavelets lapped on the glistening sand. It was a night made for romance.

"I had a wonderful day."

"If you'd gone to that party in West Hollywood with Kim and her friends, you'd have eaten a lot better."

"I like hot dogs."

"Sure. Everyone knows that hot dogs and potato chips are the only food to serve with Dom Perignon."

It was the first time today that she'd heard that gritty tone. The old Matthew was back, Leigh realized with a soft sigh. In spades. Her glance moved from his face to his right thigh, where a jagged white line cut across the darkly tanned flesh. She'd seen the scar earlier and had determined it to be a result of the wound that had won Matthew his Purple Heart.

Seeming to ignore his challenging statement, she reached out and gently traced the jagged white line with her fingernail. "Does it hurt?"

"Only on bad days."

Leigh could practically see the NO TRESPASSING signs going up all around him. "I'm sorry you were wounded," she said quietly. "Although to tell you the truth, Matthew, I'm surprised that your shoulder doesn't give you more pain than your leg."

"My shoulder?"

"That's a very large chip you're carrying around. It must get very heavy."

Matthew knew she was right. What surprised him was the hurt he detected in her voice. "You're exaggerating."

"No. I don't think I am. May I make a suggestion?"

Matthew shrugged. "You're the boss."

Determined to avoid another fight, Leigh chose to ignore

his disparaging remark. "I'll stop thinking of you as a rude, overbearing, ill-tempered snob if you stop thinking of me as an unfeeling, spoiled rich bitch."

"I never thought of you as that," he insisted, not quite truthfully. "Pampered, perhaps. And you are bossy, in your own quiet way. But I'd never accuse you of being a bitch." As her words sank in, his eyes narrowed. "A snob? Me?"

"Well, you do have a tendency to put people into nice tight little pigeonholes and you don't seem to like anyone who has any money at all . . . Did you say bossy?"

Their eyes held, each waiting for an apology from the other. Finally, they laughed and the uncomfortable moment passed.

Matthew lay down on the blue-and-black plaid blanket and folded his arms behind his head. He stared up at the vast expanse of sky. "Look at those stars," he murmured. "They look as if you could reach up and touch them."

Leigh murmured an agreement, but she wasn't looking at the sky. Her eyes were drinking in the way his gray USC T-shirt molded the hard lines of his body. Knowing it was a dangerous thing to do, she allowed her surreptitious gaze to travel down his long legs, lingering on his muscled thighs.

"Back in 'Nam there were times when I'd look up at the sky and think that those stars were the same ones that were shining back in the world. I know it probably sounds dumb, but sometimes it helped, remembering that."

It was the first glimpse of his life in Vietnam he'd shared with her. "It's not dumb," she said quietly.

Matthew turned his head toward Leigh just as her gaze returned to his face. She was trembling despite the warmth of the fire. And her eyes were far from calm. Even as he was gratified to see that he possessed some measure of control over her, he had to admit that such success was not one-sided. His own heart was pounding furiously.

"Come here."

She shook her head. "I can't."

"Can't? Or won't?"

Her mouth was so dry. Leigh took a sip of her wine. Then another. Then a gulp. Nothing helped. "I think I'm afraid," she whispered.

The sea breeze ruffled her hair. Matthew sat up and leaned toward her, brushing a few shimmering strands away from her face. The gesture, while outwardly innocent, turned out to be remarkably intimate. He could feel her skin warm under his touch, a heat that had nothing to do with the nearby fire. A heat that was echoed in his own body.

"That makes two of us." Cupping his fingers under her chin, he drew her to him with only that light, enticing touch.

The constant ringing was a litany of failure in his ear. Slamming down the receiver, Joshua resumed pacing the floor. Where the hell was she? He'd called both the studio and that damn beach house she'd insisted on moving into and she wasn't at either place. So what was she doing? And more important, with whom?

The phone rang. Grabbing it up, he barked out, "Leigh?"

There was a moment's silence. "Sorry, Daddy," Marissa said. "Wrong daughter."

"No daughter of mine would allow pornographic pictures to be taken of her."

"Don't hang up," Marissa said, correctly perceiving his intention. "I have a proposition I want to discuss with you."

"You and I have nothing to discuss."

"Oh, really? How would you like to see those pictures on the front page of the *Enquirer*?"

"You're under age; they wouldn't dare print them. And if they tried, I'd slap the fucking publisher with an injunction so fast he'd never know what hit him."

"For your information, Daddy dear, I turned eighteen last week. Aren't you going to wish your baby daughter a happy birthday?"

"If you sell those photos to anyone, I'll cut off your allowance."

Marissa laughed at that. "For what I could get for those photos, I wouldn't need an allowance. But as difficult as this will be for you to accept, this isn't about money."

"Since when does blackmail not involve money?"

"Please, Daddy." Marissa clucked her tongue. "Blackmail is such a nasty word, don't you think?"

He could feel his blood pressure rising. The vein at his temple pounded furiously. "What the hell would you call it?"

"Persuasion."

Joshua refilled his glass and took a long drink. "What do you want?"

"A screen test. That's all. One screen test to prove to you that I'm the answer to all Baron Studios' prayers."

"Nightmares, you mean. And you'll get a screen test over my dead body. Baron Studios doesn't hire sluts."

Instead of sounding offended, Marissa laughed. "What a joke. Not only do you hire sluts, Daddy dearest, you also screw them. In fact, now that you've brought it up, I wonder if the *Enquirer* would like a behind-the-scenes view of the Baron Studios' casting couch? It would make a nice story to go along with the pictures, don't you think?"

"If you dare sell those—"

"Sleep on it," Marissa suggested silkily. "You can give me your answer at ten o'clock Tuesday morning." She gave him an address on Wilshire, repeating it twice to make sure he'd written it down correctly. Then she hung up.

Red with rage, Joshua pushed down the disconnect button and immediately redialed. When he was greeted with that now-familiar ringing tone, he yanked the phone out of the paneled wall and flung it across the library, where it skidded to a stop atop the carpet.

"Where the hell is she?" His roar sounded like a wounded lion as it reverberated through the silent, empty house.

Leigh had never thought of herself as a sexual person. Experimental teenage fumblings in the backseat of cars at drive-in movies left her cold; in college her virginity achieved daunting proportions, making her believe herself to be the only virgin left in California and, although there had been times that she had considered going to bed with a man just to get it over with, she had never met anyone who stirred her interest enough to make the symbolic act worth the effort.

After graduation, she directed her energies into her work and never gave sex a second thought. Until Matthew St. James came into her life and turned her world upside down.

Although they'd kissed before, Leigh was not prepared for the explosion that rocketed through her as his mouth met hers. Gasping at that fiery initial contact, she tried to pull away.

"No," Matthew said. "Not yet."

His eyes reflected the flickering glow of the firelight. When they settled on her lips, Leigh felt her resistance melting away, like the foundation of a sandcastle at high tide. Reading her acceptance, Matthew returned his lips to hers.

The kiss was subtle persuasion—a feathery brushing of lips, a slow stroking of his tongue against Leigh's skin, his teeth nipping at her bottom lip. It was more temptation than proper kiss, more promise than pressure. When a rich, liquefying pleasure flowed through her, Leigh let out a shuddering little breath.

"This is crazy."

"Insane." Matthew abandoned her lips to press kisses along the curve of her jaw. His hands moved up and down her back, caressing her with a confident, practiced touch. When his fingers slipped under her T-shirt, something rippled along her skin, something alien. Exciting. Frightening. "But that doesn't stop me from wanting you."

"Nor me from wanting you."

Rising from the blanket, he pulled her to her feet and kissed her. "You deserve better."

"Better than you?"

"No. Well, that too, probably, but I was talking about the location. You're a woman who deserves silk sheets and candlelight and champagne. Not jug wine and a sleeping bag."

The mellow sounds of "If Loving You Is Wrong, I Don't Want to Be Right" floated by on the sea breeze; Leigh decided that the title was prophetic. "We have music. And hot dogs. And moonlight."

"I do believe that you're a card-carrying romantic, Ms. Baron."

"And we've already determined that you, Mr. St. James, are a dreamer. So where does that leave us?"

He traced her lips with his finger. "A dreamer and a romantic? It's a hopeless combination."

"Or a perfect one."

He gave her a long, considering look. "Perhaps." The fire was dying out, the air cooled. Although she did her best to hide it, Matthew didn't miss Leigh's slight shiver.

"You're getting cold. Want me to get the blanket?"

She shook her head. "I'd rather that you keep me warm."

Matthew needed no further invitation. Gathering her up, he carried her into the tent.

"I'm afraid I haven't had a great deal of experience," she murmured as he laid her on the down-filled sleeping bag.

"Don't worry. I have." He began to undress her, pulling her cotton shirt over her head with an abrupt movement that displayed his impatience. The bikini top followed. When he blazed a trail of kisses over her breasts, Leigh tensed.

"I'm sorry," she said.

He lifted his head. "Don't be. I was rushing things."

"It's not that."

"It's your prerogative to change your mind."

"I'm not going to change my mind." She pressed her palm against his cheek. "I'm afraid the truth is that I haven't had any experience."

The only sign of surprise Matthew allowed was a momentary hesitation that lasted no longer than a heartbeat. "All the more reason to make this last," he said, lying down beside her and drawing her to him. She was as rigid as a bar of cold steel. "I've always loved sleeping outdoors," he murmured, looking up at the star-studded sky through the mesh ceiling of the tent. "Every house should come equipped with a glass roof."

"My house has a skylight."

"Really?"

"Three, actually. One in the living room, another in the bedroom, and a third in the bathroom."

"What decadence." He pressed his lips against hers, lightly, unthreateningly. "Next time we'll make love in your bed. Or your bathtub. Think of it, Leigh, you up to your chin in bubbles, drinking champagne, the moonlight making your flesh gleam like pearls while I wash your back. Or your front." His hands caressed her breasts, his lips recaptured hers in a long, drugging kiss that took her breath away.

Her skin warmed and her blood hummed as Matthew's hands and lips moved over her. Her white shorts seemed to dissolve away and when his fingers slid under the waistband of the bottom half of her bikini, Leigh lifted her hips off the sleeping bag, straining for his touch.

"Not yet." His breath fanned the satin skin of her abdomen, moving down, following the path his fingers had blazed as they rid her of the final barrier. Closing her eyes to his beguiling touch, Leigh moved fluidly under Matthew's stroking hands. Where he led, she followed willingly, letting him bring her to higher and higher planes as he discovered flash points of pleasure that she never knew existed.

When his roving tongue slid up the sensitive skin of her inner thighs, she quivered in response and knew that, if she were capable of speech, she'd be begging him to take her now. Instead, she could only moan his name as his stabbing tongue grew greedy, turning her to quicksilver in his arms. She trembled as passion too long suppressed exploded in a dizzying release.

No longer passive, she moved under him, her hands fretting against his back, his thighs, his buttocks. With one hand never ceasing his caresses, he managed to get rid of his clothing and put the condom on with the other. Free of the barrier of material between them, Leigh gasped at the fiery feel of flesh against flesh. She wrapped her legs around his hips.

"Now," she said achingly.

"Now."

To Leigh's surprise, there was no pain, just momentary surprise as Matthew entered her. Then she was moving with him, instinctively knowing his rhythm as if they'd made love a thousand times before. And then it was coming again, the spiraling pressure stretching her body tighter than ever before, the wetness, the shattering spasm of release.

When he felt the rippling convulsions rip through Leigh's body, Matthew followed her to his own tumultuous climax.

Afterward, they lay in a tangle of arms and legs and Matthew thought about how fully, how freely Leigh had given herself to him. She'd held nothing back, surrendering completely. But who had done the surrendering? And who had emerged the victor?

He propped himself up on one elbow and looked down at her. "I don't think I'll ever get enough of you."

His frown was not that of a man who'd just experienced bliss. "You don't sound very pleased about that."

"It's not having a choice that I'm finding difficult to accept."

Leigh considered that. "You're a man used to your own choices. Making your own way."

"Yes."

"I don't think either of us had a choice, Matthew, from the beginning," she said soberly. "And although I realize that we'll have to talk about it, if you don't mind, I'd rather think about all this tomorrow."

"Tomorrow." Matthew wondered if Leigh realized that she was at her most appealing when she was being earnest. "At Tara."

She smiled at that. "At Tara," she agreed, twining her arms around his neck.

It was all either of them were to say for a long time.

The princess, clad in a jeweled white gown, lay in a glass bier. A forest of thorns had grown up around her, protecting her, shielding her, keeping her hostage. All the knights in the kingdom tried to make their way through the thick brush, but for every thorny branch they cut, a hundred would appear in its place.

A year passed. Ten. A hundred. Then one day the most handsome prince in all the kingdoms came riding by, astride a gleaming white stallion. The prince's magical sword cut a wide swath through the thicket, and soon he was lifting the glass top of the bier, freeing the princess he'd come so far to find. The moment the prince's lips touched hers, the princess awakened, tears of joy and love shining in her eyes. But as he began to lift her from the bier, a dark cloud moved across the sun and the air turned cold and dank. Like the inside of a dungeon.

It was then that the princess realized that there was no escaping the monster. The monster's claws reached out for the prince. She began to scream.

"It's all right . . . Leigh, listen to me. Everything's okay."

Leigh awoke to find herself wrapped in Matthew's arms, his lips pressed against her hair. "It's all right," he repeated, running his hands up and down her icy arms. "You're here. With me. And you're safe."

She clung to him. "I was so afraid," she whispered. She looked up at him, her eyes, illuminated by the silvered moonlight, holding a lingering dread he knew all too well. "Oh God, it always seems so real."

"I know," he said, brushing the tears off her cheeks with extraordinarily gentle hands. "Believe me, Leigh, I know."

he phone was ringing when Leigh walked in her door the following morning. She gave Matthew an apologetic glance and picked up the receiver. "Hello? Oh, hello, Daddy."

Realizing that this could be a lengthy call, Matthew began to idly roam around the room. If he'd expected Leigh's home to give him any insights into her personality, Matthew would have been disappointed. The place mirrored the same perfect, self-controlled image she presented to the world. White predominated—the glazed floor tile was the color of vanilla fudge, the walls were a stark alabaster, the modular sofa and matching chairs were wrapped in shell white cotton. Brass cachepots and candlesticks provided gleaming color but no warmth.

"I've been at the beach," he heard her say.

Unlike his own home, no magazines cluttered the nearby tables, no dirty glasses marred the white marble mantel. There was no clutter, no mess, not a speck of dust. From what he could see, everything was absolutely perfect. Matthew felt something akin to claustrophobia.

"Yes, all night. I went to a party with Kim." When Matthew looked at her, color flooded into her cheeks. The soft blush, blooming under yesterday's sun-brightened skin, drew him like a magnet. Matthew wrapped his arms around her and began wetly nuzzling her neck.

"Really, Daddy, I am twenty-five years old; far too grown up for a curfew."

"Do you have any idea what I want to do to you?" Matthew murmured in her ear.

"Stop that," she hissed when he began to unzip her shorts. "No, Daddy, not you." Kneeling, Matthew pressed his mouth against her.

Leigh gasped. Her head felt light, almost faint; her knees were turning to water, and if Matthew hadn't been holding her so tightly, she wasn't certain she could stand.

"Look, Daddy," she said on a ragged voice nothing like her usual calm one, "it's a holiday. Can we continue this conversation Tuesday at the office?"

Matthew slipped a finger into her and even as her body clutched at it, it wasn't enough. Leigh wanted all of him. Again. Now. "To tell you the truth, at this moment I don't really give a damn what Marissa's done," she said. "Daddy, I have to go. Have a nice weekend; I'll see you Tuesday."

His objections ringing in her ear, she quickly hung up, then immediately lifted the receiver and placed it in the desk drawer. "Now," she said, lifting Matthew's shirt over his head, "where were we?"

Joshua stared down at the telephone, unable to believe what had just happened. Leigh had actually hung up on him. After having spent the entire night on the beach like some tramp. And not with Kim. A woman Leigh's age was too old for slumber parties; she had been with a man.

The idea of his daughter in bed with some faceless, anonymous man made Joshua's gut clench. He popped two Rolaids into his mouth and dialed another number.

"I've got a job for you," he told the man who answered. "But you'll have to start immediately."

The voice on the other end of the line agreed, as Joshua

knew it would. Ever since some damn woman he'd been sleeping with had hit him with a phony paternity suit, he'd learned that it was worth a hefty retainer to keep the private investigator at his beck and call.

After giving the detective Leigh's Santa Monica address, Joshua resumed pacing the floor. First he'd find out who the hell his daughter was sleeping with. And then he'd get rid of the bastard, whoever he was.

By the time the sun streamed in through the skylights early Tuesday morning, there was nothing Matthew didn't know about Leigh's sleek, responsive body. No secrets had been withheld as he'd brought her to repeated orgasms.

In return, he had held nothing back, urging Leigh's tentative, exploring fingers to become more intrepid, learning to read his needs and desires as a blind woman would read Braille.

They knew everything about one another. And they knew nothing.

"I had a marvelous time this weekend," she said softly. They were sitting on her bedroom balcony. Below them, a lone beachcomber gathered shells that were scattered on the shoreline.

Now that Tuesday morning had arrived, reality had come crashing down on Leigh, making her wonder where, exactly, they would go from here. Although her behavior was an anomaly for her, she was certain that Matthew was accustomed to such sexual marathons.

She was dressed in a chic black-and-white suit from Givenchy's fall collection, her hair tucked into the chignon he'd come to hate. The black pearls gleamed at her earlobes. She was every inch the coolly efficient lady executive; looking at her, no one would suspect that she'd spent the better part of the last two days making love.

"So did I." He brushed his knuckles over her cheekbone. "I like it when we use our energy for something besides fighting."

"We're bound to have differences." She sounded cautious.

"I realize that. Don't worry, Leigh, I can keep my personal life separate from my professional one."

The implication was there, that whatever they had shared

would last beyond the weekend. The idea was both thrilling and terrifying at the same time. "That's a great deal more difficult to do when the press gets involved."

"We'll keep them out of it."

"Then we're agreed? That our relationship will remain discreet?"

Matthew had considered relationship to be one of those 1970s female words, right up there with commitment and marriage. It had been a word to be avoided at all costs. Not that he hadn't always been forthright about his lack of commitment; his short-lived affairs had always been based solely on mutual pleasure. In that respect, his personal life had always been satisfactory. If, after passions cooled, Matthew found himself from time to time experiencing disillusionment, or an odd, empty feeling, he would force those thoughts away.

But Leigh was turning out to be an entirely different matter. Because now, as he looked into her soft gray eyes, he found himself wanting to stick around for as long as this lasted.

"As much as I hate the idea of sneaking around, it's probably best."

"Oh, it is." Her relief was obvious. Relief that they'd have more nights together? he wondered. Or relief that he was willing to keep their affair secret. "You know, Matthew, a little intrigue might just add zest to things."

"Add any more zest to what we've got going between us, and I wouldn't have been able to get out of bed this morning. You wore me out, lady."

"I don't believe that's possible." Her lips curved in a soft, reminiscent smile. "In fact, if we could find a way to bottle whatever it is that keeps you going, we could probably make a fortune."

"The answer is simple." His dark eyes held her captive. "It's you."

Although they'd struggled to treat the weekend lightly, their lovemaking had catapulted them into a relationship that neither had been prepared to accept. Leigh knew that they both needed time to sort out their thoughts.

"Dinner tonight?" he asked.

She thought of all the scripts waiting to be read, the correspondence that needed to be answered. Whatever new problems her father was having with Marissa. Her life did not allow time for romantic dalliances, no matter how enticing. "What time?"

"Seven. My place."

Seven o'clock. Only eleven hours away. It seemed an eternity. "I'd love to, but I have a meeting with Christopher Burke at seven. I'd reschedule, but he's returning to Melbourne first thing tomorrow morning." Burke had been signed to direct *Dangerous*, and although the Australian was a genius at his craft, Leigh knew him to be a highly temperamental one.

"Hey, don't worry about it," Matthew said on a shrug. "It was just a thought. No big deal."

She was losing him; Leigh could see Matthew retreating behind those damn barricades again. "Make it eight-thirty." She pressed her lips against his. "And you've got yourself a date."

Joshua's first thought was that he was having a stroke when he entered the warehouse on Wilshire and found Marissa lying nude on the round bed, illuminated by a bank of klieg lights, a biker's head burrowed between her thighs. A vein throbbed wildly in his temple, his blood pounded in his ears.

"Turn those goddamn lights off," he roared.

Heads turned. Expressions ranged from surprise to fear to irritation. Marissa propped herself up on her elbows and observed her father with what appeared to be out-and-out glee.

"Hello, Daddy."

"Daddy?" Joe Bompensiero said, looking back and forth between father and daughter. "Well, shit, who would have suspected the chick was connected?"

Joshua ignored the director. "Get some clothes on. We're leaving."

"In the middle of my big scene?"

"I said, get dressed. Now."

"No."

Jeff appeared from behind the lights with the red kimono. "Come on, baby," he said under his breath. "You got your old man's attention. Let's not blow it, okay?"

"Hey, man," Bompensiero complained, "what gives you the right to come busting in here?"

"I'm Joshua Baron."

"So? I don't go fucking up your movies, why don't you just get the hell out of here and let us get back to work?"

"I'll leave as soon as you give me the film."

The director stared at him. "You gotta be kidding."

Joshua folded his arms over his chest. "I'm not leaving until I get that film."

"Perhaps I didn't make myself clear." Bompensiero made a slight gesture with his left hand; a trio of massive, stone-faced men appeared at his side. Any one of them could have played linebacker for the L.A. Rams; indeed, the largest of the three had played fullback for the Cleveland Browns. Although he'd been too slow to last more than one season in the pros, Clayton "The Crusher" Armstrong had managed to set an NFL record for broken bones inflicted on his opponents in a single season.

Joshua held his ground. "Why don't you go call your boss," he suggested. "Before you make a big mistake." He glanced around the warehouse, eyeing the crates piled nearly to the ceiling. "Interesting inventory you have here. Of course you've got purchase invoices for the electronic equipment."

A muscle began to twitch at the corner of Bompensiero's left eye. "I'll be back."

Joshua nodded. "I'll be waiting."

Less than three minutes later the director returned. "Mr. Minetti wants you to know that he was unaware that this was your daughter. The girl used a phony name. She also came to him of her own free will."

"I've no doubt of that."

"Mr. Minetti also wants you to understand that since she's legally of age, there is nothing preventing her from appearing in this film. However, having a daughter of his own, Mr. Minetti appreciates your feelings," Bompensiero allowed. "He says that the film is yours."

Joshua had never had a single doubt that things would turn out this way. He and Rocco Minetti went back a long way. Too long to let a little slut like Marissa ruin what had always been a congenial working relationship.

"Please extend my appreciation to Mr. Minetti," he said politely. His business concluded, Joshua reluctantly turned toward Marissa. His face twisted in disgust. "I'll see you this evening, at the house. Seven o'clock. Sharp."

After watching the way the tyrant of a director had bowed to her father's demands, Marissa wondered if she'd underestimated her hand. "Why can't we talk now?"

His eyes raked her kimono-clad body. "Because this isn't the place to discuss business, you're not dressed, and I have a lunch meeting with your sister and Corbett Marshall. Seven o'clock," he repeated, turning abruptly on his heel.

Leigh again. Watching her father march out of the warehouse, Marissa coldly reflected on exactly how much she loathed her sister.

Leigh was at lunch with her father and Corbett, sipping a cream soda and wondering how many hours of exercise it would take to work off the enormous sandwich she'd eaten.

"Look who's getting nabbed," Corbett said with undisguised glee. Outside the window a meter maid was citing a white Rolls belonging to Alan Bernstein, a top agent.

"That's the reason you asked for this booth, isn't it?" Leigh accused with a smile. "You enjoy watching your rivals get parking tickets."

"Best seat in the house," Corbett agreed cheerfully.

"I talked with Matthew last Friday," Leigh mentioned offhandedly. "He wasn't very happy."

"Oh?" His carefully schooled expression was one of puzzled interest, but Leigh had the feeling Corbett knew precisely what she was referring to.

"He said that had he known Brendan Farraday was going to be in *Dangerous*, he never would have signed."

Joshua's eyes narrowed. "You never mentioned that to me."

"We haven't had a chance to talk since then," Leigh said, hoping her father would not bring up their abbreviated Sunday morning conversation. "Besides, it's all straightened out."

"You know, Matthew mentioned something along the same lines to me," Corbett admitted. "But I certainly didn't expect him to go to you with his complaints."

"It came as quite a surprise. Do you know why he has such

animosity toward Brendan? It may help me know what to do if we have any problems between them once we begin filming."

"I've absolutely no idea," Corbett said, lifting his hands in a palms-up gesture. "The only other person I've ever known to dislike the guy so intensely is Tina. Did I ever tell you that she refused to marry me until I dropped Farraday from my client list?"

"I told you at the time that was a stupid, female demand," Joshua said.

"It certainly wasn't something I was very eager to do. Brendan Farraday was a very profitable client."

"Tina gets along with almost everyone," Leigh said.

"I know. That's what made her hostility toward Brendan so odd, but when I tried to get her to explain, she refused to talk about it."

"She was probably just smarting over a foiled love affair with the guy," Joshua offered. "Hell, Farraday's screwed just about every woman in town."

Corbett's eyes offered his long-time friend a silent warning. "Not Tina. Anyway, although I know I can be accused of being single-minded when it comes to business, I finally gave in to Tina's demands, rather than lose her."

"At which time Farraday began lining Alan Bernstein's pockets," Joshua said. "All in all, that little maneuver cost you one helluva lot of money."

"Tina was worth every penny."

"What a nice thing to say." Leigh smiled. "I envy you two, sometimes."

Corbett patted her hand paternalistically. "Don't you worry, sweetheart, one of these days you'll meet the man of your dreams and Tina and I will be first in line to dance at your wedding."

The man of her dreams. Although he was far from that, Leigh couldn't stop the image of Matthew's hard, tanned body from coming to the forefront of her mind. As she felt the color flood into her cheeks, she pretended a sudden interest in the scene outside the window in order to avoid her father's suddenly intense gaze.

* * *

Leigh sat in her office, stunned by the scene being played out on the television screen. A guerilla group, calling itself Black September, had taken the Israeli Olympic team hostage. As she watched the black–ski-masked terrorists on the hotel balcony in Munich, all Leigh could think was that the world must be going mad.

When her father called, insisting that she join him in the screening room, it was with a sense of relief that she darkened the nineteen-inch screen.

"Well," Joshua demanded, as the lights came back on in the screening room later that afternoon, "what do you think?"

Leigh shook her head in disbelief. Although she'd always considered herself to be a sophisticated adult, the scenes from the pornographic movie had left her momentarily speechless. Had anyone told her that Marissa was making such a film, she supposed she would not have been surprised. If she'd known exactly what such a performance entailed, she would have been stunned.

"The setting was certainly less than luxurious," she managed. "And the lighting was terrible."

"Atrocious," Joshua agreed, lighting a cigar.

"The cinematography will never win any awards."

"It was absolutely uninspired."

"You know," Leigh said cautiously, "the pornography business can be dangerous. If you'd only allow Marissa to work here, we'd be able to keep a closer eye on her activities."

"That's one thought. I told you the little bitch is threatening to blackmail me with those stills."

"I don't believe Marissa would actually carry out that threat. She's simply bluffing to get your attention."

"Well, she certainly succeeded. Aside from the bad lighting, budget set, and horrendous cinematography, what did you think of your sister's performance?"

Leigh took a deep breath and jumped into the dangerous conversational waters. "She was riveting."

"Exactly what I was thinking."

Joshua studied the glowing end of the cigar and considered his options. Only minutes before leaving his office to come to the screening room, he'd received a phone call from the de-

tective, informing him that the man Leigh had spent the weekend with was none other than Matthew St. James. When he'd
instructed Leigh to get close to their new discovery, he never
expected her to get so damn close.

A very strong part of him wanted to fire Matthew. To utilize
one of the loopholes the studio's lawyers always wrote into
the contracts. Another, more pragmatic side, realized that
Baron Studios needed a blockbuster like *Dangerous*. And like
it or not, Matthew St. James was a natural for the role; it was
as if the part had been written with him in mind.

There was, Joshua considered, a chance that were he to
succumb to Leigh's request that he cast Marissa to play the
part of Marilyn Cornell in *Dangerous*, she and Matthew would
get sexually involved. He'd been aware of Marissa's sexually
permissive behavior for years (just like her slut of a mother)
and, according to the report the detective had compiled, St.
James sure as hell hadn't spent the years since his return from
Vietnam in a monastery.

"You know," he said thoughtfully, "you may be right about
your sister."

"In what respect?"

"About her starring opposite St. James in *Dangerous*. Although this porn is unadulterated trash, she does light up a
screen. And there's always the chance that she and the guy
will strike sparks off one another."

Even as Leigh found that idea particularly unpalatable, she
couldn't repress the excitement she felt at the thought of
finally having the key roles in her pet project cast.

"I'll call her right away and give her the good news."

"She'll be at the house at seven tonight," he said. "Let's
wait until then; it'll do her good to sweat this one out."

"I suppose it wouldn't hurt," Leigh agreed. "After this
latest stunt."

"She's always been a handful." Joshua ran his fingers down
the side of Leigh's face. "Unlike her big sister. You'd never
disappoint me, would you, princess?"

Leigh wondered what her father would say if he knew that
she'd spent the weekend making love—no, she corrected
firmly, having sex—with Matthew. Disappointed would be
putting it mildly.

Before she could answer, Joshua flashed her a smile. "Why don't you come by the house for dinner tonight? I'd say that this calls for a family celebration."

She looked at him suspiciously, trying to recall the last time he'd acted as if he believed the three of them to be a family. "I'd love to, Dad, but I have other plans."

"What could be more important than toasting the success of your new picture?"

What indeed? Just the memory of Matthew's lovemaking sent a thrill of anticipation racing through her. "I'm having dinner with a friend."

"Anyone I know?"

"Actually," Leigh said with a nervous little laugh, "it's Matthew."

"St. James."

Leigh would have had to have been deaf not to hear the disapproval in her father's tone. "You're the one who told me to keep him satisfied." Damn, she'd come off sounding too defensive.

Joshua merely nodded. "So I did. I have another idea."

"What's that?"

"Bring St. James along to dinner. After all, if he and Marissa are going to play lovers, it only stands to reason that they'll be more convincing if they become well acquainted before you start to shoot." He winked. "Just think of the box office appeal if the two of them became an item. Probably increase the gross several hundred thousand dollars."

Even as she secretly agreed with him, Leigh was appalled to discover how upsetting she found that particular scenario.

"Matthew's already made plans. I don't think he'd be thrilled with me changing things at the last minute."

Joshua could feel the pressure building up behind his eye. "Well, you certainly know the man best. So, have we agreed to give your sister the part?"

"Agreed," Leigh echoed softly.

Matthew and Marissa were a casting director's dream match—Leigh had no doubt that when Matthew's smoldering danger collided with Marissa's golden fire, the result would be explosive on the big screen. So why was she feeling so apprehensive?

22

The fall of 1972 saw the reelection of Richard Nixon, which pleased Joshua, who'd given generously to CREEP, and depressed Leigh, who, knowing that she was supporting a losing cause, had voted for George McGovern on principle. The Dow closed above 1,000 for the first time in history (displaying confidence in the continuing administration, Walter Cronkite proclaimed). Dashing hopes that the war in Southeast Asia would soon be over, the Vietnam cease-fire agreement was postponed (yet again!) as North and South Vietnam negotiators continued to bicker.

Back on the homefront, an unprecedented epidemic of teacher strikes disrupted classrooms all over America. Placard-carrying men and women shared the sidewalks with the Jesus Freaks (the latest evolution in the youth movement's never-ending search for new highs) who'd taken to the streets, making parents yearn for the good old days when kids wore love beads and got stoned on pot.

Billie Jean King became a symbol for women everywhere, while Playboy Bunny impostor Gloria Steinem (brains and looks, admirer J. K. Galbraith enthused) was fast emerging as a leading cover girl of women's lib, proving to a legion of dazzled detractors that she was much more than just a pretty face.

At Baron Studios, the single most important event of the year (although David Brinkley failed to mention it on the evening news) was that *Dangerous* was finally scheduled to begin shooting.

And although Leigh knew that she should be thrilled to have achieved her long-awaited goal, she was depressed. Because her time with Matthew was rapidly drawing to a close.

"You're early."

It was four o'clock in the afternoon. The autumn sun was low on the horizon when Leigh stood on the porch of Matthew's small house, her arms filled with brown grocery bags from a nearby Ralph's. "I know. I decided to cook dinner for a change, so I took off work to go shopping."

"Amazing." Matthew took the bags out of her hands. "It's usually like pulling teeth to get you to leave that damn studio before eight or nine. And even then you insist on reading scripts in bed."

There had been times when Matthew had been irritated at being relegated to second place in her life, but not wanting to waste their time together fighting, he'd bitten back his resentment, pushing it further and further into the back of his mind.

"I'm not always reading scripts in bed." She followed him into the home she knew as well as her own.

"Thank God." Tossing the bags onto the ceramic tile counter, he took her into his arms, kissing her on the back of her neck, in a special place he'd discovered that first night she liked to be kissed. "Am I allowed to ask what precipitated this uncharacteristic display of domesticity?"

He was wearing a pair of jeans, zipped, but with the button undone. As she slipped her hands into his back pockets, Leigh reveled in the feeling of his toned, hard body against hers. "I wanted to fix you a farewell dinner."

Two months ago, Matthew had been going crazy, anxious

to begin work. Now, as his fingers expertly plucked the pins out of her hair, releasing the long blond strands, he marveled that their time together had passed so swiftly. Tomorrow he left for Paris to begin filming on *Dangerous*.

"Good-byes can wait. How about giving me a hello kiss first?"

She rubbed her breasts, clad in a silvery gray silk Ralph Lauren blouse, against his bare chest. "I thought you'd never ask."

Joshua lay on his back in a comped suite at the Lucky Nugget Hotel and Casino while a blond whore in her mid-twenties sucked enthusiastically on his limp penis. The woman, whose name was Iris, gave the best head in town. Today, however, his body refused to rise to the occasion.

"You're so tense," Iris murmured, massaging his inner thighs with her hands. "What's the matter, Daddy? You drop a bundle at the tables?"

"I wish to hell my problem was that easy to solve." Grabbing her by her long flaxen hair, he lifted her head. "Let's give it a break, okay? Before I get a blister."

"Sure thing, hon." She reached over to pour herself a glass of champagne from the silver bucket beside the round, king-size waterbed. "Want some bubbly?"

"I think I'll pass."

"Good idea. Alcohol tends to make things worse." As she sipped the icy champagne, her gray eyes lit up with the enthusiasm of yet another idea. "Remember when you got off drinking champagne from my boobs? How about giving that a try?"

At least she was trying to cheer him up. Which was a helluva lot more than his own daughter had been doing lately. Over the past two months he'd noticed a distinct change in Leigh. And although she'd become frustratingly secretive about her activities, he knew exactly who had precipitated this unwelcome change.

Matthew St. James.

Joshua hated his new star more and more with each passing day. There had been too many times lately when Leigh returned to work after a long lunch, flushed with an unmistakable glow that revealed she had been well and thoroughly fucked. By that bastard.

Although he wanted to forbid Leigh to see Matthew, Joshua forced himself to bide his time. One thing he had learned from his father was to choose his battles well. All he could do for now was assign her more and more duties to curtail the amount of time she had to spend with her illegitimate lover.

"The day *Dangerous* finishes filming," he vowed under his breath, "that bastard's balls are going to be mine."

"Well, look at that." Iris grinned lasciviously, discarded her empty glass carelessly onto the plush carpeting and lowered her silvery blond head. "I don't know what got you so turned on, Daddy, but whatever it is, hold that thought."

Leigh had never suspected how large a void Matthew's absence would leave in her life. Although they talked often on the telephone, the long-distance conversations were strained to the point of being forced.

Part of the problem, Leigh mused one night as she tossed and turned on a bed which now seemed unbearably lonely, was that she was never sure exactly how she felt about Matthew. Or if she should even think about it long enough to figure it out.

She only knew that she missed him. Desperately.

Mental images of Matthew and Ryder Long—so alike, yet so different, like opposite sides of a coin—tumbled around in her head like the facets of a kaleidoscope. Constantly changing, whirling, shifting, never leaving her at peace. Finally she surrendered. Getting up from her rumpled bed, she put on a pair of jeans, a heavy sweater, a pair of ski socks, and went out onto the balcony.

The sun was rising over the mountains behind her house, splintering the wisps of high fog with streaks of pink and lavender. By the time the sky was a wide blue bowl overhead, she'd made her decision. Going back into the house, she picked up the phone and placed three calls.

The first was to United Airlines, booking a seat on the first flight to JFK, with a connecting flight to Orly.

The second was to Meredith, instructing her secretary to reschedule her appointments.

The third was to Joshua. Despite her father's outspoken

objection to Leigh's trip, Leigh was smiling as she hung up the receiver.

Rain fell from a slate gray morning sky, drumming on the roof of the barge where Marissa lay on a narrow bunk, clad in tight jeans and a torn silk blouse. Her lover's lips burned a path across her bare shoulders, as the brown waters of the Seine lapped against the side of the barge, making it rock.

"You're mine," he muttered, his teeth nipping at her warming flesh. When he yanked her jeans down her legs, Marissa trembled in a delicious mixture of pain and pleasure.

Without warning, he grabbed her wrists in one hand and held them up over her head. His dark eyes held the untamed gleam of a predatory animal. "Say it, damnit."

"Yours," Marissa whispered.

"Louder." He unfastened his jeans with his free hand.

"I'm yours," she cried out as he crouched over her.

"That's better." When he lowered his body onto her pliant one, Matthew's lips curved into a cruel, sensual smile.

Leigh glanced at her watch as the taxi driver sped recklessly through the confusing maze of Paris traffic, horn blaring. With any luck and barring an accident, she should arrive on location about the time the crew was breaking for lunch. It was a cold gray, foggy day, but as the wipers swished back and forth across the windshield, Leigh's body warmed with anticipation of seeing Matthew again.

"Cut," shouted the director.

"Cut," echoed the assistant director.

Christopher Burke slammed his battered khaki bush hat onto the floor. "We'll have to do it again; the bloody boom operator buggered it." He glared up at the young man perched over the bed, dangling a microphone strapped to the boom. " 'Ow in the bloody hell do you expect us to get this friggin' movie made if you keep sticking the bloody microphone into the picture? Wanna tell me that? Christ, you're movin' around up there worse'n a blue-arsed fly . . . And Marissa looks like she's got the fucking measles. Where the hell are the bloody makeup people?"

Recognizing an impending tirade, Matthew left the bed

without a word and shrugged into his shirt. When a harried-looking makeup woman dashed in and began sponging Light Egyptian body makeup onto Marissa's bare shoulders and breasts, he went out on the deck and stood under a tarpaulin that had been erected to protect the crew from the rain.

Matthew had heard it said that film crews were like families. In this case, it was turning out to be more like a reunion with a bunch of relatives who couldn't stand each other. At the root of the problem was the Australian director's insistence on creating a film-noir look—high contrast and deep shadows. Moody images. Although Matthew would be the first to agree that the script was intense enough for such a treatment, they'd already shot enough film trying to render the proper mood to make three feature-length movies.

Meanwhile, the crew, particularly the camera operators, dolly grips, and boom operator, were forced to try to keep up with Burke's impromptu inspirations. In one memorable instance yesterday, the first assistant cameraman had to manually turn the camera two-hundred-and-eighty degrees from a dolly that cut through the cabin roof. When the barge began to rock dangerously on the rising water, the kid fastened his foot to the camera with C-clamps to keep from being thrown overboard.

Pulling a pack of cigarettes from his pocket, Matthew lit one, allowing his thoughts to drift—as they had on too many occasions lately—to Leigh. He had spent much of the past three weeks cursing himself a fool for letting her get under his skin. He'd wanted her—from the beginning—and he'd had her. Again and again. But each time he touched her, kissed her, felt the tremor of her body next to his, had only left him wanting more.

Their encounter hadn't gone the way it was supposed to. The plan had been to take advantage of what he knew to be their mutual attraction and make love to her. Finally, his curiosity satisfied, his desire sated, he could get on with his life.

That had been his plan. Carefully executed and expertly conceived. But then she'd surprised him with her soft admission of inexperience, something he'd hadn't expected any more than he'd expected to care so damn much for her feelings.

He inhaled, pulling the strong, acrid smoke into his lungs. It tasted lousy. That had been one of the reasons he'd given the habit up shortly after his return from 'Nam with a minimum of effort. Then, just last week, he'd broken down and bought a pack of Gauloise in the hotel gift shop. That he found himself wanting—hell, *needing*—a cigarette after all this time was additional proof that Leigh Baron was nothing but trouble. So why the hell didn't he accept one of the many enticing feminine offers he'd received since arriving in Paris and forget about Leigh? Now, before things became even more complicated. He looked up, as if seeking answers in the gloomy, overcast sky.

"God," Marissa said, joining Matthew under the tarp, scantily clad in her scarlet kimono, "you'd think the guy was Otto Preminger, the way he carries on."

Matthew shrugged.

Marissa was getting fed up with the way Matthew continued to ignore her. She still couldn't figure out how any guy could be rolling around in the sack with her one minute, then turn it off and walk out the door as if she didn't exist. If she hadn't reached down and felt his erection this morning, she would have thought Matthew was queer. "This isn't my first film, you know."

Matthew blew out a stream of smoke and studied the view, which was, in a word, magnificent. The towers of Notre Dame were at his back, the great facade of the Louvre on his right, a frieze of chimney pots on the Left Bank. From the deck of the barge, the snarling combat of traffic sounded like the sigh of wind in treetops.

"Of course the other was more fun to do; we didn't have some power-hungry director screaming 'Cut' just when the sex began to get interesting." He hadn't bothered buttoning his shirt; Marissa pressed her palms against his bare chest. "How about slipping away during lunch for a private rehearsal?"

Matthew plucked her hands off his body. "When are you going to get it through your head that I'm not interested? If you're that eager to screw someone, sweetheart, you've got plenty of candidates to choose from. Practically the entire crew, from the director right on down to the clapper loader has been panting after you since day one. And Farraday's scheduled to arrive in town next week. His reputation as a stud should satisfy even you."

"But I don't want any of them. I want you." She licked her lips suggestively. "And you can deny it all you want, Matthew St. James, but you want me too. Don't forget, I'm the girl whose boobs you just finished playing with. And I'm the one who made your cock hard."

It had been an involuntary physiological reaction, triggered by the unexpected realization that she was wearing the same scent her sister favored. "Don't flatter yourself, it had nothing to do with you."

"Why fight it, Matty? When we both know that I could give you the hottest time you've ever had." Twining her arms around his neck, she went up on her toes and kissed him with a fierce, angry passion.

"Excuse me." Leigh stood on the dock, beneath an umbrella the same dark gray as the sky, her face schooled to a composure she was a long way from feeling.

He stared at her over the top of Marissa's head, feeling surprised and guilty. Marissa resembled a cat who had just swallowed a particularly succulent canary.

"Hi, Leigh," she said breezily, not bothering to take her arms from around Matthew's neck. "What a nice surprise. Matty and I were just rehearsing our big scene."

A tabloid headline she'd seen in the airport flashed through Leigh's mind. Something about Paris and lovers, accompanied by a photo of Matthew and Marissa in a heated embrace, the Eiffel Tower in the background. She'd told herself at the time that the story was only gossip, the photo a composite. But it had done nothing to raise her spirits.

"If that kiss was any indication of what Chris has in the can," she said, "you two are going to burn up movie screens all across the country."

"Believe me, that was only a sample of what we can do when we really get going, huh, Matty?"

Matthew didn't answer. He pulled Marissa's hands away, his eyes fixed on Leigh. "I wasn't expecting you."

"Marissa," Christopher Burke shouted before Leigh could answer, "get your lovely round arse back in here, darling, we need to get a new light reading. Jaysus," he complained loudly, "where the hell does everybody get off to?"

"I'd better get back in there before he goes apeshit again," Marissa said, pressing her hand possessively against Matthew's dark cheek. The smile she turned to her sister was guileless. "It's great to see you, Leigh. Are you going to stick around and watch our big love scene this afternoon?"

"I'll be here for the next three days."

"Terrific. Matty and I are going to have to take you out on the town." With that parting remark, she went strolling back toward the cabin, her hips swinging provocatively beneath the red satin.

Matthew wanted to go to Leigh, but afraid of what she was thinking behind that smooth, polite mask, he remained where he was. "I don't suppose you'd believe me if I told you that there's absolutely nothing—less than nothing—between your sister and me."

She'd known it. But she hadn't expected to feel so relieved to hear him say the words. "I just have one question," she said as she boarded the barge and came to stand in front of him.

"What's that?"

"Have you missed me as badly as I've missed you?"

It had been so long. Three weeks. An eternity. Unable to resist, he reached out and touched her hair. "What the hell do you think?"

She wanted to touch him, to wrap her arms around his hard body and press her lips against his chest. She wanted to open herself to him—her heart, her mind, her body—here, now, before common sense and reason overcame need.

The folly of such temptation was demonstrated by the sudden arrival of Christopher Burke on deck. "Matthew, if you could be so good as to favor us with your illustrious presence—" He stopped in his tracks when he viewed Leigh. "Stone the bloody dingoes, if it isn't the lovely boss lady."

Genius or not, Leigh knew that Burke could be a tyrant on a film, and experience had taught her that he slipped into his native slang when he was at his most dictatorial. "Hello, Chris," she said, holding out her hand. "How are things going?"

He swept his hat off with a flourish. "She's jake, Leigh."

Leigh looked puzzled. "I forget, is that good or bad?"

"Oh, good enough that you don't need to be worrying."

"Yet I hear that you're using a great deal of film."

"It's important to get the right look."

"And you're running a bit behind schedule."

"We've had some hard kack—bad luck," he translated at her sharp glance. "The bloody bureaucrats wouldn't let us bring our props into the country. Said they lost the permits for our guns."

"But I thought that was taken care of the next day."

"Oh, it was. But then this bloody rain started. The beginning of the week the river was so high we couldn't get the barge under the bridges. So we had to wait."

"I see."

"But the forecast is good for next week and we'll be able to make up the lost time then."

"I certainly hope so," Leigh said. "We can't afford to go over budget on this one, Chris."

"And we won't. You have my word on it." Inquisition over, he flashed her a smile the likes of which Matthew, who had been working with the man for three weeks, had never seen. "How long are you planning to grace us with your lovely presence?"

"Three days."

"We hadn't scheduled to shoot over the weekend, but if you don't mind paying overtime, we can move things up."

"Oh, don't change the schedule on my account. As producer of this movie, I thought it might be a good idea to drop in and see how things were going." She smiled. "And being in Paris over the weekend gives me an excuse to do some shopping."

The director's relieved expression was that of a death row inmate who had just received a reprieve from the governor. "Well, you've certainly come to the right place. Are you staying at the hotel?"

"No. I was afraid my presence might put a damper on the crew's leisure time, so I booked a room at the Abbaye Saint-Germain."

"I don't think I know it."

"It's a former seventeenth-century convent not far from

here on the Left Bank. It's small and they don't take credit cards, but it's cozy and there's a lovely garden. And best of all," she said, exchanging a brief, meaningful glance with Matthew, "it's peaceful and private."

"Sounds bloody boring to me," the director decided.

Leigh smiled. "Different strokes."

"Ain't that the bloody truth, luv," Burke said. "Well, we're using up precious light. Not to mention Baron Studios' valuable time and money. You will stay and watch us shoot the next scene, won't you? It's a pivotal one. Where Ryder and Marilyn go to bed for the first time."

Leigh forced a smile. "I'm looking forward to it." Actually, she couldn't think of anything less palatable than watching Matthew in bed with her sister.

"Good. Well, Matthew, are you coming?"

With a quick, apologetic look, Matthew ground the butt of the cigarette into the deck with his heel, then followed the director into the cabin, wondering how the hell he was going to pull off a heated love scene with Leigh watching every move he made.

If there was one thing Joshua hated, it was losing control. It made him angry; when he was angry he paced. He had nearly worn a path in the carpeting of his office when the disembodied voice of his secretary came over the intercom, advising him of Jeff Martin's arrival.

"Send the young man in," he said, taking his place in the tall chair behind the desk.

Believing a good defense to be a strong offense, Jeff walked into the room as if he owned it. "So, Mr. B," he said, flinging his body into a chair without waiting for an invitation. "What gives?"

Unaccustomed to such arrogance from those privileged few who were granted access to his sanctum sanctorum, Joshua experienced a flare of annoyance. One he managed to control. "I understand that you are friends with Matthew St. James."

"Matt and I go all the way back to high school. The two of us are like that," Jeff said, holding up a pair of crossed fingers.

"My sources also tell me that you're an aspiring actor."

"In this town, who isn't?"

Joshua didn't bother to answer. The dossier the detective had gathered on Jeff Martin was remarkably detailed. From what Joshua could determine, there wasn't anything Martin wouldn't do, for a price. "As it happens, I'm in a position to offer you a part."

Jeff couldn't believe his ears. After that little debacle in the warehouse with Marissa, he'd half expected her old man to order a hit on him. And here he was, offering him a job. Something didn't fit.

"Why?"

"One of the actors working on *Dangerous* has suffered an unfortunate attack of appendicitis. He was rushed to a Paris hospital last night for emergency surgery and, although I'm told that he's doing fine, he won't recover in time to return to the set. It's not a large part, but there are a number of good lines. Are you interested?"

"Do bears shit in the woods?"

"I'll take that to be a yes. There's just one slight favor I must ask in return."

"Who do I have to kill?"

"Nothing that drastic, I assure you. I merely want you to see to it that once this picture wraps, Matthew St. James disappears from Los Angeles. Permanently. Needless to say, I will pay for any expenses you incur."

Jeff stared at the studio head for a full minute. The guy had to be kidding. Or else he was crazy to think he'd fuck over his buddy, just for a part. Not any old part, but a part in a major motion picture, he reminded himself, along with the perfect opportunity to fuck Marissa's brains out in Paris. He was wondering about the chances of making it with her on top of the Eiffel Tower when he remembered that picture on the front page of the *Enquirer* of his old pal Matt and Marissa in a clinch.

So much for the buddy system. Once a guy made the big time, he figured the world—and all the chicks in it—was his own private fucking oyster.

Jeff made his decision. "Hey, the minute the flick wraps, the dude's history."

23

Leigh was taking a bath in an ancient, claw-footed tub, thinking about Matthew when she slowly became aware of someone else in the room. Turning her head, she saw him, leaning against the doorjamb, looking sexier than ever in the faded chambray shirt and jeans he'd worn for the filming.

"I knocked, but you didn't answer."

After all they'd shared. After the hours and days and weeks of lovemaking, why did she feel so uncomfortable? "I probably didn't hear you over the running water."

He nodded. "That was undoubtedly the case. The concierge didn't blink twice when I asked her for a duplicate key."

"This is Paris."

"I still don't like knowing that any man can get into your room. Christ, Leigh, I could have been the Parisian strangler."

"Ah, but since I had to go out for a while, I told her I was expecting a very special visitor."

"That makes me feel better. I'd hate to think that just any man can talk his way into your bathroom."

"Not any man." Her lashes swept down and her fingers tightened on the bath sponge. "Only you."

The sight of her, amid all those bubbles, made him ache. But there was an emotional distance between them that kept him where he was. "You left before we had a chance to talk."

Leigh picked up a bar of fragrant soap from the tile holder and began working up a creamy lather between her palms. "By the twenty-third take, I think it was obvious to everyone that you either wanted to prolong the scene as long as possible, or I was making you unreasonably nervous."

"Which do you think it was?"

"Actually," she said in a conversational tone as she worked the lather up her arm, "I was hoping I was the cause."

"You were driving me crazy." He entered the room and squatted down beside her. "The entire time I was kissing your sister, touching her, all I could think about was how I wished that she were you."

The desire that was never far away sprang up between them, so palpable that Leigh felt as if she could put out her hand and touch it. "Marissa's very beautiful. And sexy."

"Flash and trash," Matthew said dismissively, lathering the French milled soap between his hands. When his soapy palms caressed her breasts, tingling vibrations ran from her nipples to her vagina.

"Now you're the one making me crazy."

"Really?" His fingers moved down her rib cage, over her abdomen, tangled in the silken curls at the juncture of her thighs.

When his hand pressed against the throbbing ache between her legs, Leigh leaned her head back against the blue-and-white flowered tile and closed her eyes. "Damn you, Matthew," she complained on a half-laugh, half-moan, when his fingers slipped into her, "I'm going to pay you back for this."

His thumb tantalizingly brushed against her swollen clitoris. "I certainly hope so."

Then he touched her—really touched her—and Leigh crested in a series of shuddering peaks.

* * *

"When are you leaving for Paris?" Joshua asked Brendan Farraday over double Scotches at the Polo Lounge.

"Monday. They don't begin shooting my part for another two weeks, but I figured I may as well go over early and enjoy some French pussy before I have to get down to work."

Who the hell did the guy think he was kidding? Work had never put a damper on Farraday's extracurricular fucking before, and Joshua doubted that this time would be any different. Every film Farraday had ever worked on, his expense sheets ended up being astronomical. It didn't take a CPA to realize that the actor was charging something a helluva lot juicier than coffee and croissants onto his room service bill.

"I've always enjoyed Paris," Joshua said. "French women know how to have a good time without feeling the need to put a ring through a man's nose."

"Or his prick."

One thing about Farraday, Joshua considered, the guy had a way with words. "I've got a little problem," he divulged offhandedly.

"Oh?" Farraday matched his casual tone.

"Nothing serious. Just a little cash flow problem."

"How much do you need?" Farraday didn't blink when Joshua mentioned an amount in the high six figures. "The money will be in your account when the bank opens tomorrow," he said. "I assume you'll send the appropriate papers over to my house."

"They'll be there before your morning paper." Rising from the table, Joshua reached into his pocket and pulled out his American Express card.

"I've got it," Farraday said expansively. With what he was going to end up getting in return for a few hundred grand, he could afford to be generous.

After Joshua left the restaurant, Farraday signaled the waiter for a telephone. As he placed the call that would put Joshua Baron more deeply in debt to Minetti, Farraday smiled. One of these days he and Rocco were going to end up the proud owners of Baron Studios.

Three weeks of separation had done nothing to lessen the feelings Matthew had for Leigh. If anything, the attraction was stronger than ever. The mere proximity of her body kept him in a constant state of arousal and for two days the room—the luxurious brass bed—became the center of their universe. He loved keeping her eager and pliant, yielding under his intimate touch; he thrilled at the way her gray eyes widened when he hit the right spot; he reveled in her gasps of pleasure.

She gave herself openly to him, never holding anything back. Matthew had never been with a woman who made him feel as happy and as carefree as he felt when he was making love to Leigh. Admittedly unromantic and cynical, a man who'd slept with more women than he could count, as he dressed for work that Monday morning, Matthew found himself wanting to believe that a life—a love—with one very special person might actually be conceivable.

But at the same time a lifetime of experience had taught him that the obstacles to such a storybook, happily-ever-after ending were unsurmountable.

Weren't they?

As they stood beside the taxi that was waiting to take her to the airport, Matthew couldn't miss the distress in Leigh's soft gray eyes.

"Have a good flight."

"Good luck with today's chase scene."

They laughed uneasily when they both spoke at once. Matthew slowly brushed his knuckles up the side of her face. "It was good seeing you."

"It was good, wasn't it?" Except for the silences, Leigh considered. Those fleeting moments between making love and talk about the picture. Those moments when one of them had seemed on the verge of discussing what was happening between them, only to back away.

"Do you think you'll be able to get back again, anytime soon?" Do you care about us enough to leave your precious studio? he wanted to ask, but didn't. Is this as important to you as it is to me?

"I don't know." Do you want me to come? Do you care? "Fall's such a busy time, what with all the upcoming holiday releases."

"Must be hectic."

"That's one word for it."

They were looking deep into one another's eyes, trying to divine what the other was thinking. "I'll try to clear my calendar so we can spend Christmas together," Leigh said.

"I'll book our room this afternoon."

Wrapping her in his arms, he fused his mouth against hers, his kiss hard and long, laced with a desperation he was unable to put into words. "You'd better go," he said finally. "Before you miss your plane."

"And you're late on the set." She attempted a smile that failed. "As producer of this picture, I have a responsibility to see that you show up on time."

Matthew didn't bother to try and return her smile. "I'll call you in a few days."

Tears stung behind her lids; she resolutely blinked them away. "Yes." Unable to say another word, she shoved her suitcase at the driver and escaped into the backseat of the taxi before she changed her mind and stayed here in Paris. With Matthew.

Matthew remained standing in front of the former convent watching as the driver tore off down the rue Cassette. If Leigh had glanced back out the rear window, she would have seen him watching the departing taxi thoughtfully, his face tense, troubled.

Leigh missed Matthew desperately. She missed his low, rumbling chuckle, the caress of his amber eyes when she returned home at the end of the day. She missed his tautly controlled energy, his powerful body, the melting touch of his hands. She also missed the way sleeping with him had kept her nightmares—which were beginning to return—at bay. Without her realizing it had happened, Matthew had become a crimson thread who had woven his way through the gray fabric of her life. She wondered how she had ever believed herself to be happy or satisfied without him.

Ignoring her father's relentless sulk, she returned to Paris to spend Christmas with Matthew, but the trip turned out to be a disaster. In a blatant disregard for Baron Studios' budget, Christopher Burke had arranged for the entire crew to celebrate the holiday with dinner at the Hotel Ritz. Although she'd hoped to spend a quiet, private day with Matthew, Leigh knew that if she and Matthew disappeared, the resultant gossip could be detrimental to the film. There was already enough acrimony on the set without everyone knowing that their star was sleeping with the executive producer.

The dinner began inauspiciously when Christopher Burke expounded on the superiority of Australian films compared to those coming out of America. "It's true," he pronounced loudly, "American filmmakers are only interested in the almighty fucking dollar. You Yanks," he pointed a finger at Leigh across the table, "are falling into a self-destructive trend of using flashy, shallow stories, while we Aussies still choose substance over superficiality. Art and originality before profits." He stared at her through bleary eyes, daring her to argue.

Partly because he had a point, but mostly because he'd practically emptied the outrageously expensive bottle of Château Mouton-Rothschild 1947, single-handedly, Leigh refused to be drawn into the fray. "Even if that's true," she said, feeling the need to defend her film in front of the crew who'd worked so hard, "surely you'll admit that *Dangerous* is the exception that proves the rule."

"Of course it is, luv," the director said. "Because you had the good sense to hire me to direct it."

Just when Leigh was congratulating herself on avoiding that particular minefield, they drew the ire of a haughty Gallic waiter by forestalling ordering until Marissa and Jeff arrived. They arrived thirty minutes late. Marissa, true to form, was decked out in a low-cut red dress that fit as tightly as a coat of lacquer. She was also high, flirting outrageously with every male at the table, most particularly Matthew.

Jeff, who'd already sampled more than his share of alcoholic holiday cheer, grew increasingly jealous and contentious as the meal dragged on. Before the waiter arrived with the first course of omblé-chevalier, Jeff had threatened to wipe the floor with the best boy, who being twenty and human, could not take his eyes off the lush swell of Marissa's breasts.

From there it was all downhill.

The strain of keeping up appearances during what could only be described as a debacle, followed Leigh from the din-

ing room to the bedroom, where she was forced to spend
forty-five minutes soothing Joshua, who had called to complain about being forced to spend Christmas with Tina and
Corbett instead of his own flesh and blood.

"I'm sorry," she said, turning back to Matthew, who was
lying on the bed, his head pillowed on his arms, staring up at
the ceiling.

He'd been strangely withdrawn all day and, although he'd
assured her that his attitude had nothing to do with her, Leigh
couldn't help worrying. Perhaps he'd grown tired of her. Perhaps he was wishing that she hadn't come.

"It's only natural your father would want to talk to his
daughter on Christmas Day."

She rested her head on his shoulder. "This hasn't been a
very jolly holiday, has it?"

"Don't worry about it. I've never made a big deal about
Christmas, anyway." Truthfully, Matthew had always hated
the holiday, which seemed to be created solely for families.
Christmas always reminded him that he had no one. That he
was an outsider.

"That was quite a story Brendan told about his Vietnam
Christmas show getting shelled in Pleiku."

Matthew had spent that particular Christmas in a bunker
with sandbags and steel over his head, seated on a green cot
that had been white before it had mildewed, listening to the
enemy rockets while he ate meatballs and beans in tomato
sauce, with juices, out of a can.

"The NVA was a tough audience. It's too bad they had such
poor aim."

She glanced at him curiously. "You really don't like Brendan at all, do you?"

"I thought I'd made myself clear on that point."

He had, Leigh remembered. The day before they'd made
love for the first time. She found Matthew's inexplicable enmity toward Brendan Farraday as curious now as she did then.
"Has working with him been too hard?"

"I don't want to talk about Farraday, Leigh. Not today. And
especially not with you."

Secrets. There seemed to be so many secrets between
them, Leigh thought sadly. But he was right about today not

being any time for serious discussion. Putting the subject away, she kissed his shoulder. Beneath her lips, his muscles were tightly knotted.

"You're too tense," she murmured, moving her mouth slowly down his chest. "What can I do to relax you?"

When her tongue dipped seductively into his navel, Matthew pulled her into his arms. "What you're doing isn't bad. For starters."

"For starters," Leigh agreed. Her low, throaty laugh was part honey, part smoke. When she took his sex in her hands and slipped her mouth over him, the dark shadows of the past disintegrated and there was only now. Only Leigh.

Although Matthew's lovemaking was as ardent and skilled as ever, an unrelenting tension hovered over the bed like a dark presence. When Leigh faked an orgasm for the first time, she had an uneasy, guilty feeling that she wasn't fooling Matthew for a minute.

She wasn't.

Later, as they lay side by side listening to the depressing drizzle of December rain roll down the windowpane, Matthew was the first to break the silence. "It'll get better, Leigh. When we aren't forced to crowd so much into such little pieces of time. After this damn film wraps."

Leigh touched the gold heart hanging from a slender chain around her neck—a Christmas present from Matthew—as if it were a talisman. "After *Dangerous* wraps," she whispered.

It was part promise. Part prayer.

24

March 1973

When *Dangerous* finally finished shooting, twenty-four days late and two million dollars over budget, Leigh was in Toronto, scouting locations for a project still in the development stages.

Peter Ustinov had piqued her interest in the city when he described it as "New York run by the Swiss." During the last few days, she had decided he was right. Toronto bore a remarkable resemblance to New York City. One that would permit her to film less expensively than in Manhattan. Of course, the film crew would have to mess up the gutters and spray-paint rude commands on a few of the buildings—Torontonians appeared to have a deep-seated aversion to graffiti and litter—but on the plus side, she wouldn't have to pay off street gangs to prevent them from disturbing the film set.

After spending the day trudging through slush and snow, ruining a pair of pewter gray Ferragamo boots purchased expressly for this trip, Leigh was not in the best of moods. She was having a solitary dinner in her suite on the eighteenth floor at Sutton's Place Hotel when Matthew called from France. It had been more than two months since Christmas. Sixty-eight lonely days and even lonelier nights.

"How's the sexiest woman in the world?" his deep voice rumbled over the faint hiss of thousands of miles.

Sexy. No man had ever described her that way before. Until Matthew. Leigh clasped the receiver more closely to her ear, as if she could lessen the distance between them. "I'm freezing. The forecast is for snow flurries tomorrow, so I spent the entire day trudging through Chinatown, Cabbagetown, and Kensington Market."

"Too bad I'm not there to warm you up."

"Isn't it?"

"You know, the telephone company lied."

"About what?"

"Long distance is *not* the next best thing to being there."

"I know," she whispered. For some reason she could not discern, talking to Matthew on the telephone had become more painful than pleasurable.

"Hey, the picture wrapped today. I could be in Toronto by tomorrow afternoon. Day after at the latest."

She paused. The idea was so tempting. As much as she had come to look forward to their frequent telephone conversations, the enforced separation had begun to take its toll.

"Oh, Matthew." Her throat was tight; her eyes burned. "You have to work."

How often had he heard that excuse over these past months? How many times had a planned trip to Paris fallen through at the last minute because of some perceived emergency at the studio? Too many times. Her decision to go to Toronto, just as the filming on *Dangerous* was coming to a close, only added to Matthew's suspicions that Leigh's feelings for him had begun to wane.

"We wouldn't have any time together," she said. "And knowing that you were in the city, but not being able to be with you, would be worse than having you all the way across the Atlantic. You do understand, don't you?"

No. He didn't. Even Leigh couldn't work all night, and from

Matthew's point of view, any time they could have together would be well spent. But knowing the futility of pressing his case long distance—they'd already had too many arguments each time she canceled her plans to join him in Paris—he lied.

"Sure."

"Why don't you take advantage of your free time and new-found wealth and see Europe?" she coaxed. "You've been working so hard, you deserve a vacation."

"Looking at a bunch of crumbling churches isn't my bag. Sightseeing alone sounds even worse. I'll just go back to California and get back to work."

"You can get some surfing in. You must have missed it."

There was a significant pause as Matthew failed to answer.

"Matthew, I really would rather be with you. You do know that, don't you?"

"Sure. Look, Leigh, if I'm going to get a flight home, I'd better call the airline. I'll see you soon, okay?"

"I'll be back in L.A. in two weeks," she promised. "Not a minute more."

"Two weeks."

He hung up first, leaving Leigh to vow that if she ever met Helen Gurley Brown, the first thing she'd do was ask the Cosmo girl's secret of juggling personal and professional lives.

Escondido, Mexico, was a surfer's paradise. Its variety of big barrels provided something for every mood and taste. But when Matthew arrived, the famous Mexican break was suffering from a massive wave drought, the glassy waters of the Pacific giving a convincing imitation of Lake Placid. Even the slightest hint of a swell was greeted with cheers by the surfers lining the sand and promptly assaulted.

"I don't know why the hell I let you talk me into this," Matthew complained. He'd been in Mexico for three days and so far he'd been lucky to catch four mediocre waves.

"Because Mexico's a fucking bash, man," Jeff said, winking lecherously at a comely young señorita who passed by. "And after spending all those weeks with that Nazi asshole of a director, we are in desperate need of some serious party time."

Last night Jeff had arrived back at the bungalow with two willing women and a quart of José Cuervo. When Matthew declined to join in the fun, Jeff had disappeared into the adjoining bedroom with both women. From the way the bedsprings had squeaked all night, Matthew decided that Jeff, at least, was making the most of the trip. The trouble was that Matthew wasn't interested in some anonymous vacation fuck and, since the woman he wanted was still in Toronto, he decided that he might as well get back to work.

"I think I'll go home," he said.

"Hey, man, the weather's gotta change. It'd be a bummer to come all this way, then leave right before the primo waves hit."

As much as he hated to admit it, Jeff had a point. Besides, with Leigh in Toronto, he sure as hell didn't have anyone waiting for him back home. Not that he ever had. Reminding himself that he'd always been content to be a loner, Matthew shrugged and popped the top on another bottle of Corona.

"I suppose I could stick around another day or two."

Jeff grinned his satisfaction. "Now that's the fun-lovin' dude I remember."

The beer flowed like water on the beach that afternoon. Surfers sat and waited and swapped stories of classic swells and monster curls. Exotic locations—Rarotonga, Tasmania, Sri Lanka—were spoken of with wistful longing while other, more popular sites—Ouahu's North Shore and Australia's Warriewood—were breathed with awe.

When night fell on the glassy, moonlit surf, the troop moved indoors. The drinks changed from beer to pitchers of margaritas, but the talk remained the same. Blowouts. Shark scares. Ten-foot tubes. Hot-dogging. The new macramé bikinis.

Hours later, after a surfeit of beer and margaritas, Matthew was in bed when a trio of uniformed Mexican police officers burst into the room, automatic weapons drawn.

"What the hell?"

"You are under arrest," one of the men said. He went straight to Matthew's duffel bag and pulled out a cellophane baggie. "For possession of an illegal drug."

Shaking his head to clear it of sleep and alcohol, Matthew

stared at the marijuana as if he'd never seen it before. Which he hadn't.

"You've got the wrong guy."

"You are Matthew St. James, sí?"

"Sí, but—"

"If you are Matthew St. James, señor, then we have the right man. Put on your pants and come with us, por favor."

Over the next ten days, Matthew quickly discovered the disadvantages of being arrested in a country whose law was premised on the Napoleonic Code—declaring a detainee guilty until he proved himself innocent.

He was interrogated constantly, kept awake day and night. When a lawyer finally did arrive, Matthew was not encouraged to learn that his attorney was the police captain's brother-in-law. Since he'd already decided that this particular group of cops were about as clean as the tap water, he was not surprised when a magistrate declared the evidence sufficient to hold him over for trial.

"So when do we go to trial?" Matthew asked his attorney.

The man shrugged. "The courts are crowded. Since our law allows a suspect to be held for a year without a trial, I would expect that's how long it will be before you have an opportunity to present your case."

His expression was not encouraging. And why should it be? The evidence was overwhelming and, although Matthew had continued to profess his innocence, he knew that even his own attorney had tried him and found him guilty.

"I'm going to be stuck here a year before I even go to trial?"

"Probably. Sí."

"I want to talk with the American consul," Matthew demanded, not for the first time since his incarceration.

"He's been called."

Matthew didn't believe him. There hadn't been a word from the American consulate office. "Then, damnit, I want to make a personal telephone call to the States." Surely Corbett, a lifetime wheeler-dealer, would figure out some way to get him out of this nightmare.

"I'm afraid that is up to the district attorney."

The police captain's uncle. Strike three. "I don't suppose they've found the other guy who came down here with me."

"No. Your friend seems to have disappeared."

No surprise there. Jeff was known for his expert vanishing act whenever there were cops around. "Okay. One more question."

"Sí?"

"If I'm found guilty, what kind of sentence am I looking at?"

"You have to understand, Señor St. James, in my country, possession of narcotics is a felony. It is not inconceivable that you could receive the maximum sentence."

"And that is?"

"Twelve years."

25

"I can't understand it."

"I assume we're talking about St. James again." Joshua leaned back in his chair.

They were sitting in his office and his distaste with the turn the conversation had taken was obvious. Leigh took a sip of her coffee. Since returning to Los Angeles to find Matthew gone, she had been running almost solely on caffeine. Caffeine and frazzled nerves.

"He should have returned from Europe by now."

"Leigh, you've grown up in this business; you know actors have no sense of responsibility. They're impulsive children, responding to instinct. To whatever brings them pleasure. It's difficult to hold their attention as long as it takes to shoot a picture." He shrugged. "St. James's disappearance, as you insist on calling it, is simply another case of an immature performer taking off on a binge as soon as the picture wraps."

"Matthew's different."

"So you've been saying for the past two weeks." Joshua gave her a piercing look. "If I didn't know you to be an extremely sensible young woman, I'd worry that this actor had turned your head."

"It's nothing like that," Leigh lied unconvincingly. "I'm simply worried about the way he seems to have dropped off the face of the earth. What if he's been hurt? Or worse?"

"Then *Dangerous* would get a great deal of free publicity."

Leigh had always known her father to be cold-hearted, but this time his words struck her heart like a stiletto of ice. "That's disgusting."

"That's business," he countered brusquely. "Don't tell me you've forgotten James Dean. Hell, in the three years after his death, Dean's studio got more mail addressed to him than any of its living stars. If the poor bastard had lived, he'd never have been able to live up to his publicity. . . .

"Beside, it's a moot point. St. James will be back," Joshua predicted. "When he runs out of bucks, booze, and broads."

Matthew wasn't like that. Leigh had been telling herself that ever since she had returned home from Toronto and discovered him missing. After fourteen days, she'd almost managed to convince herself.

Almost.

Marissa was naked, her voluptuous breasts bouncing on the bubbling hot waters of the Jacuzzi, garnering the full attention of the man seated across from her—Barry James, the latest candidate produced by a desperate television network in an attempt to unseat Johnny Carson as king of the night.

James, a former television game show host, had three things in common with the perennial late night television host: boyish good looks, quick wit, and multiple marriages. His current divorce was a messy affair, even for Hollywood, the details hashed out daily in the headlines. Just last week he'd been quoted as saying that after five failed marriages, he'd sworn off women forever. He had no way of knowing that such a statement was like waving a red flag in front of a bull.

Marissa, newly back from Paris, had never been able to resist a challenge. Although Jeff was all for continuing their relationship, now that they had returned to Los Angeles, she'd become bored with the predictability of their affair.

More than one psychiatrist over the years had tried to explain to Joshua that the absence of a loving male figure in her life had made Marissa intolerant of the calmness of long-term relationships. Reasonably quick to feel ignored and hurt, once the veneer of new passion wore off, her childhood pain resurfaced, causing her to rush off to the narcotic of a new love. The moment she'd seen that headline about Barry James, she'd decided to make him her new conquest.

During the three months that Barry had hosted the late night talk show, nearly every actress in town had appeared on his program; several of those had also made a starring appearance in his bedroom. "The Barry James Show" might not be the guaranteed career maker the "Tonight Show" was, but it did validate whatever publicity the studio press corps was churning out. If sleeping with the host was part of the deal, more than one budding young actress merely shrugged and decided that a blow job was a cheap price to pay for instant stardom.

Barry didn't question this obvious perk of his position; it was simply how the game was played. Having hosted innumerable asinine game shows over the years, he felt as if he'd paid his dues; now it was time to reap the rewards. To Barry, sex was a natural, everyday part of life, like eating or sleeping. It was difficult to value something in such abundant supply.

"The taping went well," he said, his gaze arrested by a drop of moisture glistening on her rosy red nipple. All his wives had been model-thin, the better to wear their expensive designer dresses. He couldn't remember when he'd been presented with such an amazing pair of tits. "You're a natural-born star, kid."

"Really?"

"Would I lie? You've got the comedic timing of Monroe with the bawdy lustiness of Mae West. The audience loved you."

"They would have loved me a helluva lot more if your producer hadn't stuck that damn handkerchief down the front of my dress." She'd worn a shimmering black-and-silver metallic dress that appeared to have been poured across her body.

"The network censors would have shut us down if we'd allowed you to go on without it."

"I bought that dress especially for you." Marissa pouted prettily. Relaxing her head along the rim of the tub, she allowed her outstretched legs to float up.

When Barry's cock hardened at the sight of that wet, flame-colored pubis, he conveniently forgot his recent vow of celibacy. "You looked fantastic, baby. Like an intergalactic Barbie doll. I can't believe you're Leigh Baron's sister." Leigh was one of the few women Barry had struck out with over the years, not for any lack of trying.

"Every family has its black sheep. By the time I was born, Leigh had already taken the role of the good sister."

He shifted positions, moving next to her in order to take her taut nipple into his mouth. "Which left you with the part of the bad sister?" he murmured around a mouthful of water-silkened flesh. Taking her hand, he wrapped her fingers around his cock.

She was floating on air. The audience had loved her, and even more important, Barry loved her. Why else would he bump that new young comedian and an over-the-hill *Sports Illustrated* swimsuit model turned actress and devote his entire hour to her?

"Sweetie, I am so bad I'm good."

He was sucking energetically on her breast. Marissa closed her eyes, fantasized becoming the sixth and final Mrs. Barry James, and obediently stroked him to climax.

Matthew watched the guard fondle the breasts of the young woman seated on his fat lap. The woman worked at the cantina; it was her job to bring the two meals a day to the jail. Enchiladas, rice, beans, tortillas, and beer for the guard, beans and water for Matthew.

In the beginning, she had angrily brushed aside the man's clumsy advances, but lately she'd begun flirting with the obese, unshaven man. She'd also taken to wearing low-cut gauze blouses that allowed an enticing view of her full, dusky breasts.

Two nights ago, she hadn't complained when he'd smacked her on her ass as she'd left the jail.

Last night she'd allowed him to kiss her.

Tonight, when the man tilted a beer to his mouth with one dark hand while pushing her blouse off her shoulders with the other, Matthew decided they were actually going to do it, right on that creaky wooden chair.

She was naked to the waist, her full skirt gathered around her thighs. The guard's beefy hand was making its way up under that cotton skirt when his head suddenly lolled. Climbing off him, the woman hitched up her blouse and watched impassively as he slid silently, bonelessly, to the floor. Then she turned toward Matthew and pressed her finger against her lips.

Matthew was not about to say a word.

He watched as she knelt beside the guard, her fingers deftly unfastening the key he wore clipped to his belt. She crossed the room and unlocked the cell door. They both went rigid when the rusty door squeaked with a noise that seemed to rival the roar of a jet airliner, but to Matthew's relief, the guard continued snoring away. The mickey the girl had slipped into the man's *cerveza* seemed to be doing its job.

Making his way quickly past the unconscious man, Matthew had no idea why this woman was helping him escape, but after nine weeks in this dank, rat-infested cellar of a Mexican jail, he decided that there was merit in the old saying about justice delayed being justice denied. And he'd been denied too damn long.

They had just stepped out on the street when a shout shattered the still night air. A moment later a bullet whizzed over Matthew's head. He took the woman's hand and began to run.

They raced through the shadows. Matthew reminded himself that he'd always been a survivor. Hadn't he survived his mother's desertion? And what about when he was twelve and living in his ninth foster home? The owner of the home, a high school wrestling coach, had made the mistake of attempting to share an intimate shower with him. He'd changed his mind when he found himself facing the business end of a switchblade.

In 'Nam the enemy shelled their compound with 120-mm mortars and artillery. During the prolonged assault, Charlie had been jumping around in the bushes, firing AK-47s and tossing grenades around like they were going out of style. Ammo kept exploding all night and, when morning finally came, and the mortars stopped and the VC had disappeared back into the thick brush, the body count was six dead and twenty-nine wounded, including Matthew, who'd taken a carbine round in the thigh.

He was put aboard a chopper and flown to the 71st Evacuation Hospital at Pleiku, where he was stitched and cleaned up just in time for that most thrilling event: the muckety-muck general's arrival (along with the ever present contingent of reporters) to give out Purple Hearts. If he could make it through that damn dog-and-pony show, Matthew considered, he could make it through anything. Even this.

Suddenly his side burned with a flash point of heat.

Matthew kept running.

26

May 1973

Leigh sat beside Kim, with Christopher Burke standing behind her as producer and director watched the editor spin her unique magic on the Moviola. Bits of conversation punctuated the steady whirring and clacking of the reels. In the background, Kim's radio was tuned to the Watergate hearings, which had finally commenced.

"I am a fucking marvelous genius," Burke declared.

"And modest too," Kim said.

"Modesty is for losers."

"Well, that description certainly doesn't fit," Leigh said. When Matthew appeared on the editing screen, Leigh felt her heart clench. "I think you're going to get another Oscar with this one, Chris."

"Of course I am, love. Does that vote of confidence mean that you're no longer angry at me?"

"I wasn't angry. I merely pointed out that you were over budget."

"To give you a masterpiece."

Perhaps not a masterpiece. But the director had succeeded beyond Leigh's wildest hopes. "It is good."

"It'll win Best Picture. Best Director. And," he said, reaching out to ruffle Kim's sleek black hair, "Best Editor."

"Thanks for the bone," Kim muttered, backing the reel up to concentrate on the scene where Ryder Long is killed in a prolonged shootout with the police, Interpol, and the FBI agent, played by Brendan Farraday, who'd tracked the pair to Barcelona.

"Hey, luv, you've done a remarkable job. Of course it helped that I gave you a near perfect film to start with." The alarm on his gold Rolex sounded. "Sorry, ladies, but I must dash. I have an important appointment."

"Appointment, my ass," Kim said after Burke had gone. "I heard him making a date with one of the extras on that space flick they're shooting on stage 17. That man is just one constant fucking machine; I'm amazed he ever gets a movie finished."

"The rumor is that he remains celibate during a shoot in order to save his creative juices for his work."

"No wonder he's a dictator on the set. And as for giving me a perfect movie, with enough miles of film to reach to the moon and back, the guy probably turns over more of a mess than any director in the business. Although I will admit that most of the clips are brilliant." Kim stopped on a scene of Marissa, kneeling over Matthew's supine body, tears flowing copiously from her dazzling green eyes. "Do you believe Burke was actually able to resist this?"

"There *are* men capable of resisting my sister's appeal."

"Name three who aren't either gay or eunuchs."

"I'll name one. Matthew."

"He'll be back, Leigh." Kim was the only one Leigh had told about her affair with Matthew. She was also the only one who knew how much Leigh was hurting.

"I went by his house again last night," she admitted.

"And?"

"His neighbor—this gorgeous, 1960s flower child type—

was sitting out on her porch, so I asked if she'd seen him. She said he'd gone to Mexico the day after he got back from Europe . . . She seemed to know him well."

"Exactly how well?"

"Well enough that we had quite an illuminating conversation about Matthew's unwillingness to commit."

"What you and Matthew had was special, Leigh."

"That's what I thought. But perhaps I was wrong." She sighed. "Lord knows, I'm no expert on affairs, and these days everyone takes sex a lot more casually." Everyone except her, apparently.

"Have you asked Corbett if he's heard from Matthew?"

"Of course. All he knows is that Matthew refused to consider any more acting roles, said that he was going back to work, and would let Corbett know when he had something for him to read. When I told Corbett about Mexico, he suggested that perhaps Matthew just wanted to go away somewhere where he could write without distractions."

Is that what he'd considered her? Leigh wondered. A distraction? Ignoring the familiar pain gripping her heart, she turned her attention back to the screen. "Let's see that one again. This time starting with the dolly shot of Marissa."

"What the fuck do you mean, he got away?" Joshua paced the floor of his office, his red face reflecting his anger.

"Hey, Mr. B," Jeff said, lifting his hands in a gesture of self-protection. "Don't blow a gasket, okay? The cops are looking for him. He won't get within fifty miles of the border."

"You'd better hope to hell he doesn't," Joshua growled.

"Hey, I'll go down and find the dude myself, if you want."

"I want you to stay the hell out of it. You're a fuck-up, Martin." It was bad enough that Leigh had learned about St. James's trip to Mexico and contacted the consular officer; now she was actually considering going to Escondido herself.

"Jesus, it's not my fault the damn greasers let him escape," Jeff complained, wiping at his nose with the back of his hand.

The prick kid was weak. Impotent. All he cared about was getting stoned and getting laid. He'd been a fool to turn over a job this important to a sniveling doper. Joshua's face twisted in disgust. "Just get the hell out of here," he growled. "I've got work to do."

As soon as he was alone, Joshua took a plastic bottle of Maalox out of his desk drawer and poured the contents down his throat. Then he reached for the telephone.

He hadn't gotten to where he was today without learning the importance of always having a backup plan.

Whoosh. Bam. Boom. Incoming artillery screamed from the blood red sky. Monkeys and birds shrieked in trees illuminated by flames; all around him men were screaming in pain. The grunt next to him took shrapnel in the face and Matthew watched in horror as the freckled young features of an Iowa farm boy turned into a mass of red clay.

He was sweating. His clothes were drenched with perspiration; rivers of salt-drenched moisture streamed down his face. Matthew saw a man and a woman arguing heatedly. But something was out of sync. They were speaking Spanish, not Vietnamese. Before Matthew could figure it out, a dark cloud of unconsciousness settled back over him and the nightmare continued. In living color.

Matthew had been gone for three months when Leigh stopped by his house yet again. When she saw the car parked in his driveway, her heart soared. It was a new Thunderbird convertible with Sonoran Mexican plates.

"Sí?" The woman who opened the door was a Mexican in her mid-twenties, her shapely body clad in tight white jeans and a red halter top. Her hair was a mass of dark curls, her eyes the color of freshly brewed coffee. She frowned when she took in the sight of Leigh, crisp and cool-looking in a cream Chanel suit, standing in her doorway.

"I'm here to see Matthew."

"Matthew is not home. Good-bye." She attempted to shut the screen door, but Leigh was quicker, grabbing hold of the edge of the door.

"Wait!"

"I told you, Matthew is not home."

Leigh's first thought was that Matthew had used some of his newfound wealth to hire a maid. But there was something about this woman, the way she was dressed, the possessive way she spoke his name that caused a rising anxiety in her chest.

"But he is in the city?"

"Sí. But he is not home."

"May I come in and wait?"

The woman didn't budge. "What do you want with mi esposo?"

Although Leigh had a working knowledge of Spanish, she was certain she must have misunderstood. "Your what?"

"Matthew is mi esposo. My husband."

No. It couldn't be. "I don't believe it."

"Es verdad." The young woman nodded her head emphatically. "You wait." She disappeared back into the house, leaving Leigh standing on the front porch, her head reeling. Down the beach, a group of exuberant volleyball players shouted out friendly insults to one another; their voices reverberated like a distant echo in her ears. A moment later the woman was back. "This is my husband," she insisted, shoving a photograph into Leigh's hand.

It was as if the moment was frozen in time. A movie moment, Leigh considered, staring down at the couple. The woman was dressed in a frothy confection of a wedding dress, a crown of flowers atop her dark head. Her eyes, looking up at Matthew, were brimming over with love. Beside Matthew was another man, obviously a priest, from his dark shirt and stiff white collar.

Reality came crashing down atop Leigh with the force of a seismic jolt. "I'm sorry to have disturbed you," she managed through lips that had turned to stone. She felt lightheaded. As if she was going to faint. But that was ridiculous. She'd never fainted in her life.

The woman shrugged. "No problema. I will tell my husband you came to see him." Her dark eyes took another long, judicious tour of Leigh. "I do not know your name."

"It doesn't matter," Leigh murmured as she backed down the steps. She felt strangely lost, as if she could no longer recognize Matthew's house and couldn't fathom how she'd gotten there. "Not any longer."

It was only a nightmare, Leigh assured herself in the car.

One of those horrifying nightmares where demons were chasing you in the dark and, just before they grabbed you, you woke up, safe and sound in the comfort of your own bed.

Later that night, as she sat on her balcony, watching the moon-gilded waters lap relentlessly against the sand, Leigh wrapped her arms around herself in a futile attempt to hold the pain and loneliness out and the tears in.

Despite the popularity of glitzy premieres, Leigh preferred sneak previews. She preferred having her films previewed by warm bodies—real people, who paid real money. Slipping into the back row of a theater in Portland, Oregon, Leigh nervously awaited the audience's reactions to *Dangerous*.

When their interest was effectively captured by the first scene, even as the opening credits continued to run, Leigh began to breath a little easier. Their attention remained riveted to the screen and by the time the outlaw Ryder Long and his now willing hostage (wielding a sawed-off shotgun) successfully robbed the Paris branch of the Credit Suisse ninety minutes later, the mood was absolutely electric.

Then came the scene that succeeded in holding an entire theater—Leigh included—spellbound.

"I can't believe we did it!" Marissa / Marilyn exclaimed when she and Ryder entered their compartment on the night train that would take them from Paris to Barcelona. "I can't believe *I* did it. God, it was wonderful! It was the most exciting thing I've ever done!"

Marissa's eyes were as bright as newly polished emeralds, her face flushed, and she was quivering with excitement like a thoroughbred at the starting gate.

Matthew / Ryder was leaning against the wall, arms folded across his chest, watching her dance around the compact compartment. "I thought fucking me was the most exciting thing you've ever done."

"Well, of course," she agreed, unzipping the leather bag as the train pulled out of the station. "That goes without saying. But robbing banks definitely comes in a close second." She turned the bag over and shook it, sending a shower of colorful banknotes streaming over the narrow bunk. "Just look at this,

Ryder," she enthused, sifting the bills through her fingers like grains of sand. "There must be a million dollars worth of francs here. At least." She began sorting through it. "Do you want to divide it now? Or later? After we get to the hotel in Barcelona."

Ryder shrugged. "I'm not so sure we should divide it."

"But you promised! Equal partners, that's what you said."

Again his shoulders, clad in a black fisherman's sweater, lifted and dropped. "I was thinking, perhaps it would add a little spice to things if we wrestled for it."

"Wrestling? Like in arm wrestling?"

"Uh-uh. Real wrestling."

"Good idea." Marilyn laughed, confident he was teasing her. "Mud or mats?"

"Actually I was thinking about the bunk. Or the floor. But I'm open for any other suggestions you might have."

Her eyes widened. Surprise, laced with wary temptation, rose in their vivid green depths. "You're not joking, are you?"

"You should know me well enough by now to know that I never joke," he said calmly. "Especially about money. So, what do you say? One pin. Winner take all."

There was a long, thoughtful moment of silence, punctuated only by the rhythmic clickety-clack of the train's wheels on the rails. "But I don't know how to wrestle." She gave a nervous little laugh. "It wasn't on the class list at Madame Fontaine's Dance Academy."

"Don't worry." He yanked his sweater over his head. "You'll get the hang of it right away. It's a lot like sex. Only in this case, it pays a lot better."

"I still don't think—"

"The only problem is that you're overdressed."

Marilyn stood very still. He quickly, deftly unbuttoned her blouse and pushed it off her shoulders onto the floor. When he reached out, she drew in a quick breath, expecting his touch, but instead his hand shot past her, plucking a crisp bill from the money strewn over the bunk.

"Think of it," he suggested silkily, stoking her throat with the bill. "This can all be yours." He trailed the paper money down the slope of her breasts, along the scalloped edge of her silk camisole. "All you have to do is pin me. Once."

"But you're so much stronger," she complained, trembling with a heady mixture of anticipation and passion. "It wouldn't be a fair fight."

Taking his finger to her shoulder, he pushed aside one of the camisole's straps. "I'll only use one hand."

He was left-handed. She looked up at him, then down at the money. "Make it your right hand and you've got yourself a deal."

His lips brushed aside the other strap; the ivory silk clung tenuously. "You've gotten tough, lady."

Marilyn's breath was audible. "I've had a good teacher."

"Let's see exactly how good." Without warning, he pulled her roughly down onto the bunk, thrust his right hand through her hair, and kissed her deep and long. She appeared on the verge of succumbing to the passion that had been building ever since the wild drive from the bank to the train station, when she suddenly remembered Ryder's challenge.

"No fair distracting me." Pulling away, she pushed as hard as she could against his chest, forcing Ryder onto his back. Hiking her skirt high onto her bare thighs, she straddled him, her palms pressing against his shoulders. "I win," she cried out triumphantly.

"That's what you think." With a move so fluid, so quick that she hadn't seen it coming, Ryder turned, sending her sprawling. Locking her in a scissors hold between his legs, he thrust his hand beneath her skirt, eliciting a soft moan of pleasure. "Lesson number one," he said. "Overconfidence can be a dangerous mistake."

"Ryder, please." She was panting like an animal, while he was not even winded, but Marilyn was not yet prepared to give up the fight. Outside the wide window the French countryside flashed by, ghostly pale in the moonlight. "Just give me a minute to catch my breath," she pleaded prettily.

"Surrender and you'll have all the time you need." He loosened his viselike grip just enough to allow her to slip free.

"Someone once told me that overconfidence can be a dangerous mistake," she panted. "You haven't won, Ryder. Not yet." She was on her knees, her hair a damp, wild tangle around her bare shoulders, her breasts heaving with exertion.

Her skin, slick with sweat, gleamed pearly in the streaming moonlight. Their eyes locked.

A man seated two seats away from Leigh groaned. Behind her a young woman sighed.

Drawing in a deep, ragged breath, Marilyn screamed and flung herself against Ryder like a wildcat. They grappled, rolling across the mattress as if chained together, an agile tangle of arms and legs. Flesh against flesh, passion exuding from every glistening pore. Mouth to mouth, hot, open, hungry. Newly minted bills clung to their skin. Ryder's heavy beard scraped the soft skin at the inside of her thigh; Marilyn's long nails raked crimson trails along his back. Shaking and rocking, listing on curves, the train raced steadily toward the Pyrenees.

For a long, immeasurable time the camera lens never lingered on any one spot. It shifted from Ryder to Marilyn and back again. Long shot. Close-up of Ryder. Close-up of Marilyn. Cut to the hexagon mirror over the sink, reflecting the sinuous movements that were like a dance as the pair twisted, turned, came together, pulled apart, created new shapes, new designs in a blinding kaleidoscope of images and sensations.

And although she'd seen the dailies innumerable times and had sat by while Kim edited the blatantly erotic clips into a dazzlingly sensual scene, Leigh found herself caught up in the audience's mood. It was quiet in the theater. But there was something lingering in the air. A hushed, almost preclimactic tension.

Marilyn was on her hands and knees, swaying with the movement of the railroad car as Ryder crouched over her like some great lion. King of the beasts, Leigh mused, experiencing a familiar painful constriction around her heart.

"I win," he growled. Lowering his warrior body in a reverse one-handed push-up, he pressed her exhausted, prone body into the mattress demanding submission.

"Yes." Struggling to fill her lungs with air, she squirmed under him pleading, cajoling, laughing, and moaning at the same time. "Damn you, Ryder Long, I knew this wasn't going to be a fair contest."

"Say it."

"You win, damnit. All right?"

"All right." It was all he'd been waiting for. Turning her over, he pinned her hands above her head with his right hand. With his left hand he scooped up a fistful of crumpled bills and rained them down on her. His eyes were intense, dark, dangerous. Then, unzipping her skirt, he began tugging it down her legs.

As the scene faded to black (something that Christopher Burke had vehemently protested, but Leigh insisted was necessary to prevent their R rating from slipping to a dreaded X), the spellbound audience finally released a long, drawn-out breath.

When she left the theater fifteen minutes later, Leigh knew that her sister's lifelong dream had come true. Because there was no longer any doubt about it; when *Dangerous* was released, Marissa Baron was going to be a star.

Two weeks after the sneak preview in Portland, Leigh struggled out of bed like a zombie. It was a typically warm California spring, but she felt colder than she'd ever felt before. Cold and numb. The nightmares had returned again, more vivid, more frightening than ever.

"I'm worried about you," Joshua said as she exited her Jaguar, parked beside his Porsche in the Baron Studios lot.

"Worried about me?" she asked vaguely, realizing that she could not remember driving into the studio from Santa Monica.

"You haven't been yourself."

"Nonsense. I've just been a bit distracted."

"That has been only too obvious. I received a call from Ed Davidson yesterday afternoon."

"Ed? Our insurance man?"

"He said that you've received two speeding tickets in the past fourteen days."

"Three, counting the one I got last night."

"Three tickets? In two weeks?"

Leigh shrugged. "Everyone in California speeds."

"You never have."

"Perhaps I'm simply making up for lost time," she suggested, not wanting to admit that she'd been surprised each time the flashing red and blue lights had appeared in her rearview mirror.

It was as if she'd been operating on autopilot, a feeling obviously shared by the officer last night, who'd requested that she take a sobriety test. She'd passed, of course. Leigh didn't need artificial anesthetics; her mind was more than capable of producing its own numbing effects.

Joshua gave her a long look. "Well, the way you've been driving lately, you're going to get your license taken away. Or end up in the morgue. I think you need to get away."

It was the same thing Kim had been telling her for days. "I don't want to take a vacation." She didn't add that work was the only thing keeping her sane.

"Who said anything about a vacation? I was talking about a job."

"What kind of job?"

"I need a location producer for *Arabian Nights*."

Arabian Nights was a film suggested by the story of Aimée Dubucq de Rivery, a convent girl captured by corsairs and thrown into the harem of the Grand Turk. It was one of the old-fashioned costume epics Baron Studios was famous for. They'd been scheduled to film the story in Egypt when the Six Day War broke out, causing the project to sit on the shelf for six years. Until Leigh revived the movie by suggesting they move the filming to the United Arab Emirates, a newly established, oil-rich federation on the Persian Gulf.

"What happened to Peter Fowler?"

"Damn fool had a heart attack."

"That's terrible. I hope it wasn't fatal."

"No. But he'll probably wish it had been when he gets out of the hospital. Turns out that he was romping around the dungeon he and Freda had built in the basement of their Pacific Palisades house with a makeup woman from Paramount. Word around town is that by the time Freda got through with her, the girl didn't have a hair left on her head."

Although she suspected the story of being an exaggeration, Leigh wouldn't want to have been attacked by the robust former actress. Freda Fowler's temper was legendary. As was her collection of bullwhips.

"I really am in a bind, princess. The film's set to begin

shooting in five days and here I am without a location producer."

A location producer was a cross between a line producer, or production manager, and babysitter, responsible for all the niggling little problems that popped up during filming. It was incredibly demanding work, requiring continual attention to detail. And it was, Leigh decided, exactly what she needed.

"All right, I'll take it."

"You're a lifesaver." Joshua smiled his satisfaction. "I took the liberty of picking up a token of my appreciation.

"You knew I'd do it, didn't you?"

"I knew you'd never let your old man down."

The blue-wrapped package contained a perfectly round black pearl ring that matched the earrings her father had given her last summer. Slipping the ring on her finger, Leigh didn't bother to answer Joshua's supremely confident statement.

There was no need; it was, after all, the truth.

27

The frantic scene at the Abu Dhabi airport was a cross between a Roman circus and a Chinese fire drill. In the noisy terminal, Leigh looked around for the driver Erin McMurphy, the film's director, had promised would meet her.

"Ms. Baron?"

A deep voice at her elbow captured her attention and Leigh turned around to find herself face to face with one of the most striking men she'd ever seen. He looked to be in his mid- to late-thirties and his dark eyes reminded her of obsidian, without the flinty hardness. His dark face was lean—all planes and hollows—with a strong, slightly hooked nose and firm lips under a black mustache. His stark features made him appear harsh and forbidding, until he flashed a dazzling smile.

"You are Ms. Baron, are you not?"

"I am."

"I am Khalil Al-Tajir." At Leigh's blank look, he elaborated. "Assistant Minister of Culture."

The man who had been assigned by the government to act as liaison between the crew from Baron Studios and the local film crew, Leigh remembered. She knew she was staring, but she couldn't help herself. He was tall, distinguished, with a great presence, yet something about him hinted of the mystic. Something that conjured up fanciful visions of romantic Arabian nights. She found herself imagining him in robes and a burnoose.

Cupping his hand under her elbow, he led her through the crush of people and away from the long lines snaking through the terminal. "If you'll come with me, Ms. Baron, I will attempt to facilitate your passage through Customs." He shepherded her down a long corridor to a narrow door.

Within a matter of minutes she had cleared Health, Security, Immigration, and Customs. When they passed the long lines once again, Leigh noticed that they had not moved forward an inch.

"They'll probably be standing there another two to four hours," Khalil commented. If she'd been grateful for Khalil's intercession earlier, now she was doubly grateful. He snapped his fingers and, as if conjured up from Aladdin's magic lamp, a porter appeared with her luggage. A long black Rolls-Royce limousine was waiting by the curb, air conditioner running. The windows of the limousine were heavily tinted in deference to the heat.

The traffic was heavy, cars bumper to bumper. Drivers seemed determined to use up every inch of available space. Leigh watched a young girl clad in blue jeans and a striped T-shirt roar past the limo on a motorbike, carrying the carcass of a dead goat on the handlebars as she manuevered her way through the crush of Toyota pickups and Land Rovers.

"Erin said she was sending a gofer to meet me."

"That was her initial intention, but since a mere gofer would not have been able to ease your way through Customs, I felt you might appreciate my personal intervention."

"I did. Thank you."

"It was my pleasure."

Khalil had never had any intention of allowing anyone else

to greet the American filmmaker. During his student years at Oxford, he'd seen Leigh's picture in a British magazine. She had been twelve years old at the time and, although his mother had married at exactly the same age, Khalil knew that in America, Leigh would be considered a mere child. That knowledge hadn't stopped him from being intrigued by the secrets he thought he saw residing in her cool gray eyes.

When she'd entered the terminal today, looking fresh and cool in ivory linen slacks and a white silk shirt, he decided that before her time in Abu Dhabi came to an end, he and the lovely Leigh Baron would be lovers.

Abu Dhabi was a beguiling mix of ancient East and modern West. Ancient mosques and minarets were silhouetted against shining glass towers. The sidewalks were as crowded as the streets, lovely young girls in scant Parisian miniskirts waiting at bus stops, side by side with veiled women who moved like shadows under layers of voluminous black cloaks.

"It's incredible," Leigh said.

"Only thirteen years ago, Abu Dhabi was a quiet Gulf village of fishermen. Then revenues skyrocketed and Sheik Zayid began spending millions to create this instant city. I was studying in England when the oil first began to flow; when I returned home, I could hardly recognize the city. There are still times when I drive down a street and see a skyscraper that I've never noticed before, as if it had sprung out of the desert overnight."

He pointed out a Bedouin family living in a goat-hair tent while their government home was being built next door. "So much is changing," he said. His soft tone made Leigh wonder if he disapproved of the instant westernization. "And although the oil reserves may have been the bounty of Allah, we must still work to appreciate what we've built. Inshallah— God willing—we will learn how to utilize our newfound wealth without destroying our society. I only pray that these threads of gold futures weaving their way through the ancient fabric of our past will create a durable tapestry."

"If what you've created this far is any indication, I think it will be more than durable. It will be exquisite."

"The goal is to rival Beirut's seaport glitter; we hope to accomplish that without losing touch with our past."

"Inshallah," Leigh echoed the newly learned term, earning an appreciative glance from Khalil. "Are you from Abu Dhabi, originally?"

"No, I am a Bedouin. Not only was I the first in my family to come to the city, I was also the first to study abroad."

"That must have taken an enormous adjustment."

"It was extremely difficult, in the beginning," he admitted. "When I returned home from reading law at Oxford, I spent three frustrating weeks trying to locate my family." He chuckled at the long-ago memory. "I was afraid all that English rain had destroyed my desert instincts."

"But you eventually found them."

"Of course." Of course, Leigh concurred silently, from what she'd seen thus far, this was a man who would always achieve whatever he'd set out to do.

She stared out the window, like a child who'd just caught her first close-up glimpse of Oz. Donkey carts and motorbikes fought for street space with flatbed trucks loaded with cement and steel, rumbling graders, dump trucks, and busloads of Pakistani construction workers. Turbaned vendors hawked their wares—dates and nuts, copper pots, leather goods, freshly killed plump pigeons—on the same streets frequented by businessmen dressed in dark European suits. It was as if the eighteenth, nineteenth, and twentieth centuries had merged together into some sci-fi time warp. Everything and everyone seemed to coexist in this strange and wonderful place.

"Would you be offended if I admitted that most of my images of your part of the world come from our American movies?"

"I can't imagine being offended by anything you might say. Or do."

His appreciative tone and warm smile encouraged her to open up to him. "When I was eight years old, my third-grade teacher, Sister Luke, asked our class what we wanted to be when we grew up. Everyone responded with the typical answers: doctor, nurse, fireman, policeman, teacher, mommy, movie star—"

"Movie star is a typical American aspiration?"

"It is in Beverly Hills. Anyway, I think I offended Sister's delicate sensibilities when I announced that I intended to be a belly dancer in the Casbah." She felt the color drifting into her cheeks. "Do you know, I've never told that story to anyone."

Khalil chuckled appreciatively. "Then I feel doubly privileged. And as enticing an image as that admittedly is, I feel obliged to point out that despite its new, modern image, Abu Dhabi is a city that can not be taken in with a single glance. It reveals itself slowly, layer by layer. Like its people."

Although his tone remained politely conversational, when his dark eyes met hers and held, Leigh experienced a vague, distant flutter somewhere deep inside her.

"This script is shit. Just like all the others."

Marissa tossed the pages onto the brick decking of the swimming pool. She had bought the Laurel Canyon house with the proceeds from *Dangerous*.

"It's not that bad," Corbett said.

"The hell it isn't. I've already told you, Corbett, I don't want to be just another pair of tits."

As she leaned toward him, her breasts overflowing the yellow crocheted bikini top, Corbett considered that no one could ever consider Marissa's tits as just another pair. "I'd say you locked yourself into that role when you went on 'The Barry James Show.' Hell, Marissa, you looked like you were going to eat that guy alive on national TV."

"The audience loved me."

"And they're going to love you in this."

"It's exploitative."

Corbett wondered why it was that actresses who used their bodies to get roles were so often the first to scream that they were being exploited. He decided against mentioning that her sister had given her an excellent opportunity to avoid typecasting with her role in *Dangerous*. It wasn't Leigh's fault that Marissa had gone on television and thrust her boobs into America's face.

"It's a comedy, a remake of a French farce. You'll be terrific."

She chewed on a ragged nail and looked down at the script. "And you really think the audience will like me in this part?"

When her gaze returned to his face, she suddenly looked like the insecure teenager Corbett knew her to be. That was the main reason he'd taken on Marissa as a client, risking Tina's tacit disapproval. Someone needed to look out for the girl, someone who cared about more than his ten percent.

"They'll love you," he repeated. "And by the time you finish filming this one, *Dangerous* will be out and, who knows, you could be swamped with scripts featuring more serious roles."

"I'd like to do something like *Klute*," she mused.

Last year's Oscar had resulted in moving Jane Fonda from the ranks of just another bimbo and wartime protester to a major force in Hollywood. Personally, Marissa had been betting against Fonda ever escaping *Barbarella*.

"Let's just take one film at a time," Corbett counseled.

"So you think I ought to sign?"

"I think it would be good for you to get back to work." Corbett had noticed that Marissa was rudderless when she wasn't working. The last few times he'd been by the house, he'd been worried about the direction in which the girl was drifting.

"Okay, I'll do it. What about the part for Jeff?"

He glanced over toward the pool, where Jeff Martin was floating nude on an air mattress. After the short-lived fling with Barry James fizzled out, Martin had reappeared. "Your father doesn't want Jeff working for Baron any longer."

"Why not?"

"I don't know," the agent answered honestly. "But he seemed emphatic about not giving him a part."

"Shit." Marissa reached for a striped canvas bag beside the lounge, took out a compact and a small vial of white powder. Ignoring Corbett's disapproving look, she sliced and fluffed the powder onto the mirror, arranged it into two neat lines, and inhaled it. The rush was instant, clearing her mind, allowing her to think clearly enough to outmaneuver her father.

"All right," she said, "we'll do it another way. Put expenses for a second makeup man into the contract, and I'll sign."

"Fine."

Corbett knew exactly who that alleged second makeup man was going to be. Perks were an accepted part of the business.

When creating a budget, it was referred to as "adding in one third for the shit," the shit being the star's entourage. Hell, he'd just finished negotiating a contract with Paramount that included salaries for the female star's private hairdresser, the hairdresser's homosexual lover, two secretaries, her personal fitness trainer, her astrologer, and the bodybuilder-chauffeur who was currently screwing the star. On top of that, the studio had agreed to lease the star's personal trailer and car, at double what it would cost to rent them from a dealer.

That was the way the game was played in the big leagues. Marissa had grown up on the playing field and had learned the subtleties of the game well.

Gathering up his papers, he prepared to leave. "One more thing."

Marissa looked up at him. "Yeah?"

"That stuff is bad news."

"You're my agent, not my keeper." Her beautiful young face turned hard as she took her dark glasses from atop her head and shielded her eyes. "Good-bye, Corbett. I'm sure you can see yourself out."

As he drove back down the winding canyon road, it crossed Corbett's mind that for all her father's denials to the contrary, Marissa was a great deal like Joshua. Both of them could be as hard as stone.

The rich, unmistakable aroma of coffee roused him. Matthew leaned up on his elbows and looked around the room that was both familiar and strange at the same time.

"You're awake." The woman sitting beside his bed smiled.

"I think I am. Unless you're another dream." But his dreams had been nightmares. This young woman was a vision.

"No dream, señor. You have been very ill."

He rubbed his face, flinching at the pain the slight movement caused. "You were shot," she explained at his questioning look.

Matthew lay back against the pillows, trying to think back through the fog of nightmares. "Someone was chasing me. The police?"

"No, an old boyfriend." She gave him an apologetic smile.

"When he gets drunk and sees me with other men, he goes a little loco. Crazy, you know?"

Matthew grimaced as he tried to sit up. It felt as if his entire chest muscle was ripped open. "What the hell did he use? An elephant gun?"

"I do not know, señor."

It was beginning to come back to him. "You're the girl from the cantina. The one who broke me out of jail."

"Sí."

"Why?"

"They are saying at the cantina that you are a movie star."

"I'm not, really."

"But you do work in Hollywood? In the movies?"

"Yeah, I guess I do." Funny how he still didn't think of himself as an actor.

She handed him a stack of drawings. "I am a seamstress and dress designer. My dream is to work in Hollywood, in the movies. Perhaps you know someone who will arrange for my green card?"

"I'm sure we can work something out. Did you know I was arrested for drug dealing?"

"Sí."

"Then you should also know that I'm innocent."

"No es importa." She shrugged. "Mi hermano said that you made someone very angry because the policia were keeping you a secret."

Her brother. Matthew vaguely recalled an argument. "He refused to let you call a doctor because he didn't want to attract the police's attention." He flexed his shoulder, studying the expertly wrapped bandage. "I guess you won the argument."

"No. I am afraid not."

"Then who took out the bullet? Surely not you?"

"No. My cousin is studying medicine at the university. He is the one who removed the bullet and taught me how to care for you." Her wide dark eyes were grave. "You became very ill, señor. You had a fever."

Another memory returned. One of a woman—an angel— bathing his heated flesh with cooling cloths. Matthew was suddenly all too aware of his unclothed state.

"What's your name?"

"Rosaria, señor," she said softly. "Rosaria Ramirez."

"Well, Rosaria, I appreciate all you've done," he said. He wrapped the top sheet around himself toga-style and walked away from the bed. "And I promise to repay you for all your troubles, as soon as I get back home." He was about to ask what had happened to his clothes, when a man entered the room. In his hand was a .38 magnum revolver, pointing at Matthew.

"As much as I would like my sister to receive a reward for her generous good deeds, I am afraid I cannot let you leave, señor."

28

*Z*apata Canyon, fifteen miles south of San Diego, was a gravelly, garbage-strewn frontier. The forbidding canyon was the largest single route of illegal entry into the United States. Los Angeles, Matthew's destination, was one hundred and forty miles and another world away.

Despite the sagging Third World shacks that leaned against the steel fence, a fiesta atmosphere existed in the dusty canyon. Food stalls proliferated, along with tables selling denim jackets as protection against the cold Pacific Coast nights. A young boy, no older than eleven, sold maps obviously stolen from a Chevron gas station. San Diego. Los Angeles. Orange County. Sacramento. Fresno. Modesto. Lands of opportunity for those willing to do the hard, physical work norteamericanos didn't want to do.

It had been more than five months since Matthew's arrest. Five long and frustrating months. Patience had never been his strong suit; now, when he could see his country on the other side of that damn fence, he just wanted to be back home.

In the beginning, Jesus Ramirez, Rosaria's brother, had not wanted anything to do with Matthew. A professional smuggler, he earned a comfortable living bringing workers and Acapulco Gold into the United States from Mexico while moving Chevys back across the border the other way. Although he willingly paid off the local authorities, he was careful not to attract undue interest from the federales. Harboring an American fugitive under his roof would do exactly that.

But then Matthew's wound became infected and Rosaria, displaying the same stubbornness that had discouraged any of the village men from proposing to her, refused to allow him to leave until he was strong enough to travel. By that time Matthew had been staying at the house long enough to involve Jesus if he was captured, so the smuggler reluctantly decided that it was in his own best interests to get the gringo back to Los Angeles. And if that weren't motivation enough, a thousand American dollars wired from Corbett Marshall had clinched the deal.

"So what do we do now?" Matthew asked.

"Wait." Jesus stopped in front of a battered blue pickup truck with TACOS VARIOS painted on the sides of the bed. After a brief discussion with the vendor, Jesus purchased two bean burritos and a bottle of beer.

"Wait for what?"

"Night. What else?" Jesus asked around a mouthful of burrito. "When we can slip past la migra."

It wasn't Immigration that Matthew was afraid of, but the Mexican police. If there was a warrant out for his arrest, he could disappear back into the slow-grinding Mexican judicial system for years. "What about the police?"

Jesus shrugged. "The policia are no problem," he said in an offhanded way that added credence to the claim that several members of the police force worked for the coyotes, or people smugglers. Also supposedly in league with the coyotes were the bandits who lurked in the dark, attacking and robbing any illegal foolish enough to try to cross the border unescorted. It was, Matthew considered, the perfect protection racket.

More than two hundred immigrants—mostly men, with the occasional woman or child—lined the fence, watching. Waiting. As they had for years. Because he'd had grown up in Southern California, Matthew was aware of the illegal's game of playing catch-me-if-you-can with the U.S. border patrol. But now, as he watched the number of heavily armed men waiting for night to fall, he realized that the game had become a great deal more dangerous.

That was why Matthew hadn't told Corbett what he was doing. Promising that he would explain once he returned to Los Angeles, he'd asked his agent to wire a thousand dollars to Jesus. He also requested that Corbett tell no one about his call. Since he was now an escaped felon, however innocent, he didn't want to involve Corbett in anything illegal. There was also the outside chance things might go wrong. If that happened, he didn't want to give Leigh any false hope.

The sun was slowly going down. The Baja air grew cooler. People began moving toward the doorways cut into the steel mesh.

"Soon," Jesus promised. "Soon, gringo, you will be home."

As a police car cruised by, Matthew suddenly felt as if he were back in the middle of a war zone. His stomach knotted and a heavy, sweet smell of death filled his nostrils, a leftover olfactory memory from Vietnam.

When the Mexican cops drove away, Matthew reminded himself that he'd always been a survivor.

Joshua watched Marissa soothe the damaged ego of a male computer student whose girlfriend had just dumped him for an illiterate, musclebound football player. The lighthearted sexual romp revolved around a young woman who'd been hired to be a house mother for a California fraternity. Although the premise was admittedly far-fetched, the vehicle was designed to display nearly every inch of Marissa's considerable attributes.

By the time the director yelled "Cut," Joshua would not have been surprised to discover that the young man's glasses were fogged.

Marissa had felt her father's presence the moment he'd arrived. Of course she'd been expecting him; the director had informed her that Joshua would be visiting the set. Fore-warned was forearmed, and after two little blue Valium and a belt of the Absolut vodka she kept stashed away in her dressing room, Marissa felt ready to face him. She had put everything she had into that scene. Now, as she walked toward Joshua, a confident smile pasted onto her face, she tried to read his expression.

"Well? What did you think?"

"Not bad."

Marissa beamed. It was the closest thing to a compliment she had ever received from her father. "You thought I was going to turn it into just another porno flick, didn't you?"

"It wouldn't have been your first one."

"That was just to get your attention."

"Well, it sure as hell did that."

"You're the one who's always saying to take risks."

He gave her a sharp look, surprised to hear his own words thrown back to him. "You rushed your lines toward the end. And you upstaged that poor kid every chance you got. But all in all, you pulled it off better than I would've expected."

"Corbett says I have a real future in romantic comedy."

"Corbett's your agent; he gets paid to say things like that."

"You said I was good."

"I said you weren't bad. There's a difference."

It was what he wasn't saying. Marissa had seen that grudg-ing look of admiration in his eyes. The knowledge that he hadn't wanted to like her performance made his reluctant acceptance even more heartwarming.

"Mr. Baron?" The young grip looked extremely nervous about interrupting the conversation between studio head and star. "I'm sorry to bother you, sir, but there's a call from your daughter. You can take it on that phone over there."

Joshua's face lit up like the Las Vegas strip. Turning his back on his younger daughter as if he'd forgotten her exis-tence, he rushed off.

"Princess," he greeted Leigh expansively, "when the hell are you coming back home? Things aren't the same around here without you, sweetheart."

Damn, damn, damn! For the first time in as long as Marissa could remember, she'd had her father all to herself. And the miracle was, they had actually been getting along. Until that bitch Leigh had called and ruined everything.

She stood all alone in the shadows, watching Joshua laugh heartily at something Leigh said. Marissa nearly choked on the scalding bitter taste of envy that rose in her throat.

Abu Dhabi seemed to be a city built upon shifting sands. Dust was everywhere. Blowing down the narrow streets, making its way through back alleys, drifting over the meat and oranges in the marketplace. Even the buildings were the color of dust—brown, ecru, umber. There were times when Leigh found the unrelenting heat and dust debilitating. Now, even after a bath, she felt as if she had dust in her pores.

"This time next week, you will be lying on the California beach," Khalil said reassuringly.

They were sitting in the lobby of her hotel, drinking the ubiquitous overly sugared hot tea. The final scenes of *Arabian Nights* were scheduled to be shot in three days. And as much as Leigh was looking forward to leaving the oppressive heat of Abu Dhabi, she also knew that she was going to leave a little bit of herself here. It was frustrating, overcrowded, parts of it malodorous, even wretched. It was also one of the most fascinating cities she'd ever known.

"Do you know," she said with a slow smile, "there are times when I feel as if you can read my mind."

How many times over the past two months had she found herself wishing for something, only to have Khalil arrive with it in hand, as if by magic, moments later? He'd eased her work considerably, including keeping his pockets filled with piasters for the baksheesh, those tips and bribes that accompanied every transaction. Except for the usual cases of diarrhea that hit the American members of the crew, the filming had gone remarkably well. Even the scenes shot out in the desert had been achieved without incident, unless one counted spitting camels and dust storms.

Khalil smiled. "While I would like to claim that I possess an Eastern mysticism, the truth is that your lovely face is quite often an open book."

"How interesting that you should say that," she murmured. "People usually accuse me of being frustratingly enigmatic."

"They don't know you."

"And you do?"

"Yes." His dark eyes met hers. "I do."

How strange that he should remind her so of Matthew, Leigh thought, experiencing an involuntary sexual pull that was both painful and exciting. "Well, you certainly don't lack self-confidence," she said, pretending a sudden interest in the wizened old man wearing a red fez who was methodically sweeping away at the ancient Persian carpet with a palm frond.

Her hotel, located on the wide, newly constructed Corniche, retained a quiet gentility suggestive of the city's colonial period. Ceiling fans churned the air, leafy palm trees grew in bright brass containers and Bedouin baskets, the furniture was solid and overstuffed. In the adjoining café, a circle of men sat cross-legged on the floor, smoking hookahs and playing cards. As yet another example of the vast changes the oil reserves had wrought, next door to the hotel, beneath a red-and-white striped awning, a lifesize cutout of Colonel Sanders greeted diners eager to sample his finger-lickin' Kentucky Fried Chicken.

"I know that you are hurting," Khalil said. "More than you are willing to admit."

"No one gets through life without a few bruises." Leigh turned her gaze away. From her vantage point beside a high, latticed window (lattices, which Khalil had explained, were designed to protect women from view), she had a dazzling view of the harbor, where ships arrived daily from all corners of the world, their holds laden with apples from Washington State, Dutch canned milk, Chinese wheelbarrows, Korean tires. Wooden dhows bobbed beside the wharfs while workmen unloaded rainbows of silk, gleaming copper and gold, carpets and pearls.

"Spoken like a true American. I suspect next you'll be giving me that tired old bromide about rolling with the punches."

"You do know me, don't you?" she said with a slight smile.

"Not as much as I'd like." Before she could respond, Khalil changed the subject, leaving Leigh to wonder if she'd only imagined the sudden intimacy in his voice. "It went well today, I think."

They'd spent the day filming in several of the neighborhood marketplaces, where Leigh had almost succumbed to the lure of a lovely gold necklace. But when the old saleswoman, with a gold nose pendant and chin tattoo, had weighed the necklace on a pair of delicate scales, then pecked out the price per gram on a Japanese calculator, figuring in, she assured Leigh, a "most generous discount," the total cost came to more than fifteen hundred dollars. More than Leigh had been prepared to pay.

"Better than well. I can't thank you enough for talking that man into allowing us to film him." The moment she'd seen the bearded bargainer in the camel bazaar, Leigh had known that she had to capture him on film. Unfortunately, he had not been willing to cooperate. Until Khalil had stepped forward and murmured a few words. A coin changed hands. The deal was done.

"Many of the older people believe that photographs constitute a threat to God's creations."

"If he really believed that, I'm surprised you were able to bribe him."

"That was his bargaining excuse. Not his belief," Khalil corrected gently. "Contrary to popular opinion, Leigh, not everything or everyone in Abu Dhabi is for sale. We Arabs survived for thousands of years with nothing but our faith in Allah, our steadfast belief in his generosity, and the strength of our families and tribes. All this oil, while inexorably altering our landscape, has not changed who we are. What we are."

Leigh blushed and looked down at her hands. "I didn't mean to imply—"

"And I didn't mean to lecture." Khalil shook his head. "I'm sorry, but there are times when I get tired of being patronized by Westerners who didn't give a damn about this part of the world until they needed our oil reserves." He reached out, as if to take her hand, then, apparently thinking better of it, withdrew. "You, on the other hand, have been a model of diplomacy, Leigh Baron. In fact, if your State Department officials and oil company executives possessed even a fraction of your discretion, the world would be a much better place." His eyes, as they settled on her face, darkened with masculine appreciation. "Not to mention a much lovelier place."

One again, Leigh felt herself blushing. But this time it was not embarrassment that caused the soft color to drift into her cheeks. "Thank you. That's a very nice thing to say."

"It's the truth. And now that today's work is completed, I have a proposition for you."

"Oh?"

"How would you like to go horseback riding?"

"Today?" Leigh glanced unenthusiastically out the window where the brilliant yellow sun still rode high in the sky.

"Tonight. I raise Arabians at my house outside the city; I'd enjoy showing them to you."

The chance to get out of the city sounded more than a little appealing. "And I'd enjoy seeing them. Very much."

"Good." Rising from his overstuffed chair, he smiled down at her. "I will pick you up at seven. It is only a short car ride to my house."

"That sounds marvelous," Leigh said, standing as well.

Taking her hand, Khalil lifted it to his lips in an Old World gesture that suited him perfectly. The light brush of his black mustache against her skin was like a flare of sparklers, but before she could pull away, he'd relinquished her hand and was on his way out of the hotel, leaving Leigh to wonder what, exactly, she'd just agreed to.

A large, unmarked delivery truck pulled up behind an abandoned mattress factory in L.A.'s warehouse district. The driver, a heavyset, dark-complected man of indeterminate age, lumbered to the back of the truck, unlocked it, then disappeared around the corner. A moment later, fifty men clutching hand-drawn maps from relatives living in the area, dispersed in all directions. Matthew was the last man to leave. He blinked, struggling to adapt his eyes to the bright California sun. He and the others had been in the truck for the last eighteen hours.

His incarceration and near brush with death had given him plenty of time to reevaluate his life. And although he hadn't come up with any answers, he did know that he'd spent a great deal of time thinking about Leigh. Wanting her. Missing her. Loving her. What they needed was time, he had considered. Time to get to know one another without outside influences like the studio, his goals, the vast differences in their upbringing.

The first thing he'd promised himself that he would do, if he survived this nightmarish ordeal, would be to take Leigh away to some distant tropical island, where they'd spend long, lazy days basking in the sun and feeding one another sweet, succulent fruit.

Passion fruit.

As he began walking toward Venice, Matthew smiled for the first time in months.

On a cool, clear night, a spirited gallop across the desert is an unforgettable experience. They could have been a million miles away from civilization; the shifting sands, dotted with oil wells painted to resemble bright birds, seemed to stretch out to infinity. A full moon hung in the wide sky overhead, lighting the world with an unearthly white glow. Spurring her sleek gray Arabian mount forward, Leigh experienced a surge of freedom like nothing she'd ever known. Beside her, dressed in fawn-colored jodhpurs, a loose white lawn shirt, and black boots, seated astride a magnificent black stallion, Khalil cut an undeniably striking figure.

"Where are we going?" she asked, after they'd been riding about thirty minutes.

"It's a special place I keep to maintain a bond with my past," he explained. "When I feel the need to escape the constant crush and clamor of the city, I come here. I think you'll like it."

Hard-pressed to think about anything she wouldn't like about this evening, Leigh returned his smile.

It was not long when she saw it. A large black-and-white tent, standing alone in what appeared to be miles of empty desert. "I'm amazed that you were able to find it."

"I may have adopted western clothes and western manners, but I still possess a few Bedouin instincts." He reined in his horse and dismounted.

"I'm glad," she said, handing him her reins. Although

Leigh was perfectly capable of dismounting by herself, she didn't argue when Khalil gripped her around her waist and lifted her down.

"Really?"

"Really. It adds a certain mystery."

He smiled at that. "Do you think so?"

"Definitely. The first time I saw you, I thought you had a hint of the mystic. These past two months have only intensified my feelings."

"I'm pleased to hear that." He pulled the flap of the tent open, gesturing her to go in. "Since my feelings about you have been building for fourteen years."

"Fourteen years?" Leigh stopped, gazing around the interior of the tent. Oriental rugs and tasseled cushions of gold- and silver-threaded Moroccan tapestry covered the floor. "But you've only known me two months."

"Ah, but I saw a picture of you when I was at Oxford. You were dressed in a long white dress with a pink satin sash. Your hair was tied back with a pink ribbon, revealing the pair of natural pearls that adorned your exquisite earlobes."

"It was the night of the Academy Awards," Leigh remembered, stunned by his total recall. Even she had forgotten the pearls—the first her father had ever given her. "I was thirteen, I think."

"You were twelve. And I believe that's when I fell in love with you."

His words hung between them, waiting for Leigh to pick up on them. She knew that he was leaving it up to her. She could turn away from what he was offering and, gentleman that she knew Khalil to be, he would never mention it again. Or she could give in to these sexual stirrings she'd been experiencing more and more frequently since arriving in Abu Dhabi.

For someone who had never thought a great deal about sex, Leigh was shocked to discover that she'd become a highly sensual person. It was as if Matthew had opened a secret door, exposing hidden desires, unknown needs.

"I can't believe you love me," she said.

The night was cool; Khalil knelt and lit a small brazier in the corner of the tent. "Why not?" he asked as he started some frankincense burning in a copper container. Leigh had learned that burning frankincense was a traditional method of entertaining guests. "You are beautiful, intelligent, sensual—"

"But you said you fell in love with me when I was a girl."

"I fell in love with the woman I saw in that little girl's eyes."

"There's something important I need to tell you."

He smiled up at her. "Do you think you could possibly impart this important information sitting down? Or do you plan to stand by the flap of the tent all night, looking as if you're prepared to bolt at the slightest touch."

Leigh entered the tent and sank into the silken comfort of the pillows. Khalil lay down beside her. In deference to the desert heat, she'd twisted her hair into a braid and tied it with a piece of white ribbon, leaving a fan of silky blond hair that Khalil brushed with a seductive touch over her cheek and down her throat. His gaze locked with Leigh's as he tugged lightly on the ribbon. A moment later it was lying on the blood red rug. Appearing fascinated with the intricate French braiding, he traced the weaving with his finger.

Leigh told herself that she should insist Khalil stop twining his fingers through the braid as he unwound it. But her words of protest remained locked in her throat.

"You have to understand," she said softly, "this isn't easy for me."

"I know." He freed her hair from the tight braid and lifted it over her shoulders.

"Until recently, I'd always kept my feelings hidden away. Where they'd be safe. Protected. But then I met"—she hesitated, unwilling or unable to say Matthew's name—"a man."

"The man who hurt you." His hands brushed against the soft slope of her breast as he arranged the silvery blond strands to his liking. If Khalil heard Leigh's soft intake of breath, he didn't comment on it. "The man you came to Abu Dhabi to forget."

"Yes."

"And now you are afraid to risk your heart yet again."

"Yes." Drawing her knees to her chest, she wrapped her arms tightly around them.

"I have never forced myself on a woman, Leigh. And I am certainly not going to begin with you." He bent his head and brushed his lips against hers. "But I am asking that you trust me. For this one night."

He pried her fingers loose, first one hand, then the other, murmuring soothing, seductive words that she recognized as Arabic. Then he lifted her right hand to his lips, slowly kissing each tingling finger, before pressing a provocative kiss against the tender skin of her palm.

Needs too long denied flared, months of pent-up yearning made her ultrasensitive flesh burn. Details blurred when Leigh slowly surrendered, luxuriating in the pure pleasure of silk being whisked over her warm skin. Through her swirling senses she could feel Khalil caressing her pliant body with wet, open-mouthed kisses. Heat from his mouth seeped into her bloodstream, causing searing flashes of pleasure.

His lips and hands were never still, moving over her flesh, leaving sparks in their wake. Wherever his lips touched, she burned—wherever his hands stroked, she flamed. Her body was molten, flowing wherever he sought to take her. The air surrounding them thickened with fire and smoke and blazing passions.

Khalil's mouth lingered at the inside of first one thigh, then the other, creating needs that grew increasingly unbearable. With fingers and teeth and tongue he drove her higher, re-lentlessly bringing her to crest after shuddering crest until her body hummed from a thousand erratic pulses and his lips were wet with her orgasms.

While Leigh was still gasping for breath, her love-slick body limp, Khalil thrust into her. He moved fast and hard, and she gave herself up to his driving rhythm. Falling back, he pulled her onto him, encouraging her to ride him wildly, his long, dark fingers grasping her hips, holding her firm. Although she would not have thought it possible, as Khalil rocked her back and forth, Leigh experienced yet another shattering climax.

When he felt her violent inner convulsions, Khalil came with an explosive shout that echoed across the vast, barren desert.

The feel of the sharp, hot needles of water pounded against his flesh. The first thing Matthew did when he arrived home was take a long, hot shower. The second thing he did was call Baron Studios.

"I'm sorry, Mr. St. James," an unfamiliar voice said, "but Ms. Baron is out of the country."

So what else was new? Although he would have preferred Leigh to have been desperately waiting by the telephone for his call, Matthew grudgingly admitted that she did have a studio to run. Perhaps she had discovered he was in Mexico and had gone searching for him. He decided he rather liked that idea.

"Where is she this time?"

He thought he detected a momentary hesitation. "Abu Dhabi."

What the hell was she doing in Abu Dhabi? He couldn't recall Leigh mentioning an upcoming trip to the Middle East. "Would you please give me her number?"

This time the silence was unmistakable. "I'm sorry, sir," the woman said after a lengthy, significant pause, "but Ms. Baron has instructed me not to give that number out."

"But—"

"I'm sorry."

"I'd like to speak with Mr. Baron."

"I'm sorry. Mr. Baron is out of town also."

"Is he in Abu Dhabi too?"

"No, Mr. St. James. Mr. Baron is in Las Vegas."

"I don't suppose you have a number for him there."

"No, sir," the secretary lied unconvincingly.

"Of course not." His mind spinning, he tried to think of a way to skirt this latest roadblock. "Okay, let's try Meredith."

"Meredith?"

"Meredith Ward. Ms. Baron's secretary."

"Ms. Ward is no longer with Baron Studios. I'm Ms. Baron's new secretary."

He'd come full circle. "And you have been instructed not to give me her number."

Again that uncomfortable little pause. "Yes, Mr. St. James. I am terribly sorry."

"You and me both, sweetheart."

Well, that was that. He knew things had been strained between them, that was why he'd wanted to go somewhere he could be alone with Leigh without the constant pressure of that goddamn studio.

Matthew could understand Leigh's drive to succeed. He could even respect it. But ambition was one thing, blind ambition yet another. As he sat in the dark and killed a bottle of bourbon, old emotions came bubbling to the surface. Feelings of resentment, mistrust, and a deep-seated insecurity he had never admitted, even to himself.

He felt betrayed that Leigh had abandoned him without so much as a backward glance. By the time the sun had risen over the nearby mountains, Matthew had vowed to never again let anything—or anyone—interfere with his plans.

Now that he had enough money to concentrate solely on his writing, he was going to become the best damn screenwriter in the business. And as far as he was concerned, Baron Studios, Joshua Baron, and particularly Leigh Baron could go straight to hell.

Because he damn well didn't need them.

Matthew St. James didn't need anyone.

He was, as the popular song lyric so succinctly put it, alone again. Naturally.

29

"You're leaving."

Leigh reached out and took Khalil's hand across the breakfast table. "Location shooting for *Arabian Nights* finished three weeks ago," she reminded him. "I should have returned home then."

With his free hand he stroked her hair, enjoying the silken feel of it against his palm. "Ah, but think what you would have missed."

"Yes." Over these past months Khalil had become incredibly dear to her. She was going to miss him. Dreadfully. But she didn't love him, although there had been several times during these last pleasure-filled weeks that she had wished she could. "You've made me so very happy," she said quietly. More than happy. The nightmares had gone, vanquished to some dark, distant part of her mind.

His face was clouded with emotions too complex for her to easily read. "As you have made me." His palm moved to her cheek. "You would make me even happier if you would agree to stay."

"I'd truly love to, but I've played hooky long enough. I must get back to my work."

"Is it your work you're so eager to return to? Or Matthew St. James?" She'd told him all about Matthew the morning after they'd made love for the first time. Since then his name had not come up.

"My work, of course. What Matthew and I had—or what I thought we had—is over."

"Then your feelings for him should not prevent you from becoming my wife."

Stunned by his out-of-the-blue proposal, Leigh mistakenly took his words for more of the lighthearted teasing that had added spice to their relationship from the beginning. "Your first wife, you mean."

"The Koran only allows a man four wives so long as he can treat them all equally—which means not only giving them equal goods, but equal time as well." He smiled. "That being the case, monogamy tends to be the rule. Marry me, Leigh, and let me treat you the way that you deserve."

He really was serious, Leigh realized. "And how is that?"

"Like a princess. No," he corrected, "a queen. Equal to the king in every way."

Even if she believed such behavior possible from a man so steeped in Arab tradition, Leigh knew that she could never love Khalil in the way he appeared to love her. In the end she would end up hurting him the way she'd been hurt. And she did care for him too much to inflict such pain.

"I do love you, Khalil. But not in that way."

"Did I ever tell you that my parents had an arranged marriage?"

"No."

"They did. Which is, of course, traditional in our culture. My mother was twelve, my father twenty-three. They met for the first time on the day of their wedding thirty-eight years ago. Today you could not find a couple who loved one another more."

"Are you saying that I could learn to love you?"

"It's been known to happen. After all, at the risk of sounding vain, I am not a totally unlovable man."

"You're the nicest man I've ever met," she said honestly. "And one of the handsomest. And the smartest, and the wonderful way you make me feel when we make love is—"

"Wait," Khalil laughed, holding up his hand. "If I am, as you say in America, such a catch, why don't you grab me?"

"I don't know." She toyed with her necklace. The gold crescent was the one she'd priced three weeks ago in the marketplace, reluctantly deciding that it was too expensive. Khalil had surprised her with the necklace the morning after they'd made love in the desert.

Putting his fingers under her chin, Khalil lifted her downcast eyes to his. When she dared to meet his gaze, Leigh viewed tender affection, blended with undisguised sympathy in his ebony eyes. "I think," he said gently, "that you are still in love with this Matthew St. James fellow."

"That's ridiculous. Why, I—"

He pressed his finger against her lips, cutting off her words. "I also think you will always be in love with him."

No. His words tolled like a curse, reverberating alarmingly through her mind. He was wrong, Leigh assured herself.

She was over Matthew.

Completely.

Wasn't she?

April 1974

The California sun was setting in a glorious blaze of smog-enhanced pink and scarlet. Billboards soared above Sunset Boulevard in a promotional blitzkrieg, blatantly begging for Oscar votes. Fans lined the concrete canyon of downtown Los Angeles and crowded into bleachers, eager for a glimpse of their favorite stars; a fleet of helicopters hovered overhead, the cameramen and -women inside filming the scene. The gas crisis was forgotten as three hundred black limousines (booked up to a year in advance by the Motion Picture Academy for the royal procession to the theater) made their way up the hill to the glass-and-concrete palace of the Los Angeles Music Center for the annual Academy Award ceremonies.

The arrivals stepped out of their limos onto the red carpet leading inside. Reporters shouted, flashbulbs exploded, fans screamed. Across the street a small clutch of hecklers waved homemade placards quoting Scripture and accusing the stars of cutting deals with the devil. A long white limo pulled up to the curb and the liveried chauffeur, handsome enough to be a leading man at any major studio, leaped out and made a low, sweeping bow reminiscent of a royal footman as he opened the wide door. A perfectly proportioned leg, encased in glittering gold hose, slid out of the car. Moments passed before a flash of gorgeous thigh followed. Their attention successfully captured, the crowd waited with bated breath. When Marissa, voluptuously clad in a clinging, gold lamé dress dripping with black bugle beads, finally emerged from the luxurious backseat of the limousine into the glare of strobe lights, the fans in the bleachers roared their approval. Tossing her artfully tousled copper hair, Marissa smiled and waved. Her fans went wild.

In contrast to Marissa's golden heat, Leigh appeared regally cool. Eschewing the Hollywood tradition of a new, one-of-a-kind gown designed specifically to make a grand entrance, she'd chosen the same dress she'd bought for the premiere of *Scattershot*. She'd been wearing the silvery blue silk Valentino the first time Matthew kissed her and if the gown brought back painful memories, Leigh refused to dwell on them. Unlike that evening, when she'd worn her hair loose because Matthew asked her to, tonight she'd swept it back into a elaborate twist at the nape of her neck, revealing the matched pair of pale blue diamonds that glittered like chips of ice at her ears.

Seated five rows behind Leigh, Matthew realized that she reminded him of a character in *The Kalevala*, a Finnish national epic he'd recently read: Loviatar, Maiden of Pain, protector of the land of Pohjoloa. A beautiful, alluring, though ultimately deadly blonde, Loviatar's dagger of ice kept her immune from any magic spells a man might try to use against her. If anyone ever wanted to make *The Kalevala* into a movie, Matthew mused, Leigh would be a natural for the part.

Her cool composure had always fascinated and infuriated him. Matthew knew she had to be nervous—hell, even *he* had unwillingly succumbed to a case of Oscar jitters—but outwardly she remained frustratingly calm. Watching Leigh politely accept accolades from stellar directors Mike Nichols and Francis Ford Coppola, he had a sudden urge to climb over the seats separating them and shake her. Or kiss her. The only problem was, Matthew knew that if he gave into either impulse, he'd never be able to stop. The wound she'd inflicted was still too raw.

Although officially billed as Hollywood's greatest show, the Academy Awards could more accurately be described as a four-hour series of prolonged after-dinner toasts, brightened this year by the sudden appearance of a nude streaker who'd sprinted across the stage. Still, the tedium of the evening did nothing to detract from Leigh's satisfaction with the Academy's acceptance of her work. Since the kidnapping of Patricia Hearst two months earlier by the Symbionese Liberation Army, *Dangerous*, which had already achieved both critical and audience acclaim, had become the talk of the town. Leigh watched with pride as her pet project garnered Oscars in eight categories, including Best Picture, Best Director, and Best Actor. And although Marissa lost to Ellen Burstyn for Best Actress, everyone in attendance knew that the younger Baron sister was the newest, brightest star in the Hollywood firmament.

It had been fifteen months since Leigh had seen Matthew. Although he had steadfastly refused (through Corbett) to do any preballot hype for the picture, the members of the Academy had found his performance as riveting as Leigh herself had, that long-ago day nearly two years ago when he'd first read for the part.

Watching Matthew receive his Oscar from celebrity presenters Shirley MacLaine and Warren Beatty, it would have been impossible to miss the energy that surrounded him like an aura. When he held the coveted gold statuette up for the photographers, accepting the thundering applause of his peers while at the same time seeming removed from it, Leigh determined that he was still the consummate loner. But instead of working against him in this establishment, herd-mentality town, such an attitude only made him more intriguing.

Matthew's gaze swept over the pavilion, unerringly settling on Leigh. For a heady second their eyes met and held and a flood of tumultuous, bittersweet memories flooded over her. It was then that Leigh realized she had unintentionally lied to Khalil. She had run from the truth long enough; it was now time to admit, at least to herself, that she'd never be entirely free of her feelings for Matthew.

He had inexorably changed her life. He had introduced her to a world of sensuality, awakened in her a hunger she'd never known existed and, when he'd cajoled, urged, and stoked it to a primitive, clamoring pitch, he'd shown her the mindless bliss of shared possession.

Matthew St. James had taken her to the very heights of ecstasy and then, in the end, he had taught her a basic lesson in human anatomy.

No woman had ever died of a broken heart.

BOOK TWO

1976

30

I

t was a time of fireworks and John Philip Sousa bands. A time when America's Bicentennial celebrations served as a catharsis for events of the past years: Watergate, Capitol Hill sex scandals, Vietnam, presidential collapse, energy crisis, bankrupt cities, rebellion, riots, and recession.

It was also a heady time to be a woman. Independent spirits were breaking free of passive, home-clinging stereotypes in increasing numbers, achieving recognition in a society where values and standards had been long set by men. "Battling Bella" Abzug, known for her big hats and gruff voice, shattered the time-honored tradition that women—and freshman members of Congress—should be seen and not heard while a new kind of First Lady, Betty Ford, openly lobbied congressmen on behalf of the ERA. Sarah Caldwell, a former Arkansas iddler known as the Divine Sarah, became the first woman ever to conduct at the Met in New York and, in a move that made headlines all over the world, ABC spent an unprecedented five million dollars to lure former ornamental "Today" girl Barbara Walters away from rival television network NBC.

In Hollywood, during this second half of the tumultuous 1970s, owning your own production company was visible proof of power and prestige. It was viewed as the holy grail. After her dazzling success with *Dangerous*, Leigh declared her independence from her father by successfully lobbying for her own company within Baron Studios. Eighteen months later, it was obvious to everyone in town that Leigh thrived in the heady, autonomous atmosphere of her Sundown Production company. (Although there were numerous rumors floating about concerning Leigh's choice of a name, what only she knew was that one of the studio lawyers was calling every five minutes, insisting she name her company something, anything, so he could finish drawing up the papers. After racking her brain for an appropriate-sounding name, when Gordon Lightfoot's "Sundown" came over the radio, Leigh unrepentantly borrowed the title as her own.)

In a bravely independent move of his own, insisting that the only way to keep his ideas a secret was to never let them out of his head, Matthew had directed and produced a poignant story about an innocent Vietnamese laundry girl killed by U.S. artillery. The movie, *Friendly Fire*, went on to win an Oscar for Best Short Film.

"When are you going to use some of that money you've been making to buy yourself a decent house?" Corbett was sitting with Matthew on the front porch of the rented, gingerbread-encrusted bungalow in Venice.

"I like it here," Matthew said. "And you sure as hell can't beat the view," he tacked on when a willowy black woman, dressed in a fluorescent yellow bikini rolled by on a pair of skates.

"I suppose it's your business if you want to live like some throwback to the 1960s," Corbett conceded. "Actually, it suits that fuck-you reputation you're rapidly achieving. Speaking of which, you were missed last night."

"Not being one of the 'in' crowd, I doubt anyone noticed my absence."

"They sure as hell did when I showed up on stage to accept your Oscar."

Matthew heard the aggravation in Corbett's voice and, while he understood his agent's feelings, he could not change who he was. What he was. "Look, I took your advice and attended that three-ring circus two years ago. Once was enough."

"Well, however much you insist that you're not an insider, I believe this says differently," Corbett said, holding up the gold statuette. "Rona Barrett referred to you as Hollywood's newest wunderkind."

"She'll latch on to another one next year. Hollywood has never been short of boy wonders," Matthew said with a shrug. "Orson Welles was only twenty-five when he received four nominations. I'm thirty-two and this film is no *Citizen Kane*."

"Your next one could be."

For the first time since Corbett had arrived to deliver the award, Matthew looked interested. "You liked it."

"*Private Screenings* is the best thing I've ever read."

Matthew could hear the hesitation in his tone. "But?"

"But you're never going to be able to afford to produce it yourself."

"Well, I'm sure as hell not letting some damned commercial studio get their hands on it. I've seen what happens to writers in this town, Corbett. They slave over a story, honing it to the best it can be. Then they turn their work of love over to the philistines, who can't resist tinkering with it until it doesn't begin to resemble the original story.

"Finally, after all this fucking around, the movie comes out and the writer is forced to suffer the pain of his movie never getting made. Instead there's this other movie, which is, more often than not, a piece of shit." Matthew's jaw firmed. "I'd rather *Private Screenings* spend eternity in my desk drawer than have some schmuck executive with a pocket calculator for a brain screw it up."

"I don't want that to happen either," Corbett agreed. "But, like it or not, a crucial, if not the most crucial problem of making a film today, is what it's going to cost. And to do this baby right is going to take more money that you can swing by yourself, Matthew. So why don't you at least let me show it to a few people I trust?"

"Do you have anyone particular in mind?"

"Not yet. Let me give it some thought." It was the first time he'd ever lied to a client and Corbett hated having to do it. Worse yet, Matthew was more than a client, he was a friend.

As he drove back down Sunset Boulevard to his office, Corbett told himself that, in this case, the ends justified the means. But that didn't make him feel any better about his subterfuge.

Leigh was feeling on top of the world. It was the morning after the Academy Award ceremony and the Los Angeles sun had valiantly managed to slice its way through the smog, splintering the sky with shafts of brilliant gold. The clarity of the bright spring day intensified the lush landscaping outside her garden suite of offices, and although air conditioning precluded opening the French doors, Leigh imagined she could smell the piquant scent of the creeping rosemary that spilled from the Mexican clay planters.

Like too many of the city's residents, Leigh would have had to plead guilty to taking the weather for granted. It took days like this to make one stop and bask in the California sunshine and, although she had never considered herself superstitious, she couldn't help feeling that this glorious day was a portent of things to come.

Last night she'd read a screenplay, not that unusual an occurrence, certainly. But this was different; never had she stayed up all night, unable to put the screenplay down.

One of the principal reasons Leigh had formed Sundown Productions was so that she could make films that otherwise might not be made. Last year, five financially successful films—*The Godfather*, *The Exorcist*, *Earthquake*, *The Towering Inferno*, and *Jaws*—had changed the course of moviemaking. Impressed by box office receipts, all the major studios had jumped on the visceral shock bandwagon, producing a festival of blood and gore.

Private Screenings, the story of an unsinkable seven-year-old orphan determined to survive the abuse inflicted on him by overly strict nuns, uncaring bureaucracies, and neglectful, often cruel foster parents, definitely bucked what Leigh considered a distressing trend. The boy survived his unhappy existence by hiding in darkened theaters during Saturday afternoon matinees, taking refuge in a fantasy life where he imagined himself to be Mighty Man—righter of wrongs, conqueror of evil. By the time she finished reading, Leigh was in tears. She was also determined that Sundown Productions make the film.

She made the call herself, too impatient to play the power game of having her secretary call Corbett's secretary.

"Good morning, Corbett," she said warmly.

"Good morning, Leigh," the agent answered. "Don't you sound in a good mood. Hot date after the Awards party last night?" It had not escaped Corbett's notice that Leigh had left her father's Oscar party minutes after her arrival. Joshua, muttering something about desertion, had sulked all night.

"Don't I wish. No, I was working. As usual."

Corbett didn't warn Leigh about the need to maintain balance in her life; she hadn't listened innumerable times before and he doubted that she would today.

"Read any good screenplays lately?" he asked with feigned casualness.

"Could be," she responded, matching his easy tone. Then, unable to restrain her enthusiasm any longer, she said, "You knew that I wouldn't be able to resist *Private Screenings*."

"You liked it."

"I loved it. It's just what I've been looking for."

"It won't be the most commercial movie Baron Studios ever made," Corbett warned.

"No. But it will certainly be one of the best. How many studios are looking at it?"

"Only Baron. For now."

Leigh breathed a sigh of relief. As unenthusiastic as she was about becoming embroiled in a bidding war, she was more concerned about losing the script to a competitor. Something she could not allow to happen. "When can we get together?"

Corbett paused, seeming to ponder the matter. "How about lunch tomorrow?"

"How about dinner tonight?"

He laughed. "Are you sure you want to sound so eager?"

"I've never been one to play coy, Corbett, and I'm sure as hell not going to start now. This new writer you've found has a rare and special talent; I don't want to take a chance on him getting away."

"Tonight it is. Where?"

"Ma Maison? Eight o'clock?"

"Terrific." He paused, then added as an afterthought, "How would you feel about meeting the writer?"

"I'd love it." Leigh hung up the telephone, smiling. It was an absolutely glorious day.

Leigh's smile faded when she received a call from Ryan McIntyre, director of Marissa's new film. Although she had failed to win an Oscar for her performance in *Dangerous*, Marissa had forged a place for herself in romantic comedies and was in constant demand, despite a growing reputation for being difficult. Leigh spent a great deal of her time soothing irate directors.

"What is it now?" she asked.

"She's locked in her dressing room, claiming cramps."

"Perhaps she really doesn't feel well."

"Leigh, it's the third time in the last two weeks she's used the same excuse. How many fucking periods can one woman have in a single month?"

Leigh thought back to when Marissa was a freshman in high school and she'd been called to the school by the dean of girls to discuss her younger sister's repeated absence in PE, due, allegedly, to menstrual cramps. Then, as now, Marissa appeared to have accomplished the impossible biological feat of having three to five periods per month.

"How many, indeed?" she murmured.

"Well, you've got to do something. She's in there, blasting that damn disco music on her stereo and eating her weight in Mallomars—speaking of which, wardrobe had to let out her clothes again last week; if the kid doesn't stop shoving cookies into her mouth she's going to balloon up to the size of Shelley Winters and she can kiss her career as a sex goddess goodbye."

"Did you personally request her presence on the set?"

"Are you kidding? You know as well as I do that this is a question of protocol, Leigh. The director is supposed to be the unchallenged boss on the set. As director, that's where I belong. On the set. If I go and get the bitch, the balance of power will shift and then we'll all be in shit city . . . I sent the AD. Three times. She won't open the damn door. Anyway," he said, after taking a much needed breath, "everyone knows you're the only one who can talk her into working when she's like this."

"Give me twenty minutes to shuffle a few appointments and I'll be over." Leigh hung up the phone and sighed. Well, it had been a nice day, while it lasted. At least she had tonight's dinner with Corbett and his new discovery to look forward to.

Ma Maison had opened to a fanfare of publicity three years ago and had rapidly become a mecca for those Beverly Hills heavy hitters who wanted to indulge in a status meal without putting on a tie. It was five minutes to eight when Leigh walked into the restaurant, had her hand air-kissed by the ebullient manager, and immediately was whisked past the waiting celebrities to the table where Corbett had already been seated.

"You get more beautiful every day," the agent greeted her with a smile. "If you'd only chosen the other side of the camera, I could have represented you and we'd have made a fortune."

"I would think one Baron sister is all any man could handle," Leigh said dryly, sitting down. After giving her drink order to the waiter, she glanced at the silver bucket beside the table, where a bottle of Moët et Chandon was nestled in a bed of cracked ice. "It's not like you to count your chickens, Corbett."

"Ah, but I have good feelings about this deal," he said. "Something tells me that you and my client are going to hit it off right away."

She folded her hands on the table. "I love the screenplay, Corbett. And I want to make this picture. But I'm not willing to give away the store to do it, either."

"I'm sure we can come to terms, Leigh. Trust me."

She always had. But there was something about Corbett

tonight. Some devilish gleam in his eyes she couldn't remember ever seeing before. "Are you keeping something from me?"

"Who, me?" He flung his hand against his shirt. "Why, everyone in town knows that I'm an open book."

"Everyone also knows that you're not above a little manipulation when you're out to clinch a deal. So, what are you up to this time?"

Before he could answer, something over Leigh's shoulder caught his attention. "Ah, here he is now."

Leigh turned around, stunned to see Matthew walking across the room. When their eyes met with the power of a sledgehammer shattering crystal, dual emotions collided inside her—the raw pain of desertion and the unequaled joy at seeing him again. Fortunately, the waiter chose that moment to arrive with her drink. She took a fortifying sip of the vodka and tonic.

Matthew looked startled and extremely uncomfortable. "Hello, Leigh."

He hadn't changed, but Leigh wondered why she thought he'd might. Almost against her will, she'd found herself looking for him last night at the Awards ceremony. She hadn't really been surprised when he didn't attend; Matthew was gaining a measure of fame as Hollywood's most reclusive maverick.

"Hello, Matthew. This is quite a surprise."

Matthew shot Corbett a dark look. "Isn't it?"

"All right, I'll admit it," Corbett said. "I set this entire thing up. But I had a good reason."

"I'd like to hear it," Matthew said, pulling out a chair. Their knees brushed slightly, creating a small shock of unwilling desire for both of them.

"So would I," Leigh said.

Matthew looked at her. "You didn't know I'd be here tonight?"

"Of course not. I'm here because Corbett promised to introduce me to the man who wrote *Private Screenings*."

"*Private Screenings*? You read my screenplay?"

She bristled at the accusation in his tone. "I didn't know it was yours. The title page listed the author as William Seymour." She took another bracing sip of her drink. Dutch courage, her father called it. "May I ask why you used a pseudonym? Were you so afraid I'd turn the project down after what you did to me?"

"Hell, lady, I didn't even know Corbett was going to let you read the damn thing. I told him a long time ago that I didn't want anything to do with Baron Studios, especially your precious Sundown Productions . . . What I did to you?"

"Disappearing like that, driving me crazy, turning up with a wife you weren't even man enough to tell me about . . . Why didn't you want Baron Studios to produce your picture?"

"Wife? What the hell are you talking about?" Realizing that he'd just garnered the avid attention of the other diners, Matthew lowered his voice. "I don't have any wife."

"Then who was that woman I saw you with at the Academy Awards?"

"I didn't attend the damn awards."

"Not last night. Two years ago. When you won for *Dangerous*."

Matthew thought back. "That was Rosaria."

"And who, exactly, is Rosaria?"

"Not that it's any of your business, but she's a friend. She saved my life in Mexico, so when I got back to the States, I asked Corbett to help get her a job."

"That's right," Corbett confirmed. "She started out as a seamstress over at MGM, but she's worked her way up to assistant costume designer."

Leigh didn't give a damn about the absent Rosaria's couture skills. Something else had caught her attention. "She saved your life?"

"She broke me out of jail, then she took care of me when my bullet wound got infected."

Leigh felt as if she'd just fallen down the rabbit hole. "Your bullet wound? You were shot? And what were you doing in jail?"

"It's a long story."

"I wanted to tell you, Leigh, but Matthew swore me to secrecy," Corbett said. "To be perfectly honest, if you'd pressured me, I probably would have caved in and told you the truth, but when you came home from Abu Dhabi and refused

to talk about Matthew, I figured whatever had happened between you two was your own business.

"But there's personal business and movie business," he
continued. "And that's where I draw the line. I put the pseudonym on the pages I sent you, Leigh, because I knew Matthew's screenplay was something special and I wanted you to
read it without prejudice. As for not being completely honest
with you, Matthew, I was afraid that if you knew Leigh was
considering the story, you'd refuse to sell it to her.

"I realize my behavior was unprofessional, but this movie
deserves to be made by a major studio. Baron Studios is the
largest, and currently the most profitable, due, in part, to
Leigh's Sundown Productions company. Also, because I consider myself to be a friend to both of you, I think it's time you
resolved your differences."

Speech made, he rose. "Enjoy the champagne. The check's
all taken care of; I'll call you both in the morning." His knowing gaze went from Matthew to Leigh and back again. "Make
that tomorrow afternoon."

They remained silent, watching him leave.

"Corbett's slipping," Leigh said finally. "He's always been
a firm believer in the studio picking up the tab."

"Like he said, there's personal business and movie business. I have a feeling that this gesture was extremely personal."

"I think so too." She paused. "Congratulations on your
Oscar."

Matthew shrugged. "All I wanted to do was to try and make
a good film. To paraphrase Richard Burton, the Oscars are
just a goddamned horse race. And to tell you the truth, it feels
strange making a film about a war tragedy and ending up with
a gold statue. Somehow, it just doesn't seem relevant."

Leigh was pleased that Matthew hadn't been blinded by
Oscar's golden light, that success hadn't changed him. On
second thought, she wondered why she thought it might have.
He'd always had a firm vision of exactly where he was going.

"That reminds me of something I once read," she said.
"They have an annual poetry contest in Barcelona. The third
prize is a silver rose, the second prize is a gold, and the writer
of the best poem gets a real rose."

"Sounds as if they've got the right idea."

"I thought so at the time . . . *Friendly Fire* was a marvelous film. Would you think me a hopeless case if I told you that I saw it three times, and cried each and every time?"

Matthew smiled. "That's worth more to me than any Oscar."

"It was really bad, wasn't it? Vietnam."

He was about to slough off her question, as he had so many times before. But something made Matthew tell the truth. "Yeah. It was rough. But I learned a long time ago that life doesn't come with a gold-plated guarantee."

"You really weren't married?"

"Never."

Leigh looked at him across a vast chasm of uncertainty. "But I went to your house. There was a woman there, a young Mexican woman who said she was your wife. She even showed me your wedding picture."

"You're joking."

"It's not exactly a joking matter, Matthew."

"Leigh, for the last time, I am not and have never been married."

She wanted to believe him. Dear God, how she wanted to believe that he had not just used her for his own ends, then thrown her away when he was finished. "But why would anyone lie about something like that?"

Matthew had had his own suspicions from the beginning, but no proof. "I've no idea. Perhaps it was one of Jeff's less than humorous practical jokes."

"Jeff? Not Jeff Martin?"

"You know him?"

"Of course. He and Marissa have been living together on and off since . . ." Her voice trailed off.

"Since that summer we met."

"Yes."

A comfortable silence settled over the table. Leigh was stunned at how right it felt to be with Matthew again. "I really did love *Private Screenings*. The story is compelling and it's written in a wonderfully terse, dramatic style that the director and actors are going to love."

They were talking about work, but their eyes were speaking

an intimate, remembered language all their own. "The same terse, dramatic style producers and executives can't understand," Matthew said with a slight smile.

"*Most* executives."

"That's right. You're one of the few studio people left in this town who loves movies."

She'd told him her feelings the night of the premiere they'd attended together almost four years ago. There were times that halcyon summer seemed a lifetime ago. Then there were those times that it seemed like yesterday.

"I'm surprised you remembered."

"Oh, I remember all right, Leigh. I remember everything."

They looked at one another and for a long, tantalizing moment the years slipped away and they were returned to that sun-kissed time when life was golden and their love shone brighter than the California sun.

"Where did you get your idea for *Private Screenings*?" she asked, seeking something, anything, to say.

"I think I could use a drink." Matthew lifted the bottle of champagne out of the ice and poured them both a glass. He downed his thirstily and poured another. "If I tell you, I wouldn't want Janet Bridges to make it part of the promotion. That is, if I decided to let Baron make the film."

"Agreed."

"Even Corbett doesn't know."

Leigh put her hand on his arm. "Matthew, I promise not to tell a soul."

He looked down at her hand, observing the way the pale shining ovals at her fingertips gleamed against his sleeve. When the vision brought back the memory of those slender hands on his body, creating havoc in every pore, he let out a long breath. "It's autobiographical."

Leigh tried to relate this remarkably successful, self-assured man with that lonely little boy. "I didn't know. You never talked much about your childhood."

"We didn't talk much about anything," Matthew reminded her. "Most of our time together we spent in bed."

"Perhaps that was part of our problem."

"Perhaps." Taking her hand in his, Matthew looked into her eyes in a way that made Leigh feel as if he could read her most innermost secrets. Remembered passion sparked, so electric it made her tremble. "How hungry are you?" he asked.

She thought about all the nights and weeks and years lost because once hurt, they'd both instinctively retreated behind the perceived safety of their emotional barricades. Even as Leigh warned herself that she could be hurt again, she found herself unable to resist. "For food?"

Matthew laughed. A deep, robust sound that Leigh had thought she would never hear again. "You're getting ahead of me."

Her heart was pounding so hard, she was amazed that the entire room hadn't heard it. "We have to talk."

"Absolutely." He touched her hair. "Your place or mine?"

"Where are you living these days?"

"I'm still renting my house in Venice."

"My place, then," Leigh decided. "It's closer."

31

The drive to Santa Monica seemed to take an eternity. Neither Leigh nor Matthew spoke. There was no need.

"Oh, shit," Matthew muttered as they walked up to the door.

Leigh looked up at him. "What's the matter?"

"When I went to the restaurant tonight I thought . . . It was supposed to be a business dinner . . . Hell, I don't exactly carry a rubber around in my wallet like some horny high school kid hoping to get lucky."

He'd always been so insistent about protecting her. That was only one of the reasons she had fallen in love with him. "Don't worry."

His jaw firmed. "I want you, Leigh. But—"

"I'm on the pill."

"Oh." Hating the idea of Leigh being with any other man, Matthew reminded himself that he certainly hadn't been celi-

bate during their separation. But damn it, although he knew
he'd be stoned by feminists the world over for harboring such
a sexist thought, casual sex was different for women. Wasn't
it? Okay, perhaps it wasn't. But that still didn't mean he had
to like picturing Leigh in some other man's arms. Or worse
yet, some other man's bed.

Sensing his discomfort, Leigh lifted her palm to his cheek.
"My periods have always been erratic, remember? My doctor
put me on the pill to keep me regular."

"Thank God for erratic periods. Because I'm not sure I
could have walked away. Not after all this time." Bending his
head, he kissed her with years of pent-up longing.

The minute they entered the house, they fell into one another's arms, kissing with a breathless lust that surprised them
both. To reach the bedroom, they would have had to cross
what seemed to be miles of glacial white tile. The journey was
too far, their hunger too overpowering. They sank onto the
soft white fur rug underfoot.

There were no words, no soft lovers' sighs. Only blurred
movement, drugged sensations, blinding passion. Leigh
heard the sound of silk ripping and welcomed it; unzipping
Matthew's pants, she released his straining penis and ran her
hot tongue along its length. A milky white droplet glistened
on the dark, plum-hued tip. She licked it off, then took him
deep in her mouth, sucking so hard Matthew thought he'd
explode.

They made love without undressing, a fierce, feverish love
tinged with animal lust. Parting her legs with his palms, he
surged into her, his long strokes plunging deep and hard,
crashing into the very heart of her. Her juices flowed in response to his thrusts and, when she came, it was with a series
of violent shudders. When her body clutched at him, Matthew
lost the last vestige of control. He poured himself into her,
and said her name, softly, over and over, as if it were a prayer.

Marissa was in a rotten mood. She'd been up all night
fighting with Jeff. During the marathon battle, he'd called her
a selfish, ball-busting bitch; she'd shot back with the accusation that he was nothing but a spaced-out gigolo. It was then
that he'd stormed out of the house, taking the Porsche, leav-

ing her with the Mercedes convertible, which he knew she hated to drive because it had a stick shift. It wasn't until after he was gone that she discovered he'd taken their cache of drugs with him.

Not that she needed the stuff. She only popped a Dexedrine in the morning to get her started, a Valium or two when her bastard director acted like Adolf Hitler, some more little orange dexies before going out, then some 'ludes or a little grass before bed to come down. And once in a while a little coke, just to make the sex hotter. Everyone did it. It was the way of life in the pharmaceutical seventies.

Driving aimlessly, rage pounding inside her like the beat of ancient drums, she found herself at the waterfront with no memory of having driven there. A weathered tavern caught her eye; needing a drink, she pulled into the parking lot. Coming in from the bright sunshine, it took her eyes a moment to adjust to the darkness. Tanya Tucker was belting out an exuberant chorus of "Delta Dawn" on the jukebox.

When she could see, Marissa took a survey of the place. A layer of cigarette smoke hung over the room like a shroud. Against the far wall were two brightly painted pinball machines and a pay telephone. The center of the floor was taken up by green-felt pool tables, and an electro-dart game hung from the ceiling. Bottles were lined up behind the bar, beer signs glowed dimly in the smoky haze.

The Driftwood's clientele appeared to have come from the merchant ships docked outside the door. The unshaven men looked strong and tough. As her eyes swept over them, they looked back at her with a mixture of curiosity and lust.

One guy in particular caught her attention. Sitting alone at the end of the bar, he was definitely no leading man. His nose was flat, and leaned to the left, as if it had been broken more than once. He had a full black beard, long oily hair, and a ragged scar carved its way from the bridge of that battered nose to the corner of his eye. He was wearing a black T-shirt with the arms raggedly cut off, displaying a tattoo of a naked woman on one bulging biceps, a dragon surrounded by flames on the other. He also had, she noticed with a slight intake of breath, the most dangerous black eyes she'd ever seen. Perfect.

As she walked straight toward him, adrenaline pumping wildly through her veins, Marissa experienced the biggest rush she'd had in years. It was, she decided, even better than drugs.

It was not easy drawing Matthew out, but when he began to relate stories of his past, Leigh began to understand that his often brusque behavior was the result of his unsettled childhood. Matthew had never experienced the closeness of a family and became uncomfortable when people got too close. Learning about his past also helped her to understand why he found trust so difficult.

"So," she said as they lay in bed late one lazy Sunday morning two weeks after their reunion, "what do you feel like doing today?"

He reached out and trailed his finger down the slope of her breast, appearing fascinated by the way her nipple pebbled under his touch. "We could spend the day right here."

How was it that after all they'd shared, she could want him again so soon? "We could. Of course, there's also the chance we could starve doing that."

His lips followed the trail his fingertip had warmed. "We could send out for pizza. Much, much later."

"I've always liked pizza."

"Or we could go to Vegas."

"Las Vegas?" Neither she nor Matthew liked to gamble. There was more than enough risk in moviemaking. "What's in Las Vegas?"

"Sinatra." His tongue cut a wet swathe across her flesh.

"I think I'll pass."

"Wayne Newton."

"Ditto," she managed, just as he took her rosy nipple between his teeth and tugged.

"The Chapel of Lights."

"What's that? A new rock group?"

"It's a wedding chapel. Have I told you that I love the taste of your skin?"

"A wedding chapel. Like in marriage?"

"Yeah. Christ, you taste good. Like temptation. Warm, moist—"

"Matthew!" Grabbing hold of his hair, she yanked his head up. "Was that a proposal?"

"Actually, now that you mention it, I suppose it was. Should I have gotten down on my knees?"

"No. I mean yes."

"Yes, I should have proposed on bended knee? Or yes, you'll marry me?"

"Yes, I'll marry you." Leigh flung her arms around his neck. "Yes, yes, yes!"

Dressing quickly, they stopped only long enough to pick up Kim and a surprised but delighted Tina and Corbett on the way to the airport.

Nearly four years after they'd first looked into each other's eyes, Leigh and Matthew were married in the Chapel of Lights. Despite the haste, despite the fact that the music was canned and the minister yet another Elvis impersonator, the wedding was everything a wedding should be. The bride, clad in a Givenchy cream silk gown and carrying a bouquet of American Beauty roses, was beautiful and the groom was handsome. When they exchanged vows, the love they shared shone brightly in their eyes.

The call came the following morning. After hanging up, Joshua stared at the phone for a long, silent time. It couldn't be. She'd never desert him. Not his princess. Not Leigh.

But she had. She'd turned her back on everything they had built together, running off after that bastard writer like a bitch in heat. He pictured the two of them, coupled together like a pair of rutting dogs. Then, to block out the image, he went into the library and drank himself into oblivion.

Marissa had just returned home from an afternoon thrashing around in a sleeper cab with a trucker from Lodi. He'd been a big mean man, obviously used to knocking women around, but she'd managed him like a pro. For three glorious hours, she'd been in complete control.

Control. God, how she loved that word!

She was flying high until Leigh's phone call brought her crashing down to earth with a resounding bang. Her gut twisted with a spasm of raw jealousy, Marissa got back in her car. But instead of returning to the Driftwood, where she'd become a regular, she headed straight for the Beverly Hills Hotel. There, stretched out by the pool, clad in skimpy bikini trunks, were the money men, working on their coppery tans as they packaged million-dollar projects before lunch.

Her eyes scanned the current crop of moguls. She caught sight of a French film director with a known taste for buxom redheads and a penchant for leather. Licking her lips, Marissa grabbed a margarita off the tray of a passing waiter and walked toward his table.

Two days after reporting Leigh and Matthew's marriage, Rona Barrett took to the airwaves once again to break the unhappy news to men all over the world. Baron Studios' reigning sex symbol and the actress voted by *Playboy* readers as the Playmate they'd most like to be stranded on a desert island with was now Mrs. Philippe Corbière.

"What the hell got into you?"

Leigh looked up to see her father storming into her office. Although still technically on her honeymoon, she'd dropped in to the office to check her mail. "Good morning to you too."

"Don't good morning me, little girl. I want to know why you ran off with that bastard."

Leigh's gray eyes turned as cold as ice. "I am twenty-nine years old, which is a far cry from a little girl, and you will not refer to my husband in that manner again."

Husband. The word burned in his gut like acid. "Why not? Since that's what he is."

Angry color heightened her cheekbones. "That's unfair. Matthew can't be held responsible for his parents' behavior."

"How about his drug bust? Can he be held responsible for that? Or didn't he tell you about it?"

"He told me. He also gave me the report from the private detective Corbett hired to investigate the arrest."

"Corbett hired a detective?" That was news to him. Joshua wondered why his old friend hadn't mentioned a detective at the time.

"Yes, and it turns out that Matthew was booked into jail under a false name, which gives credence to his claim that he was framed."

Joshua felt icy sweat pouring from under his arms. "That may be what he's claiming, but does he have any proof?"

"He doesn't need proof. I believe him."

"If any of that drug business ever comes out, the guy is going to be a dead duck in this town, Leigh. I don't want anyone at the studio involved with him. Personally or professionally."

Leigh met his aggravated look with a calm, level one of her own. "I'm sorry you feel that way. Because not only do I love Matthew, I also plan to produce his new screenplay."

"I forbid it." The thunderous rage in Joshua's eyes would have cowed a lesser woman. "If he even tries to set foot on Baron Studios property, I'll have him arrested for trespassing."

Leigh had been prepared for an argument. Even so, the depth of her father's enmity surprised her. Not that she had any intention of backing down. She had spent her childhood playing poker with movie crews. Leigh could bluff with the best of them.

"Fine. If Matthew isn't welcome here, neither am I." She began emptying her desk. "Shall I call the publicity department with the news that I'm going into independent production with my husband, or will you handle the press release?"

Leigh had grown up at Baron Studios. Joshua knew she'd never carry out her threat to leave, but he didn't dare put her to the test. There was too much of Walter Baron's damnable stubborn pride in the girl and, personal feelings aside, she was too valuable to the studio to risk losing.

"All right," he said magnanimously. "St. James can stay. So long as he makes money."

The tension between them eased slightly. Leigh went around the desk and wrapped her arms around her father. "Don't worry, Dad," she assured him, tilting her head back to give him a dazzling smile, "Matthew is going to be the best thing to happen to Baron Studios since you took over after Grandfather's death."

At the mention of his father, Joshua recalled the Draconian power the former studio Titan had wielded during his lifetime. Walter Baron would have cheerfully crushed Matthew St. James underfoot without a backward glance. And although he would prefer to do exactly that, Joshua knew he couldn't, for fear of losing Leigh. Reluctantly, he decided to do nothing. For now.

Besides, he assured himself when he returned to his office and had poured himself a stiff drink, the marriage would undoubtedly end like the majority of others in Hollywood—in divorce.

And if it didn't? Joshua vowed to do whatever it took to reclaim his daughter and poured himself another single malt Scotch.

Leigh sank down onto her chair and buried her head in her hands. She had emerged from the argument victorious. Now she was shaken by how close she had come to having to chose between the two most important men in her life.

She left the office early and returned home to an empty house and a note from Matthew.

> *Sweetheart* [it read in his bold, black script], *Tina called. She closed the deal on that house in Topanga Canyon and, since Corbett's in New York, she wanted someone to celebrate with. We're having lunch at El Cholo; why don't you join us? Or better yet—start warming up the bed. I'll be home by three.*

As much as she adored Matthew, after six days of constant togetherness, Leigh was secretly pleased to have some time to herself. She spent the next hour walking on the beach, thinking back over the years.

She'd never had any friends her own age; she'd spent all her free hours after school at the studio, following her father from set to set, sitting in a corner, watching in awe the legions of world-famous stars who trekked in and out of his office. While the other girls were devouring Nancy Drew mysteries, she was reading *Variety* and the *Hollywood Reporter*.

When her schoolmates were glued to "American Bandstand," practicing the latest dance steps in front of the television, she was learning the proper tone to take in an audition meeting. And when those same giggling girls spent Saturdays at Neiman-Marcus, trying on dress after dress, looking for the perfect one to wear to that night's dance, she was standing outside a theater in Westwood, handing out response cards to audiences at sneak previews.

Her life, as far back as she could remember, had been entwined with the studio. And Joshua. Leigh thought of all the problems they'd overcome together, the triumphs they'd shared.

She loved her father. But she loved Matthew too.

Unfortunately, their antipathy for one another was only too obvious. Sinking down onto the warm sand, Leigh watched the sunshine reflect off the glistening water and wished that she didn't feel so torn.

32

Nineteen seventy-eight was a year of discontent. The women's movement had been the watchword of the 1970s, just as civil rights had defined the turbulent 1960s, but now, as the decade drew to a close, the nation seemed to be entering a time of retrenchment and appraisal. It was as if people wanted to stop and catch a breath, to try to access how far they'd come and where, exactly, they were going.

In Hollywood, money continued to prove a prime motivating factor as the power of the studios began to be eroded even further by a new breed of financiers, wildcat investors looking for a quick, one-shot deal. The vast amounts of dollars floating around town enabled a new batch of movie stars to demand—and get—contract amounts beyond the wildest dreams of a Tyrone Power or Norma Shearer.

Unsurprisingly, the ever rising crest of dollars extended beyond the walls of the movie studios. On Rodeo Drive, that

world-famous altar of conspicuous consumption, prices rose
into the stratosphere as the necessities of modern life were
transformed into symbols of wealth by Beverly Hills matrons
willing to shell out thousands of movie dollars for Egyptian
cotton towels, silk sheets, chinchilla lap robes. Shopping became more than a pastime; it was an obsession, as New Money
mavens outbid one another in an attempt to purchase Old
Money class (or at least Hollywood's misguided idea of it).

Designer spectacles were currently in (fitted with clear glass
for those with 20/20 vision and made of lightweight aluminum frames studded with diamonds and other precious jew-
els), as was anything from Gucci or Giorgio. The message
silkscreened on a white, sixty-five-dollar cotton T-shirt displayed beneath the yellow-and-white awning in Giorgio's
storefront window said it all: *He who dies with the most toys wins.*

Shopping wasn't the only indulgence: recreational drug use
was common and sex was as popular as ever, providing constant grist for the rumor mills.

To Leigh's dismay, there had been more than one blind
article in the gossip columns these past months, hinting at
Marissa's reckless behavior.

What sizzling sexpot was seen riding off into the sunset on
the back of a Harley last week? Word around the biker
bars is that this twice-divorced star is no easy rider.

On the May morning that particular column hit the streets,
Leigh was forced to rush to the hospital, where Marissa had
just been admitted.

"This has got to stop."

Leigh took hold of Marissa's hand, surreptitiously checking
for needle marks on her arm, relieved when she didn't see
any.

Angered by the concern she viewed in Leigh's eyes, Marissa
turned her head toward the wall. "I don't know what you're
talking about. I had a little accident, that's all."

"That's the official studio line. But we know the truth. Marissa, you were beat up. You could have been killed!"

"Don't be so melodramatic."

"I'm not being melodramatic. My God, honey, have you looked in a mirror?"

The emergency room doctor had warned her that her sister's injuries looked a great deal worse than they were. But Leigh had not been able to conceal her shock when she entered the hospital room and saw Marissa's battered face. Both her eyes were rimmed with mottled purple, one was swollen shut. Her cheeks and jaw were a canvas of black and blue, and an ugly row of neat black stitches cut across her top lip.

Marissa glared at Leigh out of her good eye. "You don't have to pretend to be so upset. We both know that you've always been jealous of my looks, of the way men ogle me. Now *you* can be the beautiful sister."

"I've never been jealous of you, Mar. Not ever. From that first day Mother and Daddy brought you home from the hospital, I loved you. I still do."

"You don't have the guts to love anyone. Not really. In fact, if you don't watch it, sister dear, you're going to lose that husband of yours. Matthew is not the kind of guy to sit around and play second fiddle to another man."

"There's no other man in my life."

"Isn't there?" Marissa's cracked lips curved into a lopsided, cruel smile. "What about our dear daddy?"

"Matthew understands that Dad and I work together; it doesn't bother him," Leigh said, not quite convincingly. "Why should it?"

"Why indeed," Marissa murmured. She reached out and turned on the transistor radio Leigh had brought to the hospital. As "Stayin' Alive" blasted over the airwaves, Leigh thought fleetingly about all the people in town, her father included, who'd thought the movie *Saturday Night Fever* to be merely a "nice little story." What she wouldn't give to have the box office receipts for that runaway hit!

"Speaking of Daddy," Marissa said, breaking into Leigh's thoughts, "I don't suppose I can expect a visit?"

It was the very question Leigh had been afraid Marissa was going to ask. "You know what a hectic day it is," she said, trying to hide the anger she felt toward Joshua for refusing to come to the hospital. "What with the Academy Awards tonight, and the party afterward . . ." Her voice trailed off. "Oh, hell, Mar, I'm so sorry."

Marissa shrugged, flinching as the movement caused a jolt of pain in her cracked ribs. "That's okay. It's no secret that he and I have never been close. Not like the two of you."

There was a strange edge to Marissa's tone. The familiar anger was there, but this time there was something else. A dark, ominous note Leigh was still trying to decipher as she drove back home to prepare for the evening's festivities.

"So how is she?"

Matthew leaned against the bathroom doorframe, enjoying the view as Leigh, wrapped in a fluffy peach towel, hurriedly applied her makeup. She'd gotten caught in a traffic jam on the Santa Monica Freeway and was running late.

"She has two black eyes, a split lip, and a pair of cracked ribs. But despite the fact that she resembles an extra from a low-budget horror movie, the doctor assured me that she can leave the hospital tomorrow and return to work in about ten days, after the swelling goes down."

"She was damn lucky."

"Wasn't she?" Leigh put down the gray eyeliner pencil with a soft sigh. "I am so worried about her, Matthew, I don't know what to do."

"Perhaps the first thing you should do is quit bailing her out of these messes."

"Are you saying I should just back away and let something terrible happen to my own sister?"

"No. I'm saying that if Marissa was ever forced to face the consequences of her own behavior, she might develop some responsibility."

"She's facing the consequences," Leigh snapped back. "You didn't see her face, Matthew. I did. Do you have any idea what this will do to her self-esteem? She's always gotten by on her looks; she thinks it's the only thing people value about her."

Personally, Matthew couldn't think of anything else to value about Leigh's younger sister but her looks. And even those were too blatantly obvious for his taste.

"You know, of course, that you have emotional astigmatism where your family is concerned."

"I do not!"

"Your sister's been married twice, she's screwed practically every guy in town, and she's got more drugs in her medicine chest than Walgreen's. But you're constantly viewing her as some innocent victim of circumstances. As for your father, you refuse to admit that he's always done everything he can to break us up."

"Because it isn't true." Turning back toward the mirror, she smudged the liner at the corner of her lids, giving her eyes a smoky appearance.

"Do you honestly believe that there was no one else at Baron Studios capable of handling that Irish problem last week?"

The assistant director had run his car into a farmer's hedge after imbibing too much Guinness at a local pub a few miles outside Cork. The farmer was seeking damages for not only the hedge, but emotional trauma suffered by his livestock: two sheep, an aged, swaybacked gray horse, and a dairy cow.

"We had to send someone with the authority to make a deal with the farmer on the spot."

"You've never heard of lawyers?"

Leigh frowned at him in the mirror. "All right, perhaps my presence wasn't needed, but—"

"How about last month? The trip to Guatemala."

A visa problem. Something that admittedly could have been handled over the phone.

"And let's not forget the little trek to India the month before that," he said before she could answer. "And the three weeks in Cairo last Christmas."

How could she? She'd been surprised to run into Khalil, looking as handsome and exotic as ever. When he'd congratulated her on her marriage, she'd read the questions in his smooth dark eyes and knew he had perceived that her life with Matthew was not the nirvana she'd professed it to be.

"I don't want to fight," she said, turning toward him. "Not tonight."

She'd been planning a special surprise for two weeks. First

they'd attend the Academy Awards ceremony, where Matthew, who was now being touted as Hollywood's new genius, was reported to be a shoe-in for two Oscars this time—for his original screenplay and directing of *Private Screenings*. Afterward, she was going to plead a headache, enabling her to skip her father's party and return home early, where a carefully prepared supper would be waiting. Along with a magnum of iced champagne and a tall stack of Billie Holiday and Smokey Robinson records. After drinking the champagne and dancing to the records, they'd make love. All night long.

She went up on her toes, brushing her lips against his. "I know how you hate these celebrity things. And I truly appreciate your agreeing to come with me."

"I don't like them, but I do understand why you have to attend. And that being the case, I'm not about to sit home and sulk while one of those studio hunks escorts you."

"Thank you, darling. I promise to make it up to you as soon as we get home." She wrapped her arms around his neck; the towel slipped to the white carpeting.

"I have an idea," he said, caressing her neck, her shoulders, her breasts. "Why don't you give me a little sneak preview of things to come?"

The sexual desire swirling in his dark eyes made her knees go weak. Leigh ran her hands over the tautness of his back, reveling in the feel of the rock-hard muscles beneath his white pleated shirt. "We'll be late."

His lips nuzzled her neck. "Our categories won't come up for hours."

"What excuse would we give?"

He cupped her breast, brushing his thumb over her nipple, pleased when it hardened in response to his touch. "The cleaners sent the wrong tux." His hand moved downward. "The dog jumped on your dress with muddy feet and you had to change."

His touch was like tongues of flame, whipping at her flesh. "We don't have a dog."

"You know that and I know that. But no one else does. I've got it." His hand slipped wickedly between her legs, making her gasp with arousal. "We'll say the car broke down on the way to the Music Center."

She'd been hovering on the brink of an orgasm, with the promise of more to come, when his words reminded her of something she'd forgotten. "Oh, no."

"What's the matter now?" A moment later, the buzzer at the security gate sounded. "Who the hell is that?"

"It's probably the chauffeur."

"Chauffeur?"

"Daddy insisted on picking us up in his limousine," she said flatly. "He wanted us to arrive in style."

The mention of Joshua Baron was all it took to curb Matthew's desire. He dropped his hands to his sides. "Then you'd better get dressed. We wouldn't want to keep Daddy waiting."

Scooping up his tuxedo jacket from the arm of the chair, he left the room without a backward glance.

Closing her eyes against an impending headache, Leigh considered that it could be a very long night.

Two days later, Leigh was sitting in a booth at the Polo Lounge, having dinner with Tina. Matthew hadn't complained when she'd informed him that she wouldn't be home for dinner, but Leigh had not taken that as a sign he was over his lingering irritation. He'd barely spoken two words to her since the night of the Awards ceremony.

"God," Tina groaned, "I think I'm going to die."

"You don't look it," Leigh said unsympathetically. "In fact, you look terrific. Exercise obviously agrees with you."

"Not me. If anyone's getting anything out of these torture sessions, it's the masochist I never realized was living inside this aching body." Tina took a drink of Perrier, then looked at the cut-crystal glass as if she wished it contained something stronger. "Who the hell ever invented aerobics, anyway?"

"John Travolta?"

"Uh-uh, although I do blame him for this disco fad; it had to have been the Marquis de Sade. I'm still trying to figure out why I let you talk me into taking that class with you. Sixty minutes of the Bee Gees is fifty-nine too many minutes for me. Whatever happened to Johnny Mathis, anyway?"

Tina reached into her bag before remembering she'd quit smoking six weeks ago. She'd give this damn health kick everyone was touting two more weeks. If she didn't feel like a new woman after that, she was returning to her unchic but highly satisfying bad habits. "By the way, what does Matthew think about eating dinner alone every Tuesday and Thursday while you're trying to reach your maximum heart rate?"

"I doubt if he'd notice."

"Corbett says he's been working awfully hard on his latest screenplay."

"Obsession is more the word," Leigh countered. "Did Corbett tell you that he's been working on this story off and on for nearly ten years, ever since he got back from Vietnam?"

"I knew that." Tina picked unenthusiastically at her dry romaine. Lord, what she'd give for a nice thick steak! "But, now that you mention it, I don't believe Corbett's told me what it's about."

"That's because he doesn't know. No one does."

Tina looked up from her search for nonexistent bay shrimp. "No one? Not even you?"

Leigh's lips firmed. "Not even me."

"How strange."

"He says it's because he doesn't want to risk the story getting out prematurely."

"Well, you can't deny he's got a point. You know as well as I do that this is the smallest back-fence town in America, Leigh. News spreads faster than a fire in the canyons during the Santa Anas."

"I know that," Leigh said softly. She traced small concentric circles on the pink tablecloth with her fingernail. "But wouldn't you think he'd trust his own wife?"

Not if he saw her as his enemy's pawn, Tina mused, thinking of how many times over the past two years Matthew had come over to their house, complaining bitterly about what he viewed as Leigh's unnatural attachment to her father. Despite everything she'd done to convince him that Leigh loved him desperately, Tina could tell that the wedge Joshua had instigated into their marriage was driving them farther and farther apart.

"Marriage isn't always easy, Leigh," she said now, covering the younger woman's hand with her own. "But you and Matthew love one another. And that makes it worth fighting for."

Her words blocked by the sudden lump in her throat, Leigh

nodded. But she couldn't help wondering if she'd already lost the battle.

Less than a week after her dinner with Tina, Leigh crept into the house at dawn, tiptoeing cautiously across the white ceramic floor. When she entered the kitchen, desperate for a cup of coffee, she found Matthew seated at the table.

"Matthew! You scared me!"

The icy look he flashed her was less than encouraging. "Then we're even. Because I was scared to death most of the night. In fact, I was going to give you ten more minutes before I called the police."

"I told you when I called to cancel our dinner plans that I had to run up to Santa Barbara."

"You also said that you'd be back by midnight."

"I know, but—"

"I kept thinking of what I was going to tell the police . . . You see, Officer, I know my wife's met with a terrible accident, because she promised that she wasn't going to let anything keep us from toasting our second anniversary. Especially since she was in Rio de Janeiro for our first—a little problem with filming permits at the Corcovado, and—"

This time it was she who cut him off. "Marissa took an overdose of Seconal. She was barely conscious when I got there. I had to rush her to the hospital."

"Interesting how you arrived just in the nick of time. Isn't that a two-hour drive?"

"A little more than that."

"Yet she managed to OD and remain conscious, waiting all that time for you to arrive. Fascinating."

"Are you accusing my sister of staging a suicide attempt?"

"Damnit, Leigh!" Matthew pushed away from the table, knocking the chair over as he stood up. "Are you that blind? Can't you see that Marissa just wanted to ruin our anniversary? She took those damn pills after she called you. That way she wouldn't risk anything but a sore throat from the stomach pump."

"You don't know that," Leigh countered. A lifetime habit of defending her sister kept her from admitting that the same thought had occurred to her while she'd been pacing back and forth in the corridor outside the emergency room, waiting for the secobarbital to be pumped out of Marissa's system.

"I know that she's a ruthless, self-serving woman who nourishes grudges like other women—healthy women—nourish children. And I know that both she and your father are determined to wreck any chance for happiness that you and I might ever have."

"That's not true."

"Isn't it? Why don't you make up your mind where your loyalties lie, Leigh? With your overly possessive father and that slut of a sister, or the man who loves you."

"I suppose you're referring to yourself?" He certainly hadn't displayed any great love lately. In fact, the last time he'd held her, or kissed her, had been while she'd been getting ready for the Academy Awards last week.

"Yeah. Remember me? The husband? The guy you promised to love, honor, and cherish. Until baby sister calls from an adult motel in some sick bid for attention. Or Daddy feels a need for his dutiful surrogate wife."

All the color drained from Leigh's face. "You can't mean that the way it sounds."

His hurtful words had come from the gut, not his head, but stubborn pride, and envy of the love she so willingly bestowed on two people who didn't begin to deserve it, kept Matthew from retracting his accusation.

"What's the matter? Did I hit a little too close to home with that one?" Pent-up grievances made him rash. "Tell me something . . . If Joshua had called from that motel, would you have rushed up to spend the night with him?"

Her hand shot out. A sound like a gunshot shattered the early-morning calm. Visibly shaken, Leigh stared at her palm, resting on Matthew's rigid cheek, as if wondering who it belonged to.

"Feel better?" His voice was low, deceptively calm, but Leigh could hear the intensity shrouded just below the surface. His dark eyes had hardened, the planes of his face turned to granite.

"No." She put her hands behind her back, twisting her fingers together. Her nervousness was pulsating in the hollow of her throat as she stared at the incriminating white mark left by her palm. She'd never hit anyone in her life. What was happening to her? To them? "Oh God, I hate this," she said, sinking down onto one of the kitchen chairs. "I hate fighting with you."

Matthew watched the unshed tears glisten in her wide gray eyes and fought the urge to go to her. To comfort her. He'd been going crazy all night long worrying that Marissa had gotten her involved in something dangerous this time. For the entire two years of their marriage, he'd lived with the constant fear that one of these days Leigh was going to arrive on her rescue mission and find herself facing one of Marissa's psychotic boyfriends.

He'd sat up, hour after lonely hour, drinking too many pots of strong coffee and waiting. Images flashed through his mind, Leigh bloodied and beaten on the floor of some motel room. Leigh raped. Killed.

This obsession she had with her father and sister, this need to please, her willingness to let the pair of them walk all over her—and her marriage—was tearing his heart out piece by piece. And the damnable thing was, he couldn't even hate her for it.

"I'm going for a walk," he said. He knew he had to get out of the house before he said or did something that would destroy the final fragile bonds between them.

Leigh watched her husband storm out of the kitchen, slamming the door behind him with enough force to make the copper pots hanging on the wall tilt.

And then, giving in to the tears she'd been too proud to shed in front of Matthew, she wept.

33

December 1978

"Did you see this?"

Leigh glanced down at the paper Joshua slammed onto her desk. She'd been forewarned about the story in today's *Variety*; the reporter had called Matthew last night to confirm it.

"I haven't seen it. But I knew it was coming."

"You knew? And you didn't tell me?"

"I only found out last night. What does it say?"

"That your husband has written a screenplay about an actor turned politician. A politician with organized crime ties."

"Is that all?" Leigh asked carefully. Matthew had finally let her read the script for *The Eye of the Tiger* last night and she'd realized immediately that it held bombshell potential.

"No. It also suggests that the primary character bears a striking resemblance to Brendan Farraday."

Whom everyone knew had political ambitions, Leigh tacked on silently. "There may be a few problems," she admitted.

"But the legal department can go over them with Matthew and hash them out."

"Impossible. I want the project dropped."

"Dropped?" Leigh stared up at her father in disbelief. "You haven't even read it."

"I don't care. Baron Studios is not going to make this film. And that's final."

"I'm afraid that's not entirely your decision," she said quietly. "You authorized my autonomy six years ago when you agreed that I could start Sundown Productions."

"Damnit, you can't make this movie!"

"Why? Do you really hate Matthew so much that you'd try to block a project he's been working on for years?"

"It's not a matter of how *I* feel about the screenplay. There are other players in the game, Leigh. Players who do not want this picture made."

"Who?"

"It's better you don't know. What you must realize is that it would be better—and safer—for all of us if this script was allowed to die a natural death."

"I understand your concern, but don't you see? If we give in to these people, these outsiders, we'll be compromising everything we've worked so hard to achieve. Everything Grandfather worked for." She took a deep breath before continuing. "Matthew has written a compelling screenplay and I'm going to turn it into the best movie of the decade. Perhaps the best movie Baron Studios has ever made."

Joshua knew that his own father would have admired Leigh's steely strength. But damnit, she could end up getting them all killed. "Isn't there anything I could say to change your mind?"

"Nothing."

Heaving a sigh, Joshua turned to leave the room. Halting in the doorway, he looked back over his shoulder at the daughter who'd never given him a moment's grief until that bastard St. James had entered her life. "I love you, Leigh. And I've always acknowledged your superb judgment."

She nodded. "Thank you."

"But this time, you're making a lethal mistake."

* * *

Her father's words of warning rang in her ears like a death knell, interrupting her work, disturbing her sleep. Only Matthew's unflagging enthusiasm for his project eased her unrelenting stress. For the first time in weeks—months—they were working together during the day and making love at night with an exuberant joy she'd worried they might never recover. And that, she decided as she dressed for her father's annual Christmas gala, was worth a few sleepless nights.

Joshua's elaborate holiday decorations could have put Fantasyland to shame. Every tree on the grounds had been strung with tiny white fairy lights, filling the night with bright, twinkling stars. A twenty-five-foot, white-flocked Douglas fir claimed center stage, dressed with antique gold ornaments, majestic in silver spotlights. Waiters, clad in gold, silver, and crimson metallic harlequin costumes, circulated with gleaming gold trays upon which rested slender silver goblets of Louis Roederer Cristal champagne. At the center of each silver lamé kilted table were graceful sprays of pungent pine and holly, adorned with shiny gold, silver, and scarlet balls. Continuing the theme, battery-operated lights added sparkle to the centerpieces.

"My God, Joshua's gone and re-created the courtyard of the Sun God," Tina said as she and Corbett arrived at the Baron estate. Dressed in a gold-shot Mary McFadden chiffon evening gown, her dark hair elaborately French-braided, she was Beverly Hills chic personified.

"Either that or King Midas's winter resort," Corbett murmured, eyeing a nearby fountain that for this one memorable night was frothily spouting champagne.

"Don't blame me," a feminine voice behind them offered. "Since I've been too busy with Matthew's new screenplay to arrange any parties, Daddy hired outside help."

Tina turned and hugged Leigh, exchanging cheek kisses. "Darling, I've missed you! That damn aerobics class just isn't the same without you to keep me in step." She backed up, giving the younger woman an appreciative glance. "You look positively delicious," she decided, eyeing the pencil-slim strapless white dress embroidered with silver flowers. Leigh's hair was a silver blond froth, left free and flowing at her husband's request.

"Like an angel," Matthew said, arriving in time to hear Tina's compliment. "My angel." He put his arm around her, drawing her close.

"Gracious." Leigh blushed as she looked up at her husband, resplendent in white tie. "You keep talking like that, Mr. St. James, and people will think we're newlyweds."

"That's the way I've been feeling lately, Mrs. St. James." It was wonderful to be able to enjoy Leigh out of bed as much as in! Over these past months Matthew had felt freer, happier, than he ever could have imagined, despite a faint, lingering fear that such unmitigated joy was tempting fate.

When Leigh and Matthew exchanged a long, intimate look, Corbett cleared his throat. "Well, it was great seeing both of you," he said expansively. "But from the way Tina's tugging on my arm, I think it's time to mingle."

Engrossed in one another, neither Leigh nor Matthew noticed their departure.

"Well, that's certainly a relief," Tina said, plucking a goblet from a passing tray. "I was afraid, for a while, that they weren't going to make it."

"You weren't the only one." Corbett reached out and touched her cheek. "Sometimes I think we're the only happily married couple in this town."

"I know." She covered his hand with hers. "But I do so want Matthew and Leigh to be as happy as we are."

His gaze held a warmth that belied twenty-one years of marriage. "Impossible."

Seeking a break from the barrage of questions about Matthew's screenplay, Leigh escaped to a far corner of the garden. Had the night ever smelled so fragrantly sweet? she wondered, breathing in the scent of the bright winter flowers. Somewhere out of sight a cricket clicked his lonely song. There was a ring around the white-misted moon and Leigh was looking up at it, marveling at how near it seemed, when Brendan Farraday's booming voice shattered her introspection.

"Leigh," he said, "you're looking absolutely gorgeous tonight."

"Why, thank you, Brendan. You're looking quite handsome yourself." It was true. Like so many of Tinseltown's aging stars, Brendan actually seemed to grow more handsome—more distinguished looking—with the years.

"Yessir," he said, nodding his head as his blue eyes moved from the top of her head down to her toes, clad in silvery silk high heels. "You're quite a vision." Farraday was famed for his love of Western art and, at the moment, Leigh felt like a piece of Remington bronze he was appraising for his collection. "Your husband's a very lucky man."

Leigh smiled. "I'll tell him you said so."

"I'll be the first to admit that Matthew and I didn't really hit it off when we were working on *Dangerous,* but you know, Leigh, I do admire that young man's talent. Yessir," he said reflectively, "your husband has a rare and special gift. I'd hate to see him ruin his career."

"That isn't going to happen."

"It sure as hell might if he ends up in court defending a libel suit. Face it, Leigh, this is a company town; the powers that be in Hollywood don't like controversy. If Baron Studios insists on making this movie, you may just find the ranks closing against you."

His threat only strengthened her resolve. "Go ahead and sue," she suggested, brushing past him on her way back to the party. "It will only earn *The Eye of the Tiger* more publicity."

He grabbed hold of her arm, spinning her back toward him. "Just a minute," he ground out. "I'm not finished talking to you."

"Tough." She met his suddenly dangerous gaze unflinchingly. "Because I'm through listening."

"No you're not." As his fingers dug into the soft flesh of her upper arm, Farraday demonstrated that he had not gotten where he was by walking away from a fight. "You go ahead and make your precious picture, baby. But you'll only have yourself to blame if something happens to your husband before you ever get it to the screen."

Leigh's blood chilled; his soft words seemed to come hurling directly at her, one at a time, shattering like glass at her feet. "Are you threatening me?"

He shrugged. "Accidents happen." Point made, he released her and faded back into the shadows. A moment later, she heard him loudly enjoying something one of the guests had said, his robust laugh sounding as if nothing had happened.

Tina stood hidden in the shadows, listening to Farraday threaten Leigh. Some things—some people—never changed.

Thirty-seven years ago, she'd been a promising young actress at Baron Studios. She had appeared in three pictures when, cast in the role of a dancer who enrolls in college and falls in love with her staid mathematics professor, Tina brought three things to the screen that captured the audience's immediate attention: a pair of long, shapely legs that rivaled Betty Grable's, a cleavage that Jane Russell was rumored to have envied, and a sexy, comedic talent that Judy Holliday invented and Marilyn Monroe would later perfect.

In short, the former Teresa Salerno was a girl headed straight for the top, which was why Joshua Baron decided to cast the newcomer in Brendan Farraday's next picture. The only fly in the ointment was that Farraday had seigneurial rights, which meant, Tina's agent explained, that if Farraday didn't like her, she'd be off the picture. The agent snapped her manicured fingers. Like that.

The warning flew right over the top of Tina's head. Of course he'd like her; what was not to like? When the call came from his secretary, inviting her to a dinner party at his home, Tina vowed that by the time the evening was over, she'd have Brendan Farraday eating out of the palm of her hand. No one had ever accused Tina Salerno of not possessing self-confidence.

She arrived at Farraday's Laurel Canyon home clad in a velvet dinner dress worn by Joan Fontaine in her Oscar-winning performance in *Suspicion*. Her roommate, a costumer at RKO, had "borrowed" the dress for this important evening.

By morning, the dress was in tatters and Tina was back at her apartment, where Farraday's chauffeur had delivered her after a seemingly endless night of sexual abuse. Mottled purple and yellow bruises darkened her breasts, her legs, her buttocks. The smooth skin of her inner thighs was marred with teeth marks; blood and semen oozed out of her vagina and rectum.

"You have to call the cops," Tina's roommate insisted. "Star or not, you can't let the bastard get away with this."

"No," Tina managed through split and swollen lips. "No one would ever believe me."

"But I knew where you were going. I can testify for you."

"No!" Now that the shock was wearing off, Tina was on the verge of hysteria. Farraday's warning kept coming back to her. He had friends, important friends, who would not hesitate to kill her if she caused him any trouble. Something in his eyes had assured Tina that the movie star was telling the truth.

"At least I'm going to call a doctor."

Tina began to shake uncontrollably. "I can't risk it."

"Hey, don't worry. This guy is discreet. He does all the studio abortions."

"All right," Tina acquiesced. "But he has to swear never to tell anyone." As her roommate went out in the hall, where the building's single pay phone was located, Tina said on a ragged sob, "I got the part."

Leigh had almost managed to convince herself that Brendan Farraday's veiled threat was nothing more than the blustering of an angry man who'd drunk too much champagne, when Tina suddenly appeared from out of the shadows.

"Tina," she said with a start, "you frightened me."

"Not as much as Brendan Farraday already has, I imagine."

"You know Brendan when he's been drinking."

"Yes," Tina answered in a low, flat voice. "I know Brendan."

Leigh looked at the older woman more closely, alerted by her strangely trembling tone. Instead of the self-confidence Tina usually wore like a second skin, she looked nervous. But there was another expression on her face as well. Something that looked strangely like fear.

"Is anything wrong?"

"Yes. Something is terribly wrong." Taking a deep breath, Tina told her story falteringly, in vivid, unrelenting detail. "Of course I never went back to the studio," she said. "A few weeks later, after the bruises faded, I got a job answering the phone in a real-estate office around the corner from my apartment. After awhile, I got a license and began dabbling in sales, and one thing led to another and, well, here I am."

Leigh shook her head in shock and admiration. "This town is overrun with people who have reinvented themselves, but you've definitely outdone them all."

"I've done okay. Although I'll always regret that I couldn't have put that bastard Farraday in jail where he belongs."

"Now I understand why you've always hated him," Leigh said. "Does Corbett know?"

All the color drained from Tina's face. "Of course not. And you can't tell him."

"Why did you tell me?"

"I wanted you to understand that Brendan Farraday is a dangerous man. He's vicious, brutal, and he'd have someone killed without so much as a backwards glance." Looking nervously at the French doors, she said, "I've got to get back before Corbett starts looking for me." She placed her hand on Leigh's arm. "You have to do whatever it takes to stop this movie, Leigh. For Matthew's sake." And then she was gone.

Alone again, Leigh wrapped her arms around herself in an unconscious gesture of self-protection. She'd been so happy when she'd arrived at the party tonight. So hopeful. And then, in a few short moments, Brendan Farraday had managed to threaten everything that she held dear.

"There you are!" Matthew strode across the brick terrace toward Leigh. "I've been looking all over for you."

"I needed a breath of air."

"You're shivering." Taking off his coat, he slipped it over her bare shoulders. "Better?"

"I love you," she whispered softly, desperately. "Whatever happens, it's important that you know that."

"I do." He looked at her with a mixture of curiosity and concern. "Are you all right?"

"Of course." She took a deep breath that should have calmed her but didn't. "Can we go home now?"

Questions still lingering in his eyes, he lowered his lips to hers. "Sweetheart, I thought you'd never ask."

"I've got good news."

Leigh schooled her face to a calm, interested expression as

she faced William Zimmerman across her desk. The energetic, personable young attorney was one of Baron Studios' latest acquisitions, hired after his graduation from Stanford Law last June. In six short months he'd proven himself invaluable, and Leigh would not be at all surprised if he'd made it to the top of the department before he turned thirty.

"I'm always in the mood for good news."

"*The Eye of the Tiger* isn't going to cause any major problems."

Her stomach dropped to the floor. It was not the news she'd been hoping for. "Oh? Are you sure?"

"Well, there are a couple of scenes that could cause a problem, but nothing that can't easily be changed."

"Matthew is not willing to alter his script in order to avoid a lawsuit."

"We're only talking about a few lines, Leigh. Nothing that would diminish the integrity of the story." He looked at her curiously. "You don't seem very happy about this. I figured you'd be dancing on air."

Leigh forced a smile. "I appreciate all the work you've done, William, but I'm afraid that after examining the matter very carefully, I've come to the conclusion that making this movie would put Baron Studios in jeopardy. Something I cannot allow to happen."

"But, Leigh—"

"And that's why I'm going to ask that you render an opinion that Baron Studios should not finance this project."

He stared at her, thunderstruck. "But, Leigh, I've already told you, there isn't any problem. I don't understand, it's a terrific script, it's going to make a dynamite movie. My God, it's your very own husband's project. How can you turn it down?"

Leigh's gaze turned glacial, her words clipped. "I've explained my position. Now, will you write the opinion, or must I ask another attorney in the department to handle it for me?"

Zimmerman's shoulders slumped visibly as he pushed himself out of the chair. "Of course I'll do it."

Leigh nodded, appearing coolly satisfied, even as her heart was beating so hard and fast she wondered if she could be having a heart attack. "Thank you. Oh, and William?"

He turned in the office doorway. "Yes?"

"I'd like to keep this meeting between us, if you don't mind."

His intelligent brown eyes searched her face. "Of course."

The moment she was alone, Leigh began to tremble violently. By behaving contrary to every rule of her life, she had saved Matthew's life. But at what cost?

34

Accustomed to overcoming obstacles, Matthew took Baron Studios' legal department report with a stoicism that was second nature. He was only sorry that the decision not to fund his film had caused a renewed rift with Leigh. For some reason he could not understand, when he announced his intention to seek independent financing, she had become almost hysterical.

It wasn't like Leigh to be so emotional, Matthew mused as he left the Polo Lounge. He'd just concluded an uneventful meeting with a potential backer—a Swiss banker from Zurich—when he ran into Jeff Martin.

"Hey, dude," Jeff said, swaying dangerously on his feet. "How're they hangin'?"

"Okay," Matthew said. "How are things with you?" Not that it wasn't obvious. Jeff's long, lank hair was unwashed, tied back with a leather thong, and his square jaw was covered with a three-day stubble of beard.

"Lookin' up, man. Looking better every day."

"I'm glad."

"In fact, I'm about to hit the big time."

How many times had he heard that? "Well, good luck."

"Yessir," Jeff mumbled, more to himself than to Matthew, "old Jeff's gonna be living on Easy Street pretty soon. Thanks to old man Baron."

He'd been on the way to his car, but at Jeff's words, Matthew abruptly turned around. "Joshua?"

"You know another Baron? Except the two chicks." Jeff giggled nervously. "Whoops, sorry, dude. I just remembered, one of those chicks is your old lady, huh?"

Matthew ignored the reference to Leigh. He worried that Jeff was involved in some new scheme with Marissa and, although he personally didn't give a damn about his sister-in-law, Leigh did. The one thing their already strained marriage didn't need right now was another crisis.

"What business do you have with Baron?"

"Old Josh is my ace in the hole." He grinned. "Which, I guess, makes you the king of the deck."

"Me?"

"Sure. The way I figure it, now that you're a big honcho, Baron should be willing to pay a bundle to keep anyone from finding out that he was the one who arranged your drug bust. Speaking of which," he said, "how the hell did you ever get out of that place? The old man just about had a stroke when he found out you'd escaped."

Matthew told himself that he should be feeling something—shock, anger, disbelief. But Jeff's words only confirmed a deep-seated suspicion he'd harbored for years. A suspicion he'd never shared with anyone. Who would have believed him?

"Sounds as if you've struck pay dirt," Matthew agreed easily. "Why don't we go get a beer and you can fill me in on the details."

"Great. It'll be just like old times. The two caballeros."

"Yeah," Matthew muttered. "Just like old times."

Two hours later, after Jeff had managed to recall specific details, Matthew confirmed that this was not some hallucination born in his old friend's sodden, burned-out brain. As he left the bar, Matthew decided that the time had come for Leigh to know the truth. About everything.

"I don't believe it!" Stricken, Leigh stared at Matthew. "You're only saying this because Baron Studios refused to finance *The Eye of the Tiger*."

Matthew understood that Leigh's first reaction would be denial. It was only natural, given her close ties to her father. He had laid it all out for her, including Jeff's participation in exchange for that small part in *Dangerous*.

"It's true, Leigh."

"No!" Hair pins scattered onto the tile floor as she shook her head. "Jeff's mistaken. Or he's lying." She grasped onto that idea like a drowning woman might cling to a life raft. "That's it," she said. "Don't you see? He and Marissa cooked this up. It's just another one of Marissa's schemes to get back at Father for treating her so abominably all these years."

"Leigh. Honey." He captured her wildly moving hands. "It has to be the truth. He knew too many details."

Pulling free of Matthew's light hold, she shrunk away from him. "It's a lie," she repeated. "A filthy, rotten, hurtful lie."

"Why don't you ask Joshua?"

"That's exactly what I intend to do."

As coldly furious as he was at Joshua, and as much as he wished Leigh had accepted his words at face value, Matthew understood her need to hear the truth directly from the source. "Let's go."

"No. I have to do this myself."

He grabbed her arm. "For God's sake, Leigh, you're in no condition to drive."

"Let go of me!" She shook him away. "Leave me alone!"

Matthew watched Leigh storm from the house. A moment later, he heard the roar of the Jaguar's engine and the squeal of tires as she tore away from the house.

Some days it just didn't pay to get out of bed.

Leigh broke every speeding statute on the books racing to Beverly Hills. A million thoughts tumbled around in her brain—spinning, swirling, colliding wildly. Questions without answers. Answers to questions she'd never dared ask.

She didn't want to believe her father capable of such treachery. But then she remembered that long-ago incident with Chance Murdock, when rumors had Joshua responsible for the teen idol's arrest, and wondered.

She found Joshua in the library.

"Darling," he said, greeting her with a broad smile, "what a nice surprise! Tell me that you're staying for dinner and I'll have Maria fix your favorite—veal piccata."

Leigh ignored both his welcome and his culinary bribe. "Did you have Matthew arrested in Mexico?"

He'd been waiting for this for years. Now that the moment of truth had finally arrived, Joshua found himself strangely calm. "Where did you get an idea like that?"

He looked like the MGM lion, confidently sprawled back in his leather-tooled chair. King of the jungle. Leigh had never realized, until now, exactly how brutal her father's jungle was.

"From Matthew."

"Honey, Matthew is angry about our refusing to finance his picture. Actually, I don't blame him; I'd be madder than hell myself, under the circumstances. He's just blowing off steam."

She had observed her father in enough meetings to know when he was bluffing. She watched him watching her and felt sick. "Matthew had lunch at the Polo Lounge today. He was meeting with a Swiss financier."

"I'd like to say I wish him luck. But we both know that would be a lie."

"And you never lie, do you, Daddy?"

There was something about Leigh's tone that made Joshua break out into a sudden sweat. "Never." He pushed himself out of the chair, experiencing an attack of vertigo when he stood up. "Since it's cocktail time, I believe I'll have a drink. Can I get you anything, princess?"

"No, thank you. Matthew ran into Jeff Martin. He was drunk."

"That's hardly surprising," Joshua remarked, pouring Scotch into a glass. "The man's no damn good; he and your sister are two of a kind."

"He may have a drinking problem," Leigh acknowledged. "But he seems to have a remarkable sense of recall. He remembered everything that happened when he and Matthew went to Mexico."

"Oh?" The fingers of his right hand were numb, as if they'd gone to sleep, and pressure was building behind his eye.

"He also had some interesting things to say about a deal you supposedly made with him."

Joshua tilted his head back and poured the Scotch down his throat. The liquor coursed through him, warming his blood, easing the painful tension that seemed to have his head in a steel vise. "I knew it would have to come out one day."

"Then you did conspire to have Matthew arrested? You paid Jeff to plant those drugs on him?"

"Of course." Joshua refilled his glass. "I also arranged for that Mexican extra to play the part of his wife."

"The wedding picture was a composite."

"An especially clever one, I thought. And if you're expecting me to apologize, you're going to be disappointed, Leigh. In fact, not only am I not sorry, I'd do it all again, if it meant keeping that bastard away from you."

Leigh knew the pain and anger and recrimination would come later, once the shock had worn off. Right now, she felt numb. But she knew exactly what she had to do.

"I'm leaving Baron Studios."

Joshua would have laughed at that, but his breath was coming in short puffs, and all he could manage was a ragged snort. "You got away with that melodramatic ultimatum once, sweetheart, but it isn't going to work this time. You'll never leave Baron; the studio's in your blood. It's family. More than that overrated bastard you're living with could ever be."

Inside she was trembling like a leaf; outside Leigh appeared calm. "Matthew's illegitimacy was none of his doing," she responded icily. "Some other men are bastards by choice. My resignation will be on your desk first thing tomorrow morning." On legs that felt like rubber, she turned to walk away.

"Grandstanding doesn't suit you, Leigh," Joshua called after her. "Go ahead, leave if you want. After you discover that there's not a studio in town who'll go against me and hire you, you'll be back. On your knees." He shook his fist at her rigid back. "On your knees, girl. Damnit, do you hear me?"

She turned, her eyes like cold gray stones. "I hear you. And not that my life is any of your concern, but I have no intention of seeking employment at any other studio. I'm going into independent production with my husband. Together we're going to make *The Eye of the Tiger*."

She was going to leave him. For that bastard. For Matthew St. James. He wouldn't allow that to happen. Joshua came after her, pushing Leigh against the carved mahogany door. His body pressed against hers; his large hands tangled cruelly in her hair and, before she could cry out, his mouth was eating into hers.

As his tongue thrust past the barrier of her teeth, a flood of memories came pouring forth from some dark, secret well inside Leigh. Memories she had blocked from her conscious mind years ago.

She had been a month shy of her sixth birthday when her father had come to tuck her in to bed.

"Whose little girl are you?" he asked the familiar bedtime question, his lips grazing her temple.

"Yours," she responded as she always did.

"Such a pretty girl," he murmured, his wide hand stroking her hair. "The prettiest girl in the world." He tugged at the pink ribbon at the ruffled neck of the white cotton nightgown.

"Prettier than Laura Lang?" she asked coyly, naming one of the studio's current child stars.

"Laura Lang looks like the Wicked Witch of the West compared to my princess," Joshua said, caressing the satiny skin revealed by the now open neckline. Something in his touch was strangely different tonight. Fear skimmed up Leigh's spine. Joshua felt her slight tremor.

"Shh. It's okay," he soothed. His hand trailed farther down her flat child's chest.

"Nanny says I shouldn't let people touch me," Leigh whispered as her father's treacherous hand crept lower, making slow, concentric circles against her stomach.

"Nanny means strangers. I'm your daddy. And I love you."

"I love you too, Daddy," she said, her voice muffled by the nightgown he was tugging over her head. "More than anything."

"I know." His hands trembled as they caressed her, strok-

ing her body, playing with the soft pink folds no one ever
touched. Even Nanny, after bathing Leigh, would invariably
hand her the soft white towel, briskly instructing her to dry
her "privates." Instinctively, Leigh pressed her legs together.

"Don't turn away from your daddy." His palms pressed
lightly but firmly against her inner thighs. "I love you, princess. Let me show you how much."

He'd said the magic word. Leigh opened to him, allowing
his long fingers to invade her most secret recesses. He was
hurting her, but she didn't cry. Instead, she closed her eyes
and reminded herself that her daddy loved her.

His fingers were deep inside her now, pressing, probing.
Hurting. Daddy loves me.

His mouth covered hers, his tongue thrusting cruelly between her startled lips. Loves me.

He fumbled with his clothing, then grasped her hand and
wrapped it around his penis. It was big and strong and puls-
ing. Leigh pulled away.

"No, damnit," he muttered harshly, curving her fingers
back around his swollen penis, holding her hand in place with
his own stronger one, moving their joined hands back and
forth, faster and faster and faster until his body tensed and he
pressed his mouth against hers again, expelling a tortured cry
between her dry lips. Less than a heartbeat later, a hot, sticky
substance shot out over her stomach and thighs. He loves me.

Her father lay atop her, heavy and inert, for what seemed
an eternity. Finally he pushed himself up and, without a word,
staggered unsteadily from the room.

Leigh lay alone on her rumpled, soiled sheets, tears streaming down her face. Pain radiated outward from her violated
core like red-hot needles, and her heart was filled with fear.
She began to shiver violently.

That was how Joshua found her when he returned with a
warm washcloth and fresh sheets. Leigh concentrated on the
now soothing touch of his hands—those same hands that had
earlier caused such unexpected pain—as he bathed her in the
scented water and changed her nightgown. Then he carried
her over to the antique rocking chair in the corner, where she
curled her legs under her and watched as he stripped the bed

of the stained, flower-sprigged sheets and replaced them with crisp, ironed ones.

"Do you still love your daddy?" Joshua asked, tucking her back in the freshly made bed.

"Yes," she answered in a small voice that sounded as if it were coming from the bottom of the sea.

He ran the back of his hand down her cheek. "And I love you. More than your mother, or anyone. You're my own special princess."

She ignored a faint stab of guilt about enjoying her exalted position over her mother, choosing instead to bask in the warmth of her father's affection.

"But some people might not understand our special love." He frowned and brushed her silky hair away from her small, pale face. "Some people might want to hurt us."

"Hurt us?" Leigh asked uncomprehendingly. "Why?"

"Because they're jealous. They might even try to take you away from me."

Her child's heart froze; the shivering began anew. "No!"

Joshua took hold of her icy, trembling hands and lifted them to his lips. "I won't let them," he promised. "But you're going to have to help."

Her father was so strong. So brave. So important. How could a little girl like her help him with anything? "How?"

"We have to keep tonight a secret," he said, his eyes locking on to hers as if he could see all the way to the depths of her soul. "Our own special secret."

It would be years before Leigh fully understood the pact she had entered into that night.

"Our own secret," she repeated gravely.

"No!" Pushing against his shoulders, Leigh broke free of her father's smothering hold. "Let go of me!"

His face was the color of paste, his eyes glazed, beads of sweat glistening on his upper lip. "You've got the wrong idea," he stammered, reaching for her once again.

"Don't touch me," she shrieked, recoiling, slapping away at his outstretched hands. "Don't you understand? I remember. I remember everything."

Her words were an indistinct rumbling in his ears. A terrible pain stabbed into his temple like a sword of flame. "Princess—"

"Don't you ever call me that again, you selfish, unfeeling son of a bitch. Goddamnit, I remember!"

A veil was coming over his eyes. Fireworks were exploding in his brain. "You can't talk to me like that. I'm your father."

"You're a dirty, child-molesting pervert." Feelings of betrayal came boiling to the surface—furious, bitter feelings she had kept locked away for years.

He tried to explain, to tell her about Signe's infidelity, his own impotence, but the words were blocked by some towering, unseen barricade in his brain and wouldn't come.

Leigh's angry words were like bullets, coming fast and hard, striking him without pity. Joshua lurched, then crumpled to the floor.

35

The hours dragged by while Leigh waited for some word of her father's condition. She'd ridden with him in the ambulance to the hospital, racked with guilt as the paramedics struggled to keep him alive.

A pretty blond candy striper brought her a cup of coffee from the vending machine down the hall. It tasted like battery acid, but she drank it, in lieu of anything stronger. She listened to the anonymous, disembodied voices paging doctors, announcing indecipherable codes.

Shortly after arriving at the hospital, she telephoned Matthew, only to have their housekeeper tell her that he'd gone out. No, he hadn't said when he'd be back. Feeling as if her entire life was crumbling down around her, all Leigh could do was leave a message. And pray.

The shift changed. New nurses, their virginal white uniforms starched and clean, their manner brisk and efficient, came on duty. Leigh's vigil continued.

"Ms. Baron?" A solemn-faced doctor clad in rumpled white slacks, white shoes, and a long white lab jacket appeared in the doorway. He looked every bit as exhausted as Leigh felt.

"Yes?"

"I'm Dr. Britton. Since your father's doctor is attending a medical conference in New York, I've been assigned his case."

"I've been so worried. Is he—" She couldn't say the word.

"Your father has suffered a cerebral vascular accident. A stroke. But he's holding his own. For now. He's been moved to ICU."

"May I see him?"

He shook his head. "I'm afraid that wouldn't be advisable. He's still unconscious."

"But—"

"He wouldn't even know you were there." His intelligent blue eyes professionally examined her too pale face. "Go home, Ms. Baron," he suggested gently. "Get some rest."

"I can't leave without seeing my father. Please. Tell me. Is he going to live?"

"I can't promise anything at this point. The next few days will determine his prognosis for recovery."

Leigh wondered how she would ever be able to look at her father—think of him—without the treachery of his actions standing between them. She could not forgive Joshua, but neither could she ignore the gravity of his condition. Or the inescapable fact that she was responsible for his stroke. All her life she'd believed that if she could only avoid tension and controversy, everything would turn out all right. And what had she done? The first time she lost her temper and fought back, she'd nearly killed her father.

"If he dies, it'll be my fault. We had an argument." She drew in a long, shuddering breath. "I said some terrible things."

Putting aside professional distance, he took hold of her ice cold hand. "Every family argues."

"We never did. I always tried to live up to my father's expectations." Oh God, she thought, she was already talking about Joshua as if he were dead.

"Every family," the doctor repeated gently. "Even the famous ones." He squeezed her fingers. "Believe it or not, there are times my children dare argue with me. And in the event the worst-case scenario does occur, it's important for you to know that you didn't kill your father, Ms. Baron. His records indicate that he's had high blood pressure for several years. He could have had this stroke at any time—on the golf course, the tennis court, at work."

"But he didn't," Leigh said on something perilously close to a sob. "Don't you see, he had it with me. Because of me."

He eyed her more intently. "I don't normally believe in prescribing sedatives, but I think in your case—"

"No." Leigh drew in another deep breath. "I'll be fine. As soon as I see my father."

"You're a stubborn young woman, aren't you, Ms. Baron?"

"That's what I've been told."

The doctor rubbed his weary face with his hand, making Leigh suddenly feel sorry for him, surrounded by so much suffering and death. "You may see him for ten minutes," he decided.

"Every hour?"

"You're staying all night." It was not a question.

"I'm staying until my father regains consciousness."

"I'd hate to ever have to negotiate a contract with you," he relented on a sigh. "All right. Ten minutes every hour."

She had never expected any other outcome.

The ICU was blindingly lit. Nurses moved across the shiny tile floors on silent, rubber-soled shoes, their starched skirts making a soft, swishing sound as they went from patient to patient. The hushed room smelled like disinfectant and disease and death.

Joshua regained consciousness in the early hours of the morning. Leigh was standing beside his bed, watching the machines whisper and beep as they measured out his life. After a lifetime of thinking of her father as larger than life, she was stunned to see him looking so weak. So helpless. His skin was the flat color of putty, he was paralyzed, and he'd lost the power of speech. All he could do was stare impotently up at her, his pleading eyes moist with tears.

He was, Leigh reminded herself, guilty of the most pernicious behavior. She'd always thought of herself as a truthful person, yet in order to protect his own selfish interests, her father had encouraged her to spend years lying to herself. So many lies. So much deception.

Matthew found Leigh pacing the floor of the waiting room. She was wearing the same ivory suit she'd had on when she left the house late yesterday afternoon to go confront her father.

"I just heard."

His day-old growth of beard suggested that he'd spent the night away from home. With another woman? When that thought didn't wound her to the core, Leigh realized that even if her husband had been out committing adultery, at this moment, she was simply too emotionally drained to care.

"I left word with Ingrid."

"Have you been alone all this time?"

She looked around the deserted room as if surprised by his question. "Yes."

"Why didn't you call Tina and Corbett? Or Kim?"

She brushed at the wrinkles crisscrossing her silk skirt. "I didn't think of it."

"I'll call."

"No." Leigh lowered her eyes, terrified that he might view her secret shame. She felt as if a scarlet A had been emblazoned on her chest. "Really, Matthew, I just want to be alone right now."

He was going to lose her. Matthew could feel it coming and was damned if he knew how to stop it. "Alone with Joshua, you mean."

"They don't know if he's going to live or die. I'm all he has. If I desert him now, that might make a difference. And if he died because of me, I'd never forgive myself."

"You take too much responsibility onto yourself, Leigh. You always have. Your father, Marissa, the studio. You can't control the entire world."

They were standing at opposite ends of the small room, like combatants. "I don't want to control the entire world," she argued weakly. "Just my own little corner of it."

"Sometimes we can't even do that. No matter how hard we try."

"He needs me," she whispered.

If he dragged Leigh away now, with her father's life hanging in the balance, and the bastard died, Matthew knew it would haunt her—and their marriage—forever. "All right. I can understand the emotional strain you're under right now. So at least tell me that when I go to the studio to clear out my office, I can pack your things as well."

It was one thing to turn her back on the studio when her father was capable of running things. But now . . . oh, God, he'd been right about her all along, she realized unhappily. The studio was in her blood. It was the embodiment of the only family she'd ever known.

"Matthew, I can't. Not now." She dragged her trembling fingers through her hair. "Baron Studios has been in the family for more than half a century. It's my roots. I can't just turn my back on it and allow it to go under without a Baron at the helm. What about all the people who work there? I have to think of them."

He'd never known roots. There had been times, during his marriage to Leigh, that Matthew had actually believed that he might be developing some, putting them down in the sandy soil of Santa Monica, building a life not only for them, but for future generations. Obviously he'd been wrong.

It was bad enough that she was staying here at the hospital, with his enemy, but to choose Joshua Baron's empire over their marriage . . . Matthew could only view her behavior as betrayal.

"Is there any chance of changing your mind?" His voice was even. Calm. Only his rigid jaw and his white-knuckled clenched fists revealed his smoldering anger.

Leigh bit her lip. "No."

He exhaled a long, weary breath. "Then I'll be moving out of the house."

Why couldn't he understand? Her heart torn, Leigh could think of no words to stop him. It appeared that her choice was between the death of her marriage or the death of her father. Along with the business both her father and grandfather had struggled so hard to keep in the family. As much as she loved Matthew, as much as she wished she could bridge the distance that yawned between them, Leigh felt as if she had no choice.

"If that's really what you want to do."

"I'll be staying at the Wilshire."

"Fine." The problems between them could be ironed out, Leigh tried to tell herself. She loved Matthew. And he loved her. He'd be back.

"If you'd send my files and any mail I might get, I'd appreciate it."

"Of course."

They were hurting one another, but unable to stop, both had retreated behind their separate barricades of unbreachable pride. "Well, I guess I'd better be going."

Her throat burning, Leigh turned away, unwilling to watch Matthew walk away from everything they'd worked to build together.

Hours later Joshua's doctor put his foot down and threatened to withdraw her visiting privileges unless she got some rest. As she drove through the dark and deserted streets to Santa Monica, images and conversations whirled around in her mind. Her confrontation with her father, the horrible sight of him falling to the floor, the painful image of Matthew's rigid face as he forced her to choose between love and responsibility.

She entered her house, went into the bathroom, and stared at the wan, guilty face she saw in the mirror. "It was just a fluke," she whispered. "Just a one-time thing. He was drunk. I remember the smell of liquor on his breath." She dragged her hands through her hair. "It was just a fluke," she repeated. Then she dropped to her knees and was violently sick in the toilet bowl.

Much later, seeking something to do to take her mind off problems she was not yet prepared to confront, Leigh went into the kitchen and surveyed the contents of the refrigerator. Sitting down at the kitchen table, she made a list for the housekeeper, adding the beer Matthew preferred before she remembered she wouldn't need to buy it anymore.

Someday, she assured herself, all this would seem like a story. An old movie that Baron Studios had produced and then put away in the vault. A movie that was forgotten long before the delicate celluloid film turned to dust.

But as she stared unseeingly into the well of darkness out the window, Leigh knew that the scene she and Matthew had played out in the hospital waiting room was no movie. It was her marriage that had disintegrated to dust.

Unable to deal with such a devastating loss while her father's life hung in the balance, Leigh pushed it away, deep inside her brain, where she wouldn't have to look at it.

Only later, when her heart stopped pounding so painfully, perhaps she'd figure out how to go on living.

The princess was lying on a towering stack of fluffy goosedown mattresses. She was crying. Tears ran backward into her long blond hair. They turned to blood, staining her gossamer silk nightgown.

"I'm trying to get Donna Summer to record the title song for *After Dark*," Leigh said. She was feeding Joshua a spoonful of puréed lamb.

It had been four months since his stroke, a month since he'd been released from the hospital, and his recovery was progressing frustratingly but predictably slowly. His once hard body, unexercised for too long, had turned flaccid; his speech center had been damaged, causing him to become angry at his clumsy tongue. Since Leigh was the only person who could understand him, Joshua had grown more and more dependent on her.

In the beginning, she attempted to keep her visits to two a day—morning and evening—but Joshua's tantrums made her worry that he'd have another stroke. Rather than risk his life, she moved into one of the guest bedrooms of the palatial Beverly Hills mansion. Now that her memory of that infamous night had returned, Leigh's own room held too many painful memories. As it was, her feelings of love and hate and guilt were impossible to sort out, so she pushed them away into a distant corner of her mind and forced herself to concentrate on the present. And all the demands that had been placed upon her.

"Er," Joshua rolled his eyes. Lamb spattered onto the royal blue silk of his pajama top. She still hadn't forgiven him, but Leigh couldn't help pitying her father. All her life, she'd viewed him as strong, invincible. Now, his once vigorous body wasted, his razor-sharp mind dulled and increasingly forgetful, he was heartbreakingly pathetic.

"I know you wanted Cher." Leigh scooped the spilled food up and put it on the side of the plate. "But I got a call from Donna's agent last week and he told me that she's got a single on her new album that's really hot. In fact," she said, feeding him a bite of strained carrots, "it's titled 'Hot Stuff.' "

"Aater." Holding out a glass of water, she waited as he struggled to take a drink through the bent plastic straw. "I heard the song last night and it's going to be a big hit. If I'd only known about it a few months ago, we could have changed the name of the movie and used it for the title song. Also, Donna's first-lady-of-lust image certainly goes along with Marissa's role in the movie.

"So," Leigh said, patting his wet lips with a napkin, "I'm going to do my damndest to sign her." Ignoring Joshua's obvious irritation at the way she'd overrode his wishes, Leigh smiled encouragingly. "And now that we've dispensed with business, how about a little stroll around the room?"

She had hired round-the-clock nursing care and a therapist visited every day, putting Joshua through an intensive series of exercises to build strength back into his muscles. But he insisted that Leigh assist him in his effort to walk again.

Over these past months Leigh had begun to feel as if she was existing in two separate dimensions of time and space. During the day she divided her time between running Baron Studios and spending as much time as necessary with her father. But at night, after the large house grew quiet, she grieved for her fractured marriage. The nightmares, which she hadn't experienced for years, had returned with a vengeance, leaving her feeling exhausted, frightened, and ashamed.

Unsurprisingly, the columnists were having a field day with their separation. Rumors had Matthew sleeping with half the women in town, something that did not surprise Leigh. After all, she reasoned, he'd always been an intensely sexual man; she could not have expected him to remain celibate. Still, the rumors hurt. More than she ever would have thought possible.

Because the truth, as painful as it was to accept, was that she had not yet begun to get over Matthew. She wasn't certain she ever would.

36

July 1979

Matthew had not expected the divorce hearing to hurt so much. At least Leigh hadn't shown up; he wasn't sure he could have handled seeing her. He left the courthouse feeling a rare need for companionship. He drove to Tina and Corbett's house.

"How are you, dear?" Tina asked as she embraced him. Her sharp gaze took in the gaunt hollows under his cheeks, the bruised-looking patches under his eyes.

Matthew shrugged. "A little shell-shocked."

"Divorce is never easy," Corbett said knowingly. His first marriage had ended in a bitterly contested divorce. He'd met Tina while looking for some place to live after moving out of the Malibu Colony home he had shared with his wife of five years, a stunningly beautiful but manic-depressive actress. That painful experience had made him all the more determined to make this marriage work. "I know it's early, but you look like a man who could use a drink."

"I sure as hell wouldn't turn one down."

"So," Corbett said, handing him a glass of the bourbon he knew Matthew preferred on the rare occasions he drank hard liquor, "how's everything else going?"

"We begin shooting the outdoor scenes for *Unholy Matrimony* next week, if the weather holds in San Francisco."

Unholy Matrimony was a story about the disintegration of a marriage. Like all of Matthew's movies, the black comedy was intensely personal. Writing the screenplay had been cathartic; now he merely wanted to get it finished and in the can so he could get on with his life.

"You've been working awfully hard. Have you thought about taking a vacation after you wrap this one up?" Corbett asked.

"I don't need a vacation," Matthew said. "What I need is to go back to work and bring *The Eye of the Tiger* to the screen."

"That isn't going to be easy," Corbett pointed out. "In the first place, you're going to need Pentagon cooperation, and we both know they're not going to be enthusiastic about helping you make an antiwar movie."

"I can do it without the Pentagon," Matthew countered. "And it's not antiwar. It simply shows another side that the nightly news never revealed."

"Washington aside, there are a lot of people in the industry who don't want to see your movie made either."

"Since I've been having doors closed in my face all over town, that little fact sank in a long time ago."

"It's only 1979, Matthew. The war's only been over for four years; give people time to gain some perspective."

"I'll give them all the time they need. But once *Unholy Matrimony* wraps, I'm not going to let anything sidetrack me again. I've been working on this for more than a decade, Corbett. I refuse to give it up."

Corbett shrugged, knowing when he was licked. No wonder Matthew and Leigh's marriage had failed; he'd never met two more intransigent people.

"I certainly admire your fortitude, Matthew," Tina said with a smile. "Even if you are giving my husband ulcers."

The chiming of the doorbell forestalled Matthew's response. A moment later, the housekeeper appeared in the doorway with Leigh.

"Well, goodness." For a woman renowned for her ability to handle difficult situations, Tina was obviously flustered. "Leigh, darling. What a nice surprise!"

Leigh stood frozen to the spot, staring at Matthew, who looked unflinchingly back. "I had some papers for Corbett to sign. Allison Wainwright's contract." Was that soft, trembling voice really hers? Tearing her eyes from Matthew, she turned toward the agent. "I know how anxious Allison's been, so since your secretary said you were working at home this morning, I thought I'd drop them by."

Actually, Leigh had been depressed all morning by the thought of her marriage to Matthew being irrevocably severed. She'd come here seeking moral support, but Leigh was not prepared to reveal that little secret in front of the very man who'd deserted her. She watched Matthew turn his back on her and refill his glass. Bourbon? At eleven o'clock in the morning?

The atmosphere in the room turned as thick as winter fog. Corbett was the first to break the strained silence. "Thanks, Leigh. But you needn't have gone out of your way."

"I was in the neighborhood; it wasn't any trouble."

"Well, Allison will certainly appreciate your effort."

Another long, uncomfortable silence settled over them. "Gracious," Tina said suddenly, "I've forgotten my manners. Leigh, dear, have you had breakfast? Guadalupe made some marvelous blueberry muffins this morning, perhaps I could interest you in one. Or some coffee?"

"No, thank you, I've already eaten. Joshua refuses to do his exercises unless I have breakfast with him every morning before I leave for the studio." She'd been referring to her father by his given name ever since his stroke; although still irrevocably bound to him, she could no longer call him Daddy.

Hearing Joshua's name on Leigh's lips—lips he could still taste, after all this time—Matthew's eyes turned hard. "I've got to go. Thanks for the drink."

With that he was gone. Out of the house. Out of her life.

Back at her office, Leigh struggled to carry on while her soul was splintered. Determined never to be hurt by any man again, she vowed to direct her energies toward the single aspect of her life where she still maintained control—Baron Studios.

* * *

The walls were white and sterile. A white sink took up the corner of the room. The only furniture was a black swivel stool, an orange molded plastic chair, and a high, narrow hospital bed, covered with a clean sheet of white paper. Beside the bed was an aluminum tray upon which rested an assortment of stainless steel surgical instruments.

"Put this on," the nurse said, handing Marissa a muddy blue paper gown. The woman's expression was studiously remote, offering neither disapproval nor comfort. "The doctor will be with you as soon as he can, although I'm afraid he's running an hour or so behind schedule. It's been a hectic morning."

It wasn't exactly a banner day for her either, Marissa thought, undressing. Despite instructions to refrain from medication for twenty-four hours, she'd been popping Valium like Life Savers, but they could have been saccharine for all the good they were doing her.

It wasn't that she was all that upset about the abortion. Neither was she worried about the publicity; she'd used a false name and had arrived at the clinic wearing a long, straight brown wig, loose cotton top, and faded jeans that made her resemble all the other girls waiting nervously in the outer room. It was just that Marissa hated pain. Unless of course, that pain accompanied sex, which was precisely what had gotten her in this predicament in the first place.

Tossing her clothes onto the chair, she ran her hands over her still-flat stomach. Her breasts were unusually tender, but there were no visible signs of her pregnancy. Her eyes drifted to a calendar on the wall. July 25. The date rang a distant bell. Suddenly Marissa remembered that today was the day Leigh and Matthew's divorce was final.

An idea flashed through her mind. A thought so delicious that it caused goose bumps to rise on her bare flesh. There was so much to do. And so few hours in which to do it, Marissa considered, practically throwing on her faded top and jeans.

"I've changed my mind," she called out to the receptionist as she dashed out of the clinic. The woman, appearing accustomed to such behavior, merely shrugged and didn't bother to answer.

* * *

Matthew was alone in his penthouse suite at the Beverly Wilshire, methodically emptying a new bottle of Jack Daniel's and proceeding, for the first time in his life, to get roaring, disgustingly drunk. When he'd bought the bourbon that afternoon, the headline on the tabloid next to the cash register in the liquor store had screamed out at him: FAIRY-TALE MARRIAGE OF BEAUTIFUL BARON AND MAVERICK COMMONER REACHES FINAL FADE-OUT.

"Some fairy tale," he muttered, downing the liquor. The Eagles' "Heartache Tonight" prophetically came over the radio. Damn. The bottle was nearly empty. He'd have to call room service and have them send another one up. "A fractured fairy tale, maybe," he decided. "Written by the Brothers Grimm."

Perhaps he ought to have a woman sent up too, Matthew decided drunkenly. A tall blonde with big breasts and a willing eagerness to please. Despite the tabloid rumors to the contrary, he hadn't been with a woman since Leigh. Because the damnable truth of the matter was, as furious as he was with his ex-wife, he couldn't imagine making love to any other woman. He couldn't get Leigh out of his mind; it was as if her image had been imprinted on his lids, so that were he to close his eyes, he could still see her.

He was just about to dial the phone when there was a knock at the door. "That was fast." He opened the door to find Marissa clad in a filmy white dress that draped softly over her breasts. The dress was vaguely familiar; after a moment's consideration, Matthew remembered that he'd bought an identical one for Leigh for her last birthday. She was holding a bottle of vintage Krug.

"Hello, Matthew," she said, giving him a dazzling smile that showed all her straight white teeth. "I thought you could use some company."

"Even if I did, which I damn well don't, I sure as hell wouldn't send for you."

With a deftness that the most tenacious of vacuum salesmen would have envied, Marissa stuck her white high heel in the door, preventing him from closing her out. "Don't be so sure," she said silkily. "After all, brother-in-law, you and I have a great deal in common."

"That'll be the day. And as of this morning, I'm no longer

your brother-in-law. Good-bye, Marissa."

She glanced past him. "Do you have company?"

"Not yet."

"Good." Sidling past the half-closed door, she entered the darkened room. "Where are the glasses? I've never been good at this, but I think it's about . . . ah, here it goes." She nodded her approval when the cork popped with the retort of a rifle shot. Ignoring Matthew's blistering gaze, she poured the effervescent gold champagne into two stemmed glasses. "To freedom," she said, lifting one of the glasses in a toast.

Matthew shook his head wearily. "Marissa, I'm really not up to your antics tonight, I've had a long day and—"

"And you need a shoulder to cry on." She handed him a glass. She was standing very close to him, and Matthew could detect the painfully familiar scent of white roses that Leigh had always favored. "You're dead wrong about us not having anything in common, Matthew."

He took a long swallow of the icy champagne because the bourbon bottle was empty. "Name one thing."

"We've both been treated abominably by Leigh and Joshua. We both know the pain of betrayal."

"Leigh never betrayed me." He'd come to the reluctant conclusion that her own private sense of honor would not permit her to leave a helpless man, especially if that man was her father. The divorce was as much his fault as hers, he'd realized today while he sat in that courtroom, watching marriage after marriage disintegrate until it was his turn. He never should have issued such an impossible ultimatum.

"Don't tell me you didn't know?" she asked with feigned innocence.

"Know what?" Matthew refilled his glass, ignoring the froth of white foam that spilled over onto the carpeting.

"That Leigh blocked *The Eye of the Tiger*."

"That's not true." He was too startled to pretend not to be stricken by Marissa's information. He'd known that there was a conspiracy to keep his story from the screen, but never, in a million years, would he have ever suspected his own wife. Leigh had been completely supportive of the project. She'd told him so, hundreds of times. Thousands. "Leigh was behind me, all the way. It was the legal department's decision."

"At Leigh's instruction."

"I don't believe it."

"Perhaps this will clarify a few things." She reached into her white satin bag and took out a piece of paper. "It's a confidential memo William Zimmerman sent to Leigh, asking her to reconsider her decision to shelve *The Eye of the Tiger*."

The words blurred on the page as Matthew attempted to concentrate on their meaning. "Where the hell did you get this?"

She flashed him her deadly siren's smile. "I never reveal my sources. But it's not a forgery, if that's what you're thinking. In fact, you can ask Leigh yourself."

"I might just do that."

"Good. It really was to be expected, Matthew. Leigh would never go against Joshua. Not after all they've shared. Unfortunately for you—and your precious project—their relationship has always been a great deal more intimate than anyone would suspect."

"Now what the hell are you talking about?"

Her bright green eyes watched him with the clinical detachment of a physician about to pull the plug on a cancerous geriatric patient. "I'm talking about how many different ways there are for a father and daughter to love one another."

The all too obvious suggestion hung murderously in the air. Matthew reminded himself that Marissa had always been jealous of Leigh. For years she'd displayed an intense sibling rivalry that bordered on obsession. This was simply one more ugly example of Marissa's hatred for her sister.

"You're sick."

"Oh, one of the Baron sisters is sick, all right. But it isn't me." She dipped her finger into the champagne, then traced the outline of his rigidly set lips. "One night, when I was about nine, I heard my mother and father arguing. They were shouting, something that never happened in our proper, polite household. Being a naturally curious child, I sneaked downstairs. My father wanted a divorce to marry some slut of an actress he'd been screwing. It was then that Mother, understandably not eager to surrender her exalted position in Beverly Hills society as Mrs. Joshua Baron, threatened to reveal Daddy's little secret. The one about him fucking his own daughter." She gave him another sly, feline smile. "Believe me, Matthew, the daughter in question was not yours truly."

"Why should I believe anything you say? Besides, Leigh was a virgin."

Marissa laughed at that, a cold, cruel sound that ripped at his soul. "Goodness, you are naive, aren't you darling?" she purred, trailing her hand down his cheek. A muscle clenched under her fingertip. "Any girl can fake that; you've no idea how many times I've been a born-again virgin."

He wouldn't believe it. Despite his feelings about Leigh's defection, he had always considered her the single pure and beautiful thing in his life.

"Think about it," she suggested. "Think about all the times you've seen Joshua look at Leigh in a way that was anything but paternal. Remember how she ignored you every time Daddy crooked his little finger. And the way she stayed with him, even after she learned that he was the one who arranged for your arrest.

"Oh, yes," she said at his sharp glance, venom dripping from every word. "I know all about that too. I'm a clever girl, Matthew. I've had to be, you see, in order to survive. That's another thing we have in common." Her lips were but a whisper away from his; her breath fanned his face. The scent of white roses swirled in his head like an inhaled drug. "I make it a point to know everything about everyone, and I know that Leigh and her beloved daddy have been sleeping together for years."

Marissa taunted Matthew with intimate details of Joshua's sexual habits, Leigh's undaughterlike responses.

"What do you think they're doing now?" she asked. "locked away all alone together in that Beverly Hills mansion? What kind of physical therapy do you think your precious Leigh is giving Joshua, even as we speak?"

The devastating image of Leigh lying in her father's arms the very night their divorce became final was more than Matthew's alcohol-drugged mind could take. He struck out blindly, striking a woman for the first time in his life.

"Bitch!"

Marissa didn't hesitate to slap back. "Bastard!"

She began savagely attacking him, raking her fingernails

down his cheek, biting his hand when he tried to pull her away.

"Damn you," he growled, managing to jerk both her hands behind her back. Her champagne glass dropped to the carpet to lie unnoticed beside his. "Damn you to hell."

"You're just pissed because your precious wife liked fucking her own father better than you," Marissa shot back. Her shoulders ached, her ear was ringing from the force of his hand, and the murderous flame in his eyes was making her wet between the thighs. "What's the matter, Matthew, couldn't you make it in bed? Couldn't you get it up? Was that why Leigh ended up choosing Daddy?"

In response, he yanked her against him and Marissa experienced a surge of exhilaration like nothing she'd ever known She felt his tumescent penis against her belly. He'd freed her hands and she thrust her fingers into his hair, holding his head as she kissed him. A deep soul kiss that shattered the last of his self-control.

Her perfume confused him, even as his body, so long denied, reacted to her erotic, seductive movements. "Damn you," he said, dragging her roughly to the floor, "damn you for betraying me."

Marissa was like an animal in heat; moisture like warm honey flowed between her legs, every pore of her body painfully sensitized, like a thousand, a million, hungry little mouths. Yanking down the zipper of his pants, she clutched at him, pressing her palm against his groin.

Matthew shoved up her white chiffon skirt and pushed her legs apart. The lips of her vagina were darkly pink and glisteningly wet. He loved the taste of Leigh—a warm, seashell taste that had always reminded him of that first time they'd made love at the beach. He loved the softness of her public curls, like silver silk against his lips. But Joshua had been there before him. Touching. Taking.

"Goddamnit, I trusted you," he panted. "You're the only one." When he surged into her, Marissa cried out in victory and lifted her hips off the carpet to meet his angry thrusts. "The only one."

He pounded into her responsive body and, when he exploded in a violent and joyless climax, all Matthew could think about was punishing Leigh.

37

Joshua Baron was dead.

Newsweek called it "the passing of an era." *Time*'s cover story was "The king is dead." The *Hollywood Reporter*, proclaiming that "Baron Studios has lost its crown prince," ran a photograph of Marissa flinging herself atop the flower-draped coffin. The photo was picked up by the wire services and circulated around the world, which had been Marissa's intention when she'd thought up the dramatic stunt. Everyone who even aspired to be someone had shown up at the funeral, which was, *Variety* reported, "the media event of the year."

Father Timothy O'Bannion had to shout over the hovering helicopters. "Earth to earth, ashes to ashes, dust to dust; in sure and certain hope of the Resurrection unto eternal life."

He sprinkled holy water from a gold censor onto the gleaming ebony coffin. The sun glancing off the white marble angel standing eternal guard over Signe Baron momentarily

blinded Leigh when she stepped forward to accept the handful of earth the priest extended her.

Keeping her eyes directed straight ahead, Leigh sprinkled
the dirt into the grave. She flinched when she heard the small
clods hitting her father's casket. The sweet scent of hothouse
flowers nauseated her.

She'd been expecting this day for months, but Leigh was
still benumbed with shock. During the mass for the Dead, the
priest's words droned in her ear, as incomprehensible as the
humming of a swarm of angry bees. A soft chorus of *Amens*
signaled the conclusion of the graveside services. Leigh
barely heard the condolences offered her.

"Leigh." Corbett touched her arm. "The limo's waiting."

She looked around, surprised to see that everyone but
Tina, Corbett, and Kim had drifted away. Marissa was already
in the limousine, reportedly attempting to compose herself.
"I'd like a moment alone, if you don't mind."

"Of course," Tina said. "We'll wait for you in the car."

Leigh looked down at the coffin for a long, thoughtful time.
"I want to forgive you," she whispered. "There have even
been times when I think that I have." She drew in a long,
shuddering breath. "The problem is, I'm not sure that I'll
ever be able to forgive myself." Her head bowed by a combination of pain and guilt, Leigh turned away.

Matthew stood alone on a hillside, overlooking Joshua's
Forest Lawn burial site. He could see the slender, grieving
woman dressed in unrelieved black, and he felt as if there was
a dark hole where his heart used to be.

Marissa was on her feet, her cheeks flushed. "What the fuck
do you mean, I don't get any part of Baron Studios? Whether
the prick bastard liked it or not, I was his daughter. I deserve
half!"

Ira Friedman, Joshua's attorney, winced at Marissa's vocab-
ulary. It was two days after the funeral and he'd been working
overtime preparing for the reading of Joshua's will.

"Joshua left a letter explaining all that. A letter he asked
that I read to everyone assembled here today."

"This had damn well better be good," Marissa said, flinging
herself back down in the chair.

A stunned hush fell over the room after Friedman had read the brief letter in which Joshua revealed that he'd been in Greece when his wife had gotten pregnant with her second child. Signe had refused to reveal the name of Marissa's natural father. She had also admitted Joshua's lack of paternity from the beginning.

" 'And since I have generously given the girl known as Marissa Baron my name,' " Friedman concluded, " 'as well as providing her with a gracious upbringing and generous income, I feel I have dispatched any moral obligation I may have toward my wife's daughter. Therefore, in accordance with the agreement made with my wife, and witnessed by my attorney, Marissa Baron is not entitled to any further monies or property from my estate.' " He frowned as he folded the paper. "I'm sorry, Ms. Baron."

"Oh, you'll be sorry all right," Marissa exploded. "You'll all be sorry!"

Hating Joshua for striking back at her from beyond the grave, Marissa escaped the room, slamming the door behind her.

"I can't believe it." Leigh sat stunned, staring down at the papers Ira Friedman handed her. "Not only is Marissa not Joshua's daughter, now you're telling me that Brendan Farraday owns twenty-four percent of Baron Studios? But it's always been privately owned."

"It was owned by your father, who had authority to do anything he wanted with it. And apparently," Friedman said, "he gave twenty-four percent of it to Farraday as collateral."

All the little pieces of her father's strange behavior concerning Baron Studios' finances over the past years suddenly fell into place. There had been times when Leigh paced the floor for nights on end, worried that they'd be forced to declare bankruptcy. Each time, Joshua had shown up in the nick of time, just like the cavalry in those Westerns Baron Studios had made in the 1950s. Now that she knew where the money had come from, the image of Brendan Farraday wearing a white hat didn't fit.

"And how much did you say Kate Farrell owns?"

"Three percent."

"I hadn't realized she was still alive," Leigh murmured, trying to recall what she knew about the former actress.

Fifty years earlier, Kate Farrell had been a major star. Exuding sex from every pore, she had been able to suggest an amazing range of emotions with merely an arched eyebrow or pursed lips. Walter Baron had discovered her playing the piano in the sheet music department at Newberry's, recognized a gold mine when he saw one, and immediately signed her to a long-term contract with Baron Studios. Playing opposite such dissimilar talents as Valentino and Charlie Chaplin, her star took off like a blazing comet when the studio's publicity department blithely changed the birthplace on her biography from Maine to Georgia and began calling her the Vamp of Savannah.

By 1920 Baron Studios was paying her more than three thousand dollars per week, a mind-boggling salary for the time. That was one reason, many Hollywood wags suggested, that Walter proposed; always desperate for money to keep the studio afloat, by marrying his biggest star he kept her salary in the family.

Despite unequaled success in business, Kate and Walter found marriage a more difficult partnership. They divorced at the height of her success and, when the studio head could not afford the cash settlement her lawyers were demanding, a deal was cut for a percentage of the studio, where Kate continued to work to rave audience reviews.

Then, on October 6, 1927, Kate's star came crashing down to earth. In a Broadway theater, two thousand miles from where Kate was miming the part of Anna Karenina on a Baron Studios' sound stage, audiences were watching Al Jolson in *The Jazz Singer* and liking what they heard. The immediate success of that first talkie marked the end of an era. Kate's crisp New England accent was not only unsuited for a vamp from Savannah, Georgia, but her voice was too high to survive the temperamental performance of the early microphones. She retired, becoming more and more reclusive as she grew older.

"So," Leigh mused, "with Farraday owning twenty-four percent and Kate Farrell owning three, that leaves me with seventy-three percent."

"A majority," Friedman agreed.

Neither mentioned Marissa, despite the fact that her lingering fury settled over the room like a dark, wet blanket.

"God, Kate Farrell," Kim exclaimed. "I thought she was dead." It was a week after the lawyer's bombshell and, concerned about the weight Leigh had lost, Kim had invited her to dinner.

Leigh shrugged, pushing the untouched stir-fry around on her plate. "So did I. No one has seen her for years. I checked with accounting; they've been sending quarterly checks to her San Francisco attorneys."

"Then she must live in the Bay area. Unless she really is dead and her lawyers have been forging her name and cashing her checks. Hey," Kim insisted, as Leigh laughed, for the first time in months, "it's not that incredible. Why, just the other day, I was getting my hair done and heard the most amazing story about the lawyers who handled the Benny Todd estate . . . You know, that ninety-year-old character actor who married the sixteen-year-old daughter of his live-in nurse? Well, anyway . . ."

As Kim shared the outrageous, juicy piece of gossip, Leigh felt the chains that had been wrapped around her heart loosen ever so slightly. It was going to be all right. She was going to be all right.

Brendan Farraday sat by his pool, idly leafing through his mail. One letter in particular caught his attention. It was from Mark Longworth, the son of Reece Longworth, Signe Baron's attorney. The lawyer had died of a heart attack last month.

In the letter, the younger Longworth explained that while cleaning out his father's files, he had discovered a sealed envelope, along with a letter to Reece, instructing the attorney to forward the envelope to Brendan Farraday in the event of Signe Baron's death. Longworth had no idea why Signe's instructions had not been carried out and he felt obliged to deliver the letter to its rightful owner.

When he opened the enclosed envelope, a thousand memories flooded over Farraday. He'd met Signe at one of

Rocco Minetti's parties, and although he knew that the crime boss had slept with Joshua Baron's wife, he hadn't been able to understand the attraction. Until Signe practically attacked him on the floor of Rocco's sybaritic bathroom. Stunned to discover such unbridled passion lurking beneath that cool, elegant exterior, Brendan was hooked. Their affair had been one of reckless danger: they made love in her pink-and-gilt bathroom while one of Baron's famous parties was going on downstairs, in her Silver Cloud Rolls-Royce parked on Mulholland Drive, on the black leather couch in his dressing room at Baron Studios. It had been a period of insanity and, if he had been, as Signe had often claimed, like a drug flowing through her veins, he had been no less addicted. Time after time they'd break the affair off, only to come together again with a force more powerful than before.

Farraday's blood turned cold when he read the letter. He read it again. And again. But the faded lavender cursive handwriting never changed. Marissa was not Joshua Baron's daughter, but his. Farraday felt no stirrings of belated parental emotion, but he did realize that fate had just dealt him an extremely valuable card. Now all he had to do was figure out how—and when—to play it.

Who was he, the man who had fathered her, then abandoned her without so much as a backward glance? Was he someone in the industry? An actor, a director, perhaps even an agent? Did she know him? Did he know he had a daughter? Did he know that *she* was his daughter?

Part of Marissa was glad that she wasn't Joshua Baron's child. She'd hated the man all of her life, it should have come as a relief that she shared none of the bastard's blood. But then she thought of Leigh. And how, by an accident of birth, her sister had just been handed a multibillion-dollar business.

While she had received absolutely nothing. Nada. Zip.

Marissa stood in front of her dressing room mirror, glared into her own glitteringly furious eyes, and swore revenge.

38

"You have got to be crazy!"

Tina stared at Leigh as if she'd just grown a second head. It had only been three weeks since Joshua's death and, although Leigh seemed to be holding up well enough, this latest idea indicated that perhaps she was still in a state of shock.

"This is something I have to do," Leigh insisted.

They were in the foyer of the Beverly Hills estate, clipboards in hand as they took inventory of the furnishings. When she'd first decided to sell the home she'd grown up in, Leigh had expected to feel a pang of loss. Instead, whenever she looked at Tina's blue-and-gold sign on the rolling expanse of green lawn, she only felt relief.

Perhaps, by getting rid of the house that had harbored her secret sin for so many years, she could free herself from the demons torturing her mind on an almost nightly basis.

"You'll be making one of the biggest mistakes of your life

if you hand over that stock to Marissa," Tina warned.

"That's what Ira Friedman said." Leigh picked up a Sèvres vase. "What do you think? Storage? Or shall I throw it in with the stuff that stays?"

"Storage; it's too valuable to give away. And getting back to what we were discussing before you changed the subject, although I usually dislike lawyers on principle, Ira Friedman makes sense. Honey, I understand how you could feel some guilt about inheriting the studio, but it's not exactly as if Marissa were starving. She's making a fortune, as you well know, since she's making most of her pictures for Baron Studios."

"I know." Leigh sighed. "It's just that she missed so much. When she was a little girl, she would practically do cartwheels every time Joshua came home, trying unsuccessfully to get his attention. While I didn't have to do a thing."

"That's not exactly true," Tina felt obliged to point out. "You were a model daughter: bright, cheerful, hard-working, reliable . . ."

Sexually available, Leigh tacked on mentally, feeling the now familiar cloud of guilt settle back over her. What would Tina say if she knew the truth? "You're making me sound like a Girl Scout," she protested softly. "The point I'm trying to make is that Marissa has been looking for love her entire life and always ends up getting her teeth kicked in. I want to try and make it up to her. Besides, now that Joshua's no longer alive to come between us, there's an outside chance that Marissa and I might finally become friends."

"Well, I still think that you're making an enormous mistake," Tina said. "But it's your life. And your studio."

Leigh had spent a lifetime overlooking the obvious signs of her younger sister's malevolence and Tina knew that nothing she could say now would make one iota's difference. It was just too bad, the older woman considered. She resumed taking inventory, wishing that Signe had run off with Marissa's father, whoever he was, before the girl was born. That way everyone would have been spared a great deal of grief.

"Until death we do part." Matthew uttered his wedding vows with all the enthusiasm of a condemned man on the way to the gallows. Which was exactly how he viewed his situation.

He'd been stunned when Marissa had shown up at his suite at the Wilshire with the news that she was pregnant. The first time in his life he'd foregone protection and, here he was, months away from fatherhood.

He spent a long and sleepless night remembering his own tortured past, the childish taunts and jeers that had been the legacy of his illegitimacy. Unable to allow his child to grow up with such a stigma, Matthew had reluctantly agreed to marriage. It was, he told himself, his only choice.

Matthew lay on his back beside his new wife in their Reno hotel room, trying his damnedest to avoid touching her, and wished that it was Leigh who was having his baby.

Leigh couldn't have avoided the picture of Matthew and Marissa leaving the Reno chapel if she'd wanted to. Turning on the television midway through the evening newscast, expecting to view the reassuring presence of Walter Cronkite in his anchor seat, Leigh was stricken when instead, her sister and ex-husband's wedding picture flashed onto the screen. The scene caused a flashback in her mind. A flashback of another wedding photograph. That earlier picture had been a fake; this one, unfortunately, was all too real.

Why hadn't Marissa said anything? Leigh had called her two days ago with the news that she was giving her a significant block—twenty-five percent—of Baron Studios stock. At the time, Marissa had sounded ecstatic, reminding Leigh of the times she'd given in to Marissa's insatiable appetite for anything and everything belonging to her sister.

When Marissa was six, she'd stolen a stuffed tiger from atop Leigh's bed; at eleven, it had been a tube of lipstick and a crystal atomizer filled with Miss Dior. By her thirteenth birthday, she'd graduated to "borrowing" clothes; at fifteen with only her driver's permit, she'd taken some friends for a spin in Leigh's Jaguar. It had taken twenty-five hundred dollars and three weeks to put the car back in running condition after the accident.

Leigh had always overlooked Marissa's transgressions. But how could she overlook her own sister stealing the only man she'd ever loved?

* * *

Matthew stood in middle of the room, glaring down at Marissa, who was sprawled on the bed. A half-empty bottle of white rum sat on the bedside table beside a lipstick-stained glass. She was dressed in the black satin nightgown she'd been wearing when he left this morning for his meeting with his banker. After the meeting, he'd had lunch with Tina and Corbett, then attended a meeting of neighbors trying to protect the beach from encroaching development.

"What the hell do I have to do? Lock you up and post a guard at the door?"

Marissa glared back. "If you were ever home, perhaps I wouldn't have to drink. You've been ignoring me since the day we got married."

"I haven't been ignoring you," Matthew insisted. "I've been trying to get my movie produced."

"While I go crazy sitting around here with nothing to do all day."

He'd tried to make the best of a bad situation. After returning from Reno, Matthew was determined that he would not make the same mistakes with his child that Joshua had made with Marissa. He would not be a father in name only. He wanted the baby to feel from the very beginning that he had been born into a real family. Something both he and Marissa had missed.

With that in mind, Matthew had tried to treat Marissa with, if not passion, at least respect. Unfortunately, his wife's unceasing quest for attention reminded Matthew of trying to capture the tiny beads of mercury that spilled out of a broken thermometer. Just when you thought you had them, they slipped out of reach. Little by little, he had begun to discover that life with such an egocentric woman was a marriage made in hell.

"The doctor told you that you're not supposed to drink." He poured the rum down the drain in the adjoining bathroom.

"Hey, I just bought that bottle."

"It's not good for the baby."

"The baby, the baby," Marissa taunted. "Christ, that's all I ever hear. Why don't you quit thinking about this damn kid for a change and think about me?" She watched him take a clean shirt out of the dresser drawer. "Now what are you doing?"

"I've got to go out. I only came home to see how you were and to change clothes."

"Where are you going?"

"I have a meeting; I'll be at the Wilshire if you need me."

"You always say you're at a meeting. But you're really sleeping with Leigh again, aren't you?"

"Don't be ridiculous. I haven't seen your sister in months."

"Half-sister," she corrected bitterly. "And if you leave now, you won't hear my big surprise."

"What's that?" He glanced at his watch. If he didn't leave soon, he was going to be late.

"I've got a new role in a romantic suspense," Marissa said with a broad, excited smile. "It's called *Dangerous Passions* and I play a librarian who gets involved in a spy caper. I get beaten up and nearly raped by the villain, chased by the CIA, and ravished throughout the entire movie by the hero. Christopher Burke is directing."

"Well, that should certainly give you an incentive to get back on your feet after the baby's born." Matthew experienced a fleeting stab of pity for Marissa. How would he like it if he couldn't work for months? How would he feel if he was forced to sit around the house and watch soap operas and television game shows all day? He would, he answered himself with brutal honesty, go start raving mad.

"Not after," she corrected. "Before. We begin filming next week. It's going to be a real blast: Venice, Rome, Paris, Milan, Sri Lanka—"

"Wait a goddamn minute." He stopped in his selection of ties. "You can't make this movie. Not now."

"Why not?"

"Shit, Marissa, in case you've forgotten, you're pregnant. You can't be traipsing all over the world. Especially with Burke, who considers a movie some kind of damn Iron Man competition. If nothing else, how sexy do you think you'll look, running around Rome in a maternity dress?"

"Burke's already thought of that; the costume designer is working on a corset that'll hide everything."

"What about rest? Location shooting is rough enough, but

this one sounds like an absolute nightmare."

"You're not going to stop me from making this movie, Matthew. Besides," she said dangerously, "think what fun you and my slut sister can have with me out of town."

That did it. "I told you," he said as he took off his old shirt and put on the new, "I haven't seen Leigh in months. I haven't thought about her in months."

"If I believed that," Marissa said, "you and I just might have something to discuss. But we both know that while I'm here alone tonight watching Barry James on television, you're going to be fucking Leigh's brains out."

"Christ, you are really sick. Don't bother to wait up; I'll be late."

"So what else is new?" she screamed after him. She waited until she heard his car pull out of the driveway. Then she picked up the telephone. "He's gone," she purred into the mouthpiece. "Hurry over. Oh, and bring some rum. I seem to have run out."

Matthew sat in the restaurant across from the man who held his future in his hands. "I'm sorry to be late," he apologized to his dinner companion. "A little family matter." He forced a grin he was a long way from feeling. "You know how pregnant women are."

Khalil Al-Tajir studied this man who had, for so many years, held claim to Leigh's heart. "Never having been a father-to-be, I'm afraid that I wouldn't know firsthand, although I have heard tales of mood swings and strange cravings."

"That's part of it."

"Excuse my curiosity, but were you not once married to your wife's sister? The lovely Leigh Baron."

Even her name could cause his heart to lurch. "Yes, Leigh and I were married."

Khalil gave him a long, unfathomable look. "Some men are doubly blessed," he said finally. "Now, tell me about this screenplay of yours, *The Eye of the Tiger*. I hear it is quite controversial."

"Oh, God, that was good." Marissa was panting and her skin glistened with a faint sheen of perspiration. The bedroom exuded a feral smell of wanton sex.

"You're not so bad, yourself. For an old pregnant lady," Jeff said, taking her hard brown nipple between his teeth. When he bit her, hard, Marissa yelped.

Jeff wondered how Matthew would react if he knew he was balling his wife. Since his acting career had stalled before it ever got off the ground, Jeff relished this personal triumph over his former buddy, who'd reached such an enviable pinnacle of success. Perhaps next time he ought to bring his Polaroid, he considered. Take a few candids for Matthew to put in the family album.

"New game," he decided, leaving the bed long enough to take four silk Hermès scarves from her drawer. In a flash, he'd tied her, spread-eagle, on her stomach. "You're a beautiful slave girl," he said, "captured in the Spice Islands." He retrieved his leather belt from a nearby chair and whipped her once across the buttocks.

"Ow!"

"Shut up, wench. I am the captain of this slave ship," he said, running his fingers over the red welt. "Every trip I select one woman to train into the proper ways of servitude." His hands, as they caressed her stinging flesh, were making her ache.

"I'll never submit," she said, getting into the spirit of this latest game. "I'd rather die."

"Now that would be a real waste of good pussy." He snapped the belt again, this time across the top of her thighs, and Marissa felt a delicious tingling between her legs. "No, I think we'll just break you in nice and slow."

As she wiggled beneath him, pretending to resist, Marissa hoped that her husband would stay gone for a very long time.

Sri Lanka was a world apart, a land of ancient mysteries. Ancient Arab mariners knew the teardrop island off the coast of India as Serendip, and an eighteenth-century British writer, describing it as a world of unexpected delights, coined the word "serendipity." To the Chinese, Sri Lanka was known as the Island of Gems, referring to its natural abundance of gemstones; rubies, cat's-eyes, sapphires the size of wrens' eggs. In Hindu epic, the name meant Resplendent Land.

A mystical island shrouded in blue-gray mist and antiquities, it was a place of scenic glories and ancient buried cities, home to beautiful, sari-draped women and saffron-robed monks. But to Marissa, the country formerly known as Ceylon was monsoons, a nearly impenetrable tangle of vines, sweltering shade, leeches, and the rank, unrelenting smell of decay as fallen limbs and dead trees rotted moistly underfoot.

She had been riding atop one of the country's ubiquitous elephants for hours, while Christopher Burke, demonstrating his typical perfectionism, struggled to capture the scene in all its glory before losing the day's light. Her dress, designed to conceal her pregnancy, had enough boning to qualify as heavy armor. She'd been suffering from cramps all morning and even the fresh coconut milk that their native guide had assured her would settle her distressed stomach had not helped.

It was late afternoon, and she'd been atop the beast for hours, when Marissa felt something warm and wet on the inside of her thigh. Lifting her skirt, she saw the dark red stain slowly oozing down her leg.

"Oh, my God," she cried out, her voice laced with panic. "I'm going to bleed to death in this fucking jungle!"

"I'm sorry." Matthew stood in the doorway, his expression as bleak as she'd ever seen it.

She'd been rushed by Land Rover to the capital city of Colombo, but Marissa could remember little of the trip. "You warned me the movie would be too much of a strain. So now you get to say I told you so. You should be feeling real smug."

Funny how the death of a child changed so many things. Matthew hadn't suddenly fallen in love with his wife when he'd heard about her miscarriage, yet he did regret the loss of a life they'd created together. And as furious as he was at Marissa for putting their unborn baby at risk, he also felt an unexpected surge of pity for what she'd been through.

He crossed the hospital room to stand beside the bed. Instincts older than time made him brush her damp hair from her forehead. "Smug is hardly the word," he said quietly. "How are you?"

"Sore as hell. When are they letting me out of this fucking place?"

"In a couple of days. You've experienced a lot of bleeding; the doctor wants to keep an eye on you."

Marissa cringed as she saw a gecko climbing the wall, searching out insects. "I hate it here. I want to go home. Now."

Her voice held an edge of hysteria. Matthew reminded himself that she'd been through a harrowing experience and deserved careful handling. "I can't see anything wrong with moving you to the hotel," he decided. "We can hire a nurse to stay with you until you're strong enough to travel."

"It sure as hell won't be soon enough."

"I spoke with Leigh as soon as I got Burke's call. She's chartering a plane to take you back to Los Angeles."

A familiar jealousy reared its ugly green head. "Interesting how Leigh was the first person you called."

Matthew recognized the tone immediately. It was the low, distant rumbling sound a volcano makes shortly before it erupts. "You're making this movie for Baron Studios; Leigh's head of the studio."

"How kind of you to remind me of that," Marissa snapped. "Let's also not forget how she wormed her way into those executive offices—by fucking her father."

Instead of feeling the shaft of pain her words had once caused, Matthew merely exhaled a weary sigh. This scene was so familiar he could act it out in his sleep. Marissa was on a tear and he decided that it definitely said something about her recuperative powers that she could suffer a dangerous miscarriage in the middle of a jungle and still muster up enough energy for a temper tantrum.

"Let's not get into that again," he suggested mildly. "You need your rest."

"What I need is to get even with that slut once and for all!" Marissa stormed, her beautiful face twisted with hatred. "I thought I'd done that when I took you away from her, but no, the minute I'm out of town, you two are back in bed together, laughing at me."

"That's ridiculous. In the first place, you didn't take anyone away from anybody. Leigh and I were divorced when you and I got married."

"But you loved her. Didn't you, Matthew? In spite of everything, in spite of her choosing to stay with your worst enemy, you couldn't get her out of your mind. Don't you think I knew that?'' she snarled. "Why the hell do you think I bought a dress just like hers and wore her perfume the night your divorce was final? Because I knew that what you wanted most in the world was to fuck my sister. And what you wanted second most was to punish her for her dirty little secret. So I simply obliged you. On both counts.''

He'd suspected as much for a long time, but his self-esteem hadn't wanted to admit that he could have been so easily manipulated. "I think it's time for me to go.''

"Back to Leigh?''

"No. Back to my own life. Where I used to maintain some semblance of control.''

He was walking away from her. Just like all the others. Just like her natural father, who hadn't even stuck around long enough for her to know his identity.

"Go ahead and leave,'' she shrieked after him. "But there's one more thing you need to know. That wasn't even your baby they tossed out in the trash this morning. It was Jeff Martin's. I was pregnant that night you raped me, Matthew. And I've been sleeping with Jeff every chance I could get since we got married. So what do you think of that?''

Matthew turned, his steady dark eyes those of a stranger. "I think,'' he said quietly, "that you and Martin are a match made in hell. And I'm sure you'll both make each other miserable, a state of mind which you, in particular, seem to enjoy. Good-bye, Marissa. It's been . . . interesting.''

He walked out the door. When Marissa's water glass shattered against the doorframe, inches from his head, Matthew didn't bother to look back.

BOOK THREE

January 1981

39

Marissa read the listing of Academy Award nominations in the morning *Variety* and grew increasingly furious. As usual, Leigh and Matthew's names topped the list. It wasn't fair that their lives were going so well when hers was falling apart.

Marissa had carefully cultivated her resentment toward Leigh, feeding it regular doses of hatred and jealousy. She had thought that she'd ruin her sister's life by taking Matthew away from her, but Leigh seemed to thrive on running Baron Studios, which just went to show what a heartless bitch she really was. Only last week, she'd pulled Marissa off a movie, accusing her of being irresponsible and uncooperative. It wasn't enough that Leigh owned Baron Studios, she'd seen to it that her sister couldn't even work there.

And if that weren't enough, she'd actually had the nerve to suggest that Marissa enter a drug rehab program. Marissa hadn't been fooled by Leigh's phony concern; it was obvious that she just wanted to lock her away so that people would forget any other Baron sister had ever existed.

Marissa thought back to her sister's cool, collected attitude when she informed her that she was being replaced; anger curled through her like dark smoke.

"You made a big mistake, sister dear," she murmured, reaching for the pretty white stuff that always made her feel better. "One you're going to regret the rest of your life."

Leigh hadn't wanted to attend Christopher Burke's party to celebrate *Dangerous Passion*'s five Oscar nominations (Best Director, Best Cinematography, Best Original Screenplay, Best Actor, and Best Picture), but as head of Baron Studios, she knew she should at least put in an appearance.

Fortunately, Khalil telephoned with the happy news that he was planning to be in L.A. on business and would like to see her. When Leigh invited him to escort her to the party, Khalil had immediately accepted.

Burke's Malibu beach house overflowed with good cheer, fine wine, and congratulations. The guest list was strictly A, all the movers and shakers in the industry gathered to honor one of their own. By entertainment standards, Leigh supposed the party was a success—the rooms were too crowded to escape talking to everyone, the noise level too loud to hear what anyone was saying. When she couldn't listen to another word, when she'd had her fill of stuffed mushrooms, when the scent of cigarette smoke and perfume made her head ache, Leigh decided to go down to the beach for some fresh air.

"Can you believe all these people!" Jill Cocheran shouted over the din. The DJ hired for the evening had just put Eddie Rabbitt's "I Love a Rainy Night" on the turntable, while nearby a crowd gathered around the large-screen television to watch the arrival home of the American hostages after four hundred and forty-four days of captivity in Iran. "Ah feel like an itty-bitty sardine, stuffed into one of those funny flat cans. All we need is some oil to make things more interesting."

"Remind me to stop at a Ralph's on the way home," Matthew said. "We'll pick some up and make our own party."

"Matthew St. James!" She slapped his arm playfully. "Just when I begin to think you're the biggest stick-in-the-mud God ever put down on this green earth, you turn right around and surprise me." Jill smiled up at him. She was dressed like a lady pirate in a white satin blouse with billowy sleeves and black velvet knickers. A crimson sash was wrapped around her waist and enormous gold loops dangled from her earlobes. "Ah suppose that's why Ah allow you to drift in and out of my life, without ever stopping long enough to put down roots."

"I tried that once. It didn't work." He looked at her curiously. "Besides, since when did you want to settle down?"

"Ah don't, really. But Ah have to tell you, Matthew, if you ever got a hankering to get serious, Ah might just change my mind." When he looked concerned, she threw back her head and laughed. "Lordy, you shouldn't take a girl so literally. Go mingle, Matthew, before one of us says something we'll regret in the morning." Smiling at him, she melded into the crowd.

The glittery, gossipy gathering was the first time he'd been out on the town since his divorce from Marissa. Maybe Jill was right, maybe he was a stick-in-the-mud. Worse yet, perhaps he was getting old.

Now there was a depressing thought.

Ten minutes after his arrival, Matthew had already had enough. Since Jill seemed to be having the time of her life, boisterously lip-syncing "Nine to Five" to the delight of the guests gathered around her, he decided to take a solitary stroll on the beach.

Leigh saw him coming toward her. Telling herself that it was just a coincidence, that he hadn't followed her out to the beach, she leveled her eyes at Matthew and took a deep breath.

"Hello, Matthew."

"Leigh."

Standing beside the water, the moonlight tangled in her silvery hair, she was more beautiful than ever. But too thin, he thought, measuring her slender frame with a practiced eye. He'd explored every inch of her body, he knew it intimately. There were too many nights, even after all these years, that seductive visions of it infiltrated his sleep.

"I came out for a breath of fresh air," she said. "It was getting rather crowded."

"A typical Leigh Baron understatement." His tone softened his accusation.

The initial pain of seeing him passed. "I'm surprised to see you here, Matthew. This isn't exactly your type of party."

"I came with a friend. Jill Cocheran." Aching to touch her, he stuck his hands in his pockets and rocked back and forth on the balls of his feet.

"Ah." Leigh nodded. "The photographer who made your chest world famous."

A little pool of silence settled over them.

"Khalil says he's thinking of investing in *The Eye of the Tiger*," she said finally. She hadn't been surprised when Khalil had given up his cultural ministry position and established a syndicate to finance motion pictures. His interest in all aspects of the movie business had been more than obvious that long-ago summer he'd served as Abu Dhabi's liaison during the shooting of *Arabian Nights*.

William Zimmerman's memo to Leigh about rejecting his screenplay flashed through Matthew's mind. "That's right. It's taken a couple years of negotiations, but it looks as if we're finally on the verge of putting a package together. Now all we have to do is find a studio."

"I'm pleased things are working out for you."

"Are you?"

Leigh flinched at his cold tone as if he'd struck her. What did he know? "Of course."

He wanted to ask her why she'd blocked his project. Instead, he succumbed to temptation and reached out, brushing away the errant strands of hair the sea breeze had blown against her cheek.

"I've always liked your hair down."

Leigh swallowed. "I know."

"You were wearing it down that first night too." His hand moved down the side of her face.

"You've an excellent memory."

"You're a difficult woman to forget, Leigh. I know because I've tried."

"Matthew—"

"I remember thinking that you had the face of a Botticelli angel. I'd never seen a woman as beautiful—or as dangerous—as you."

"Dangerous?"

He wanted her so much at that moment that he experienced

a surge of anger at his lack of control. After all these years, after two painful separations, you'd think he would have learned his lesson where this woman was concerned. "Dangerous," he repeated. "Actually, a siren came to mind."

"Considering that sirens are infamous for luring men to their deaths, that's not a very complimentary description."

"Perhaps not." His gut twisted at the memory of her betrayal and he felt a dark sense of devastation that anyone so lovely could be so treacherous. Marissa's machinations, at least, had been blatantly obvious, so long as he'd remained sober enough to avoid her snares. Too many of Leigh's thoughts remained hidden. "But my feelings for you always seemed to prove fatal, in the end."

If he had struck her, it would have been less painful. Leigh let out a shuddering breath. She'd no idea he harbored such resentment. "I'm sorry you feel that way," she said, wrapping herself in her protective cloak of self-restraint. "Perhaps you should leave now, before you fall prey to my fatal attraction."

He could feel the steel curtain drop between them and Matthew realized he'd struck a nerve. When would they stop hurting each other? he wondered bleakly. When would they let go? "Oh, hell, I'm the one who's sorry. Come here." Putting his arm around her, Matthew drew her to him, feeling her familiar shape against his.

Leigh put her head on his shoulder and basked in the solid strength that had always been both comforting and exciting at the same time. "Why?"

Her mouth muffled against his jacket, he barely heard her. But he knew what she was thinking. Because the same painful thoughts were tumbling around in his own mind. He brushed her hair aside and pressed his lips against her fragrant neck. "Why couldn't we make it work?" he asked softly. "Or why can't we stay away from one another?"

She tilted her head back to look up at him. In the streaming silver moonlight, her lashes were tangled and wet. "Both."

A single tear glistened on her cheek like a diamond; he brushed it away. Matthew felt her heart thudding against his, felt her tremors, and he, a man who never gave in to impulse, lowered his mouth to hers.

Leigh moaned, feeling a shock like a seismic jolt shoot

through her. Wrapping her arms around his waist, she surrendered to the feel of his tongue sweeping her mouth.

"Christ, how I want you," he said, kissing her cheeks, her chin, her temple. Her face and lips tasted like tears. "I've wanted you from the first minute I saw you." His hands slipped beneath her royal blue velvet jacket, pushing aside the draped neckline of her dress to caress her breasts. Her engorged breasts filled his hands, his stroking fingers made her nipples tingle with anticipation. "Come home with me, Leigh. It used to make me crazy, thinking about the past, about you and Joshua, but being without you is worse." Matthew's words slashed through the passion clouding her mind.

"What are you talking about?"

"I know." Her warm flesh was like liquid satin, her scent alone was enough to make him hard, and the taste of her lips threatened to drive him over the edge. "About you and your father. But I can understand how it happened: in the beginning you were a child, he forced you. Later, you were afraid to reject him."

"You have it all wrong." Leigh backed away, nearly stumbling in the soft sand. "It wasn't like that . . . Oh, my God."

The shame of anyone—but especially this man whom she'd loved for so many years—knowing her sin was too much to bear. Emotions she'd kept safely locked away since that afternoon she'd remembered her father's betrayal came flooding back over her in waves. Sinking to her knees, she covered her mouth with her hands and began rocking back and forth. An eerie keening sound came from between her fingers.

"Shit, Leigh, I'm sorry." Squatting down beside her, Matthew tried to pry her fingers away, but his efforts only succeeded in intensifying her crying.

"Go away, Matthew. I don't ever want to see you again."

"That's going to be a little difficult. With both of us working in the same business. In the same town."

"Would you please just go?" Uncovering her face, she looked up at him. Her eyes had the fixed, glazed stare of combat veterans. An icy fear, like nothing he'd known since Vietnam, washed over him.

"I'll find Khalil."

"No!"

"Tina, then." When she didn't answer, Matthew took off

running across the beach toward the house.

He found Tina at the buffet table, and to Matthew's dismay, she was unmoved by his appeal.

"You and Leigh have been playing this same ridiculous game for nine years," she said, plucking a batter-fried hibiscus blossom stuffed with cheese from a nearby platter, "and I'm tired of watching foolish pride get between two people who obviously belong together. Might I suggest, Matthew," she said archly, "that if you really care about Leigh, you should be the one to take care of her."

"I tried, but she won't let me." His fingers closed around her arm. "Damnit, Tina, something's terribly wrong with her and you have to help. Before she does something that we'll all regret."

She looked up at him, surprised by his uncharacteristically emotional appeal. His dark eyes were filled with an unspeakable fear that touched a chord of apprehension deep inside her. "Where is she?"

Taking her arm, he guided her through the crush of people. Once outside, he pointed to where Leigh remained on the deserted beach, a small, isolated figure rocking silently back and forth.

"Damn you, Matthew St. James," Tina hissed, her own dark eyes shooting furious sparks. "What the hell have you done now?"

Not giving him a chance to answer, Tina took off her high heels and began running across the sand in her stocking feet.

Matthew stood on the balcony, watching and waiting. When he saw Leigh turn to Tina, and allow the older woman to take her into her arms, he felt a draining sense of relief.

"There you are!" Jill came out onto the terrace, a pair of stemmed glasses in her hands. "Ah brought you a drink."

Matthew cast one last glance toward the beach, where Leigh was rising unsteadily to her feet. "I think I'd rather go home."

Jill dumped the champagne into a nearby planter filled with ferns. "Lover, you must've been readin' mah mind."

"You have no idea how much I've missed being with you like this," Khalil murmured, taking Leigh in his arms. A change had come over her; a pall he was certain had something to do with Matthew's presence at the party. "How much

I've missed making love to you. I've never forgotten, you know."

"Neither have I." It was true. Her time with Khalil had been a magical, wonderful fantasy.

They were sitting in the moon-spangled darkness of her living room. Leigh had lit a trio of white beeswax candles immediately upon arriving home, and now, as he examined her face, illuminated by the flickering candlelight, Khalil considered that Leigh was a woman who would only grow more beautiful with the soft patina of years. He'd never seen her look so lovely. Or so sad.

"I had hoped that we might resume our relationship where it left off," he murmured, bending his head and giving her a slow, exploratory kiss.

So had she. Finally taking Kim's advice that she had mourned her dead marriage long enough, Leigh had had every intention of going to bed with Khalil tonight. But as his lips touched hers, it was Matthew's lips she was tasting, and when his hand slipped inside her dress to caress her breasts, it was Matthew's hand warming her naked skin.

"Oh, Khalil." She placed her palm on his dark cheek. "I know that I gave you that impression when you called, and again earlier this evening, but . . . oh, damn. I can't seem to do anything right anymore."

Turning his head, he pressed his lips against her fingertips. "You still love him."

"Yes."

"Then why do you not go to him?"

Such a simple question. Such complex answers. "It's difficult to explain," she insisted, rising from the couch. She began pacing the room.

"My grandmother used to cite an old Arab proverb," he said. "Perhaps you have heard it: Pride goeth before a fall."

She managed a weak smile. "That's an Arab proverb?"

"It could well be. After all, the West has borrowed many things from our culture. But whatever its origins, Leigh, it remains the truth."

"It's not anything as simple as pride. If that were the case, I'd go to Matthew on my knees and beg him to take me back."

It was Khalil's turn to smile. "Why do I have a difficult time picturing such a scenario?"

"All right, perhaps I wouldn't exactly beg. But it's a moot point."

Matthew knew. It did not matter how he knew—although she realized that once the shock had lessened, she would be frantic to know—but rather that he did.

"Whatever your problem, Leigh, you and Matthew are intelligent people. You can work it out, so long as you're both willing to take the risk."

He'd hit too close to the mark. "I know you mean well, Khalil, but I don't want to talk about this anymore." Leigh turned on a lamp, flooding the room with light. "Besides, there's something else you and I need to talk about."

"What's that?"

"*The Eye of the Tiger*. Matthew says you've got a package together. That you're looking for a studio."

Leaning back, he lit a slim dark cigarette and viewed her with interest. "Are you asking as a woman in love? Or as a studio executive who knows a good screenplay when she reads it?"

"You can't let him make that movie!"

There was an edge of uncharacteristic hysteria to her voice that had him instantly alert. "Why not? It's a compelling screenplay, as you no doubt know, since you were married to Matthew during the time he was writing it."

She sank back down beside him on the couch. "They'll kill him."

"Matthew thinks not."

She stared at him. "Matthew? He's been threatened too?"

Things clicked into place and Khalil finally understood the reason why Baron Studios had turned down Matthew's screenplay. "Darling Leigh," he clucked, "for a brilliant woman, you seem to wear blinders where Matthew St. James is concerned. Of course he's been threatened, you gorgeous, foolish woman. Did you think they'd stop with you? Knowing how obsessed the man is with getting this movie made? Matthew is not a man to run from a fight, Leigh. Surely that's one of the things that attracted you to him in the first place."

"He's too damn stubborn for his own good."

"This sounds to me like a case of the pot calling the kettle black."

When she shot him a sharp look, Khalil grinned. "Simply

another old Arab proverb." Standing, he took hold of her hands and pulled her to her feet in front of him. "And now that I have done my duty as an escort and bestowed my wealth of knowledge concerning the war between the sexes, I think it is time that I returned to my hotel. Unless you've changed your mind about making love to me."

When he waggled his dark brows in a frankly lecherous manner, Leigh laughed. "I really have missed you," she said as she walked him to the door. "You always made me believe that anything was possible."

He looked at her with astonishment. "But it is." Cupping her chin with his fingers, he tilted her head back for a soft, undemanding kiss. "He loves you, Leigh. And you love him. That should be enough."

It should be, Leigh considered much later. But it wasn't. When she lay alone in her empty bed, memories of Matthew— the touch of his hands and lips—unleashed a flood of erotic memories. Her body was seized with an expectancy bordering on agony and, seeking relief, Leigh put her hand between her legs, finding it to be, as always, a poor substitution for the real thing.

They were lying in bed in Matthew's Malibu home. Not eager to return to hotel life, he'd bought the house after his divorce from Marissa had become final.

"It's okay, you know." Jill went up on one elbow and looked down into Matthew's grimly set face. "It happens to lots of men."

"Not me."

"Sugah, you are many wonderful things," Jill drawled, tracing his tense lips with a scarlet fingernail. "Smart, talented, sexy as all get-out, but you are not Superman."

"So tell me something I don't know." Realizing how petulant he sounded, Matthew grimaced. "I'm sorry. I didn't mean to be such rotten company."

"Don't apologize for being in love, Matthew." Leaving the bed, she began to pick up her scattered clothing from the floor. "Actually, Ah think it's kind of sweet," she said, stepping into a pair of red bikini underpants.

"What the hell are you talking about?"

"It's obvious what's wrong," she said, her voice muffled by

the billowy satin blouse she'd pulled over her head. "You are so in love with your first wife, making love to any other woman would be like committing adultery." She grinned at him, her blond head popping back into view. "Some girls might consider you old-fashioned, Matthew St. James. But Ah think you're the sweetest, most romantic man Ah've ever met." Bending down, she gave him a quick kiss. "Ah wonder if Leigh Baron realizes what a lucky woman she is."

"I rather doubt it."

"Well then, you're just going to have to see that she does. Aren't you? Don't get up," she said, pushing him back against the pillows. "Ah think Ah'm going to go back to the party. The night is still young and there was this cute little ole rock musician who looked as if he'd like a chance to ring mah chimes." Tugging on her impossibly high heels, she wagged her fingers at him and left.

Matthew laughed, thinking that Jill's carefree, no-strings-attached attitude reminded him a lot of Lana Parker. Or Lana as she'd been back when they were neighbors. The last he had heard from the attractive ex-hippie, she was married to a stockbroker from an establishment California family and had just given birth to a son, whom she'd named Jason Ashby Palmer Kirkland III. That, more than anything, had proven to Matthew that the flower generation had moved on to greener pastures.

So much had changed, he reflected. He'd come a helluva long way from that starving would-be writer with the hit-and-run sexual habits who seldom took the same woman to bed twice. He'd grown more successful than his wildest dreams, and he knew that there were any number of beautiful, sexy women who'd willingly tumble into bed with him at the crook of his little finger.

But he didn't want any of those women.

Damnit, he wanted Leigh. There. He'd finally put aside his wounded pride long enough to admit it. The next thing to do was to come up with some way to get her back.

In his bed. And in his life. Forever.

"I don't believe this!"

Marissa stared at the letter in her hand. The once ivory parchment stationery had yellowed and years had faded the lavender ink, but the handwriting was instantly recognizable.

"Since your mother would have no reason to lie about such a thing, I have to assume it's true," Brendan said, handing her the gin and tonic she'd asked for. "And the timing fits."

"You were having an affair with my mother? Right under Joshua's nose?"

"Yes."

"I love it," Marissa decided, leaning back in the chair and crossing her legs. "The old bastard was cuckolded by his biggest star. Delicious." She took a sip of her drink. "Did he know?"

"I didn't think so at the time. But of course I had no idea that he and Signe weren't sleeping together. When she got pregnant, she assured me it was Joshua's child."

Marissa glanced down at the letter again, then looked up at Brendan. "So, you're my father."

He nodded. "It appears I am."

"Well, imagine that."

She thought back to that time in Paris, during the filming of *Dangerous*. Furious at Matthew's continual rejections, she'd put on her most alluring nightgown and was headed down the hall to Farraday's room, where she knew, from the looks he'd been giving her all week, that she wouldn't be turned down. As fate would have it, that was the moment that Jeff had shown up with the news that he'd gotten a bit part in the movie. She laughed at how close she'd come to committing the same incestuous act that she'd held against Leigh all these years.

"I hadn't realized you'd find your paternity so amusing."

"Sorry. Private joke." She looked at him expectantly. "Well, Daddy dear, what do we do now?"

"Funny you should ask that question," Farraday said, opening a thick manila file. "I thought you and I might enter into a joint business venture. But since we're family, I'm going to be up front with you, Marissa, and tell you that it'll involve ruining your sister."

A burst of pure pleasure surged through her. Marissa licked her lips, leaned forward, and gave him her full attention.

"Where do I sign?"

40

"I can't believe you're doing this to me."

Leigh faced her sister across the room. Marissa was having a late breakfast in bed, clad in a white satin nightgown and matching bed jacket trimmed in ostrich feathers. The outfit could have easily belonged to Jean Harlow, but strangely enough, Leigh considered, it suited Marissa perfectly.

"For God's sake, Mar, we're sisters! Baron Studios has always been in our family. I never would have given you that stock if I'd known you'd go in with Farraday."

Marissa tossed her head. "To set the record straight, you're only my half-sister, remember? Actually, I'm relieved that Joshua wasn't my natural father. Considering his penchant for perversity."

Comprehension thundered down on Leigh, almost staggering in its enormity. "You knew," she said faintly. "All these years, you knew."

"Of course." The raw pain in Leigh's eyes thrilled Marissa and she was tempted to reveal her own father's identity. Then she remembered what Brendan had said about the damage such a revelation could do to his political career. Although Marissa was totally apolitical, the promises he'd made to her—money, power, half interest in one of the casinos planned for Palm Springs—kept her silent.

"You're the one who told Matthew," Leigh said, more to herself than her sister.

"Wow, when you start putting two and two together, you're a regular whiz kid." Marissa spread orange marmalade onto a toasted English muffin. "Are you sure you don't want breakfast?"

"I'm not hungry." Her stomach was gripped with escalating waves of nausea.

Marissa shrugged her satin-clad shoulders. "Suit yourself."

"Why?" Leigh whispered.

"Why?" Marissa eyed her over the rim of her coffee cup. "Why did I tell Matthew about you having sex with your daddy? Or why am I going to take your precious studio away from you?"

"Both, I guess."

"Christ, you are incredible!" Marissa slammed her cup down onto her saucer. Coffee splattered onto the peach satin comforter and went unnoticed. "I hate you. It's as simple as that. I've always hated you. For years I struggled in your shadow, waiting for a single word, a look from the man I thought to be my father. But all he ever wanted was you. It was always Leigh this, Leigh that."

She laughed, a dangerous, brittle sound that struck at the very core of Leigh's soul. "All those years," she said, her eyes glittering with absolute malice. "I knocked myself out to get the bastard's attention, when I could have simply spread my legs. Like his precious princess."

"You're disgusting."

"I've done a lot of things in my life. But at least I didn't get to the top by screwing my father," Marissa spat back.

Faced with her sister's naked jealousy, Leigh felt as if a blindfold had been taken from her eyes. She was finally forced to recognize a malevolence and ruthlessness she could only begin to understand.

"You and Farraday aren't going to succeed," she warned. "I've sacrificed too much for Baron Studios to simply roll over and let you two ruin it."

"Then I guess it's all-out war." Marissa lifted her fluted glass. The pale orange mimosa sparkled in the morning sunlight. "May the best woman win."

The sisters faced each other. Leigh's expression revealed cold, steely determination; Marissa's heated one was filled with provocative defiance. The rivalry between them was finally out in the open and Leigh realized that neither of them would emerge from the upcoming battle unscathed.

San Francisco was wrapped in its familiar blanket of fog. The American Airlines jet had been circling for what seemed like hours and, seated in first class, Leigh grew increasingly frustrated.

She'd come to the city to meet with Kate Farrell's attorneys. They had remained adamant on the telephone about maintaining the former actress's privacy, but she hoped that if she could only talk with them face to face, she could convince the lawyers to arrange a meeting with their client. Because if she couldn't talk Kate Farrell into voting with her, Baron Studios was going to end up owned by Rocco Minetti's development company and run by Marissa and Brendan Farraday.

Leigh glanced at her watch for the third time in five minutes, as if it might speed things up. It didn't.

Matthew sat out on his terrace, watching the waves wash against the shore. Something had been teasing his mind all morning. Something he'd read in this morning's *L.A. Times* article profiling gubernatorial candidates. Although the election was still months away, Brendan Farraday was considered an almost sure bet to win. Tax reform had cut deeply into revenues, which had caused a cutback in the services the taxpayers had come to take for granted. Apparently, increasing numbers of Californians viewed legalized gambling as the answer to all their fiscal woes.

He'd known Brendan Farraday had been a truckdriver

before becoming a star; the story had been the thing of legends, along with Lana Turner's famed soda counter stool at Schwab's, and in a lesser way, his own discovery pouring drinks at Joshua Baron's party. What he hadn't realized was that Farraday was originally from Nevada, gambling capital of America.

Interesting.

The last time he'd been in Las Vegas was when he and Leigh had been married. Perhaps it was time he made another trip.

"Are you saying that I enjoyed my incestuous relationship with my father?"

Harriet Singer, a motherly-looking psychologist in her fifties, leaned back in her chair and observed Leigh over linked fingers. "I was merely suggesting that when a relationship which begins in innocence and trust takes on undercurrents of secrecy and danger, that danger can become enticing," she said calmly. "Fear, mixed with pleasure, can be like playing with fire."

Leigh had spent three hours a week for the past two months with Dr. Singer, trying to untangle the Freudian knot that was her relationship with her father, and not one minute of those hours had been the least bit easy. "But I didn't remember anything for so many years. And even then I didn't begin to remember all the other times." There'd been too many to count, she'd discovered under hypnosis. Beginning when she was five, ending when her period had begun at thirteen. "How could I have blocked something like that out?"

"It wasn't that difficult. You simply created another self, a little girl with memories and experiences separate from your own. Whenever your father approached you, you turned into that other little girl."

"She sent messages to me. Through my dreams."

"Yes."

Leigh dragged her hands over her face. "The monster wasn't just my father, was it? It was also my other self. My mother's jealous rival. That precocious little girl who liked having her daddy all to herself." Leigh exhaled a long, rippling sign. "No wonder my mother never displayed any warmth or love. She must have hated me."

"You can't take the blame for whatever problems your parents had with their marriage," Harriet advised sternly. "Whatever pact they made, they were adults. While you were merely a child. A child who survived by forgetting."

Not entirely. The shadows had always been there, disappearing before she could make out their shapes.

For eight weeks, Leigh had done all the talking. Now, for the first time, Harriet seemed inclined to offer the reassurance Leigh needed. "You have to understand that while you went to school, or work," the psychologist continued, "made friends and gained experiences, your other self remained a child, unable to deal with complex emotions, difficult moral decisions."

"Is she the reason I've always been afraid to love?"

"Perhaps. Love is never easy. Even for a rational adult." She smiled. "Do you know, every once in a while, I look across the breakfast table at my husband—who I've loved for nearly thirty years—and ask myself, who is this man? And what the hell is he doing here in my kitchen?" When Leigh smiled, as she was supposed to, Harriet Singer nodded, satisfied. "There's something else you need to consider."

"I'm not certain I can take much more," Leigh said.

"You're a tough lady, Leigh Baron. What you've achieved proves that. Which brings us to my next point: growing up in a dysfunctional family, you viewed home as a dangerous, treacherous place, while the outside world—the public arena that frightens most children—was an unknown place, therefore a place of hope."

"Are you saying that part of my success comes from the fact that my father molested me?"

"That's a bit simplistic, but yes, it's possible that besides causing you a great deal of pain and mental anguish, his behavior also contributed to your willingness to take risks."

Leigh thought about that for a long moment. "I still can't understand what made him do it," she said quietly.

"You'll probably never be able to understand," Harriet advised. "But what you must do, Leigh, is to forgive. You must forgive your father, so you can forgive yourself."

*　*　*

Something was in the air. The sun was low, though it wouldn't set for another hour. The cool wind whipping off the ocean carried the pungent scent of salt and a Pacific storm that had been threatening all day. The sea swirled angrily, the white spray rising high and wide; dark clouds raced by overhead.

The turbulent weather fit Leigh's mood perfectly. Needing to be alone, she walked along the hard-packed sand at the water's edge. Her mind was in turmoil: thoughts spun wildly, memories colliding into shattered dreams, reckless hopes overrun by fears.

She'd always thought of herself as a survivor. If anyone had ever asked, she would have said her best attributes were her resiliency and her persistence in the face of seemingly overwhelming odds. Her determination to save Baron Studios, at whatever the cost, was a prime example of her perseverance. Unfortunately, her marriage had been a different story.

When it came to Matthew, she'd been a coward from the first. She'd run away from her feelings for him, and even after making love, she remained afraid to open herself up to all the relationship could offer. Instead of tracking him down and confronting him about his alleged marriage, she'd gone running off to Abu Dhabi like some flighty heroine out of a nineteenth-century novel. Even after that misunderstanding had finally been smoothed over enough to allow them to marry, she continued to hold something back.

Matthew had been right all those times he accused her of running all over the globe on errands any mid-level employee could have performed. The cold, unattractive truth was that she'd welcomed those trips because they kept her marriage—and Matthew—from becoming the single most important thing in her life. She had stood impotently by while he walked out of the hospital the day after her father's stroke; she had remained silent when he subsequently filed for divorce. She hadn't even raised a hand to stop him from marrying Marissa, even though the thought of him making love to her sister was almost more than she could bear.

During the sessions with Harriet Singer, she had come to understand that her almost obsessive perfectionism stemmed from a child's mistaken belief that she should have been able to control something that was beyond her control. She also was finally able to believe that she was the victim. She had nothing to feel guilty about.

And perhaps most important, she realized that she had become a prisoner of her own defenses; her shell, which had always protected her from being hurt, now seemed like a cage.

A cage she desperately wanted to escape.

The man lay in the shadows, watching. Waiting. He was clad in a hooded black wet suit and his face was darkened, as if for jungle combat. The waterproof bag he carried with him contained coils of double wire, four small round blasting caps, a radio receiver, and enough C-4 plastic explosive to powder the Coliseum. The fog had rolled in, wrapping the house in a thick gray blanket, obscuring the thin sickle of moon, muffling the night sounds. Crickets chirped; nearby a dog barked. As the hours passed, the fog became thicker and the night grew silent. And still the man waited.

Master Sergeant John Hill had been a member of Delta Force, an elite team that originated in the jungles of Vietnam. While stationed in Nha Trang, he'd seen a recruitment flyer stating that the Army was looking for a few good infantrymen, men guaranteed a medal, a body bag, or both. They should be loners, able to work independently, and possess a streak of paranoia.

Although Hill qualified in all three categories, so did a lot of other in-country soldiers. What earned him a coveted place on Delta Force was a passion for demolition and a love of loud noises.

Earlier, the lone commando had disabled the complex alarm system with a skill that suggested such sabotage was all in a night's work, and now, as he made his way toward the house, blending quickness with a pantherlike agility, Sergeant John Hill was smiling. It was good to be working again.

41

The shrill ringing of the phone jerked Matthew from a deep, dreamless sleep. Groping for the receiver, he muttered, "Yeah?"

There was only silence on the other end of the line.

"Hello?" he said with obvious irritation. "Who's there?"

Another pause. Then finally, "Hello, Matthew? It's Leigh."

She need not have given her name. Did she think he could ever forget her soft, musical voice? He turned on the bedside lamp as he sat up. "Leigh? Are you all right? Is something wrong?"

No, I'm not all right and everything is wrong. "I need to talk with you," she said instead. "Could I come over?"

"Leigh, it's"—he glanced at the clock radio—"almost two o'clock in the morning and there's a bitch of a fog out there. You know how dangerous this road can be." She sure as hell should, Matthew considered, since her mother had died on it. "Tell you what, why don't I come to you?"

"I couldn't ask you to do that. I'm sorry, Matthew, I didn't realize how late it was."

"But if it's important—"

"It's nothing that can't wait until a more reasonable hour. Are you free for breakfast later this morning?"

"Sure."

"Fine. Why don't you come by around eight and I'll make a Mexican omelet."

"Sounds great," he agreed instantly. "Leigh?"

"Yes?"

"Are you sure you're all right?"

"Positive. My only problem is that I have difficulty reading a clock properly. Good night, Matthew, I'm really sorry to have bothered you."

"No bother," he said to the dial tone. She'd already hung up.

"What the hell was that all about?" he wondered out loud. He turned off the lamp and prepared to go back to sleep.

The explosion lit up the sky, shaking the earth with such force that neighbors, jerked from sleep, could only surmise that Southern California had just been hit with a major earthquake. The Big One. Windows shattered, the shrill shriek of burglar alarms rent the night air, followed by the wail of sirens as fire trucks and police cars rushed to the site.

Where the house had once stood, a pile of rubble was engulfed in flames. A crater large enough to house the Goodyear blimp had swallowed two bedrooms and the den.

"Wow," one rookie cop breathed in awe as he stared at what had only minutes before been a prime piece of California real estate. "Whose place was it?"

"Belonged to that movie guy," his partner said, watching the sparks shoot into the sky. "St. James. Matthew St. James."

While the firefighters waged a futile battle, far out on the darkened water, beyond the breakers, Master Sergeant John Hill looked on with a rush of physical satisfaction that was almost sexual. His assignment completed, he started the engine and piloted the Zodiac down the coast, toward Mexico.

* * *

"You really needn't have come," Leigh said. She put a pot of water on for tea. "I would have never forgiven myself if something had happened to you on that road."

"You sounded upset," Matthew said simply. "And I couldn't get back to sleep, knowing that something was bothering you bad enough to have you pacing the floor at two in the morning."

"Oh, Matthew." Leigh sank down onto a rattan barstool at the counter. "I really don't know where to start."

"How about at the beginning?"

She dragged her hands through her hair. "There's something I have to say first."

She looked so distressed, so uncharacteristically unnerved, that it was all Matthew could do not to take her in his arms. "What's that?"

"I love you. I always have."

"I know."

"What?"

"There was a time when I was so angry at you that I didn't believe you knew the meaning of the word. Perhaps I'm finally growing up, because lately I've decided that perhaps it was the very fact that you loved me which made you so unreachable."

How could he know something that had taken her so long to understand? The sudden whistle of the teakettle shattered the moment into a thousand crystalline pieces. "The water's ready." She crossed the room, taking the steaming copper kettle from the burner. "How do you know me so well?" she murmured, as she poured the water over the tea bag.

"I've been thinking about us, Leigh. A helluva lot, actually, if you want to know the truth."

"Really?" She carried the tea to the table, the sudden rattling of the china cups against their saucers sounding unnaturally loud in the nighttime stillness of the house. Leigh was appalled to discover that her hands were shaking.

"Really. And I've come to the conclusion that part of the problem was that we were too much alike."

"We were both afraid to open up."

"I'm not one of those people who think our entire futures are determined by when our mothers stopped breast feeding.

But it doesn't take a Ph.D. in psychology to realize that our pasts do play an important part in our futures. I think our major problem was that you were always afraid of losing my love, while I expected to lose yours."

"Which made us overly defensive."

"That thought has crossed my mind."

Leigh took a deep breath, garnering the strength to continue. "Marissa didn't exactly lie."

"About you scuttling *The Eye of the Tiger*, or . . ." A muscle twitched along Matthew's jaw, but his voice remained calm. "The other."

He couldn't even say it out loud. This wasn't going to be at all easy, Leigh thought. "I think I'd like a drink." She reached up in the cupboard and took down the bottle of Courvoisier Napoleon. "Would you like a glass?"

"Am I going to need one?"

She met his steady gaze without flinching. "You just might."

Matthew reminded himself that he loved Leigh enough to forgive her anything. "Perhaps I will have a drink," he decided.

Leigh poured the cognac into a pair of glasses. She handed one to Matthew, then took a sip of her own. The alcohol warmed her, but it didn't make what she had to say any easier.

"I did ask William Zimmerman to block your project," she admitted. "But I was trying to save your life."

She told him about Brendan Farraday's threat and the reason she'd taken it seriously, leaving out Tina's revelation, which was, Leigh had determined, no one's business.

"So, as much as I hated doing it, I honestly didn't feel I had a choice."

"You could have come to me."

"And you would have refused to drop the project."

"Of course. But at least we could have worked together to get Farraday out of the picture. And if we had taken care of the guy back then," he pointed out succinctly, "he wouldn't be trying to take Baron Studios away from you today."

"You know about that?"

"Leigh," Matthew said patiently, "you're the one who taught me what a small town this is, remember?"

"Are you saying that everyone knows about Farraday and Marissa trying to take over the studio?"

"I'm afraid so."

"How does the grapevine view my chances?"

"Do you want the honest answer?"

"Yes."

"Slim to none."

She tilted her jaw in that way he remembered with a mixture of fondness and frustration. "I'm going to stop them, Matthew. I don't know how, but I will."

He lifted his glass. "I have no doubt you will, sweetheart. Besides, I'm working on something myself; we just might manage to kill two birds with one stone."

"What does that mean?"

He shrugged. "I'll tell you later, if my hunch pans out. So, now I finally understand about *The Eye of the Tiger*."

"And?"

"And although I wish you'd told me, I appreciate your doing your wifely best to save your husband's life."

A pregnant silence settled over them. "Now comes the hard part," Leigh said softly.

Her hands were trembling as she refilled her glass. Matthew put his hand over the top of his, declining her offer. Whatever she had to say about her relationship with her late father, he knew that if he didn't stay sober, he'd only end up making a bad situation even worse.

They were facing one another, barstools swiveled together, knees touching. "Let's continue this conversation somewhere else," he suggested, taking her hand. "Somewhere a little more conducive to intimacy."

He led her down the hall, into the sitting area of their former bedroom. The cozy niche had always been a refuge from the turmoil of their lives, a place where they could shut out the rest of the world.

"All right," he said, putting his arm around her and drawing her close, "I'm ready." And he was, he realized, feeling the familiar warmth of her body against his. There was nothing she could tell him that would make a difference.

Basking in his solid, reassuring strength, Leigh put her head on his shoulder and closed her eyes. "It happened a long time ago," she managed in a voice that was little more than a whisper. "For years, my mind blocked it out."

Matthew felt a flood of relief. If she'd been routinely sleeping with Joshua, like Marissa had alleged, how could she have blocked out such behavior? "He raped you?"

"No. Well, not exactly. Oh God, it's so complicated."

In a faltering voice, she told him everything—about Joshua's betrayal, about her repression that never allowed her to understand or admit, the power her father had wielded over her. She told him about her shock when the truth had come hurtling back, fear that she had caused Joshua's stroke, and the lingering sense of guilt that by setting herself above her mother and sister, by being Joshua's "princess," she had willingly contributed to her own molestation.

When she finally finished, the sky was tinged with a soft pink tint. Leigh felt drained.

"Christ, we really do belong together," he said.

Leigh looked up at him. "You don't sound very happy about that," she ventured.

"It's not that. I was just thinking that for two supposedly intelligent people, we've been a real pair of jackasses." He bent his head and brushed her trembling lips with his. "I never, ever, loved Marissa. I only married her because I didn't want my child to grow up a bastard."

She remembered what he'd told her of his own childhood. "I'd hoped at the time that might be the case." She pressed her hand against his cheek. "I'm sorry you lost the baby, Matthew," she said compassionately.

He laughed at that, but the sound held no humor. "It turned out that it wasn't mine after all."

"I suppose I should be surprised, but I'm not."

There was one thing more, one thing he needed to tell her. "The reason I thought it might be was because I did have sex with her the night our divorce was final," he admitted.

"You don't need to tell me—"

"Yes," he cut her off. "I do. Because I don't want any more secrets between us, Leigh. Never again."

She nodded, her heart in her eyes as she looked up at him.

"After seeing you that morning at Corbett and Tina's, looking so beautiful and unattainable, I went back to the hotel and indulged in a bout of self-pitying, solitary drinking. Not that it's any excuse, but I was pretty drunk when Marissa showed up, goading me about your blocking my project. I thought I could handle that, but when she told me about you and Joshua . . ." He paused. "Well, I don't want to go into details, but her accusations hit pretty hard."

"I've got a good idea of what they were," Leigh murmured.

He ran his hand down her hair. "Even then," he said, "in my mind, it was you, Leigh. I wanted to punish you, to hurt you like you'd hurt me, but all I succeeded in doing was punishing us both even more."

"Oh, Matthew." Tears streamed silently down her cheeks. Leigh dashed them away with the back of her hand. "What a mess we've made of things."

"Shh." The years of separation fell away as he nuzzled her neck and throat with his lips. "That's all in the past." Unfastening the ribbon tie at her waist, he slipped her ivory satin robe off her shoulders. She was wearing a sea green satin chemise, the lace bodice so sheer it could have been spun from spiderwebs.

Leigh's hands delved under Matthew's black fisherman's sweater to stray over his chest. Her fingers wove their way through the forest of dark curls as her lips sought his.

They kissed a long, luxurious time; then they stood and held each other, swaying together in the misty pearl light of dawn, as if dancing to music only they could hear.

They walked hand in hand the few feet to the bed. They undressed each other, slowly, reverently. Then they were lying naked on the crisp Porthault sheets, Matthew kissing her sensitive breasts as he caressed her from her shoulders to her thighs. His hands tempted, his mouth seduced. His tongue, as it slipped between her parted lips, promised.

In turn, Leigh made love to him, her lips and hands moving over him in blissful familiarity, like a love song whose music stays forever in your mind. Wherever his fingers lingered, she flamed; wherever her hands played, he burned.

Their lovemaking was so intolerably beautiful, so exquisitely sensual, that Leigh could only close her eyes and ride the spiraling passion that carried her higher and higher. Outside, the sun rose over the horizon, drowning them in a shower of golden warmth. The pace quickened; hands that were once content to loiter now moved more urgently. Soft sighs became throaty moans. Tender kisses grew eager, hungry.

When he did not thrust into her as she expected, but instead penetrated her with tantalizing slowness, her hot wetness surged forward to welcome him. She was already on the brink and he'd no sooner begun to move inside her when the first pulsating wave crashed over her, followed by another, then another. Feeling her contractions along the length of his penis excited Matthew to new heights of passion, and he plunged into her with a deep, rhythmic stroke. The sound of the surf roared in his ears as Matthew was overcome by an incomparable pleasure that went on, and on, and on. A blood red haze appeared before his eyes. Then everything went dark and he collapsed on Leigh's pliant flesh, his body spent.

Their lovemaking had been both redemption and pledge and, when she lay quietly in his arms, Leigh wept again. This time, however, her tears were born not of sorrow, or regret, but love.

42

For some reason she knew had everything to do with Matthew, Leigh felt uncharacteristically domestic. She was briskly whipping eggs in a blue Pyrex bowl for that omelet she'd promised while he showered, when the phone rang.

"Hello?"

"Leigh, it's Tina."

"Good morning, Tina. Isn't it an absolutely beautiful day?"

"Actually, dear, it's begun to rain."

"Really?" Leigh glanced out the window. "Goodness, I could have sworn the sun was shining." She laughed.

"I'm afraid I didn't call to give you a weather report."

Belatedly noticing the strain in Tina's voice, Leigh put the bowl down on the counter. "Something's wrong. It's not Corbett?"

"No, he's fine. Well, not fine, but considering . . . Leigh, dear, I think I'd better come over."

Dread was a cold, wet thing, covering her like a shroud. "Just tell me. Is it Marissa?"

"No." Tina's ragged intake of breath came over the wire. "Honey, it's Matthew."

"Matthew?" Involuntarily, Leigh glanced in the direction of the bedroom with its adjoining bath. "What about Matthew?"

"There's no easy way to say this. He's dead."

"Dead?" For one horrible second, the words struck at the very core of her heart. But relief quickly swept over her when the man in question entered the kitchen, clad in a pair of low-slung jeans, water sparkling like diamonds in his black chest hair. "Tina, wherever did you get an idea like that?"

"His home was blown up last night, honey. The arson squad is going through the rubble, but the police say they don't expect to find any suvivors."

White spots swam on a sea of black velvet behind her eyes. Leigh slumped down onto the barstool, dropping the receiver.

Alarmed, Matthew put his arm around her while scooping up the phone with his free hand. "Who the hell is this?"

There was a startled gasp on the other end of the line. "Matthew?"

"Tina?"

"Oh, thank God, you're safe."

She sounded every bit as bad as Leigh looked. "Of course I'm safe. Why wouldn't I be?" Listening to Tina's explanation, Matthew's frown deepened. "Thanks for calling," he said. "If you don't mind, I think I'd better take care of Leigh. Sure. We'll come by right after I talk to the police." He replaced the receiver in the wall cradle. "Tina says the news is reporting that the explosion occurred at two-thirty."

"Oh, my God." Fate was such a delicate, unpredictable thing. If she hadn't called him, if he hadn't decided not to wait until morning . . .

"Looks as if this time you really did save my life," he said, wrapping her in his arms and pressing his lips against her brow.

Leigh slumped against his reassuring strength. "What do we do now?"

Putting his fingers under her chin, he tilted her head back and kissed her. "First we have breakfast. Next I suppose we ought to call the police. Then I promised that we'd drop by to prove to Tina and Corbett that you didn't just finish making mad, passionate love to a ghost. And after we take care of all those mundane social duties, we come back here and see how many ways we can think up to drive one another crazy."

As he unfastened the sash to her short robe, Leigh could think of innumerable ways without even trying. "There's one thing we have to do before that."

"What's that?" He lowered his lips to her breast, his tongue flicking enticingly at her nipple.

"We have to stop by the studio."

"Take the day off."

"But there's a contract I want to draw up."

He lifted his head, instantly alert. "What contract is that?"

"You are going to let Baron Studios make *The Eye of the Tiger*, aren't you?"

A few hours ago, nothing could have pleased him more. But that was before Farraday's hired killer had blown his house to kingdom come.

"I don't want to do anything that might put you at risk, Leigh."

"For just one fleeting moment, when Tina told me that you were dead, I felt as if I'd died." She pressed her hand against his cheek. "We're in this together, Matthew," she insisted. "This time we're going to be partners. In everything."

Matthew thanked whatever gods or fates had seen fit to give him yet another chance with this woman. "If you really want to make this movie, there's something you should know. Something you never asked."

"Whether the story really is true."

"Yeah. Remember Farraday's entertainment tours?"

"Of course. They practically made him a hero. With the government facing more and more protesters, they appreciated having a famous name like Brendan Farraday support their undeclared little war. And even those of us who didn't approve of the war gave Brendan credit for trying to make life a little better for the soldiers who were risking their lives over there."

"Yeah, the guy was a real Boy Scout," Matthew muttered. "The real reason Farraday made all those trips to Vietnam was to keep a tight control on the drug cartel he'd built."

"How can you know such a thing?"

"One of the guys in my unit was working for Farraday. Trouble was, after about three months he got a little greedy and began doing some dealing on the side. Shortly after that, Farraday came into camp with a bunch of pretty blond USO girls. When he left the guy was dead. Shot right through the right eye on his way to the latrine. The official report was death by a VC sniper. But there were a lot of us who knew Farraday had ordered the hit."

"Other people knew about this?"

"There's no point in killing someone unless you let other people realize that it could also happen to them. I think Murphy was killed more as an example than for revenge."

"Why didn't you tell anyone?"

"Are you kidding? Who'd believe the word of a bastard grunt like me against a man like Brendan Farraday? You said it yourself, sweetheart, the man was a hero."

"So why are you opening things up again?"

"In the first place, I'm only admitting to you that this story is factual. And in the second place, I'm more of a match for Farraday now." He gave her a long, probing look. "And now that you know the truth, if you don't want to get involved in making this movie, I'll understand."

Leigh told herself that after Tina's horrendous story about Farraday brutally raping her, she shouldn't be surprised to discover that the actor had been leading a double life. But she was. "I meant what I said, Matthew. We're partners, all the way."

He'd never loved her more than he did at this moment. "Well then, partner," he drawled, punctuating his words with kisses, "how about going back to bed and consummating the deal?"

"But I was going to make you breakfast."

"Leigh, darling . . . man does not live by omelets alone."

He lifted her into his arms and headed decisively for the bedroom. Leigh could not think of a single objection.

It wasn't easy being a woman in these new, undefined 1980s. Betty Friedan, who'd once jokingly referred to herself as "the Pope of women," the very same woman who'd written the feminist bible, *The Feminine Mystique*, founded the National Organization of Women, and led the nationwide Women's Strike for Equality (the largest demonstration of its kind since the days of the suffragists), had published another book proclaiming that a new set of constraints was forcing women to deny themselves the pleasures of home and families.

On the other hand, *The Cinderella Complex* claimed that personal psychological dependency was the chief force holding women down.

She was certain that she'd never suffered from the Cinderella Complex, but Leigh had to admit that perhaps Friedan's new Second Stage idea had merit. Because the more time she spent with Matthew, the more she found herself fantasizing about a real home. With children.

There were no witnesses to the violent demolition of Matthew's house. After rumors of mob threats against him were uncovered by a reporter at WBC, Matthew's script became front-page news and the pressure from the press built with each passing day. Along with the media attention, the armed guards stationed at Leigh's house and the studio only added to the unrelenting stress.

"I only have two days until that damn stockholder's meeting Marissa and Farraday called," Leigh complained when she returned to Matthew's office at the studio after a meeting with her attorneys. "What am I going to do?"

Matthew glanced up from the stack of computer sheets he'd been studying. The cost estimates were substantial; fortunately Khalil had offered unlimited resources. "I'd suggest that you talk Kate Farrell into voting with you, instead of those two rattlesnakes."

"How can I do that, when I don't even know where the woman is?"

Matthew handed her an envelope.

"What is this? A plane ticket? To Klamath Falls, Oregon?"

"Kate Farrell has a ranch there," he said mildly. "She's expecting us for lunch tomorrow."

"What?"

"Her lawyers called while you were out."

"There are two tickets here . . . Us?" She stared at him as his words sank in. "You're coming with me?" In the past, aside from his own films, he'd never displayed a modicum of interest in Baron Studios.

"Hey, we're a team, remember? Partners."

"But I thought you resented my feelings about Baron Studios."

"It was your father's interference I resented," Matthew corrected quietly. "There were admittedly times I thought you were overly obsessive about the studio, but I didn't really want to change you, Leigh. I merely wanted you to expand your horizons, to realize that there was a lot more to life than work."

Like love. And commitment. She perched on the edge of his desk. Her emotions, no longer guarded, were in her eyes, on her smiling lips, in the trembling of her hands as she framed his face between her palms. "I love you, Matthew St. James. And as soon as we get home, I'm going to spend the rest of the night showing you exactly how much."

Matthew closed the cover on the cost sheets. "Sweetheart, that's the best offer I've had all day."

Their lips were inches apart when the intercom buzzed. "I could learn to hate that thing," Matthew muttered. He pressed the button. "Yes, Marge?"

"I'm sorry to bother you and Ms. Baron," the secretary said, "but there's someone waiting in the lobby I think you'll want to see."

"Not another reporter?"

"No, sir. It's Miss Farrell."

Matthew and Leigh exchanged a look. "Kate Farrell?" Leigh asked.

"That's the name she gave to the guard," the secretary confirmed.

"Please," Leigh said, "have the guard send her up. On

second thought," she decided, "we'll go meet her."

"Yes, Ms. Baron."

"I wonder what made her come here?" Leigh said as she
and Matthew left the office.

"Your guess is as good as mine. It's too bad, though."

"What's too bad?"

"That she decided to come here. Personally, I liked the idea
of visiting her ranch."

"Really?" She glanced up at him. "I wouldn't have thought
rural life to be your cup of tea."

"True enough," he agreed easily. "But the idea of tumbling
you in a hayloft was extremely attractive."

"You're incorrigible," she said with a smile.

"I know; actually, I've always considered it one of my more
endearing traits. . . . My God, look at that," he said as they
approached the lobby. "It really is her."

The small, reed-thin woman was obviously in her late seventies or early eighties, and the unmistakable aroma of horses
and hay clung to clothing more suitable to a ranch hand than
a former movie queen—jeans, a red-and-black checked shirt,
and cowboy boots. Still, the resemblance to the earlier silent
movie sex symbol was unmistakable. Her warm brown eyes
still slanted catlike at the corners, her heart-shaped face possessed those same amazing cheekbones, and in a burst of old
Hollywood glamour, her once sparkling auburn hair had been
dyed a vivid orange.

"Miss Farrell," Leigh greeted her warmly, taking both the
woman's hands in her own, "how nice to finally meet you."

"I'll bet you thought I'd died years ago," Kate said with a
forthrightness usually attributed to the very young or the very
elderly.

"Not at all," Leigh responded, not quite truthfully. Only a
few months ago, had anyone asked, she would have guessed
that the former actress was no longer living.

Kate gave Leigh a long, measuring look. "You've got your
grandfather's chin," she determined. "Are you as stubborn as
Walter, as well?"

"I've been accused of being tenacious."

The old woman nodded. "Good. Women have to be tough
if they're going to succeed in this business. I'm still furious at

Lillian Gish for saying that directing was no job for a lady. That was, of course, after she'd tried directing that silent movie in New York. Hell, just because she couldn't cut it on the business end of a camera was no reason to help the men keep the doors closed against the rest of us."

"But you did direct a flapper flim for Paramount," Matthew recalled.

Kate's dark eyes lit up. "I've heard you were an intelligent man, Matthew St. James. But I hadn't known that you were a collector of ancient movie trivia. There are very few people who know about that film." She sighed. "You know, I rather liked telling people what to do. I think I would have made a successful director, but Walter had other ideas about the direction my career should take, and once Walter Baron made his mind up about something, it was no longer up for debate." She gave them both an appraising look. "But of course you two young people have already discovered the perils of mixing moviemaking and marriage."

Matthew put his arm around Leigh's waist. "We're working on it."

Kate nodded, apparently satisfied. "Good. I've followed both your careers with interest and, although each of you is quite successful on your own, together I believe you can build an even greater dynasty than Walter—or Joshua—ever dreamed of."

"Thank you for the vote of confidence," Leigh said. "Does that mean I have your support at the stockholders' meeting?"

"My dear, you had my vote even before those thugs showed up at my ranch last night."

"Thugs?" Matthew asked, instantly alert.

Kate glanced around the room, as if seeking out spies. "Why don't we go for a drive along the beach," she suggested.

They drove up the Coast Highway, with Kate explaining about the pair of men who'd shown up unannounced and uninvited at her Oregon ranch, suggesting that Brendan Farraday would appreciate her vote.

"Of course I feigned ignorance in the entire battle," she said with a self-satisfied grin. "Then, when they pulled out the proxy for me to sign, I simply fainted. Oh, not really, dear," she said at Leigh's concerned look. "I was merely acting. I still can, you know," she said to Matthew.

He smiled. "I've no doubt of that. Talent like yours doesn't disappear, it merely ages, like fine wine."

"Oh, I do like this man," Kate said to Leigh. "You mustn't let him get away this time."

"I've no intention of it," Leigh answered, exchanging a quick, fond glance with Matthew.

"Good. Now where was I? Oh yes. Anyway, my housekeeper, who isn't such a bad actress herself, assured the men that I often have such spells and that I'd be fully recovered by morning. Or at least well enough to sign their papers."

"And that satisfied them?" Matthew asked, his doubt obvious.

"They didn't have any choice but to agree. I was, after all, unconscious. They left, promising to return first thing in the morning. Of course the moment they left the house, I called the airline and booked a seat on the first flight out of Klamath Falls. Then, afraid they might be watching the house, I put on the clothes I wear to muck out the stalls, figuring that if they did see me leave, they'd think I was one of the hands.

"That's why I'm dressed this way," she explained. "Usually I'm much better turned out for traveling. Anyway, I went out to the barn, took the old pickup we use for hauling hay, and hightailed it to the airport." She cackled delightedly. "I figure that, by now, Farraday should be chewing their behinds off for letting a senile old woman get the best of them."

"I am glad you've come," Leigh said, "but you must understand, Miss Farrell, these are very dangerous men."

"You must call me Kate, dear," she said, patting Leigh's hand with her beringed one. Blue veins crisscrossed the back of Kate Farrell's hand, but her soft skin was the color of gardenias, free of the age spots suffered by so many of her contemporaries. "And of course I know that those men were dangerous. I may be old, but I'm not stupid. If their suits hadn't tipped me off first thing—they looked like extras from an Edward G. Robinson movie—the guns they were wearing under their jackets would have probably given me a clue." She peered at them with bright brown eyes that reminded Leigh of a curious bird. "Now that I've managed to escape their trap, what do we do next?"

"The first thing we need to do is find you someplace to stay where we can keep you under wraps for the next two days," Matthew mused. "Unfortunately, while they may look like something from an old gangster movie, the bullets these guys use are all too real."

"I heard about your house," Kate said matter-of-factly. "Lucky you weren't in it; they'd still be picking up pieces of you off the Catalina coast."

When Matthew chuckled appreciatively at Kate's forthright speech, Leigh repressed a shiver. She'd tried to put it behind her, but she couldn't forget how close she'd come to losing Matthew forever.

"How about Corbett and Tina's house?" Leigh suggested. "I don't think Farraday would ever think to look there."

Matthew nodded. "Good idea."

"I'd like that," Kate decided. "Corbett Marshall's grandfather, George, was my banker, you know. Back when I was still working at the Famous Players Lasky Studio on Long Island. He even proposed to me. Three times. I turned him down each and every time."

Her eyes turned thoughtful. "I'd already decided that if he asked once more, I'd accept. But he didn't, and I ended up marrying Walter Baron instead, which didn't last the year. Walter was a hard man. I've heard his son was nearly as ruthless." She looked at Leigh expectantly, as if expecting Joshua's daughter to confirm her statement.

"Joshua Baron was an extremely complex man," Matthew said quietly, coming to Leigh's rescue. He squeezed Leigh's hand, assuring her that he'd managed to put the past—and Joshua's treachery—behind them.

"That's probably what they said about Genghis Khan," Kate offered on a cackle. "The way I've heard it, other movie moguls may kill to eat, but Joshua Baron killed for fun."

Neither Matthew nor Leigh answered. Unfortunately, it was all too true.

"I have a gift for you. Something you might just find exciting," Matthew said later that evening. They were sitting out on the bedroom balcony, watching the sun sink into the ocean.

Leigh smiled up at him. Soft pleasure lingered in her eyes. "Something else?" They'd made love earlier, and for some reason she was not about to analyze, each time she and Matthew made love, it was as if it were the first time. "I'm not sure how much excitement I can take for one day."

He went back into the house. Moments later he returned with a manila envelope. "I thought you might like to take this to your meeting."

Leigh pulled out the sheaf of papers. She began to read, her curiosity replaced by incredulity. "Farraday used to transport contraband for Rocco Minetti?" she asked unbelievingly. "How did you find that out?"

"I've had a detective digging into the guy's background for a few months. They did a pretty good job of covering up, but these prove that Brendan Farraday—the former Arnie Stoller—is not the Boy Scout he's perceived to be."

"If this ever got out, his campaign would be finished," she murmured.

"Deader than a doornail," he agreed cheerfully, leaning back in his chair and stretching his long legs out in front of him. "The way I figure it, Farraday will gladly sign over his twenty-four percent in the studio in exchange for this little blast from his past. As big a fish as Baron Studios is, it's still small potatoes compared to the power he'd gain if he was elected governor."

The idea was so tempting. Even though now, thanks to Kate Farrell, she would be able to fend off Farraday and Marissa's takeover attempt, so long as he possessed his stock, Farraday would still have a vote on the board of Baron Studios, something that was anathema to Leigh.

"If I make that deal with Farraday," she said slowly, "I'll practically be putting him and his mobster cronies in the governor's mansion." She shook her head, giving the papers one last wistful glance before sliding them back into the envelope. "I have to turn these over to the attorney general."

"My darling Leigh," Matthew said on a slow sigh, "sometimes, for an intelligent woman, you demonstrate a remarkable lack of street smarts. Didn't your father teach you that when you're negotiating, you should always hold one vital piece of information back?"

"Yes, but—"

"Was it Hedda Hopper or Louella Parsons who said that the deeper you dig, the dirtier it gets?" Matthew asked. "Anyway, here's the smoking gun that's going to get Farraday out of our hair for good," he said, handing her one more piece of paper.

Leigh's eyes widened as she read the information on the page. "I don't believe it! Brendan Farraday killed his father?"

"Actually, Arnie Stoller is the one who blew his old man away," Matthew said. "But since they're one and the same, I believe that the Nevada police will be quite pleased to be able to close their files." He grinned. "I would have notified them earlier, but I wanted to give you an opportunity to buy back Farraday's shares before he's arrested. There's no point in tying up so much of the studio's stock in a civil lawsuit for the next twenty years."

"I hesitate to say this, because it's going to sound like dialogue from an old silent movie, but you really have saved the studio." There was a tremor in her voice. She stood up and looked down at him with uncensored admiration and love. "How can I ever repay you?"

"Don't worry," Matthew said cheerfully. He pulled her down onto his lap. "We're both intelligent people. If we put our heads together, I'm sure we'll think of something."

43

To Leigh's vast relief, the stockholders' meeting held no surprises. Farraday's eyes had narrowed dangerously when she'd entered the room with Kate Farrell, but the voting was cut and dry and over in minutes. Relieved to have won, Leigh experienced a stab of regret for lost opportunities when Marrisa stormed out of the conference room, swearing to make Leigh pay once and for all. She'd heard those words too many times to count. Still, Leigh couldn't help wishing that there had been some way to reach her sister. Unfortunately, the seeds of jealousy planted by Joshua so long ago had borne a bitter fruit.

"Oh, Brendan," Leigh said casually as the actor turned politician left the room, "there's just one more little thing."

He turned in the doorway and glared back at her. "What?"

"I'd like to purchase your shares."

Had it not been for the reassuring presence of Matthew, waiting just outside the door, Leigh would have been frightened by the rage in his stormy blue eyes. "It'll be a cold day in hell before I sell those shares to you."

"Better bundle up, Brendan," Leigh countered. "Because there's a blizzard on the way. You see, I have big plans for Baron Studios. Plans which do not involve crooks." She held out the detective's report, holding back the same pages Matthew had initially kept from her. "I don't believe the voters would be so eager to elect a man with crime ties."

"What the fuck are you talking about?" he growled, snapping the pages from her hand. He perused them quickly, his complexion turning grayer with each line.

"I'll pay exactly what my father owed you," she said, taking out her checkbook. "Not one penny more."

He snapped the check from her outstretched hand. "Your sister's right. You are a cunt."

Her cool expression didn't waver. "Please close the door on your way out, Brendan."

A moment later he was gone, leaving Leigh bathed in a cooling flood of relief.

"Hey, bartender." Marissa waved her empty glass. "Why don't you hustle that good-looking ass? A girl could die of thirst in this joint before she got a refill!" She had been drinking steadily for four hours, but unfortunately she still wasn't drunk enough to forget the way Leigh had treated her. Fucking bitch. Where was it written that she always won?

The shift had changed and the evening bartender, a good-looking Muscle Beach Adonis, and new to the Driftwood, gave Marissa a long, surprised look. "Hey, you're Marissa Baron."

"Bull's-eye. Give the hunk a Kewpie doll." She leaned her elbows on the bar and licked her lips lasciviously. "Unless there's something else you'd rather have, Mr. Tall, Dark, and Hung."

Taking away her empty glass, he replaced it with another. "Sorry," he said easily. "But I'm afraid you'd be wasting your time."

"Shit. I should've guessed from the tight pants. Only queers advertise that openly."

Instead of appearing offended by her attitude, he grinned. "My daddy always said that if you don't have any meat to sell, take the sign out of the window. On the other hand, some-times it pays to keep the sign up.''

"Well, from what I can see, you'll never be accused of false advertising," Marissa said, her gaze dropping pointedly to his groin. "But that still doesn't solve my problem of what I'm going to do tonight."

"Perhaps the gentleman at the end of the bar might have some ideas," the bartender suggested. "He offered to buy your drink."

Marissa turned. When she viewed the familiar face, her lips curved into a slow, sensual smile. "Jeffy. It's been a long time."

Jeff Martin slid off the stool and came to stand beside her. "Too fucking long, if you ask me. I've missed you, babe."

He didn't look anything like the drop-dead handsome gigolo she'd met nine years earlier. His complexion was sal-low; his once sun-gilded hair hung lank; there was a faraway, remote look in his eyes; and, as he wiped his nose with the back of his hand, she noticed a distinct tremor.

But what the hell, Marissa decided, so long as the guy could still fuck like Superman, what did she care what he looked like?

"You got any stuff?"

He grinned, reminding her of the devil-may-care Jeff of old. "Funny you should bring that up. I just scored some ace coke that should make a dynamite speedball. If you've got the guts to try it."

She tossed back the rest of the rum. "Sweetie, you are playing my song."

After Leigh's treachery, she needed something special to lift her spirits, Marissa told herself as she left the Driftwood with Jeff. Tomorrow she'd figure out a way to get even.

"You are an extremely accomplished actress, my dear," Kate said. Leigh and Matthew had taken her to dinner to celebrate their victory. "That was quite the scene you pulled off this afternoon."

"Are you sure Farraday couldn't see my knees shaking?"

"She looked as cool as a cucumber," Kate told Matthew. "You would have been proud."

"I always am."

"Are you certain that you can't stay a few days longer?" Leigh asked.

"More than sure," Kate said emphatically. "I've enjoyed my visit, but I've got a mare set to foal and a garden to plant. Besides," she said with a wink, "I need to leave before those pesky reporters discover that I'm in town and plaster my picture all over the front pages of those horrible supermarket tabloids. I've always felt it's better for fans to remember me the way I was—a vamp—instead of a shriveled up old woman."

"You're not that at all," Leigh protested. "In fact, you look lovely." Kat had discarded her disguise. She was wearing a vintage forest green Mainbocher suit that carried a faint, underlying scent of mothballs and a matching green hat with a perky yellow-and-black feather. An exquisitely matched pair of Canary diamonds set in antique gold twinkled at her ears. "I don't know how to thank you," Leigh said.

"Simple. As as stockholder in this studio, I want to see some profits. And although I realize that three percent doesn't give me a very large voice in the day-to-day operations, if you ask me, you ought to get this fellow back on the payroll." The feather bobbed when she tilted her head toward Matthew.

Leigh's eyes met Matthew's. "That's precisely what I intend to do."

The police were waiting for them when they arrived home. "What in the world?" Leigh murmured when she saw the marked cars parked in her driveway. "Did you turn Farraday in so soon?"

"No. I wanted to give you time to file the papers."

"Then if it isn't about Farraday . . ." Ice skimmed up her spine. "Oh, my God. Marissa," she whispered, clinging to his arm.

"You don't know that for certain." But Matthew had seen the way Marissa had stormed out of the office. He had lived with her for those few hellish weeks. He knew exactly how self-destructive Leigh's sister could be. And that was before she'd slipped so deeply into her Götterdämmerung of drugs and alcohol.

"Ms. Baron?" The officer's face was solemn, his blue eyes offering sympathy.

"Yes, I'm Leigh Baron." Her fingers closed more tightly on Matthew's arm as her premonition increased. "Is something wrong, Officer?"

He took his cap off. "I'm sorry, Ms. Baron. But it's your sister."

Leigh had been expecting this for years. But that didn't stop her knees from almost buckling. "Is she—"

"I'm sorry, ma'am. But she's dead." He looked nervous, as if expecting her to fall apart, to get hysterical, or start screaming or something, Leigh thought. "We can't be certain until the autopsy, but from the drug paraphernalia scattered around the bedroom and the needle marks on her arm, the suspected cause of death is an overdose."

An image of Marissa, lying dead on her peach satin bed, her arms riddled with needle marks, made Leigh's heart clench. She closed her eyes, hoping that when she opened them the patrolman would be gone, that this would turn out to be a horrible nightmare. She opened them again. No such luck. Unfortunately, it was all too real.

"Uh, if you don't mind, Ms. Baron," the young patrolman said hesitantly, "we need someone to come to the morgue and identify the body."

Body. She'd never noticed what a final ring that word had to it. Feeling strangely faint, she leaned against the reassuring pressure of Matthew's arm around her waist. "Of course," she murmured. Her words were a distant hum in her ear, like the sound of the sea that supposedly lingered in a conch shell.

Leigh was grateful for Matthew's lack of conversation when they returned from the Los Angeles County morgue later that night. Her brain felt strangely numb and her stomach felt as if it were riding a rollercoaster. She couldn't get the sight of Marissa sliding back into that horrible drawer, as if she were being hidden away in some oversize safe deposit box, out of her mind.

Even her father's death had not left Leigh feeling so bereft; after the horror of his initial stroke, Joshua's death had been expected; the second stroke, which had taken his life during his sleep, had seemed peaceful by comparison. But Marissa

had died violently. The bruises on her face and body and the
needle marks in her arm had attested to that.

The unwelcome vision lingered before her eyes. Leigh
moaned softly and pressed her fingertips against her closed
lids. Without taking his attention from his driving, Matthew
took her hand in his.

It had definitely been a day of contrasts. When she continued to see Marissa's atypically calm but waxen features,
Leigh tried to remember that a few short hours earlier, she'd
been floating on air.

If Joshua's funeral had resembled that of a head of state or
Far Eastern potentate, Marissa's was a media circus, the likes
of which Tinseltown hadn't witnessed since the death of
Valentino. Guards had to be posted at the funeral home to
keep the hordes of fans from storming the doors in order to
catch a glimpse of Marissa's body. Cars were backed up for
miles on both the Golden State and Ventura Freeways and, on
the surface streets surrounding Forest Lawn, traffic had
ground to a standstill. Crowds of fans covered the lush, rolling green hills.

"My God, it looks like a Rose Bowl float," Tina said to her
husband, when they saw the flower-draped white coffin. "I
doubt that there's a flower left growing anywhere in the Western world."

"You know what they say," Corbett answered quietly.
"Give the folks a good show, and they'll all come. And Marissa, for better or worse, gave the people one helluva show."

"Amen to that," Tina murmured.

The helicopters were back, circling the burial site, their
rotors blowing delicate petals from the acres of hothouse
flowers. Leigh ignored them. She'd said her final good-byes
to her sister at two o'clock this morning, in the privacy of the
mortuary's silent chapel. She found this elaborate ceremony
something painful to endure, but she knew it was what Marissa would have wanted.

"Marissa would be pleased by the turnout," Leigh said.

Matthew decided not to state his opinion that Marissa had
lost her ability to be pleased by anything years ago. "Ironic,
isn't it?"

She looked up at him. "What?"

"The goddess of love, eventually dying from a lack of love."

His words, Leigh considered, were unhappily all too true.

They were leaving the funeral, Khalil on one side of Leigh, Matthew on the other, when one reporter burst from behind the police barricade. "Ms. Baron, Mr. St. James," Peter Bradshaw of WBC shouted. He ran across the lawn, his jean-clad cameraman, attached by an electronic umbilical cord, following on his heels. "If I could just have a minute."

Matthew's arm curved possessively around Leigh's shoulder. Khalil hovered protectively beside her. "Can't you see Ms. Baron is in mourning?" Matthew growled. "What is it with you guys, anyway?"

The TV reporter appeared uncowed by Matthew's blistering glare. "I'm just doing my job, Mr. St. James. There's a rumor going around that Marissa Baron's death was a mob hit. Those same rumors say that Baron Studios is going to cave in to mob threats against your life and shelve *The Eye of the Tiger*. Would either of you like to comment?" He thrust a microphone in front of them.

"Damnit," Matthew complained, "don't you have any respect for the dead? Why don't you let it go?"

"I'm sorry, Mr. St. James," Bradshaw persisted unrepentantly, "but this is a big story; it isn't going to go away just because you don't want to talk about it."

"Look." Matthew brushed the microphone away as if it were a pesky fly. "I'm giving you ten seconds to get out of here; then you'll be arrested for trespassing."

Determined not to allow the reporter from the upstart television network an exclusive, the other reporters descended on the threesome as they walked toward the waiting limousine. Flashbulbs exploded, blinding Leigh; microphones were shoved into her face; the unintelligible shouted questions were a cacophony of raised voices.

Realizing the futility of answering their questions here, Leigh stopped long enough to issue a brief statement. It took an effort, but she remained calm, drawing herself up to her full height. "Mr. St. James and I will be holding a press conference tomorrow morning at ten o'clock in the press room at Baron Studios. We'll both make a brief statement and then we'll answer any questions you wish to ask." She took off her

sunglasses, her soft gray eyes looking directly into Bradshaw's. "Now, if you don't mind, I would like to mourn my
sister in peace."

Peter Bradshaw hadn't gotten what he wanted—an exclusive—but at least he'd gotten the ball rolling. Beside, he decided as he looked up into Matthew St. James's glowering
face, it would definitely be pushing his luck to stay around
here any longer.

"Ten o'clock," he said, backing away as he saw the police-
men headed his way. "I'll be looking forward to it."

"Are you sure you want to do this?" Matthew asked con-
cernedly as they entered the back seat of the limousine.

"We can't keep dodging the issue, Matthew," she said wearily. "It's time to face it head-on."

Khalil, seated across from the couple, looked at Leigh, his
concern evident in his solemn dark eyes. "Are you certain
you're up to the rigor of a new conference? It has been an
exhausting three days, made worse by your insistence to plan
every detail of your sister's funeral yourself. Why don't you
simply issue a statement through your attorney?"

"Khalil's right," Matthew said. "A statement should keep
the vultures at bay for a while. Besides," he pointed out,
"once the police arrest Farraday, Minetti won't have a candidate to run, so the mob will back off."

"Until the next time," Leigh tilted her chin. "I'm not going
to allow myself to be bullied by anyone, Matthew."

Khalil and Matthew exchanged a look. They both knew
Leigh well enough to realize that attempting to change her
mind would be a waste of time. And they both loved her
enough to worry that, by standing up to Minetti publicly, she
could be risking her life.

44

Jeff Martin was desperate.

His hands, seldom steady these days, shook like a leaf in a hurricane as he clung to the telephone receiver. "Hey, Mr. Minetti," he whined, "you got the wrong guy."

"No. I don't. You see, Martin, Marissa Baron called Brendan Farraday the night of her death. She said she had left the Driftwood with you."

"Hey, the chick didn't make any calls!"

There was a momentary silence on the other end of the phone. "Now that you've admitted you were with her, after all, let me tell you she told Farraday you were in the john."

"Okay, so I was with her. So what?"

"I have to assume the man who was with her that night is also the man who injected her with the cocaine and heroin that killed her."

Sweat poured down Jeff's face, from under his arms, his

crotch. "Hey, Mr. Minetti, it was an accident, okay? I didn't mean to kill the chick. Hell, I liked her. Besides, she had this habit of picking up guys, strangers, you know. It could've been anyone."

"But it wasn't anyone, Martin. It was you."

Jeff dragged his hands through his lank dishwater blond hair. "I told you, it was a fucking accident!"

"And the bruises?"

"What can I say? The chick liked it rough, and I didn't mind obliging her. Is there a law against a little S & M between friends?"

"You're not getting my point, Martin," Rocco Minetti said with a cold, deadly calm. "If it hadn't been for those fresh bruises, the police undoubtedly would have written the Baron woman's death off as accidental. Now they've called homicide in, which is more attention than we'd like with Brendan's upcoming campaign on the line."

"I'll tell you what, just extend me a little bread and I'll blow town," Jeff said. "I'll go to Mexico. Colombia. Brazil. Somewhere the cops'll never find me."

"I'm sorry, Martin," Minetti said, "but you've become a dangerous liability. There's nothing I can do to help you." He hung up.

His final words rang in Jeff's ears like a death knell. "Shit!" The shout echoed off the bare walls of the apartment. Minetti was going to have him killed. And there was nothing he could do about it. Not a fucking thing. Except run like hell.

Throwing his few possessions into a duffel bag, Jeff ran from the apartment, no destination in mind. He only knew that he had to get the hell out of here before Minetti's hit men arrived.

His head was pounding and a needlike pain was radiating under his skin. When he realized Marissa was dead, he'd taken off, leaving all his stash behind. He'd been three days with nothing but some grass and a few 'ludes and he was about to go out of his fucking mind.

Desperate for relief, he went into a liquor store and bought a pint of whiskey. As he counted the rumpled bills out onto the counter, he noticed the L.A. *Times* headline: STUDIO TO BREAK SILENCE ON ST. JAMES'S SCREENPLAY. Rubbing his watery eyes with his fingers, he tried to focus on the swimming black print, his alcohol-sodden brain remembering something about Minetti wanting to keep Matthew's script from the screen.

That was it!

The way to get back into Rocco Minetti's good graces.

He'd blow Matthew away.

"Damnit, Leigh," Matthew said the next morning, "you don't have to do this." He looked like a man who wanted to lay down the law, if he could only figure out how to make it stick. "The police should have Farraday in custody before the news crews ever get their cameras set up. It'll be over."

"With men like Minetti, it's never over." Leigh pushed herself up from the table. "Unless people stand up and refuse to be intimidated." She pressed her hand against her stomach, where giant condors were flapping their wings. "Are you ready to go?"

"In a minute." He drew her into his arms and kissed her long and hard. "Now, I'm ready," he said, when they came up for air.

Flashbulbs popped like gunfire the moment they entered the room. Along with all three major television networks, WBC had sent a camera crew, which certainly wasn't surprising, since Peter Bradshaw had broken the story, setting off the chain reaction that had brought them all here today.

Jockeying for position with the network crews were jean-clad, T-shirted cameramen and -women from local television stations. Beside them stood the field reporters—the men bronze, blond, and handsome; the women tawny, blond, and beautiful, proving that the California girl popularized by all those Beach Boys songs was alive and well and living in Hollywood. Behind these uniformly attractive golden individuals, notebooks in hand, were the print journalists, delegated, as always, to the back of the room.

Posted on either side of the doorway were two Brinks guards, their eyes alert as their gazes continually swept the crowded room. Only moments earlier the uniformed men had delivered a million dollars in newly minted thousand-dollar bills to Leigh Baron. They had remained to ensure that none of those crisp green portraits of Grover Cleveland fell into the wrong hands.

Leigh was not surprised by the turnout. Viewed by many to be Hollywood's reigning royalty, she and Matthew had lived in glass houses for years.

As they'd decided, Leigh spoke first. "Ladies and gentlemen, I have a few things to say before turning the microphone over to Mr. St. James. The first is of a personal nature. As you all know, I had the unhappy task of burying my sister yesterday. During the past four days, I have been informed of stories suggesting that her death was a homicide. There have even been rumors that she died of a mob hit. Those stories are blantantly false.

"The sad fact is that my sister was a very troubled woman. She had become addicted to drugs and alcohol, and although her friends and family did everything in our power to help her, unfortunately, in the end, it wasn't enough. And while I will always regret not being able to save her from the destructive powers of her addictions, I hope that her death will serve as a warning to those in our community who consider recreational drugs to be both safe and fashionable.

"I also want to say that Marissa's addiction did not take away from her tremendous talent, nor did it diminish the pleasure she gave so many moviegoers during her too short career. And although we had our differences, both personal and professional, there was never a time when I stopped loving my sister. And I can only hope that she has found the peace which eluded her for so much of her life."

The room was as still as a tomb. Leigh took a deep breath, glancing down at Matthew for moral support before continuing.

"Now, for the persistent rumors that Baron Studios intends to shelve *The Eye of the Tiger* because of certain unsavory elements in our community, I will admit that both Mr. St. James and I have received numerous threats."

A low murmur of interest rippled through the assembled group of reporters.

"Most of those threats were anonymous, which only proves the cowardice of the people we are dealing with. Others were

more forthright, Brendan Farraday being one of the individuals who felt obliged to warn me against making Mr. St. James's
movie.''

The murmurs turned into a noisy buzz of excitement.

"But Baron Studios will not bow to pressures from people
like this,'' she insisted, her voice growing stronger with each
word. "We will bring *The Eye of the Tiger* to the screen. Baron
Studios believes that the period of national denial concerning
the Vietnam war has gone on too long. It's time people had
an opportunity to view a slice of life from this era, written by
a man who was there.

"And we are so certain that there is a demand for this film
that we are pledging a one-million-dollar advertising budget.'' Reaching into the attaché case, she pulled out the neatly
stacked bills and held them up for everyone to see.

Flashbulbs exploded. Portable videocams hummed. Excitement rippled through the crowd like a shot of adrenaline; it
was obvious that the reporters were dying to dash out of the
room and file the story of the year. But they wouldn't. Not
until they'd heard from the man standing next to her.

"And now I'd like to introduce the writer of *The Eye of the
Tiger*, a man whose credentials speak for themselves, Matthew
St. James.''

Introductions were unnecessary, Leigh knew as she sat back
down. They all knew him. For much of the last decade the
name had appeared, larger than life, on movie screens in
darkened theaters all over the world. SCREENPLAY BY MAT-
THEW ST. JAMES. DIRECTED BY MATTHEW ST. JAMES. A MAT-
THEW ST. JAMES PRODUCTION. Once he had been the bane of
Joshua Baron's existence. Today Matthew St. James was the
ace up the sleeve of Baron Studios. In Hollywood vernacular,
he had the world by the balls.

Leigh watched Matthew weave his seductive spell over his
audience. Then her gaze drifted slowly over the rapt crowd,
returning momentarily to a man standing at the front of the
room, his eyes unblinkingly riveted on Matthew. The lack of
a camera revealed that he wasn't a photographer. And he
wasn't carrying one of those long slender notebooks favored
by reporters the world over. Nor did he have a portable recorder in the hand that was visible. His other hand, she noted

with slow-building apprehension, was tucked away in the pocket of his faded denim jacket.

Too late, she recognized him. Jeff Martin. Before she could determine what he was doing here, staring through watery blue eyes at Matthew with such concentration, she saw it. The gun. Pointedly directly at Matthew.

No! Events seemed to slow to the agonizing pace of ten frames per minute. She grabbed the bronze bust of her father, Joshua Baron, from its marble pedestal beside her, and hurled it at the gunman. Then she screamed.

The sudden sound of the shot ricocheted around the room like the snap of a firecracker. The riveting explosion was instantly followed by another. Then a third.

After what seemed an eternity, the reporters began to react, shouting and shoving violently, trying to force their way to the front of the room. A blood red haze covered Leigh's eyes; someone a long distance away was calling for an ambulance. Instinctively she reached out for Matthew.

"Matthew?" she asked in a voice that was little more than a whisper.

Matthew was on his knees beside her, brushing the strands of blood-splattered hair from her forehead. "I'm here, Leigh. Don't worry, darling. Everything's going to be all right."

She was going to die. Just when things were finally beginning to work out for them. "I love you." Her lips moved, but no sound escaped.

Just as their fingers touched, Leigh surrendered to the darkness.

45

It was bedlam.

At the same time Leigh was being rushed into the hospital emergency room, a parking garage under construction next door to the hospital had collapsed, burying three construction workers and injuring scores more. Within minutes, the emergency room was overflowing with patients, doctors, nurses, and paramedics.

Matthew could understand that he was in the way, hovering beside the gurney, but he didn't want to leave Leigh's side. Finally, a harried young resident, clad in unconventional wrinkled chinos, a Grateful Dead T-shirt, a pair of high-top basketball shoes, and a blue L.A. Angels baseball cap managed to convince him that he'd be helping Leigh more by allowing the doctors to get on with their work.

"What the hell is taking them so long?" Matthew ground out. He paced the floor of the private waiting room the hospital administrator had commandeered for him, away from the prying eyes of reporters. The rigid lines bracketing his mouth were deeper and harsher than usual.

"Matthew, you saw the chaos in that emergency room," Khalil said. "The fact that Leigh is not their first priority can only mean that she's not as badly injured as the others." His voice was calm, but the ashtray beside him, filling up with cigarette butts, told its own story.

Triage. Matthew remembered lying on the ground, watching the nurse at the evacuation unit in Vietnam separate the incoming wounded by the gravity of their wounds. "If anything happens to her . . ." His voice drifted off, his words choked by the gigantic lump in his throat.

"I know." Khalil ground out his cigarette and immediately lit another. "I suppose it is no secret that I love her."

"No."

Khalil eyed Matthew through a haze of blue smoke. "Will that present a problem?"

Matthew stopped pacing long enough to consider Khalil's question. "There was a time when I found trust an impossible thing," he said finally. "In those days I would have seen you as a threat."

"And now?"

"And now I consider you my friend. As well as Leigh's."

Khalil nodded, satisfied. He hadn't wanted to give up his ties, however innocent, to Leigh, but at the same time, he didn't want to be responsible for keeping Matthew and her apart. "I tried to make a place in her heart," he said. "But you were always there. You are, my friend, a very fortunate man."

"I know." He resumed pacing the floor. Matthew hoped that his luck held up.

Leigh opened her eyes, disoriented by her strange surroundings. She blinked in an attempt to clear her mind.

"Thank God, you're awake."

At the wonderfully familiar voice, Leigh concentrated on focusing on the man seated beside the bed. "Matthew?"

"Right here, sweetheart." He stood up, coming to stand over her. "How are you feeling?"

"Thirsty," she decided. "My mouth feels all fuzzy."

"That's from the shot they gave you before they stitched you up."

"And I feel like I'm riding a merry-go-round. A flying one."

He brushed her blood-matted hair back from her forehead. "Think of it as a cheap drunk."

She half smiled. "But I never get drunk." She pressed her fingertips against her temple, where a row of dark black stitches cut a path through her hair. "I'm so dizzy."

He bent down and brushed a kiss against her dry lips. "Why don't you get some sleep," he suggested.

Exhausted from trying to keep her eyes open, she allowed her lids to drift down. "You'll stay?"

"Forever," he said.

It was early evening when she woke again.

"How are you feeling?" Matthew asked.

"I'm fine," she assured him.

"Are you sure?"

She nodded, wishing she hadn't done so when boulders tumbled around in her head. "Did you say something about stitches the last time you were in here?"

"Don't worry, the scar will never show under your hair."

"I wasn't worried about that. I was trying to remember what happened."

"Jeff tried to shoot me, but that bronze bust of Joshua you threw at him made his shot go astray and it grazed your scalp." He frowned. "You had no damn business risking your life like that. If anything had happened to you . . ."

Leigh could remember the panic she'd felt when she saw the gun aimed at Matthew. "I couldn't let you be killed. What happened to Jeff?"

"The guards shot him. He's dead." It took every ounce of Matthew's self-control not to shout at her for putting herself in danger. Realizing that she'd already been through enough, he took her hand and lifted it to his lips. "That's twice you've saved my life. I'll have to think of some way to repay you."

"Jewelry is always nice," Leigh mused. "I've always been a sucker for sapphires. And emeralds aren't too bad either. But do you know what I'd really like?"

"Name it and it's yours."

"A plain gold band," Leigh suggested softly.

"Funny you should mention that." Matthew reached into his pocket and pulled out a box. Leigh's heart was pounding a million miles a minute. She lifted the lid.

"Oh, Matthew." Tears sprang to her eyes when she viewed the ring resting on its bed of royal blue velvet. Three brilliantly cut diamonds glittered on a wide platinum band. "It's absolutely exquisite."

"Three stones," he said, taking her hand and slipping it on her finger. "One for each of the times we've been together, but don't get any ideas about going for a quartet, lady, because this time is going to last forever."

"Forever," she agreed, holding her hand up. The diamonds caught light, breaking it into tiny white hot flames.

He bent his head, intent on kissing her, when there was a knock on the hospital room door. "Mr. St. James?" The floor nurse popped her head into the room. "I hate to interrupt, but you asked me to tell you when the news came on."

Matthew smiled. "Thank you, Mrs. Wilkinson." He picked up the remote control beside Leigh's bed and aimed it at the television hung on the wall.

"I'm not certain I'm ready to see myself being shot, Matthew," Leigh said hesitantly.

"Sorry to disappoint you, sweetheart, but you are old news."

"Then what . . . ? Oh, it's Brendan."

"Uh-uh. Arnie Stoller." They both watched the actor being taken from the backseat of the patrol car, his wrists bound by a pair of stainless steel handcuffs.

"Well, that's that," Matthew said, turning the screen black again. "Farraday's out of the picture and, thanks to you standing up to him publicly the way you did, Minetti won't dare do anything to disrupt *The Eye of the Tiger*. So, as soon as we spring you from this joint, we can start celebrating our upcoming nuptials in style."

"In bed, you mean," Leigh said with a saucy grin.

"Hey, don't blame me if that's my favorite style." When he bent his head and kissed her lingeringly, Leigh forgot all about her headache. "I have another proposition for you," he said.

"What's that?"

"We've been doing so well working together on *The Eye of the Tiger*, what would you say to collaborating on another Baron Studios production?"

"Any time," she answered without hesitation. "Do you have something in mind?" She hadn't known he'd been working on another screenplay.

Matthew sat down on the edge of the bed, took her hand in his, and laced their fingers together. "All my life, I avoided becoming involved with anyone," he said. "And then I fell in love with you and discovered that I wanted commitments. Strings. A long, luxurious lifetime of strings."

"I want that too," she said softly.

"I know. And as happy as that makes me, I've recently discovered that I'm a selfish man. I want it all, Leigh." He took a deep breath. "I want to have a child with you."

"Only one?"

"That depends on you. Although I'm certainly open for negotiation on the number and gender."

She looked up into the dark eyes that were filled with promises. "There's nothing I'd love more than to have babies with you," she answered truthfully. "And now that you bring it up, two would be nice, three even better . . . But, there's just one thing."

His heart clenched. "What's that?"

"Well, I *am* thirty-four years old, Matthew. Do you think that's too old to begin a family?"

Matthew had never loved Leigh more than he did at that moment. He drew her into his arms, unable to remember when he'd ever felt so happy. "Positively ancient," he said. "All the more reason to get started as soon as possible."